I0582651

THE
AGE
OF
RESONANCE

KATHRYN KNOWLES

MAD
ENDEAVOUR

This is a work of fiction. Names, characters, places, and incidents are the product of the author's imagination or are used fictitiously. Any resemblance to actual events, locales, or persons, living or dead, is coincidental.

Copyright © 2022 by Kathryn Knowles

Illustrations copyright © 2022 by Kathryn Knowles

Cover Design by Maria Spada

Edited by Rebecca Fisher

First Mad Endeavour Edition: November 2022

All rights reserved.

The scanning, uploading, and distribution of this book without permission is a theft of the author's intellectual property. If you would like permission to use material from the book (other than for review purposes), please contact info@madendeavour.com. Thank you for your support of the author's rights.

Identifiers:

ISBN 978-1-998781-00-3 (hardcover)

ISBN 978-1-7778470-8-1 (trade paperback)

ISBN 978-1-7778470-9-8 (ebook)

Mad Endeavour

www.madendeavour.com

For Mom.

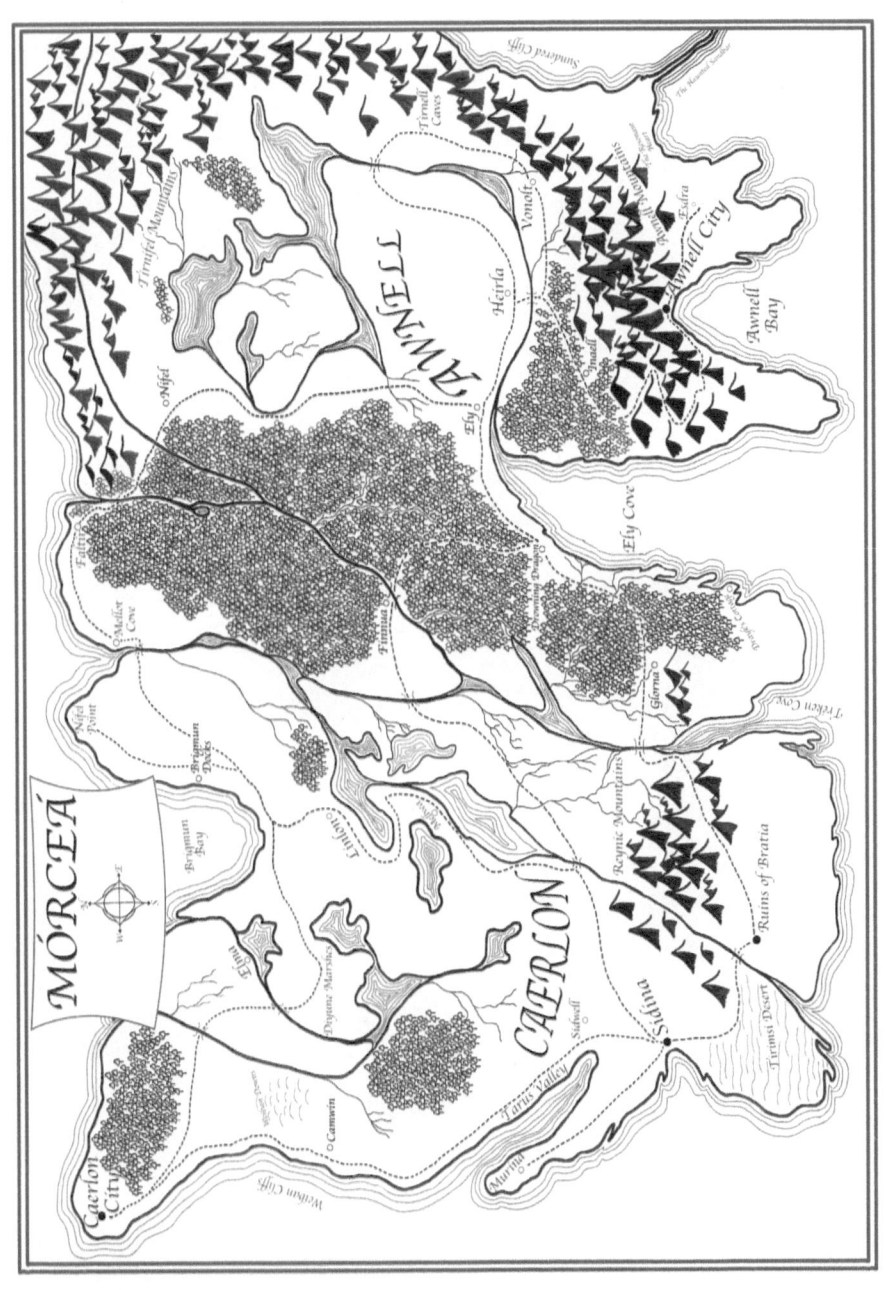

PROLOGUE

LORD ZADÍLAR

THE ILLUSIONIST

L ord Zadílar arrived at the Great Hall of his estate to find the party in full swing. The enormous room had been lavishly decorated. Garlands of flowers adorned the walls, framing the rows of windows and paintings. One long table stretched the length of the room, draped in multicoloured silk tablecloths and bearing countless platters of food and wine. Dozens of candelabras hung from the ceiling, swinging gently, as if stirred by the evening's excitement. In the middle of the room, seated beneath the grand southern archway, Sidina's best musicians guided and steered the revelry.

The sound of laughter and delight was as intoxicating as ever.

"Zad!" cried a group of people near the door, beckoning for him to join them. He smiled indulgently and wagged his finger.

"I'll join you in a moment," he called, waving his empty glass as an explanation. Then he made his way to the table at the edge of the room where the food and drinks were waiting. He'd imported all the best spiced wines for the evening, but right now, he wanted something a little stronger. He poured himself a generous helping of sourwood rum and snatched a

KATHRYN KNOWLES

pastry off a nearby plate. Then he turned to gaze at the jovial crowd of people. Hundreds of people had come out for the celebration, including several delegations from Caerlon.

Initially, the presence of so many firkon had dampened the mood, since most people feared the kingdom's warriors. The firkon were trained to intimidate, never letting their guard down. But the alcohol and music had worked their magic. Now that the party was under way, the lads seemed more relaxed. They weren't here to work after all, they were here to celebrate.

King Casréyan had signed the order today. From now on, every piece of iron, every weapon, shield, and sword would be purchased from the ironworkers in Sidina. It was an enormous contract for the city, one that meant Zadílar's people were finally and forever secure. His city was rich, and everyone in it would prosper. All those years of backbreaking labour, excavation, and training had paid off. Sidina had become *irreplaceable*. The official weapons dealer for the Kingdom of Caerlon.

And that was only the contract that existed on paper. There was still the tacit agreement with Awnell—the agreement only he and his stewards knew about. For years, that income had been the backbone of Sidina's economy, and the only thing keeping it afloat. But not anymore. Now Zad controlled the entire weapons industry for all of Mórceá, and that kind of control was invaluable.

All it would take would be a little hint here, a suggestion there... Yes. He was finally where he wanted to be.

Zad finished his pastry and re-joined the party, chatting with different people, telling stories, and laughing at jokes. This was his life. Working the room and learning whose strings he could pull to get what he wanted. His work was never over. The people of Sidina relied on him.

"Zad, come settle something for us!" called a young firkon he vaguely recognized. A bristly goatee stuck out like cactus spines on the man's pointed chin, and long strands of scraggly hair framed his dark, keen eyes. He beckoned for Zad to join his group.

Zad strolled over, wracking his brain to remember the man's name. *Was it Slanvil? Sledrir?*

"Slaedir and I were wondering," said one of the other men. *Slaedir. That's it.*

"Was it twenty thousand or forty thousand gold pieces you won in that bet with Lord Birmedel?" The firkon all grinned at each other.

"Ah..." Zad sipped his drink and chuckled. "It was thirty thousand pieces and his three fastest horses." Lowering his voice to a conspiratorial whisper, he added, "And then I turned around and sold the horses back to one of Birmedel's stewards for ten thousand a head." Zad winked at them and they hooted and roared, clapping him on the back in congratulations.

"Never bet with Lord Zadilar!" cried one of the men. "He's twice as cunning as the rest of us and four times as sly!"

Zad chuckled. "Now, now, I never lied to Birmedel. I merely obfuscated the rules of the bet a little. It's not my fault the man didn't think to ask the right questions."

"Well..." said Slaedir, smirking. "Any man stupid enough to bet on a horserace without first examining the beasts deserves to have his money taken. I never bet unless I know I'll win."

There was an oddly harsh quality to Slaedir's tone, which Zad found distasteful. But he raised his drink to Slaedir in salute. "A wise decision," he said with practiced diplomacy.

"Oh, come on, Slaed," interjected another firkon with scorn, "I know you bet heavily on the tournament this year and you still lost."

Slaedir's face flushed. "I didn't lose," he said through gritted teeth. "I never bet that I'd make it to the final round."

One of the other men snorted. "Yeah, you should be glad you didn't, otherwise you'd be dead right now. No one's ever going to beat Hamir and claim the maífirkon title." He exchanged knowing and proud glances with the other firkon. These men obviously respected their leader.

"Care to bet on that?" asked Zad jokingly. He had been eyeing Slaedir and noticed a fierce shadow pass through the man's eyes. There was no doubt in Zad's mind. This man would stop at nothing to take the maífirkon title in the next tournament. Zad suppressed a shudder at the thought. He didn't know Slaedir well, but his instincts about people were never wrong. This was not a man who should be given more power. Unfortunately, those were the men who usually ended up with all of it.

So, as objectionable as it was, Zad would endeavour to befriend the man in the coming years. It was imperative that he keep the maífirkon on his side.

As the evening progressed, Zad made a point of talking with everyone. Several groups of miners had clumped around the table, eating their weight in food and discussing the recent advances in drilling and blasting involving something called explosives; the tradesmen and shopkeepers exchanged business advice over glasses of haymead; the entertainers and musicians took turns performing and socializing; and the metalcraft designers eagerly interrogated the visiting firkon, keen to know what they liked and disliked about their current armour.

Many firkon were delighted to attend such a boisterous party since Caerlon City rarely hosted events anymore. Zad suspected the stories about Casréyan were true—that he had grown paranoid and reclusive of late, and that he was increasingly obsessed with finding the infamous Relics of Illayan.

Zad had never put much stock in fantasies or legends like that. Certainly, the relics were an intriguing idea. But he had far more pressing concerns. The real world was wearisome enough, without wasting his time on silly daydreams.

The moon had fully risen outside the window, its pale light blanching the hall, and the noise level was reaching an all-time high as the celebrations extended into the night. Zad was standing in the middle of the room, chatting with a group of craftsmen, when he noticed a strange buzz pass through the crowd. He glanced around, trying to understand the source, but he couldn't see anything through the hordes of people. However, all the eyes in the room seemed to follow something as it moved towards him.

Moments later, a small, bedraggled-looking figure pushed through the crowd to stop in front of Zadílar. The person was stooped, wearing a heavy cloak to conceal their features. They almost looked like a beggar, but something about that didn't seem right.

"Can I help you?" asked Zad uncertainly. He glanced back at his guards and saw them exchanging nervous looks. *Never a good sign.* Zadílar tensed. The guards jostled through the crowd in a hurry, and Zad's heart raced.

The entire energy in the room shifted in an instant. Before Zad could do anything, the beggar took a step forward. Only then did Zad see the knife in the beggar's hand and the tears streaking their face.

"Lord Zadílar supports a corrupt and vicious king. We must end the profiteering!" the beggar cried to the crowd. The nearby firkon launched forward, but they were too slow. A flash of silver slashed the air, and a sharp pain ignited in Zadílar's gut.

He crumpled to the ground, clutching the wound, as a crowd of panicked faces appeared around him. He could just make out the image of three firkon wrestling the beggar onto the ground, but then the image blurred. Zadílar's eyes fogged. His vision slid, and the room spun in nauseating circles. He was losing control.

Zad lifted his hands. The sight of so much blood churned his stomach and he retched. Blinding pain exploded as his muscles contracted, and he let out a cry as someone pressed down on his abdomen, trying to stop the bleeding.

"I-I'm dying," he spluttered, his temperature rising and his heart hammering against his ribs. He had never felt anything this painful before. The agony continued to grow, mounting inside of him, getting worse and worse.

Until he lost consciousness.

Everything was dark. Panicked voices shouted nearby, but Zad couldn't make sense of the words.

"Go fetch the healer," said someone he didn't recognize.

Zad tried to open his eyes, but nothing happened. His body was numb except for the searing pain in his stomach. He tried to focus on the pain because it was the only thing he understood at that moment, but even the pain felt wrong. It had begun as a sharp, hot throbbing, localized in one area, but now it was creeping farther into his body. It seeped into his veins and his bones, burning as it moved.

Then he convulsed, and the movement made everything worse.

"What's happening now?" the same panicked voice asked.

Zad slid in and out of darkness and agony. Each time he awoke, he heard voices and felt someone prodding at the raw wound in his stomach. He wanted to tell them to stop. They were making it so much worse.

But he couldn't speak.

The burning in his veins reached his neck, scorching his throat. He was screaming, gurgling and choking on the fire. Someone wrestled with his limbs, trying to force him to remain still, but he couldn't stop. He needed to get it out of him.

With tremendous effort, he wrenched open his eyes. Blurry faces hovered around him in the dark, but they were unrecognizable to him. Meaningless shapes his eyes couldn't understand.

He tried to ask what was happening, but the pain exploded through him again. His eyes snapped shut, and he plunged into darkness once more.

The next time Zad awoke, he felt groggy and heavy, but his thoughts were clearer. The pain in his body had subsided, though every inch of him ached like it had been flayed raw. He opened his eyes and blinked the sleep away before glancing around. It was daylight now. He was inside his bedchamber, all alone except for a man standing near the window with his hands clasped behind his back.

"What happened?" asked Zad, his throat raspy and sore. The man by the window gave a little start and approached the bedside.

"You're awake." He sounded relieved as he hurried to pour a glass of water and help Zad drink.

Zad's throat was so dry it scraped as he tried to swallow, and he coughed, aggravating the pain in his stomach. He gasped and tensed up, which only made things worse.

Then he held his breath, waiting for the pain to subside. "Right," he exhaled, nodding as memories of the party swam in a jumble through his mind.

"The wound was deep and required surgery," said the other man, indicating a collection of medical utensils and vials on the bedtable. "It seems the blade was also laced with poison. You've been on the brink of death for days. If I hadn't gotten here when I did..." The man trailed off, looking exhausted and relieved.

"Who are you? Where's the city healer?" asked Zad. It frightened him to hear how close he'd come to dying, but his fatigue was stronger than his alarm at the moment.

"My name is Dyanyn," said the man, helping Zad to take another drink. "One of your stewards sent for me when you were overtaken by convulsions and your healer couldn't identify the cause." He examined Zad for a moment.

"How did you figure it out, then?" Zad didn't mean to sound

rude, but he made it a point to employ the best people at his estate. He found it difficult to imagine this man could do something his own healer couldn't.

Dyanyn shrugged. "I have skills most healers do not," he replied vaguely. "But it's no surprise your healer was lost. This poison is extremely rare—so rare that, in all my life, I have only seen its effects twice. Fortunately, I have never forgotten how it works, nor how to mix the antidote."

He sounded pleased with himself, but not in a boastful way. Zad found that honest self-assurance refreshing.

"Thank you," he said, eyeing the man. Now that his strength was returning, Zad could see more clearly. Dyanyn was quite young for such an accomplished healer. He looked to be in his twenties, with delicate features and sandy blonde hair that had been bleached by the sun. He obviously wasn't a wealthy man. His shabby brown tunic was frayed on the sleeves, and his vest was dotted with several patched holes. He wore a strange pouch holstered to his shoulder, so it hung down near his ribs.

The image of the pouch conjured a distant memory in Zad's mind. He'd heard stories about healers, ancient people with unparalleled skill and knowledge.

"Wait... are you a Heiltúir?" he asked, not daring to believe it was possible. No one he knew had ever met a Heiltúir before. Most people assumed the ancient race of healers had been eradicated during the Quiescence Wars, but there were still occasional stories—tales of healers who travelled the continent, saving people from even the most desperate illnesses.

Dyanyn inclined his head. "I am," he replied.

Zadílar stared at him in wonder. As a young man, he'd often fantasized about meeting a Heiltúir and learning the truth about their race, but he'd never really believed... And definitely not under conditions such as these...

"Thank the Natures you were nearby," he whispered,

closing his eyes. Zad had never been one for religion or faith, but right now, he appreciated whatever forces had led this man to his door.

"Actually," said Dyanyn with a smile in his voice, "I have permanently settled in a town not far from here. Murina."

It took Zad a moment to process that. "What, really?" He opened his eyes to stare at the young healer. "Why settle in a small coastal town when you could move to one of the cities? With skills like yours, you could be one of the most sought-after, one of the wealthiest—"

Dyanyn laughed—a rich, melodic laugh that warmed Zad from the inside out. His kind eyes twinkled with indulgent pity. "And why would I want that?"

Zad gaped at him for a moment.

"No," continued Dyanyn. "In Murina, I have found something infinitely more precious, something more valuable than all the gold and all the power in Mórceá." He beamed at Zadílar. "I have found happiness."

"Happiness?" repeated Zad.

"Mmm." Dyanyn closed his eyes momentarily. "My wife and our baby daughter..." He opened his eyes and grinned from ear to ear. "What more could I hope to have?"

Zad opened his mouth to respond and then closed it again, not sure what he intended to say. Dyanyn was right. That sounded like a dream life, something he, Zad, could never have.

"And," said Dyanyn with a slight grin, "I might add that *stabbings* are exceedingly rare in small towns like Murina. I'd call that an excellent reason to prefer a small town to a city, wouldn't you?"

Zad laughed and immediately regretted it as pain blasted through his body again.

"Ah, apologies," said Dyanyn, grimacing, "Though laughter has many healing properties, perhaps it is not the best treatment for a gaping stomach wound."

Zad winced and shook his head. He reached down and touched the wad of bandages wrapped around his abdomen.

"So... a Heiltúir?" he asked to distract himself from the pain. "What does that actually mean—if you don't mind me asking? I've always wanted to know... Do you have special healing abilities, then? Or is it just a title?"

Dyanyn smiled. "No, we do not possess any mystical ability. It is more a predisposition, a heritage. Although..." He paused thoughtfully. "There is reason to believe our people have stronger memories. For instance, I can remember every book I've ever read, every remedy I've ever made, but my memory seems selective. I remember things as they relate to healing. I remember every moment I spent with my mother, who was a Heiltúir like me, but my memories of my father seem more rudimentary—more ordinary. I can remember the exact properties of every herb and every mixture I've ever concocted. But I cannot tell you the lyrics to the song my wife sang to me last week—which is rather unfair, if you ask me. I think I'd prefer to remember the song."

Zad suppressed a laugh and clenched his jaw at the pain mounting in his gut.

Dyanyn pulled the satchel off his shoulder and began rifling through it as he continued his explanation. "In addition to our memories, we also seem to possess a natural... let's call it *empathy*, for lack of a better word. More often than not, I can tell instinctively what is wrong with someone before I've even examined them. Like now... I can sense the pain you must be experiencing. I can see it in the air like a wave around you. So" —he pulled a vial of opaque liquid from his pouch and held it up—"I offer you some pain reliever."

Zad chuckled and sighed in relief. "Yes, please," he said, wincing as he aggravated the wound again.

It took less than five minutes for the healer's medicine to

take effect. It astonished Zad how much more comfortable he felt.

"Now, you mustn't try to move," warned Dyanyn. "The pain may be gone, but the injury is not. That wound will take weeks to heal properly, so you must rest. I have prepared a sedative if you'd like it." He held out a second vial of a darker liquid.

Zad took the sedative and drifted into a deep, comfortable sleep.

It wasn't until the pain reliever wore off that he awoke again. The room was dark. The fire in the grate gave off a warm light, but the candles on the tables had burned low. It took a moment before he spotted Dyanyn sitting in a chair by the window.

Dyanyn sat with his legs crossed and his fingers pressed together, humming to himself. The tune had a spirited melody, and it was strangely comforting. Like a mixture between a madrigal and a lullaby.

Zad wasn't sure how long he listened to Dyanyn hum, but when the melody ended, Dyanyn turned to find Zad watching him.

"So..." Zad's voice was tired and groggy. "I didn't see everything that happened the other night. Did they catch the person who stabbed me?"

Dyanyn stood up and walked over to the bed. "Yes," he replied, but he wore a tight frown on his face. "The firkon apprehended the man immediately. It seems he was a disgruntled blacksmith from a village outside Caerlon City whose livelihood will be impacted by the new trade deal. I believe there were also some implications of abuse from the king's delegates in the village... not surprising to hear, I'm afraid."

Zad nodded. He was relieved they had caught his attacker, but it saddened him to learn the man's motivation.

"I believe the fîrkon have scheduled his execution for later this week." Dyanyn spoke in a cool voice that clearly communicated his disapproval.

"You don't agree with the punishment?" Zad asked. In the dim light, he could just make out Dyanyn's sour expression, and it made him slightly ashamed of himself. For some reason, he really wanted this man to respect him.

"*A Heiltúir is first and foremost honest. We do not mete out death, nor do we fear it. Our sacred knowledge is our gift and our privilege, and we use it, not for glory or for fame, but for peace.*" Dyanyn recited the words calmly. "I cannot condone murder, no matter how it presents itself... even under the guise of justice." He spread his hands before him, palms up in a gesture of tired resignation.

Zad shifted uncomfortably. Looking at Dyanyn now, he realized this young man might be the only truly decent person he'd ever met. "I have no authority over the fîrkon," he said, averting his eyes.

There was a brief pause before Dyanyn responded. "I know that," he said kindly. "And that man tried to kill you..."

Zad nodded, remembering the accusations the man had made about him before plunging the poisoned blade into his gut. "It's not true what he said about me," blurted Zad before he could stop himself. "About supporting Casréyan and profiteering... I don't really agree with the king's actions, and I don't want to support his tyranny." Zad didn't know what had possessed him to say those words out loud, but they poured out of him so fast he couldn't believe it. He'd never admitted the truth to anyone before, not even his closest stewards, and now he'd told this perfect stranger? He wished he could take it back, but it was too late now. All of his years of careful planning and game playing were undone in an instant. He'd left himself vulnerable and exposed.

Dyanyn nodded and put his hand firmly on Zad's shoulder

to calm him. *"The illusionist dazzles with one hand and manipulates with the other,"* he spoke in a soft, ruminative tone. "Have you ever heard that phrase?"

Zad looked at him, surprised, and shook his head.

"It is an old coastal proverb, I believe. And it seems a fitting description for you."

"What do you mean?" Zad tried to sit up straighter in his bed, but the pain undermined his effort and he slumped back down.

Dyanyn shrugged. "It's a dangerous risk you take, but I see the benefits as well as the costs. It is easier to manipulate your audience when you have their trust." Dyanyn looked Zad directly in the eyes. "Not everyone understands the complexities and nuance of political gambling, but I do. And you may rely on my secrecy. You are not a wicked man, Lord Zadílar Aí-Sidina."

In an instant, Zad's fear and shame melted away. His body relaxed and the rest of his pain subsided into the background. He hadn't realized how much he'd needed to hear that.

Dyanyn remained by Zad's side for the next several days, and they got to know each other well. Dyanyn had spent his life travelling all over Mórceá, working as a healer. First as his mother's apprentice, then on his own after his mother's death. He spoke with authority on matters of philosophy, social justice, and art. He understood love and loss, life and death. And through everything he'd seen and done, Dyanyn had never allowed his spirit to tarnish. He had an air of optimism that Zad had never seen.

The more Zad learned about him, the more he admired Dyanyn. He wished he could live his own life as honourably as the healer did. But sooner or later, Zad's wound would heal, and he would need to re-join the world and reclaim his role in it.

After a week had passed, Dyanyn informed Zad that he needed to return to Murina. "You are recovering nicely now. I believe your healer can take you the rest of the way, and I really must get back to my family."

"Of course," said Zad, but he struggled to hide his disappointment. "It's strange... I know I nearly died, but I don't think I've ever been this rested before in my life." He blinked and turned to look at Dyanyn. "Thank you."

Dyanyn inclined his head. "I wouldn't recommend getting stabbed again, though. Once was quite enough."

Dyanyn finished packing his supplies and scribbled out a description of the remedies and ingredients Zad should continue to take for the next several months. When he was ready to leave, he turned to bid farewell.

"Wait!" Zad said, aghast. "I haven't paid you." He sat up straighter in the bed and gestured towards the door. "I need one of my stewards to—"

But Dyanyn cut him off, waving his hand in the air. "No payment, please."

Zad frowned. "But you saved my life. I owe you everything. I need to repay you somehow."

Dyanyn smiled. "You can repay me by counting me your friend, and allowing me to count you as mine." He stared at Zad with a resolute expression, and Zad realized there was no point in arguing.

"Very well," he said reluctantly, "but promise me this, then. Promise me that if you ever need anything—"

"You'll be the first person I come to," replied Dyanyn. He smiled again and took Zad's hand in farewell. "Lord Zadílar, I wish you all the best for health and happiness. May we meet again."

Zad watched him go, feeling strangely forlorn. He didn't

want to return to his life of deceit. He longed to follow Dyanyn back to his world of honour and integrity, a world where Zad could be himself. His true self. Not the persona he'd adopted all those years ago.

But he didn't belong in that world. Zad wasn't a Heiltúir or any kind of healer. He wasn't a father or a husband. He was a politician. An *illusionist*.

And he had work to do.

PART I

1

TÚIR-AVLEA

Catanya and Drayk stood together in the forest, battered and exhausted, cloaked in the shadow of an enormous mountain. Its towering, oppressive outline cleaved the sky in half, while beams of late afternoon sun radiated behind it, streaking shades of yellow and coral across the otherwise clear blue canvas.

Catanya craned her neck and squinted at the mountaintop. It glittered and shimmered, reflecting light in all directions, as if a star perched atop its peak. Then she turned her gaze back to the strange old woman now standing across from her and Drayk.

"You are most welcome here," said the stranger, smiling as she circled them appraisingly. Her loose, flowing white robes bunched at her feet, and her willowy hair hung in wisps beneath a thin circlet of woven silver and partially wilted yew branches.

After narrowly surviving the strangest, most perilous journey of their lives, Catanya and Drayk hadn't seen another living person in what felt like ages. Catanya wasn't entirely sure what to say or how to react. Her nerves were frayed and she didn't know if she should try to be polite, or brace for another attack. Drayk, she noticed, kept his hand poised on his sword, as if preparing to fight.

"Oh, you're a powerful one, aren't you?" The old woman stopped walking and looked at Catanya, her bushy eyebrows dancing close to her feathery hairline. "Yes, I can feel it." She closed her eyes and inhaled. "We've been waiting for you."

"What do you mean?" Catanya cast an uncertain glance at Drayk. "And who are you?"

The old woman chuckled and her eyes crinkled. "I have already told you. My name is Laylian, Maílehr of Túir-Avlea. I'm so pleased to meet you. Of course, we knew you would come."

"You know who we are?" asked Drayk, not moving his hand from his sword.

"Hmm, interesting question." Laylian screwed up her face and took a long pause before saying, "Do you?"

A bewildered silence filled the space between them. Catanya wasn't sure how to respond, and from his unsettled expression, neither did Drayk.

"Mmm, I thought as much," said Laylian, seemingly unconcerned by their confusion. "Well, let's start with names, shall we? I've told you mine, but you haven't told me yours." She looked at them expectantly.

Catanya and Drayk exchanged baffled looks, but Catanya shrugged and told her their names.

"Catanya and Drayk," repeated Laylian. "Lovely. Well, you've made it through the journey. Now, if you'll follow me, I'll take you into the mountain." She turned and beckoned for them to join her. "Come along, then."

Catanya hesitated. But something told her to trust this woman, a warmth or a connection running between them. It was strong and stable, like a cord connecting them together. Catanya's stress slipped away and she inhaled a deep, relaxing breath before moving to follow Laylian. But Drayk's hand on her arm held her back.

"What?" she whispered, seeing his apprehensive frown. "This is why we're here, isn't it?"

Drayk wavered, looking around through the trees as if searching for something. He sighed and glanced in Laylian's direction, then he nodded and followed Catanya forward.

Laylian moved surprisingly fast for her age as she climbed across the uneven forest floor with ease. She zig-zagged through the trees, following some unknown route. But several times she stopped dead in her tracks, mumbled something under her breath, and then turned to walk in the opposite direction.

"Oh, drat, where did it go?" she muttered, craning her neck up and turning on the spot as though trying to orient herself.

Catanya stopped beside her. "Um, is everything okay?"

"Oh yes. I know it's around here somewhere." She chuckled happily to herself. "Sometimes I let my mind wander and then I can't find it again when I need it." She began humming and wandering around with no apparent aim. "Think it over, think it under, left—no. No, I left through the left so it's... Right this way!" she called back at them, and took off confidently in the opposite direction. "It's funny how everything looks different when you're showing it to someone else."

"This woman has lost her mind," whispered Drayk as they followed her deeper into the forest.

"Not lost!" called Laylian, chuckling again. "Only misplaced."

Catanya couldn't help agreeing with Drayk. The old woman seemed confused and disoriented. Catanya was beginning to question whether Laylian should be trying to lead them anywhere when the old woman came to a sudden halt. Catanya nearly ran into her.

"Here we are," announced Laylian. She stepped off the path

and stooped beneath a pair of ancient trees, whose upper branches had curved and tangled together to form a sort of gable.

Catanya and Drayk followed her under the trees, and descended into a massive stone hollow sunken into the base of the mountain. Thick layers of springy green moss cloaked the entire area, and a fine, gentle mist dangled in the air. The terrain was uneven, littered with remnants of broken basalt columns, like geometric stepping stones laid out in disorganized patterns. The columns grew taller and more compact, merging into the sheer wall of the mountain and giving it a corrugated, rippled appearance. And directly ahead, carved into the mountain wall, was a simple archway, just large enough for them to pass through.

A prickling sensation spread across Catanya's skin, and she shuddered. She glanced through the archway, but saw nothing more than damp earth and rock.

"What do you think?" Laylian stared at her, wearing an expectant grin. But Catanya didn't know what to think.

"Are we going through there?" asked Drayk.

"We are," said Laylian, nodding and smiling. Then she stepped confidently forward, through the archway, and out of sight into the mountain.

Catanya gave Drayk a weary but confident look, then she took a deep breath and followed Laylian through the arch.

Catanya had expected a dark, earthen passage, twisting beneath the mountain. Instead, the tunnel inclined beneath her feet, leading her up until she emerged onto an open stone staircase, bathed in the dimming daylight. It extended up the steep rock face like a jagged vine, and wrapped around the mountainside, out of view.

Laylian was visible ahead, climbing the narrow stairs with ease. "Come along," she called, beckoning for them to follow her.

The uneven stones were smooth and slippery, so Catanya climbed with care, making sure each foot was sturdy before lifting the other. Drayk followed, muttering under his breath, "Oh, sure, a crumbling, magical staircase on the sheer edge of a mountain, what could go wrong?"

Catanya suppressed a nervous laugh and continued climbing.

They followed Laylian in silence for several minutes. The staircase rose up the rocky mountainside, carrying them above the treeline. The burnt orange sun blazed into view as the stairs curved towards the western slope. It hung low in the sky, beginning its nighttime descent, but its rays were still warm and bright, illuminating the path.

Catanya paused on the stairs and squinted at the horizon and the forest below. From here, she thought she could just see the entrance to the Shrouded Caves. But the dark forest and the sunset's oversaturation made it difficult to discern. Birds soared over the canopy, and every once in a while, Catanya thought she noticed a shadowy figure pass between the trees.

The Dead Wood.

Only a few hours had passed since she'd stood in those trees, speaking with her ancestor's ghost.

You have made many sacrifices already, but there will be more, Ana, the first Queen of Awnell, had told her.

Catanya shuddered, wondering what other sacrifices she'd be forced to make before this was over.

"All right, love?" asked Drayk, catching up to her and pausing to follow her gaze. "Not afraid of heights, are you?" He leaned over the edge of the mountain to survey the precipitous drop.

Catanya shook her head. Without speaking, she turned and resumed her upward climb.

They continued for almost an hour before the terrain began to change. It grew more sloped and rolling until the solid rock gave way to earthier ground with scattered trees and vegetation that grew denser the farther they walked. About a third of the way up the mountain, the stairs levelled out, leading them onto a wide, grassy plateau. The plateau protruded from the thick forest now blanketing the surrounding slopes. And the rest of the enormous mountain stretched above, like a great bulwark, protecting this private copse. At the centre of the plateau, Laylian waited for them, standing beside a simple stone structure.

"Nearly there now," she said with a smile.

But Catanya's eyes were drawn towards the stone structure. She stepped away from Drayk, her feet carrying her forward almost unconsciously. The structure stood alone, hazy and shimmering in the setting sunlight, like a mirage on the empty plain. It was another archway—a freestanding stone arbor, wreathed in blossoming moonflower vines, the flowers strangely vibrant despite the ever-present sun.

A bristling energy seemed to emanate from the arbor. Catanya reached out towards it, and the energy rippled as it connected with her outstretched hand. A tingling sensation spread from her fingertips, creeping along her forearm towards her chest. A sudden jolt shocked her out of her trance, and she dropped her arm.

She was still staring at the arbor when Drayk stepped up beside her.

"When darkness lights the day," he mumbled, forehead creased.

Catanya blinked and stared at him. "What?"

Drayk shrugged. "It's an old saying—I read it in a book when I was young." He cast a glance at Laylian before circling the arbor to examine it. As he walked, he cleared his throat and recited the words, "*The moonlit flower shines just out of sight, but when darkness lights the day, change will stir the night.*"

He made eye contact with Catanya through the open arch,

but Catanya didn't know what to say. He took his time surveying the arbor, then he crossed back around to stand with her.

"You know me—not one for poetry, but I always liked that saying..." he muttered, trailing off into silence.

"Are you ready?" asked Laylian in a gentle voice.

Catanya turned towards her. The old woman wore a kind, sympathetic smile, like she understood the swarm of emotions and thoughts swirling inside Catanya's head.

Catanya took a deep breath and nodded.

"Then follow me," said Laylian, before she stepped through the archway and vanished completely.

Catanya and Drayk gaped at the arbor. Then Drayk craned his neck around, as if searching for a sign of Laylian on the other side. But the old woman was gone.

Energy bristled along Catanya's skin and she shivered.

Drayk let out a nervous laugh. "Well..." He took a deep breath and held his hand out for Catanya. "Onwards?" The corner of his mouth twitched like he wanted to laugh.

Catanya smiled and laid her palm on his. "Onwards," she said.

Then, together, they stepped through the arch.

The glade transformed before their eyes. They were still on the plateau, bordered by dense forest with the mountain rising before them. But now the area was full of people moving about, talking happily while tending gardens and preparing food.

The glade appeared to be the centre of a small community, and everyone was out finishing their work, or else enjoying the last rays of sunlight. The landscape teemed with life and a buoyant energy. A narrow stream cut down from the mountain, trickling across the plateau to form an unnaturally circular pond at the centre. Flowers and plants of all different varieties decorated the grassy floor in a mosaic of colours. Squirrels and rabbits scurried through vibrant, overflowing gardens, and birds fluttered in the skies, chirruping, and singing their varied melodies. Scattered throughout the bordering forest, dozens of linen tents and wooden cabins were visible in all different shapes and sizes. Twisting paths wove through the forest in every direction, and countless garlands draped between the tree branches, hanging lanterns that shone like captive stars.

Catanya's jaw dropped as she gazed around at the enchanted place—at all the people living together and thriving without a care in the world. Couples sang and groups of children chased each other across the glade. The entire place glowed with the smiles of the people living in it, and it was mesmerizing.

"Túir-Avlea," said Drayk under his breath, and he sounded a little dumbstruck.

Catanya nodded. "I never pictured anything quite so..." She trailed off, lost for words as she watched a small group of butterflies land on a nearby bush.

"You like it?" asked Laylian, drawing her attention away from the butterflies. The old woman stood a few feet away, accompanied by a tall man and young woman. "This is Viena and Lynor," she said, introducing the strangers. "I asked them to arrange tents for you."

"We've been expecting you for a while," said the man named Lynor. He was thin and reedy, and his sandy-blonde hair fell in waves over his shoulders. Viena, on the other hand, was short and stout. She had thick hair that jutted out wildly in every direction. They both wore kind, eager expressions.

"You must both be so tired," said Laylian. "Why don't you get settled in? Have a rest, and then join us for the bonfire tonight. I promise you are quite safe here."

Catanya didn't need her to say it, she could sense it in the air. This place was peaceful. She had never seen anything quite so beautiful or so serene. She knew she was safe. Nothing bad could ever happen here.

A wide smile cracked through Catanya's fatigue and all the tension of the last several weeks melted away. It had all been worth it. The arduous journey, the near-death experiences, everything she and Drayk had endured to get here had been worth it.

They followed Viena and Lynor, who led the way through the community and into the trees. As they passed the other people, they were greeted with smiles and waves like old friends reuniting after a long absence.

"This place is unbelievable," whispered Drayk. He seemed genuinely intrigued as he took in his surroundings.

"Your tent is this way," said Viena, motioning for Catanya to follow her in the opposite direction of Lynor and Drayk.

Catanya hesitated, looking back at Drayk, but he was preoccupied, grinning and waving at a group of young people gathered outside a nearby cabin. Catanya had to fight the urge to roll her eyes. She turned to follow Viena along the winding path, leaving Drayk to his flirtation.

Before long, they arrived outside a cozy-looking tent. It was nestled between two large trees and made of the same natural linens, wools, and furs that everyone was wearing. Viena pulled back the canopy and led the way inside. Several mismatched rugs covered the forest floor. There was a small table in one corner and a large, comfortable-looking sleeping pallet in the other.

"I've laid out some fresh clothes for you if you want." Viena indicated the linen dress draped over the foot of the bed. "If you want to wash up, I can take you to the pool."

Catanya couldn't think of anything that sounded better right now. She followed Viena back into the forest in search of the pool.

The first sign of it came with the sound of rushing water. Viena pulled back a thick bush to reveal a small waterfall running through a gap in the mountain face and emptying into a shallow spring. The water glittered like sapphires, and a gentle steam rose from its surface.

"I'll leave you to it," said Viena, smiling as she turned and walked back the way they'd come.

Catanya stepped forward eagerly and laid the white linen dress on one of the nearby rocks. She kicked off her sweaty boots and felt the soft, springy grass beneath her aching feet. Her clothes were filthy, covered in salt water, dirt, and grime, not to mention her own sweat and blood. The leather clothes of Awnell had withstood the journey well, but the material chafed and itched.

As she peeled the filthy clothes away from her skin, she noted all her cuts and bruises. Some were healing, but other wounds had reopened, smarting as she tugged the clothes away. The gash on her hand was recent. She'd grazed it, falling in the Dead Wood, and streaks of smeared blood had dried on her palm. Catanya tossed the sullied leather uniform aside and examined her body in more detail. Her once robust frame had worn thin, and her sinewy muscles, crafted by months of training in Awnell, stuck out prominently beneath her papery skin.

The warm steam rising from the spring clung to her bare skin as she approached the edge. A set of carved stone steps led down and she descended into the hot water, allowing it to rise up her body until it was over her shoulders.

The water was unbelievably soothing as it washed away the ordeal of the last few weeks. The spring was deep enough for her to swim a few lengths, stretching out her aching muscles. She paddled forward and stopped beneath the waterfall, letting the stream of cooler water rain upon her head. She pulled her hair out of its ties and watched it float around her.

There was an enchanted quality about this place. It reminded Catanya of the last time she'd been swimming outside like this. She instinctively glanced behind her, almost hopeful, but nobody was there.

"Of course," she said to herself, chuckling ruefully. A slight ache swelled inside her chest, a pain she hadn't had time to acknowledge much in recent weeks. But it was still there, weighing on her whenever she tried to sleep or whenever she allowed herself to reminisce. The pain of losing Jémys would never disappear completely, but she hoped it would fade over time. Unlike everyone else she'd loved and lost, at least Jémys was alive, somewhere out there. He'd chosen to leave, to separate himself from her and the damage that followed in her wake. She preferred to find contentment in that, rather than sadness. She loved him, and it was enough for her to know he was okay. It would be selfish of her to expect anything more.

After she'd washed and returned to her tent, Catanya realized how tired she was. She lay down on the soft bedding, closed her eyes, and drifted immediately off to sleep. And for the first time in as long as she could remember, she slept a dreamless sleep.

When she awoke, it was dark. It took her a minute to remember where she was. She rolled onto her back, staring up at the roof of the tent. The faint glow of the moon was visible through the thin linen. The soothing sounds of crickets and toads filled the night air as a gentle breeze rustled through the trees outside.

She lay there, enjoying the peace and calm as she ran over the last several hours in her mind. Now that she was rested, she could think more clearly, and she realized she had so many questions. Questions about the journey here, the lessons she'd learned along the way. Questions about her powers and her destiny.

Now was her chance to get answers.

She stood up and crossed the tent, brushing through the canopy door and out into the forest. She had expected it to be pitch-black, but the warm glow of lanterns brightened the path out to the glade. They hung from the tree branches every few feet, flooding the forest floor with dancing light.

Catanya made her way along the twisting paths, enjoying the hypnotic ambiance of the place. A gentle hum of voices in the distance grew louder as she approached the clearing. When she emerged from the forest, she found the entire community gathered together around a roaring fire.

Excitement buzzed in the air, as everyone bustled about, preparing food and drinks. Catanya cast around, looking for Laylian. Instead, her eyes fell on Drayk. He stood near the pond, watching a small group of children laugh and chase each other nearby.

Catanya walked towards him, noting how strange it was to see Drayk wearing the airy clothes they'd given him. The linen pants and tunic were loose and rumpled. And what was more, he didn't appear to be wearing any of his weapons. Catanya had never seen Drayk without his sword. It was odd. His posture seemed entirely different—easier and more open. He didn't look like himself at all.

"You look relaxed," she said, stopping a few feet from him.

Drayk turned towards her, surprised. He was clean and shaven, and he looked bright, despite his slightly gaunt features. The journey here had taken a toll on both their bodies, and Drayk's frame looked just as attenuated as hers.

"It's strange," he said, frowning and examining the glade.

Catanya didn't need him to explain. "I know. This place is so peaceful, so calm... but there's something else too. Something in the air, some sort of energy."

Drayk nodded, and then, leaning towards her, he said in a low voice, "How did they know to expect us?"

"There have been signs for months now," said a voice behind them.

They turned to see Laylian walking along the stream nearby.

"Signs?" repeated Catanya.

"Yes. It has been in the stars, in the smoke—a shift in the air." She stopped in front of them, with her hands behind her back, gazing at the sky. "The world's Resonance has ruptured and there is a war coming. It's becoming clearer every day. For ages, signs have been pointing to a moment when our limited reserve of Resonance would meet with a much stronger source. Well, it seems that moment is now." She turned her eyes back down to them and smiled.

"So, you're telling me you can predict the future?" asked Drayk.

Laylian laughed. "Of course not! No one can see the future. We have simply learned to watch and interpret..."

They paused, waiting for her to continue, but she just turned abruptly and said, "You are hungry. Let's eat!"

It was a meal unlike any Catanya had ever experienced. Everyone chatted happily as they gathered around the fire, roasting nuts, meats, and vegetables, and passing around stacks of warm flatbread and baskets of fresh fruit. The carafes of spiced wine tasted more complex and more wonderful than any wine Catanya had ever tried before. And there was no formality or awkwardness in any of the activities. Everyone moved around the glade, interacting with each other, lounging in the soft grass, and splashing in the stream.

After a while, when everyone had finished eating, they assembled around the fire again. Lynor stood up and the atmosphere around the fire pit shifted. The excitement was palpable in the air. Catanya couldn't help but join in, though she didn't understand why.

Then Lynor cleared his throat and began to sing in the most piercingly clear voice Catanya had ever heard.

> In the light of the setting sun,
> We join together in song.
> We carry our hearts in our hands
> And feel our arms growing strong.
>
> We know the time will come soon
> When, our hearts, we need to set free,
> Free to follow their paths,
> The paths we may never see.
>
> But fear not the unknown path,
> In the light of the setting sun,
> When your heart has wandered away,
> Your journey has just begun.

The song had a gentle melody, and Catanya found it soothing. It reminded her of the songs she used to sing to the girls at Camlee Lodge to help them sleep.

Lynor sang several songs that night. Songs about love and history, and some songs in languages Catanya didn't know. Before long, several others had joined him, and the children shouted requests for their favourites.

Catanya laughed as she watched the children clamouring over each other. Then she noticed Viena making her way through the crowd.

"He has a beautiful voice, doesn't he?" asked Viena, taking a seat beside Catanya and gesturing at Lynor.

"It's incredible," said Catanya. "I don't think I've ever heard anything quite so beautiful."

"No. Not even the best singers in Awnell," said Drayk,

34

nodding. He looked as serene as Catanya felt, lounging with his back against a rock and his arms draped over his knees.

"Awnell?" Viena looked at them curiously.

"Oh…" Catanya faltered, looking from Viena to Drayk. She hadn't considered it before, but the people of Túir-Avlea had left Mórceá long before the formation of the kingdoms. They had sealed themselves off in order to remain safe. Of course, they wouldn't know anything about Awnell… or Caerlon.

"It's a kingdom and a city on the mainland," said Drayk, shrugging.

Viena's face brightened with curiosity, and she leaned forward. "What's it like? What's the world like beyond the shoal?" Catanya could tell she'd been waiting all evening to ask them this question.

"Oh, well…" Catanya bit her lip. She didn't really know how to respond. Viena's enthusiastic expression was so innocent and optimistic. She reminded Catanya of her younger self—the version of herself who had been safe in her naïveté, dreaming of a world beyond her small community. Catanya didn't want to be the one to shatter the fantasy for Viena.

"Have you never been beyond the shoal?" asked Drayk, sitting up straighter and saving Catanya the trouble of finding a response.

"No, I was born here. We all were. But I've heard so many stories about the outside world," said Viena. "It sounds amazing." She stared at them expectantly.

"It can be," said Drayk with a smile.

Catanya sighed and rubbed her forehead. "But it can also be horrible," she said quietly, exchanging glances with Drayk.

"Yes, but that's only because the Resonance is out of balance," declared Viena. "And Laylian says the Resonance will be restored soon, and we can all leave here."

"Is that what you want? To leave here?" It surprised Catanya to hear it. She couldn't imagine anyone ever wanting to leave this place.

Viena shrugged. "I love it here. It's my home. But I want to know what else is out there. I want to see the world."

Catanya sighed sadly to herself. "You might not like what you see," she said. She was reminded even more strongly of her younger self. It made her ache for those simpler times.

"But that doesn't mean it's not worth it," said Drayk with a hint of annoyance. He shot Catanya a reproving look.

Catanya opened her mouth to retort, but at that moment, the singing stopped. Laylian stood up in front of everyone with her hands out in a welcoming gesture.

"Good evening, everyone," she greeted them all with a smile. "Tonight is a very special night. It is the night that we've been waiting for. Tonight, we welcome Catanya and Drayk into our community." She paused and gestured towards them.

Everyone's eyes followed her movement, searching out the newcomers.

"I'm sure most of you felt the surge in power when they crossed through the archway into the mountain earlier today," continued Laylian. A murmur went through the crowd and the level of excitement seemed to increase. "This mountain has been our home for generations. Ever since we were forced into hiding during the Quiescence Wars, this mountain has protected us. It kept us safe, kept us alive, and our Resonance survived the decimation. Only those who live here remember how to embrace it and live with it. And only those who welcome the truth—those who open themselves and their senses, seeking harmony with the Natures—can survive the journey to find us. The trials of the Natures."

A shiver of realization ran down Catanya's spine as she exchanged looks with Drayk. The trials of the Natures—the haunted voices on the wind, the torturous images in the fire, the ice that had forced their confessions, the claustrophobic helplessness of the caves—each step had exposed them to one of the Natures, and each step had brought them close to death, but together, they'd made it through. Together, they'd survived.

Catanya instinctively reached for Drayk's hand in the darkness and he grasped it tightly.

But what about the Dead Wood... What Nature had been at play there?

Laylian cleared her throat and took a deep breath before continuing. "There was a time, long ago, when the people of Mórceá lived in peace with one another. We were connected by an energy that flowed through everything and everyone. Those of us who could relate to that energy—who could interact with it—had learned to bend it and influence it. We could unite with the world around us and let its magic flow through us.

"Some were more adept than others, and one man"—she shook her head in disappointment—"one man became infatuated with it. He craved more and more until finally he sought to control it all."

One man, thought Catanya bitterly. Maílater Caer, the founder of Caerlon. The one responsible for generations of injustice, pain, and bloodshed. How could one man have caused so much damage?

"The other practitioners tried to warn him, but he would not listen. Eventually he turned on them all. He siphoned their Resonance for himself and slaughtered nearly every one of them." Laylian paused, closing her eyes as if in remembrance. Grief and pain were etched through the lines on her face. "But the more power he took within himself, the more that power came to control him instead."

Catanya's stomach clenched.

"Resonance was never meant to be harnessed in that way. It was never meant to be controlled by one person alone. It is too powerful. Too strong. The power of the natural world does not want to be contained. It wants to be free, as it was meant to be. As it will be again soon.

"Centuries ago, when our people sealed this mountain off from the world, we swore it was only temporary. One day the binding magic would splinter. The Resonance would grow too powerful to be contained, and it would tear apart, returning to its natural state... So, for generations, we've waited. We've lived here together, safely removed from the dangers of war and tyranny. And generation to generation we've passed on our knowledge. We alone know how to live in harmony with the Natures. We alone know how to tap into Resonance without allowing it to consume us. Now the time has come for us to share that knowledge with our new friends." She gestured towards Catanya and Drayk. "We will help them on their path."

There was a long pause as everyone turned to stare at Catanya again.

"But for now, sleep!" called Laylian, clapping her hands together and shocking everyone out of their trances.

A wave of mingled groans and laughter ran through the group as everyone stood up and filtered off for the evening. As they passed Catanya, they all smiled, greeting her with warm words of welcome or the occasional pat on the back.

But Catanya barely noticed. She made her way through the crowd towards the fire where Laylian stood chatting and bidding goodnight to people in passing.

"Is that true?" she asked when she reached the old woman.

"Of course, it's true," said Laylian, smiling and turning away from the dwindling group of people.

"So, you are going to help me, then?"

"My dear, I have the impression it will be you who helps us in the end, but for now, yes. I will help you as best I can."

"How?" asked Drayk, who had just arrived beside Catanya.

"Oh, I have a few ideas," muttered Laylian absentmindedly. "We'll get started in the morning, how's that?"

Catanya nodded, unsure if she felt relieved or nervous. "Thank you."

As Catanya turned to walk away she heard Laylian saying to Drayk, "Speaking of paths, I'd say it's almost time for you to choose yours, wouldn't you agree? I believe you've got an important role to play."

"Me?" Drayk was surprised. "How can I be important?"

"Oh, nonsense! Everyone is important... which, of course, really means no one is important, doesn't it? So, I suppose there's no reason not to try, now, is there?" She laughed heartily to herself and walked away.

Catanya smiled and waited for Drayk to join her. She took his hand once again and said, "Everyone is important. I like that thought."

Drayk shook his head and chuckled as they walked back towards their tents.

2

THE NEW MAÍFÍRKON

Diyah stood in her chambers, staring at her reflection in the mirror and trying to decide what to do.

Julyán had won the Maífírkon Tournament. Not Slaedir. *Julyán*. How did she feel about that?

Diyah ran her shaky hands through her hair, confused.

The initial rush of adrenaline had worn off and now she had to face reality. Slaedir, the man who'd tortured her and tormented her for months, was finally gone. Watching Julyán take Slaedir's life had been a strange, overwhelming experience. Diyah found she felt no remorse for her present state of relief. Slaedir was dead and she was pleased. It brought her comfort to know that appalling monster was gone, and he couldn't hurt anyone else.

But what about Julyán? Her conversation with him before the final round had rattled her.

All I've ever wanted is to see that bastard dead at my feet, to finally make him suffer—make him pay. I've waited long enough.

His determination to win had seemed like more than a professional rivalry. It had seemed personal. And Slaedir had killed Julyán's father, hadn't he? If this had all been about revenge for him, then what would Julyán do next?

Tonight was the grand banquet—the ceremony to swear in the new maífirkon. Diyah had promised herself that she wouldn't attend. Before the final round, she'd been certain. She'd refused to accept a fate where she was forced into an abusive, loveless marriage with Caerlon's maífirkon, and she'd known what she was going to do. The vials were ready to go in her pocket.

Diyah pulled them out and stared at them momentarily. The plan had seemed so simple, so solid. But that was before. Before all these questions, and before...

You're not going to stop me? Not even if you win? Diyah had been so frightened when he'd discovered her plan, but Julyán hadn't reacted the way she'd thought he would. He hadn't tried to stop her or dissuade her at all..

No... My victory will be its own reward.

His sole focus had been Slaedir, nothing more. He'd lied to everyone, including his brother, concealing his true intentions with a masterful level of control unlike anything Diyah had ever seen. What was he hiding?

She closed her eyes in frustration and shoved the vials back into her pocket. The curiosity was too strong. She needed answers, she needed to talk to him. It was the only thing she knew for sure.

Diyah had seen Julyán briefly after the tournament to tend his wounds, but he'd barely spoken two words to her. Servants and courtiers had bustled in and out, eager to congratulate their new maífirkon. She needed an opportunity to be alone with him.

If she truly wanted answers, there was only one way to get them.

Diyah glanced in the mirror one last time, decided she

looked presentable enough—not that she cared—and set out for the banquet.

When she arrived, the festive grandeur of it all temporarily floored her. The Great Hall was adorned with shining silk banners that hung from the ceiling. The violet and gold colours were overwhelmingly bright, flaunting their obnoxious royal pride in the aftermath of a gruesome tournament. Enormous tables ran down the sides of the room, piled high with platters of every kind of food: roasted chicken, salted pork, lamb shanks, tureens of seared vegetables, and trays of fruits and cheeses. There were jugs of bark-beer and haymead, carafes of spiced wine and sourwood rum, and a dessert table full of the most elaborate cakes and pies Diyah had ever seen. The hall was packed with people dressed in their finest clothes, and the gentle hum of a harp somewhere told Diyah there would be music and possibly dancing later in the evening.

"Diyah," said Fehla, breaking free from the crowd to find her. She looked regal in an elaborate, deep blue gown with a wide neckline. As always, a delicate gold circlet sat perched on her head. "I was starting to worry you weren't coming." She glanced nervously back at her son, who lounged in his throne, surrounded by simpering courtiers. "Julyán told Cadyan you wouldn't be here."

"Oh, well..." Diyah shrugged. She didn't want to tell Fehla about her plan, nor the conversation with Julyán that had put it on hold. "Have you seen Julyán? I need to talk to him."

"He's over there." Fehla pointed towards the table in the corner.

Julyán stood there, looking remarkably neat and stately in his ceremonial uniform. It was a deep plum surcoat with long sleeves and a standing collar. Intricate golden embroidery circled the neckline and continued along the front where the laces held it together. A thick black belt was fastened across his waist, awaiting its new sword. And his long black cloak hung off his shoulders, giving him an even more intimidating presence than usual. The uniform had been custom fitted for him and it was hard not to notice how well-built he was underneath it all.

Julyán turned to see her watching him, and an expression of pleasant surprise crossed his face. He took a sip of his wine and placed it back down on the table as he walked to meet her. He strode through the crowd, ignoring several people's attempts to engage him in conversation. The crowd seemed to part for him instinctively, clearing a path for their new maífírkon. Diyah wasn't sure if it was respect or fear that motivated them. She supposed it was both.

As he came closer, Diyah noticed that the deep plum colour of his uniform accentuated the colour of his eyes. The gold highlights reflected the light of the many candles above, shimmering as he moved.

"I'm surprised to see you," he said when he was standing right in front of her and Fehla. Several bruises and cuts disrupted his smooth, dark complexion, but his eyes seemed especially bright as he searched Diyah's face. "I didn't think you were coming. I thought—"

"Well, that *was* the plan," said Diyah. "But there's something I need to know first."

Julyán's face fell slightly. He waited as Fehla's attention was drawn away and the queen left them alone. Then he spoke in a low, almost wary voice. "What do you need to know?"

Diyah thought back to their interaction this morning, before the final round. The way he'd spoken to her about Jémys. She'd seen it in him then, the sadness and regret. And so much anger.

Diyah hesitated, a little nervous to begin. Then she took a deep breath and looked him straight in the eye. "I need to know why," she said. "This morning you told me your victory would be its own reward. That you'd waited years to see Slaedir dead. Why? Why was it so important to you that you win that tournament? I don't believe you really care about being Caerlon's maífírkon. So, what was it really about?"

Julyán's posture stiffened and he clenched his jaw. "Just let it go," he muttered, trying to turn away.

"No." Diyah spoke in a hard whisper as she moved to block his path. "I need to know."

"No, you don't!" he retorted. "And you don't really want to know."

"Yes, I do! And while we're at it, I want to know why you're working so hard to make Jémys hate you."

"It's none of your business."

Their angry whispers were attracting attention. Julyán shook his head and tried to walk away.

Diyah grabbed his hand with hers and held it fast. "You said it was easier for Jémys to hate you than to accept the truth. Well, that's not good enough for me. I want the truth. And I won't stop pushing until I get it."

Julyán stared at their interlocked hands, frowning. Then he turned his gaze up to the ceiling.

"Please, Julyán," she urged in a softer voice. "I need to know."

With his eyes still trained on the ceiling, Julyán spoke through clenched teeth, like he was struggling to let the words out. "I needed to win," he said. "I needed to watch Slaedir die, and I needed to be the one to kill him."

"But why?"

Julyán turned his eyes to rest on her, his head tilted like he was weighing his options. "You know why."

Diyah's breath caught in her throat. "Please tell me," she said, pressing him to continue.

Julyán sighed in resignation and pulled her away from the crowd. He looked around to make sure no one was listening, then took a deep breath and continued, "Because I swore to myself over ten years ago that I would do it. I swore I would kill the man who killed my father and I would have my revenge." He was barely moving his lips. "That's all I have ever wanted."

It surprised Diyah to see Julyán shaking slightly as he spoke. She squeezed his hand to encourage him to keep talking.

"It was Casréyan's order, of course, but still... I never forgot what that man did. The way he carved and sliced into my father. The smile on his face as my father screamed..."

Diyah's insides twisted. She could picture the scene so clearly. It would be a long time before she forgot Slaedir's predatory smile.

"So, when they brought me to join the firkon, I vowed to make him pay," continued Julyán. "I spent years working for him, keeping my head down. Waiting."

"But Jémys told me..." Diyah trailed off, searching for the words. "Jémys said they executed your father. He said your father dissented, and that you... you told..." Diyah looked at him apologetically.

"Jémys never knew the truth," muttered Julyán. "Only my father and I did."

"So... what is the truth?"

Julyán averted his eyes, shaking his head.

"Please," she whispered, not letting go of his hand.

Julyán sighed heavily and closed his eyes. "Casréyan was coming for *me*. He wanted to punish me—most likely kill me— but my father intervened." He opened his eyes and looked back down at Diyah, a strained intensity visible behind his usual mask of indifference. "My father pleaded with them to spare my life but they wouldn't listen. He tried to fight, to stop them, but Casréyan declared his actions to be treason. He ordered Slaedir to execute my father. But not before promising him I would suffer a fate worse than death... They made me watch... I watched Slaedir torture and kill my father."

Horror stole the warmth from Diyah's body, and she shivered. She listened in silence, struggling to keep the disgust from her face. The party raged around them, but the noise and high-spirited energy felt miles away.

Julyán turned to watch a group of courtiers laughing and talking nearby. "We were a noble family, and I was the first-born son," he continued in a quieter voice. "So, instead of killing me, they brought me to join the fírkon earlier than expected. They stripped our family of its title and reduced them to poverty while I started my training. Well," he turned back to Diyah with a humourless smile, "they claimed they were training me, but it was more than that... they were breaking me. It was my father's punishment... and mine," he finished, shrugging as if the memories didn't hurt.

"But why?" Diyah's eyes filled with tears as she tried not to imagine what Julyán had endured as a boy. "Why did they want to kill you?"

"Because in Casréyan's mind, I had done something unfor-givable," he said in a blank voice.

When he didn't offer any more information, Diyah urged him to continue. "What did you do?" she asked.

He looked at her, clearly reluctant to tell her the truth. "I insulted the crown—humiliated them," he said. He saw the dissatisfied look on her face and sighed. "I had an altercation with one of the royal family. It was just a simple exchange between young boys, but... Casréyan would never allow his family to be shamed like that. He was a petty man, and I had demeaned his son... I had to pay. He came looking for me in Mellot Cove that evening..." He trailed off, avoiding her stare, and Diyah suddenly realized what he meant.

"No!" she gasped, as a lump formed in her throat. "No! I don't believe it." She shook her head, staring up at him. It couldn't be true...

That day over ten years ago near Mellot Cove. Julyán had defended a little girl in the woods, standing up to the young prince of Caerlon. And the king had tried to kill him for it.

Julyán just shrugged.

A long pause settled between them, as Diyah absorbed everything. "I'm so sorry," she said, on the verge of tears. "I'm so sorry." She put her hand on his arm but he pulled it away.

"I don't want your pity," he said.

"But... but this is all *my* fault." The memory of that day in the woods had always been a good one, something to remind her of the strength and kindness that still existed in Mórceá. But now... Tears trickled down her face. She couldn't bear to think about it.

"No, it's not," said Julyán. "And I don't want your guilt any more than I want your pity." He backed away from her. "I tried to tell you that you didn't want to know. But now you do, and I don't need your sympathy. I got what I wanted. Slaedir is dead. I killed him."

"But—"

"Let it go," he said coldly.

Just then, Jémys emerged from the crowd to stop at Diyah's side. "Are you all right, Diyah?" He was glaring at Julyán. "What did you say to her?"

"No, Jémys, it's fine." Diyah wiped the tears from her cheeks. "Julyán was just telling me—"

"I'm surprised to see you here, little brother," said Julyán, cutting Diyah off before she could continue. He angled away from her, re-establishing his guarded distance. "I thought you'd still be licking your wounds."

Diyah blinked, taken aback by Julyán's sudden change.

Jémys pursed his lips, his face set in defiance. "You know, it's fitting that you should be the next maífirkon," he spat. "First Slaedir, now you... both men responsible for my father's death, and both men murderers and cowards alike. I can only hope you meet the same fate as your predecessor."

Diyah opened her mouth to retort but Julyán cut her off again.

"Careful, Jémie. Don't forget you're one of my fírkon. I'm your leader now." He smirked, glancing only briefly at Diyah.

Diyah frowned, shaking her head in disbelief. She couldn't understand why Julyán was still lying to his brother. The tournament was over, Slaedir was gone. He didn't need to act like this anymore.

Diyah took a reflexive step back from him, and his eyes tracked her movement, darkening slightly.

"Well, don't let me keep you," he snapped at her. "I know you have something pressing to do tonight, don't you?"

He turned to walk away, and Diyah cursed herself for letting him see her uneasiness. Before she realized what she was doing, she called after him, "I'm staying right here!"

Julyán stopped in his tracks and looked back at her. His emotions always so carefully guarded, Diyah wasn't sure what she read on his face then. Was it confusion? Surprise? Curiosity? However, he was spared from having to reply by Cadyan's sudden appearance.

"Well, I think it's time we get this ceremony started," said Cadyan, clapping him on the shoulder. "Don't you think?" He sounded impatient, like his mind was distracted.

"Yes, Your Majesty." Julyán gave Diyah one last searching look before following his king through the crowd.

The ceremony that followed was something Diyah would never forget. The sight of Julyán kneeling before Cadyan and pledging his eternal allegiance sent chills running down her spine. Despite everything he'd just told her, Julyán still seemed every bit the loyal soldier.

"*I pledge my life and my sword to the promotion and protection of Caerlon and its one true ruler.*" Julyán spoke in a clear, ringing voice. "*I vow to remain faithful to the king, never cause him harm, and never act against him or the interests of his kingdom. I will lead his armies with honour and without deceit, with this sole purpose: to uphold the glory and majesty of Caerlon and its king.*"

Diyah thought she noticed a slight hesitation as Julyán recited the oath. She looked around the room, but no one else seemed to notice anything.

"Now, Julyán, I mark you as the rightful maífirkon of Caerlon," said Cadyan as he pulled a red-hot iron out of the kiln at his side and pressed it into Julyán's skin above his heart. Julyán didn't even flinch as the metal seared his flesh, leaving a clear imprint of the royal insignia on his chest. He simply re-tied the laces on his uniform and turned his gaze back towards his king.

"Now take this sword, the sword of the maífirkon. May it serve you as it has served those who came before you."

Diyah saw a definite shadow pass over Julyán's face as he reached out and took the gilded sword that once belonged to his enemy—the sword that had killed his father.

"Now rise," commanded Cadyan.

As Julyán stood beside him, Cadyan grasped his hand in brotherhood and raised it above their heads, calling out to the crowd, "For Caerlon, for Might, and for Glory!"

"For Caerlon, for Might, and for Glory!" echoed the crowd as they raised their glasses in salute to their new maífirkon.

The crowd parted and all the firkon stepped forward, forming a line down the aisle in front of Julyán and Cadyan. One by one, the firkon knelt before the dais and presented their swords at their new leader's feet (even Jémys, though he knelt only briefly and wore a sour expression throughout the entire process). It was remarkable watching them pledge their service to Julyán, given they'd all been vying for the same post less than a week before.

Diyah had gotten to know most of the firkon during the tournament, healing them after every round. She recognized Holun, the man who'd nearly killed Julyán. He looked very calm, presenting his weapon at his new leader's feet. Diyah didn't know how Julyán could trust any of these men. What was stopping them from simply stabbing their new maífirkon in the back when he wasn't looking?

But of course, the answer was obvious. It was the same thing that prevented anyone from rising up or acting out.

Cadyan.

Cadyan and Julyán were a team now, and it made Diyah's skin crawl. She couldn't reconcile Julyán's past with his apparent loyalty to the king. Surely Cadyan was every bit as responsible for his father's death as Slaedir. How could Julyán stand beside the king with such composure?

In fact, how could any of these men trust a man who commanded them to fight and die and proclaimed it entertainment?

Diyah watched the next group of firkon step up to Julyán. These men were younger, the boys who'd barely survived their first tournament. Some still wore bandages or walked with limps—injuries they'd bear for the rest of their lives.

Then came the new Awnadh-firkon. Astonishingly few of them had any injuries. It reminded Diyah how adept they were. The Awnadh warriors had made it through the tournament with the fewest casualties and the fewest injuries. The worst injury was a man named Bir, a burly man with a long, braided beard. He'd lost his hand in his fight with Slaedir.

Diyah watched him approach Julyán, and noticed, with pleasant surprise, that he'd fashioned himself a wooden hand. It was bluntly carved from some dark lumber, likely a piece of scrap firewood. The shape was crude, with only two fingers fully hewn from the block, but it was impressive nonetheless. Rey had told Diyah that Bir was a carpenter. It lifted her spirits to think he'd managed to carve something suitable in less than a week and with only one hand. It gave her hope that there was life after the tournament for some of these men.

Diyah watched with particular interest as a tall, serious man stepped forward and presented his weapon at Julyán's feet. Rey, the ex-lieutenant of Awnell. He'd betrayed his queen and his kingdom, siding with Cadyan during the battle for Awnell. Now he was declaring his allegiance to Julyán. She couldn't hear what they were saying, but Julyán's body language told her there was no trust between them.

In all the uproar of the final round Diyah had almost forgotten about Rey. The former lieutenant of Awnell was another mystery she yearned to understand. Why had he let Jémys win their match in the tournament? Was it possible he'd just made a mistake? Rey was supposed to be the greatest fighter in Awnell, but that didn't mean he was perfect, did it?

Diyah sipped a glass of haymead and watched Rey for the next few minutes. He looked uncomfortable, wandering around near the entrance as though waiting for something to happen. He stopped beside the door just as another man joined him. They looked around to make sure no one was watching and then stepped outside.

Diyah hesitated only briefly, and then curiosity got the better of her. She placed her cup on the table, glanced around quickly, and slipped out the door after them.

After a few minutes searching the corridors, she heard voices coming from a small room near the armoury. She crouched behind a statue so she would be out of sight while she listened.

"Should we tell her?" came a voice through the door. "She needs to know it's working. Slaedir is dead. Our secret is safe."

"I did," said Rey. "But we can't risk making too many visits to the dungeon, it'll arouse suspicion."

Diyah held her breath, listening. If they were visiting the dungeons, then that meant...

"Okay, but then what? What's next? Did Ayr tell you how long it would take?"

"No. We'll just have to be patient and follow our orders."

I knew it, thought Diyah. Her instinct was right. Rey and his men had been lying this entire time. They never truly defected to Caerlon. They were still loyal to their queen, and they'd been following her orders all along. *I'll bet Ayr told them not to hurt Jémys*, she thought.

"Any progress?" asked Rey with a more urgent tone.

"I'm getting close," responded a new female voice. "He trusts me and his spirit is weakening. He's getting sloppy, so it shouldn't be long now." Diyah thought she recognized the voice, but she couldn't place it. And she hadn't seen anyone else leaving with Rey and his soldier.

"Good, just make sure you take care of him when it's done."

"Obviously." The woman sounded irritable. There was a long pause. Diyah thought maybe they were done, but then the woman spoke again in an eager whisper. "So, do you really think she can do it?"

"Ayr believes in her," said Rey.

Who are they talking about now? Diyah's heart pounded. She strained to hear the hushed voices through the door.

"And Cadyan thinks she's dead so he won't be expecting it. We'll have the element of surprise."

Diyah almost lost her footing and stumbled. She couldn't believe what she'd just heard. Then she leaned forward so her ear was closer to the door.

"And you're sure she's not dead?"

"I'm sure," said Rey.

"And we're certain she'll come here? She'll come face her brother?" asked the woman with a hint of doubt in her voice.

"Absolutely. Let's just hope she's mastered her powers by then."

As Diyah made her way back into the banquet hall, her head was spinning. Her heart felt lighter than it had in months. She looked around at everyone packed into the room—all these people she hated—and had to resist the urge to laugh.

Catanya was alive. Awnell had never been defeated, they

were just biding their time and distracting Caerlon until Catanya could make it back.

Diyah could have cried with joy. She stood, surrounded by people celebrating their new maífirkon, as a warm glow formed inside her. A glow that nothing could extinguish. She spent the rest of the evening watching the proceedings with a great deal more interest.

Catanya was alive and none of these people suspected a thing. Catanya was *alive*. There was still hope.

As the evening wound to an end, Cadyan stood in front of the crowd one last time to announce that the maífirkon's wedding would take place two nights later.

Diyah felt dozens of eyes on her again, but she didn't care. She and Julyán locked eyes across the room, and she knew she was making the right decision. She had hope again—hope that there was more to Julyán than he let on, and hope that Catanya was coming to save them all.

3

THE AGE OF RESONANCE

Catanya awoke early from another dreamless sleep. It had been a long time since she'd felt this rested. She swung her legs off the side of the sleeping pallet and stood up, stretching her body. Though still sore from her journey, her muscles felt much better after a full night's sleep in a comfortable place.

The pale light told Catanya it was just before dawn. Birds chirped in the trees nearby. The soft dewy air was refreshing on her face as she stepped out of her tent and inhaled deeply.

She was eager to find Laylian and finally learn about her magic, but a large part of her also longed to enjoy this sense of repose for as long as possible.

Making her way slowly along the path towards the glade, she was amazed again by how beautiful this place was. The trees were enormous and ancient. Their moss-covered limbs sprawled and tangled together, with bark that peeled to form patterns and faces. The garlands of lanterns that hung between the branches still gave off a faint pearly glow, fading into the misty blue tinge of the new dawn light.

The entire place had a mesmerizing and dreamlike quality

that spoke to the artist in her. She could imagine herself sitting here for hours, drawing the lines of the trees and the curves of the branches as they stretched towards the sky. She could sketch the shadows as the rays of light peeked through the canopy, highlighting the leaf-strewn floor in patches of emerald and sage.

Catanya had never felt this way about a place before. She had never known in her bones that she belonged somewhere. Until now.

She made her way along the path until she spotted a figure standing in a small clearing a few feet away. As she moved closer, she realized it was Laylian.

Her long white hair fluttered around her head, like feathers in the breeze, and it dangled messily from underneath the same wilting wreath she'd worn the day before. A serviceable-looking, long brown vest hung open over her flowing robes. The robes looked a little too big for her as they bunched up around her ankles. Catanya wondered how Laylian didn't trip on the hem when she walked. But right now, the old woman stood still, gazing up at the canopy of trees.

Catanya was on the verge of joining her when she stopped, wondering if Laylian wanted to be alone.

"Don't be silly," said Laylian. She turned to look at Catanya and smiled, her bright eyes twinkling beneath her bushy white eyebrows.

"Sorry, I didn't mean to disturb you," said Catanya.

"Nonsense." Laylian brushed away the comment and turned back to stare at the trees. "Have you ever noticed the different timbres of the trees?"

Catanya opened her mouth to respond, frowned, and closed it again without saying a word. She wasn't at all sure what Laylian meant.

"This one here is mellow," continued Laylian, apparently unaware of Catanya's confusion. "It's croakier than it used to be." She stepped forward and laid her hand on the trunk of a mid-sized oak. "Ah, yes, age comes to us all in the end." She chuckled merrily and began humming to herself as she walked in circles around the clearing, pressing her hand against each of the trees.

Catanya cleared her throat. She didn't want to interrupt, but she had the impression Laylian might have forgotten she was here.

Laylian gave a little start. "Listen," she said, beckoning for Catanya to join her. "Come on."

Catanya felt a little bewildered, but she did as instructed. Stepping forward, she held up her hands and tried to imitate Laylian's gestures. She even leaned her head in closer, straining to hear anything other than the general hum of the forest.

"Mmm, nothing?" asked Laylian, eyeing her.

Catanya bit her lip. "No, sorry. What should I be hearing?"

"Should?" Laylian frowned thoughtfully, she repeated the word a few times as though trying to understand it, and then she shrugged. "I don't know much about oughts and shoulds, I'm more concerned with wills and shalls!"

Catanya just stared at her, completely nonplussed, but Laylian seemed to find it all amusing. "You might not hear it now, but you will." She sounded confident.

Catanya frowned, trying to understand. "Are you talking about Resonance?"

Laylian smiled and nodded. Then she motioned for Catanya to walk with her.

They set off together through the forest, taking no path in particular. Laylian made several stops, exploring the surroundings with eagerness and childlike wonder, as if she were seeing everything for the first time.

"Every creature on this earth is capable of Resonance to a certain degree," she said after a while. "However, very few people are ever aware of that connection enough to use it. In the years leading up to the Quiescence Wars, the practice of Resonance was at its most prevalent..." She trailed off, distracted as a bright yellow bird flew past them, tweeting happily. She tracked its movements for a few minutes, watching with apparent glee as it landed on a nearby log and began rooting around for insects to eat.

"What was I saying?" She frowned, picking at a spot on her chin. "Oh yes." She chuckled and started walking again. "In the days before the wars—the Golden Age of Resonance, if you will—when the maílehrs took apprentices and the old religion was still heavily practiced, there was a great deal of debate about the true nature of Resonance. Some believed it was the will of the Natures acting through us, others believed it was an affliction that needed to be cured. I have always been of the belief that Resonance is a relationship of *harmony*. It is a powerful connection, which exists in all of us no matter how small or how unacknowledged. And, as with all relationships, this connection can be wholesome or it can be destructive. There is nothing inherently good or evil about Resonance, it is the people who determine its purpose."

Catanya's mind raced as she tried to take in everything she was hearing. This was all new to her. She had never understood Resonance beyond the vague concepts she'd heard as a child. Most people in Caerlon had been taught that it was an uncontrollable and dangerous force, one that caused years of pain and suffering. They believed Maílater Caer had been their saviour, the hero who'd abolished its rampant spread and destructive force.

But regardless of what Caerlon claimed, most people still told stories of Resonance, tales of magic and legends of kind practitioners who would save them from their troubles. It had become a metaphor for hope and kindness in a time when there was so little of each. But those stories were so fantastical, so over-embellished that no one believed them. No one really knew the truth anymore.

"Now that being said, there are what you might call two *variations* of Resonance," continued Laylian, and Catanya hung on every word. "The first and most common is Resonance with the physical Natures. This can be anything ranging from a gentle connection with one Nature—such as a sailor might hold for the sea or a farmer might have for the land—to a full mastery of invoking and materializing."

"Invoking and materializing?" asked Catanya.

Laylian smiled and nodded. Then she closed her eyes and a powerful breeze blew through the area ahead, lifting an assortment of leaves and twigs into the air in a delicate wave that settled back down to the ground gently.

"Invoking is the easiest," said Laylian calmly. "Materializing takes some more effort."

Catanya was still gazing at the spot where the leaves had landed so she didn't immediately notice the small flame Laylian held in her hand.

"Oh—" She jumped back in surprise. Laylian relaxed so the flame disappeared into a wisp of smoke.

"Most of us here in Túir-Avlea can still perform small acts of Resonance like that." She brushed the remaining smoke away and continued walking. "Enough to keep our little community alive and thriving, but nothing that could be considered *earth-shattering*." She chuckled at her use of words.

"And the second form of Resonance? What about that?" asked Catanya, hurrying after her.

"Ah, yes..." Laylian had a strange, far-off look in her eye. "The second form has always been rare and, therefore, much more difficult. Even in the years before the wars, there were only two or three people who ever truly learned to master it." She smiled sadly and took a deep breath before continuing. "While the first form involves connecting with the physical

Natures, the second involves connecting with the Spirits themselves."

Catanya frowned. "I'm not sure I know what that means," she said. "What Spirits?" The old religion worshipped the Natures, but Catanya had never heard people talk about spirits before.

Laylian chuckled and shook her head. "*The* Spirits—the souls and the energy of every living creature past, present, and future," she said, as if it were the most obvious thing in the world.

"Oh... right..." Catanya wasn't sure that explanation made anything clearer.

Laylian took Catanya's arm and pulled her along the path towards a small grassy dell. "Imagine a stream of energy—a life force—flowing between us. It is between you and me here"— she released Catanya's arm and gestured to the forest— "between the trees, the grass, the birds, and insects. Map it out in your mind, follow it along and watch how it connects every-thing. There are no breaks or gaps in it. It just flows. Even after our bodies decay and return to the Earth, that stream continues to flow. That essence is what we mean by 'the Spirits'. And they are waiting for you to connect with them." She smiled at Catanya expectantly.

"R-right now?" asked Catanya, flabbergasted.

Laylian chuckled. "No, we must work up to that. You cannot run before you walk. That is how accidents happen." She gave Catanya a meaningful and sympathetic smile.

"Accidents?" Catanya's mouth went dry. Did Laylian know about the times when Catanya's power had overwhelmed her? That time in Finnua, or Awnell? Or that time in the cabin?

"Mmm..." Laylian nodded. "The Resonance in you is very strong, Catanya, I can feel it itching and scratching away inside. I expect it has been a constant struggle for you. The Spirits converge around you and they want to be set free. It will take a long time before you can control them completely."

Catanya was somehow both comforted and disappointed to hear that. "So, how do I learn to control them, then?" she asked after a while, trying to ignore the tightness in her stomach.

Laylian paused and tilted her head to the side like she was examining her. "You begin as every student begins. One step at a time." She grinned widely and scrambled onto the grass where she sprawled out on her back, facing the small patch of sky between the trees. "Come on." She patted the ground next to her.

Catanya was taken aback. "All right..." She stretched out on the forest floor beside Laylian, feeling more than a little silly.

"Good, good." Laylian sounded cheerful. "Now, the first thing you must do is learn to attune yourself to the Natures, beginning with the Earth. Let the energy flow from the ground and into your body. Stretch out with your spirit and listen to the vibrations and the intonations. Focus on letting them pass through you and then back into the Earth."

Catanya wasn't sure what that meant. She closed her eyes and focused her attention on the areas where her body touched the Earth. The back of her head, her shoulders, and so on.

Laylian clicked her tongue reprovingly. "No, no, silly. Don't connect physically, connect emotionally. You are stretching the wrong muscles."

"How did you—"

"I can feel it," she said simply.

So, Catanya tried again. This time, she tried to reach out with her mind, she tried to imagine the Earth speaking with her. She imagined what its voice would sound like, what words it would say.

Still nothing.

Catanya let out a sigh of frustration.

"Steady, Catanya," said Laylian in a soothing voice. "Have patience."

Catanya took a deep breath to force her frustration back in check and tried again. This time she imagined she was part of the Earth—that she could feel everything it felt and do everything it did. She imagined stretching herself beneath the trees, the trickling stream cutting through her.

At one point she thought she detected a slight tingling on the back of her neck, but it was gone almost as soon as it came.

They lay there for what seemed like hours, as Catanya struggled to stretch her mind out into the Earth. Finally, Laylian rose to her feet. "Excellent start," she said.

"Really?" Catanya opened her eyes and frowned up at the old woman. It seemed like they'd just wasted an entire morning lying in the grass.

"Oh yes. A very promising beginning." Laylian held out her hand for Catanya and pulled her onto her feet with surprising strength.

"I don't feel any different," said Catanya.

"Well, of course, no one ever *feels* different, you just *do* different."

Catanya frowned and decided not to respond. She found Laylian a little baffling still. Sometimes she seemed like a wise teacher, and other times she just seemed like a foolish old bat.

Laylian grinned at Catanya like she seemed to know exactly what was on her mind.

Together, they turned and walked along the main path leading out of the forest. As they emerged into the glade, the area was buzzing with activity. Catanya spotted Drayk standing nearby. He held himself with confidence and ease, with one foot on a log and his hand on his knee. Viena and a group of eager teenagers surrounded him, bombarding him with questions about the world outside the mountain. He seemed to be rather enjoying himself as he spun wild tales about his exploits.

Catanya smiled to herself as she headed over to join him.

"And then what did you do?" asked one of the boys—a blonde, freckled teen whose dewy features had almost settled into manhood. The eager look on his face told Catanya he was more than a little taken with Drayk.

"Then we ran," Drayk declared with a laugh. "As fast as our feet would fly. And before they realized what had happened, we were long gone, never to be seen or heard from again."

Everyone roared. Drayk turned to find Catanya standing next to him. "Oh, hello." He grinned at the amusement on her face. Then his eyes lit up with curiosity and he stepped away from the group. "So how did it go?" he asked.

Catanya shrugged. "I'm not sure. Laylian seemed pleased, but if you ask me, I just lay there like a lump for hours." She snorted humourlessly.

Drayk patted her on the back. "Well, it's bound to take some time, right? But you'll figure it out. I know you will." He gave her a confident smile. "Now, have you met everyone?" he asked, gesturing to the group of people around him.

Drayk introduced her to the group, which included Viena, a wiry girl with short black hair named Elmia, a towering young lad, Broinan, who looked like he'd been stretched too tall too fast, and Sprale, the freckled boy whose eyes kept flicking eagerly back to Drayk. The four young people seemed overcome with curiosity about the newcomers and their lives in the outside world.

"What's it like living in a city?" asked Broinan in a surprisingly deep voice.

Elmia inched closer, trying to get around the tall boy. "Have you ever been on a ship?" she asked.

"Exactly how far is it from Caerlon to Awnell?"

The questions tumbled out of them so fast that Catanya and Drayk barely had time to respond.

"I haven't been able to get away from them all morning," said Drayk in a low voice so only Catanya could hear.

Catanya snorted. "Yeah, you love it," she said with a wry smile.

Drayk gave her a playful grin and shrugged. "True."

"So, what clothes do people wear in Awnell?" asked Viena, her tone inquisitive and persistent. Catanya noticed she was scribbling their responses in a small, handmade notebook. The cover was rawhide, and the pages were likely birch bark or calf skin.

"Whenever possible, none at all," replied Drayk, wagging his eyebrows. Catanya smacked him on the back of the head.

"Just picture the clothes we were wearing when we arrived here, but cleaner," she said, shaking her head at the amused expression on Drayk's face. "Why do you ask?" She turned her attention back to Viena.

"I want to know everything about the world outside Túir-Avlea."

"Viena's a writer," chimed in Sprale. "She writes tales of adventure to keep herself from going mad with restlessness and boredom."

The others laughed and Viena shrugged. "I enjoy it," she said unapologetically. "And when the Resonance is back in balance and we can finally leave, I'm going out there to experience some of these things myself."

Catanya smiled, thinking once again how strongly Viena reminded her of her younger self.

"I'm sure you will," said Drayk with the same confident smile he'd given Catanya moments before.

The glade was filling up now as preparations began for the midday meal. The group of eager listeners was forced to disperse in order to help with the work.

After they'd finished eating, Laylian suggested Catanya spend some time getting to know her environment. *Attuning,* she had called it, which was apparently the first step in mastering Resonance.

So Catanya spent the afternoon exploring the central glade and trying to connect with it. She sat for a while, breathing the refreshing Wind as it brushed against her face. Then she spent some time near the stream, listening to the gentle trickle of the Water against the rocks.

When that didn't work, she decided to explore the community a bit more intently. She wandered along the paths, stopping to chat with people and learn how they lived. The longer she spent interacting with the people, the more she discovered the small moments of Resonance woven into everyday life in Túir-Avlea. It was just like Laylian said, nothing earth-shattering, but it was clear everyone used their Resonance to support the community.

Whether it was the streams that somehow flowed uphill into the gardens, the plants growing out of season, or the unnaturally perfect temperature in the air, the entire place brimmed with life and energy.

The sun was approaching the horizon, and Catanya was wandering the paths through the forest when she heard a new sound coming through the trees. Someone was singing nearby. A gentle melody wove through the air with such grace it seemed even the birds were compelled to listen.

Then a second voice joined, moving in perfect harmony.

Catanya couldn't resist heading towards the sound. She reached the end of her path and arrived at a small tent surrounded by sprawling gardens.

She recognized Lynor standing among the bushes. He was singing with a woman as they worked in the garden, and every few minutes they made eye contact across the garden and smiled. Their love and affection were palpable in the air.

Suddenly the melody swelled. Two more voices joined the

song. Catanya cast around for the source and spotted two young children carrying baskets out to their parents.

The family continued to sing while they worked. It seemed natural, unrehearsed. They created beautiful music together, almost effortlessly.

"Hello!"

Catanya blinked and realized the song had ended. One of the children stood in front of her, sporting a wide grin full of missing teeth.

"You're one of the new people who came through the arch," said the young girl with a matter-of-fact, eager tone. She looked to be about six or seven years old.

"I am," said Catanya, smiling down at her.

"My name is Heena," she said, placing her basket on the floor, and beaming up at her. "What are you doing at our tent?"

"I heard you singing." Catanya looked over at the garden and saw the others coming to join her.

"Catanya." Lynor wiped his hands on a cloth before taking her hands in greeting. "May I introduce you to my family? This is my wife, Emra." Unlike her husband, who was tall and reedy, Emra was short and dark. Her cheeks were ruddy and flushed and her face glowed with happiness. "And you've met my daughter, Heena. This is my son, Flian."

Flian waved, but stood behind his father, peering around his leg like he was nervous to approach.

"Catanya heard us singing," said Heena proudly. "Did you like the song?"

"I've never heard anything more beautiful," said Catanya. "Do you sing together often?"

"Every day," said Emra, beaming at her kids. "It's how we stay attuned to each other, and to the Natures."

"Really?" Catanya was curious. She hadn't considered the possibility of attuning to another person.

Lynor nodded. "Everyone has a unique process. For us, we find singing helps us connect."

"Flian and I love to sing!" said Heena, as she tried to beckon her little brother forward, but Flian's cheeks flushed, and he took another step behind his father.

Emra patted her daughter on the shoulder and shook her head. Then she turned back to Catanya with a sympathetic smile. "How is *your* attuning going?" she asked.

"Um..." Catanya rubbed her neck. "I don't think I've made much progress yet. Maybe I should try singing."

Lynor and Emra exchanged smiles.

"You can certainly try that, if you like," said Lynor. "There's no one right way to attune. You need to find whatever speaks to you. What calms you and gives you connection to the world around you?"

Catanya thought about that for a moment. "I like to draw," she said, shrugging. She wasn't sure how that could help her with Resonance.

Emra smiled. "Perfect. I'd start there."

***

The next few days passed in much the same manner, and Catanya continued to struggle with attuning. She decided to try Emra's suggestion, and asked Viena if she could borrow some writing supplies. Viena gave Catanya some loose leaflets from her notebook, a handmade writing brush, and a small vial of ink made of pine sap.

It took Catanya a while to get used to the rustic materials, but once she found a rhythm, she started to draw. She moved through the glade, drawing trees and people, sketching the movement of the breeze and the stream. But still nothing seemed to change.

Despite her lack of progress, Catanya was beginning to feel

at home within the community. Every morning she rose with the sun and joined the others for breakfast in the glade. She spent her mornings drawing and trying to attune, or else helping to harvest and prepare food. In the afternoons, she walked with Laylian along the winding paths, asking questions about Resonance. Other days she observed the maílehr's lessons with the younger community members still learning to master their own powers. At night, Catanya joined the fire celebrations, listening to the singers and storytellers and enjoying the gentle companionship.

The rhythm and the pace of life in Túir-Avlea was familiar to her. It reminded her of Finnua, and she couldn't help thinking Jémys would have loved it here. These people were free in a way his people had never been. There was so much joy and happiness in the air and a genuine sense of safety that made it truly peaceful. Wherever Jémys was now, she hoped he'd found some peace and safety of his own, someplace he could heal from the tragedies she'd inflicted on him. But part of her was truly sorry he'd never see this wondrous place. She would have loved to share this with him.

It surprised her, however, to see how well Drayk seemed to adapt to the pace of life in Túir-Avlea. She had assumed he'd grow restless and bored after a few days. If she didn't know him better, she would have said he was settling in quite nicely, spending his days helping with repairs and chores or else chatting with the other residents. It was a side of Drayk she'd never seen. A peaceful, almost humble side of him.

But Catanya knew him well enough to recognize the undercurrent of anticipation beneath his relaxed exterior. It was built into him. Instincts honed by years of fighting and fleeing. Drayk had lived his entire life on the run from one nightmare to another. It was in his blood. He thrived on adventure and danger. He wasn't really content to live like this, pursuing everyday activities and living in tranquillity. It wasn't who he was. The constant peace and quietude were bound to be uncomfortable for him, and she recognized how hard he was working to keep his usual manner under control. She heard it in the timbre of his laughs and saw it in the twitch of his jaw as he pretended to enjoy the day-to-day life.

It was clear to her that Drayk was trying to give her the space she needed to learn. He seemed to understand, without being told, that this was going to take her some time. He was trying not to rush her or add any pressure to the situation.

So, one evening, as everyone gathered together by the fire, listening to Lynor sing and enjoying the beautiful spring evening, Catanya took Drayk by the hand and led him away from the group.

"I want to thank you," she said in a quiet voice.

"Thank me?" he replied, eyebrows raised. "For what, love?"

"For being here with me. And for coming with me on this journey. I know it hasn't been easy and I know how uncomfortable you are, sitting around here just waiting for me to figure this out, so I want you to know I appreciate it." She looked him in the eye as she said it.

Drayk seemed surprised. "Ah, well, this place isn't so bad." He gestured around at the festivities. "And how many people can say they've been to Túir-Avlea, right?"

"True," said Catanya. "So, I suppose you should thank me for taking you on the adventure of a lifetime. The kind of adventure Viena could write about."

Drayk chuckled and wrapped his arm around her shoulders. "Yes, but the adventure's not over yet, is it?" he whispered in her ear as they walked back towards the fire. "Seems to me the best part is yet to come."

Catanya grinned to herself, comforted by the thought that whatever came next for her, Drayk would be by her side.

They walked through the festivities together, listening to different songs, and watching the dancers try to keep time with the music. Catanya continued to sketch: pictures of the people living here; memories of her time in Faltir with Diyah; Finnua with Jémys; Awnell with Drayk.

She enjoyed watching the young people swoon around Drayk now, listening to his stories of the outside world. She tried to capture his contagious energy on the page, wondering what it was about him that drew people in.

After a while, she noticed a clump of children forming near the far side of the fire.

"Tell us a story, Maílehr Laylian!" squeaked a young, eager voice.

"Yes, please tell us a story."

"A story? But I have so many stories, how will I ever decide which one to tell?" asked Laylian.

"Tell the one about the Earth and its friends."

"Yeah!"

"Oh yes, that is a good one, isn't it?" said Laylian, grinning. "All right, then, gather around."

Catanya smiled to herself. She watched all the children clambering around Laylian, who settled down on the ground, waiting for them to sit still.

Catanya nudged Drayk and the two of them walked over to listen as the maílehr began her story.

"Long ago, before our ancestors, before time, before there was anything—there were Spirits," she began in a well-rehearsed tone.

"Ghosts?" shouted one of the youngest kids, round eyes bulging with fear.

Catanya listened with amusement as the children argued over whether ghosts and spirits were the same thing. She pulled a fresh leaflet out of her stack and sat down to sketch the story as it unfolded.

Drayk sat beside her, and she leaned against him for support. His warm body was comforting.

"These Spirits were lost," continued Laylian as if there had been no interruption. She spread her hands through the air, fingers fluttering. "They were completely adrift, floating around without a home, without anything to hold on to. They needed something more—someplace they could live and take shelter. So, they created the Earth."

"How did they make it?" asked one of the little boys.

"With magic!" shouted another child, glaring at him as though the answer was obvious.

Catanya laughed and exchanged grins with Drayk, who was watching the scene with delight.

"Well, before long, the Spirits grew cold," continued Laylian, with a slightly dramatic tone. "They weren't used to staying in one place for so long, and the stagnation chilled them. They needed a way to stay warm. So, the Spirits created Fire."

Oohs and ahhs came from the group of children. Catanya resisted the urge to giggle.

"But now that they had a warm home, the Spirits noticed the Earth beginning to wither and parch," said Laylian, her eyebrows pinched in affected worry. "The ground cracked and chipped away. They realized the Earth needed something to move with it and keep its essence strong. So, the Spirits created Water."

"That's my favourite part," said one of the little girls.

Drayk snorted, and he and Catanya exchanged amused expressions. Catanya continued to sketch. An image of swirling fire and water surrounded by rocks and trees. Before the ink dried, she used her thumb to smudge the shapes, giving the illusion of movement.

"But before long, the Earth and Water grew disconnected. Everything slowed until eventually... it stopped," said Laylian, lurching forward suddenly and causing several of the children to jump. "The Earth and Water had no way to communicate, no way to understand each other. So, the Spirits created the Wind.

"The Wind could carry messages across the Earth and the seas, connecting it all together and giving shape to a new world. And this... this is when something truly miraculous happened." Laylian paused for dramatic effect and when she continued, it was with a much softer voice. "Because the Spirits had created something so complex and so united, they found they were finally able to rest, to find peace."

"You mean they weren't lost anymore?"

Laylian smiled and shook her head. "And the Earth can still feel their feet walking across its back, the Wind listens to all of their stories, the Water knows their passions and moods, and the Fire warms their hearts."

"Wow," whispered the youngest boy.

Laylian grinned. "So, you see, the Natures belong to the Spirits, as the Spirits do to them. They protect each other, and so they protect us."

As she finished the story, Laylian glanced up to see Catanya and Drayk sitting nearby. She stood up, leaving the children to their excited chatter, and walked over to join them. Spotting the incredulity on Drayk's face, she said, "You don't believe?"

Drayk scrunched up his face in polite scepticism.

"It's a nice story though," mused Catanya. Something about it had struck a chord with her. She had never thought of the Natures as actual beings before, with the ability to learn and to grow. It was interesting.

She stared down at her drawing, watching the swirls and shapes interact on the page. It almost seemed to come alive before her eyes.

"Ah, yes." Laylian was watching her. "You understand now, don't you?"

Drayk looked curiously from one to the other. "Understand what?" he asked.

"How to take the first step," said Laylian. Then she walked away from them, humming disjointedly to herself.

Catanya held out her hands and stared at them for a moment.

"What are you thinking?" asked Drayk nervously.

"I want to try something," she said, beckoning for him to follow her as she sprinted over to the little pond at the centre of the glade. She set her drawings down and held out her palms towards the Water, feeling the Wind swirl through her fingers. Closing her eyes, she imagined the Water as a living being, growing and learning from the people around it. Then she opened her eyes and focused on trying to communicate with it, trying to show it what she saw in her mind.

A handful of droplets rose into the air like rain moving in the wrong direction. Catanya centred her thoughts on them, coaxing them together. More droplets joined to form a puddle that twisted like a warped sheet of glass. She moved her hands, moulding it into distinctive shapes. Different images streamed together, following the current of her thoughts. She pictured the faces of the people she loved and watched them flicker to life in the waves, and then she thought about birds flying, horses running, and ships sailing. The Water moved gracefully between images without resistance. When the last ship reached the horizon, Catanya lowered her hands, and the droplets dissipated into a shimmering mist.

"You did it," said Drayk quietly. "How do you feel?" He was looking at her as if searching for a sign of fatigue.

"I feel... good," she replied, taking his hand and smiling. *Good* wasn't the right word, but she found she didn't know how to describe it. She wasn't weak or tired. Instead, an intense and exhilarating strength coursed through her body. She felt more alive than ever.

4

THE WEDDING

Despite her newfound hope and optimism, it surprised Diyah to discover how quickly a new sense of apprehension was able to creep in. The last two days had been a whirlwind of wedding preparations and anxiety. Everything was happening so fast. Diyah barely had time to accept it.

She hadn't spoken with Jémys or Fehla since the end of the tournament. They still didn't know Catanya was alive. They didn't understand why Diyah was suddenly willing to proceed with the marriage to Julyán. Diyah wished she could explain it to them, to make them understand. But the ongoing wedding preparations meant she was almost never alone, and she couldn't risk being overheard.

Jémys had taken the end of the tournament very hard. He seemed to feel responsible for leaving Diyah in her current situation, and he was clearly wracked with guilt. But Diyah wasn't sorry. She told herself it was all worth it if she would get to see Catanya again.

She tried to tell herself that was all there was to it. It was all about Catanya. But deep down, Diyah had another reason as well. Something that had started long before she'd discovered Catanya was still alive. It wasn't something she was prepared to admit to anyone, but a part of her was intrigued by Julyán. In-between fits of anxiety and apprehension, she thought she felt something akin to excitement as well.

She hadn't had another chance to speak to Julyán since the banquet either. But he'd finally opened up to her that night, and Diyah wasn't going to let him revert to his old, detached manner. She recognized it now, all those moments when she'd glimpsed the person he used to be, struggling to break through his icy exterior. Diyah was convinced he could be that person again in time. It wouldn't be easy, but as long as she was stuck in Caerlon, caught in this forced arrangement with him, she was determined to help him find his way back.

The day of the wedding arrived in a flurry of mixed emotions. At times, Diyah was calm and centred—confident in her decision. Other times, she succumbed to a type of frenetic panic unlike anything she'd ever experienced. Time was racing by unnaturally fast. She spent the afternoon cooped up with half a dozen maids, getting ready for the evening's ceremony.

First, they brought in a large cast iron bathtub, helping her to bathe. They scrubbed at her skin until it was almost raw. They scraped at Diyah's fingers in a vain attempt to clean the residue of minerals and herbs from under her nails, and they struggled to doff the calluses from her fingertips. Then, they tugged and twisted Diyah's hair, pinning it up in uncomfortable bundles.

Next came the dress. It was custom made for the occasion by Cadyan's own seamster, and Diyah had never worn anything so extravagant. The dress was made of ivory silk that hung close against her body. The stiff bodice was decorated with patterns of violet and pink flowers. Her sleeves were sheer lavender chiffon that cascaded towards her wrists and draped along her sides, exposing the ivory silk beneath. The maids tried to offer her a mirror, but Diyah refused. She didn't think she could stand to see her reflection, done up like a decorative gift for the new maífirkon.

Someone thumped on the door and Diyah gave a start.

"Let's go, we're late," called a guard from outside.

Diyah exchanged looks with the maids in the room. Most of them stared at her with proud eyes, admiring their work. But one maid met Diyah's gaze with a stiff expression and nodded, as if she understood everything Diyah was going through. The small sign of respect was enough. It reminded Diyah of her own dignity, giving her the strength to move forward.

As the guards escorted Diyah to the throne room, she clung hard to that sense of dignity, trying to prevent her nerves from taking control.

A draught whistled through the window, rustling the hem of her dress. She shivered beneath the sheer material, pining for her normal clothes—her thick wool kirtle and durable aprons.

This elaborate dress made her feel exposed and on display. Furthermore, the outfit was painfully tight. Diyah's breaths came in laboured bursts, and she clutched at her bodice, wishing she could loosen the ties.

The sun had set and the corridors were dark and unusually empty. The torchlight cast strange, distorted shadows on the walls. Diyah and her two guards were the only souls in sight.

Finally, they rounded the corner into the entrance hall, and she saw the enormous ebony door ahead. The ceremonial guards on either side wore their usual hauberks and surcoats. But their weapons gleamed especially bright. Like they'd polished them for the occasion.

Diyah supposed this was a mark of respect, but it just made her queasy.

It'll be okay, she thought. Her footsteps echoed off the stone walls, and she forced herself to focus on the sound, counting her steps to the door. One, two, three...

The wedding is just a façade, anyway. It won't change anything for you, not really. You'll still be the same Diyah you've always been.

Four. Five.

Besides... it's only for a short time. It won't be long before Catanya returns.

Six.

And maybe Julyán... maybe...

Seven. Eight...

Diyah slowed her pace as she arrived outside the door.

She heard the guards talking, but she couldn't make out any words. Diyah drew a long, shuddering breath and shoved her anxiety aside. It was too late to change her mind. Even if she wanted to.

The guards pushed open the door, and a wall of sound burst forth like a tidal wave. Hundreds of people were packed into the throne room for the wedding. Courtiers, firkon, servants, city workers—it seemed as though everyone in Caerlon City had come out for the event.

Cadyan sat in his throne at the end of the room, surveying the crowd with a self-satisfied smirk. The chaplain stood beside him, looking especially old and frail in his usual grey robes. A tall pedestal had been placed between them, with a small oil lamp and a wide, unlit candle perched on it.

Julyán stepped out of the crowd and joined Diyah by the door. He wore the same ceremonial uniform he'd worn on the night of the tournament banquet. The dark purple with golden embroidery looked especially flattering tonight. The high collar accentuated his jawline and Diyah realized his face was smooth shaven. He looked cleaner than usual. His bruises had nearly all healed, and his hair had been recently trimmed.

His expression softened slightly as he took in her appearance.

"Shall we?"

Diyah tried not to tremble as he took her hand and led her down the aisle, towards the throne.

A hush fell over the crowd as they passed. The silence amplified the sounds of their feet echoing off the stone floor, and the gentle swish of her dress fabric. Diyah swallowed hard and focused on walking, ignoring the hundreds of eyes following her.

They slowed their pace and came to a halt before the dais. Julyán bent one knee to kneel before his king, and Diyah begrudgingly followed suit. She glanced up in time to see Cadyan sneering at her. Rage burned in her chest. She loathed Cadyan with every fibre of her being, but she forced her face into a benign smile.

Cadyan still thought he was punishing her. He imagined her standing there resigned, weak and submissive, but he was mistaken. Despite all his soldiers and servants, all his limitless power, he didn't know anything about her. He didn't know how much had changed for her in the last few days, and he didn't know what was coming for him. Diyah couldn't wait to see the look on his face when he realized Catanya was alive. When he finally got what he deserved.

Cadyan beckoned for them to stand, and the chaplain stepped forward to greet them. He looked wan and overtired, but he wore a kind smile.

"Welcome, everyone," he called to the room in a thin, reedy voice. "Tonight, we gather to witness and celebrate the official union between these two people. Julyán Aí-Finnua, Maífirkon of Caerlon, and Diyah Aí-Murina, Court Physician of Caerlon. This ceremony marks the beginning of your journey, as sanctioned by our king."

The chaplain cleared his throat and averted his eyes, as if ashamed of the part he played in all this. He knew this wasn't their decision, but he was just as trapped as they were.

"As you begin your journey together," he continued, looking back at them. "I must encourage you to remember what matters most. It is the respect you share for each other, which will see you through the years ahead. Respect is the foundation of any strong relationship. Without it, there can be no loyalty or trust. There can be no love."

He paused here. Diyah swallowed hard and glanced at Julyán. He met her gaze with the same unreadable expression he always wore, but Diyah thought she noticed a gleam in his eye.

She didn't hear what the chaplain said next, but she felt Julyán's hand take hers again. He faced forward as he recited his vows.

"I promise to share my life with you, I will be faithful and honest in the understanding that though we are two people, there is only one life before us. I commit myself to you as husband, companion, and friend for all the risings and settings of the sun."

As Diyah recited her vows in turn, her stomach did an uncomfortable flip.

"Now together we light this candle as a symbol of the warmth we hold in our hearts." They spoke in unison as they lifted the lamp off the altar and used it to light the candle in front of them. They stood in silence, watching the wax melt. It pooled at the centre of the candle and dripped down the edges. The flame flickered and danced as the wick slowly burned.

When most of the candle had melted, they grasped each other's hands and held them out in front of the pedestal. The chaplain lifted the candle and poured the melted wax over their entwined hands. Diyah winced at the pain but she didn't withdraw, knowing it would be taken as a sign of bad luck. They watched the wax dry, sealing their hands together.

The ceremony ended as the chaplain broke the wax seal

binding them and presented them as husband and wife to the people watching.

"You have pledged yourselves to each other in the presence of your king. May the promises you made today carry you forward in love and harmony for the rest of your days. Now, let us celebrate your commitment." The chaplain shook his head as he turned away.

The crowd erupted into applause, cheering and whistling. Diyah's insides twisted as she stared out at the swarm of faces, searching for a sign of Fehla or Jémys, but she couldn't find them. Diyah hoped she could explain everything to them tonight. It pained her that they still didn't know about Catanya.

But as she continued to scan the crowd, she realized every eye in the room was trained on her and Julyán. There would be no privacy this evening. The truth would have to wait a little longer.

The crowd parted to make room for dancing. Diyah had never had much opportunity to dance before. Celebrations had always been scarce in Faltir, and even then, she'd tried her best to avoid them. So, when she stepped out onto the dance floor with Julyán, she felt supremely graceless and uncoordinated.

Julyán was surprisingly adept as he steered her around the room in smooth movements. She supposed she shouldn't be surprised, given how agile he had been in the tournament arena. Yet somehow, she'd never imagined him doing any activity that didn't involve weapons or fighting—or just standing around, brooding and being intimidating.

Diyah glanced up, curious to see his face, but he kept his gaze trained on the crowd, his expression as serious as always.

Maybe he's just focusing on the steps as much as I am, she thought and almost laughed out loud.

She wanted to speak to him. To say something, anything to break the awkwardness, but her mind had gone blank. All she could think about was his hand on the small of her back and their movement together.

When the music slowed and they came to a halt, she felt light-headed and dizzy.

"I…"

She gestured to the table in the corner, signalling that she needed a drink. Then, without looking at him, she turned and walked away, trying not to move too fast.

She stopped at the refreshment table, taking slow, steadying breaths. She lifted a wine glass and raised it to her lips, but her hands shook so badly she nearly spilled its contents down her front. So, rather than risk embarrassing herself and staining her dress, she lowered the glass again without taking a sip.

"You look simply marvellous, my dear," said a familiar voice next to her.

Lord Zadílar emerged from the crowd beside her. His ashy hair was neatly styled, and he wore a bright blue jacket with silver embroidery. The colours seemed out of place amidst the sea of purple and gold firkon uniforms.

"What are you doing here?" She hadn't expected to see him, and it caught her off guard. She glanced around reflexively to check that no one was watching, but, of course, the entire room was packed with people. And Diyah was one of the principal sources of interest.

"Why, I came for the wedding, of course!" he declared, inclining his head towards her. His tone was as light and carefree as always, but there was a seriousness in his eyes that didn't quite match his celebratory words.

Diyah just nodded and tried again to drink from her glass, this time with more success. "I need to thank you," she managed to say, and she turned to face him again. "For the girls, I—"

"My dear, we need never speak of that." He cut her off in the same light tone, but it was clear from his expression that he was warning her not to continue. "And right now, I have new interests..." His eyes scanned the room. "I spoke with your husband."

Husband. That would take some getting used to. "Really?" she asked, trying to keep her voice even.

"Yes... Now, over the years, I've never really gotten to know Julyán. He always seemed so..." Zadílar waved his hand around as though searching for the right word.

"Reserved?" suggested Diyah, chancing a glance at Julyán across the room. He was standing with Cadyan, listening to the king talk with his hands clasped behind his back and his face set in a serious expression.

"Mmm... I was going to say *unyielding* but I think your word is kinder." Zadílar grinned at her and lifted a glass off the table.

Diyah let out a feeble laugh. Her stomach was in knots and she was having trouble matching his calm demeanour.

"I must say, though," continued Zadílar, "he is a very intriguing young man. I had never noticed it before. His sedated presence is well-practised, allowing him to pass unnoticed by most. But now that I look more closely, I think there is a great deal more to our new maífirkon than meets the eye. Wouldn't you agree?"

Diyah nodded and took a sip from her glass. "Yes, there is," she replied, lost in her own thoughts. It took her a moment to realize how intently Zadílar was watching her. His eyes continued their usual twinkle, but his gaze was intense and deeply curious, belying his act. He stared at her like he was trying to read her mind. Diyah's cheeks burned hot with embarrassment.

"Ah, yes." His posture softened, and he let out a long exhale. Diyah hadn't realized how tense he'd been until this moment. "Well, I believe congratulations are in order, then, aren't they?" He took Diyah's hand in his, careful not to touch the spots that were sore from the wax. "My dear, I hope by now you trust that I only want good things for you in this world. And if you ever need anything..." He trailed off, holding her gaze. Then he smiled a little sadly, patted her on the arm, and walked away.

Diyah watched him go, feeling self-conscious and a little exposed. She wasn't sure how, but it seemed Zadílar understood exactly what she was thinking. No pity or regret had tinged his eyes when he'd congratulated her. Unlike everyone else this evening, Diyah had the sense he truly meant it.

Somehow that made her feel much better and much worse all at the same time.

As the evening progressed, Diyah was forced to accept the compliments of hundreds of people she barely knew or cared about. After a few hours she grew weary of all the unspoken pity and indirect prying.

"Oh, congratulations," simpered one woman Diyah recognized from the tournament. One of the gossipers who'd been snickering about the thought of Diyah's forced marriage to Slaedir. "I always knew it would turn out this way."

A group of nearby women giggled.

Diyah's temper flared, but she bit her tongue to keep from reacting.

"And Julyán is *so* handsome, isn't he?" asked the woman, with a sly glance at Diyah.

"Mmm." Diyah tried not to react, but this comment broke through her defences. "Yes, I suppose he is," she mumbled, glancing in his direction. The heat rose in her face once more. She had done a good job thus far of pretending to be okay, but as the night drew on, she was getting nervous again.

Just then, Fehla appeared. "That's quite enough gossip for one evening," she said in a cool voice, glaring at the women gathered around Diyah.

"My queen." The women all bowed and scurried away, looking chastened.

"Are you all right?" asked Fehla, as the last gossiper disappeared into the crowd.

Gratitude swelled inside Diyah. "Yes, I'm fine. Thank you for that."

"Of course. I well remember how fatiguing it is. All their indiscreet questions and impertinent curiosity." Her lip curled in disgust and her eyes glazed, as if lost in an unpleasant memory. Fehla shuddered and brought her attention back from wherever it had wandered. "I'm sorry this is happening to you, Diyah. I would have given anything to prevent it."

Diyah rubbed her neck, a lump forming in her throat. There was something she wanted to ask Fehla, but she wasn't sure how. "I... I'm worried about tonight," she said, doing her best not to sound childish.

"Tonight?"

"Yes." Diyah stared at her feet and fumbled with the hem on her sleeve. "I've never... I don't know... what to expect... what *expectations—*"

"Ah, yes, I see," said Fehla, nodding.

Diyah was relieved not to have to explain further. She wasn't exactly scared, but she never liked feeling inexperienced, or admitting she didn't know what to do. "It's just... I always imagined it differently. I imagined I'd be in love..."

"I know," said Fehla, patting her arm. "But in my experience, marriage and physical intercourse have very little to do with love."

Diyah's insides squirmed, and she chanced a half-glance at Julyán across the room. He was standing with a group of fírkon, listening to them talk and sipping a glass of wine. She recognized Holun and some others from the tournament. It struck her again how casual they all seemed, talking and smiling with their new maífírkon as if the tournament had never happened. As if they hadn't all desperately wanted to win.

But for Julyán, the tournament had simply been a means to

an end, a way to exact his revenge on Slaedir. Did he even want to be maífírkon? Did he even want to be married to Diyah?

"Don't let him know you're scared," said Fehla, wrenching Diyah back to their conversation. "Don't give him the power."

Diyah was taken aback by the hardness in Fehla's voice. "Right," she said, regretting entering into the conversation. This wasn't what she'd wanted to hear. She didn't think it was fair to compare Julyán and Casréyan. They weren't the same kind of men at all, and Diyah's situation wasn't the same as Fehla's had been.

Diyah cast around for a change of subject but couldn't think of anything. She noticed Julyán withdraw from the group of fírkon. He was alone now, walking down the side of the room and watching the dancers. Once again, she noted how the crowd instinctively parted for him. They didn't even seem aware they were doing it. He strolled through the crowd in Diyah's direction, apparently unaware of where he was heading.

But then Jémys appeared and pulled Julyán aside. They weren't very far from Diyah and Fehla, so Diyah caught a few snippets of their conversation.

"Deserves so much better than this," she heard Jémys say. He looked flushed and angry. "You have no idea. Diyah is one of the best people I've ever met. Intelligent, kind, passionate..." He descended into an angry whisper and Diyah couldn't make out what he said next.

Julyán's eyes flicked in her direction and his expression softened as he saw her watching them. He gave his brother a half-smile and pushed past him without saying a word, walking towards Diyah. "It's getting late," he said, holding out his hand for her.

Diyah's heart thumped in her throat, but she nodded and took Julyán's hand. She sensed Fehla's gaze on her, but she couldn't bring herself to face the queen. Her eyes fell on Jémys, who was watching them, wearing a mixture of pity and regret. His expression made her feel even worse.

She appreciated how much Fehla and Jémys cared about her, how worried they were. But this wasn't about them. This was about her and Julyán.

Diyah and Julyán took their time walking through the corridors to the third floor. Neither of them spoke a word. The corridors were quiet and dark, but they seemed less menacing than they had earlier this evening. The guards stationed in the doorways and corridors averted their eyes as they passed.

This area of the castle was heavily protected. The maífírkon's quarters were in the same area as the royal quarters. Fehla's room was down the hall, and so was Cadyan's.

Diyah pushed that thought out of her mind as they arrived outside their new, shared rooms. Julyán held the door open for her and she stepped inside. It was larger than the physician's quarters, and the furniture was much grander and more ornate. The bed at the far corner was wider than any Diyah had ever seen. She tried not to look at it as she crossed the room to the large gilded mirror near the wardrobe.

For the first time that day, she stared at her reflection, hardly able to recognize herself. Her hair was tied in an elegant mass of curls and braids atop her head with several coils slipping out of the knot to drape along her neck. She ran her hands down the front of her dress, the smooth material sliding between her fingers.

She hadn't noticed before, but fine gold embroidery outlined the square neckline. And she remarked how the pale lavender bodice seemed to echo the deep plum of Julyán's ceremonial uniform.

She sensed Julyán's eyes on her and she looked up to see him watching her from near the doorway.

"I've never had a dress like this," she said, turning away

from the mirror to face him. The dress was still uncomfortable, but Diyah couldn't deny that it was pretty.

Julyán smiled faintly and removed his cloak, draping it over a chair. Then he walked to the table by the window and began pouring two glasses of wine.

Now that they were alone, Diyah wasn't sure what to say or do next. Her mind was a jumble of conflicting emotions and desires, and she had so many questions for him.

"Are you going to tell Jémys about your father?" she blurted before she could stop herself. It wasn't the most burning question rattling around in her mind, but for some reason it's the one that came out first.

Julyán glanced at her, startled. "No," he said, recorking the wine bottle and turning to face her, holding out one of the glasses.

"Oh..." She took a long, shaky breath and urged her trembling legs forward, crossing the distance between them. "Why not?" she asked, taking the proffered glass, her fingers brushing against his.

To her surprise Julyán let go and withdrew, walking away to stand by the fire on the other side of the room. "It won't change anything," he said with a sigh. "I'm not the brother he remembers. I can never be him again."

Diyah sipped from her glass, trying to conceal her disappointment. It was a small consolation that the wine tasted wonderful. The spices were blended perfectly, and it had a faint tartness that tied it all together. It warmed her from the inside out, helping to calm her nerves.

She took another sip and drifted over to the bed, perching lightly on the edge and watching him across the room. He had his back to her. The fire illuminated his silhouette as he stood with his hand on the mantle, gazing into the flames. He was tall and strong like his brother, but he had a very different presence. It was imposing—stiff and guarded like someone who had forgotten how to relax.

For some reason, his tension emboldened her to continue.

"So, who are you, then?" she asked.

He turned to face her. "What do you mean?"

"Well, you're not who I thought you were at all. You're not the ruthless, cold-hearted warrior you want everyone to think you are. But you're not the boy I remember either so... who are you?"

Julyán frowned and swirled his wine glass as he thought about his answer. "I'm not sure," he said, and he looked disconcerted.

Diyah nodded. She found the silence uncomfortable, so she plowed on. "Well, you got your revenge. Now what? What do you actually want?"

"I don't know," he replied, shaking his head. "I don't know what I want now... For as long as I can remember I've only ever wanted one thing." He turned his attention back to the fire.

Diyah hesitated, and then cleared her throat. "Just one?" she asked, her cheeks burning.

He looked back at her curiously.

Diyah shrugged. "Well, I had hoped a part of you wanted your brother back..." She took another sip so she wouldn't have to look at him as she said what she was about to say. "And I had thought... maybe there was a part of you that wanted me."

The silence between them seemed to stretch on forever, as Diyah held her breath, waiting for Julyán to respond.

"I do," he said finally.

An unexpected heat spread through Diyah's chest, and her stomach fluttered. As she looked up at him, she thought she saw a slight colour in his cheeks that hadn't been there before. If she didn't know better, she would have said he was embarrassed.

"So, tell me, what is it that *you* want?" he asked, abruptly shifting the focus away from himself.

"Me? I want... I want..." She shook her head and sighed. "There are so many things I want."

"Such as?"

Diyah smiled to herself. Her heart raced in her chest. For a moment she wondered if she would be brave enough to do it... Brave enough to admit what she wanted to do. But then she stood up and, finishing her wine in one gulp, walked over to place her cup on the mantle next to his. Julyán watched her without saying a word. As she turned to face him, it struck her again how green his eyes were, how vivid. She took a deep breath, raised herself up on her toes, and pressed her lips against his just briefly before pulling away.

Julyán didn't react. He stood motionless, his posture somehow even more rigid than before. "Really?" he asked, and he sounded genuinely surprised.

Diyah smiled and shrugged.

Julyán stared searchingly into her face, but she was determined not to seem nervous. She kissed him again. Julyán seemed to hesitate, but then he placed his hand gently on her back, holding her in the embrace. Her body trembled as she wrapped her arms around his neck.

But Julyán's body was warm and strong. As he pulled her tighter into his arms, her tension melted away. He had one hand on her waist and the other found its way up to her head. He pulled the pins out of her hair one by one, letting the strands fall down her neck and onto her shoulders. When he dropped the last pin on the floor, he pulled back and gazed at her, brushing the hair out of her face. Diyah had never seen such tenderness in his expression before. It made her ache, thinking how much of himself he kept hidden from the world.

Slowly, his hand slid down her neck to rest above her heart. They paused like this for a moment, the heat of their bodies building between them. Then Diyah brought her hands up to the laces on her bodice. As she began untying them, she turned her eyes to meet his, and he seemed to understand. His hands joined hers and before long her bodice was lying on the floor at her feet.

Diyah wanted to see him, to feel his skin against hers. Her heart raced and she fumbled with the ties on his uniform. Julyán unfastened his belt and laid his sword on the mantle just as Diyah finished untying his coat. With one swift movement, as if he couldn't wait any longer to hold her, he cast it off and pulled her back into his arms.

His lips pressed against hers more fervently and he gripped her body, squeezing it firmly against his own. The soft silk of her dress swam across her skin. His hands ran down her waist and over her legs until he lifted her up into his arms. Diyah didn't want anything between them anymore. She clutched at his tunic and yanked it over his head as he carried her over to the bed.

His right arm was still wrapped in bandages, but he gave no indication his wound was bothering him. Despite his countless scars, his skin was surprisingly soft against her lips. She kissed his neck and his chest as he laid her down. But he winced when she grazed the brand over his heart, burying his face in her neck. His mouth found hers again, and he ran his fingers up her thigh.

Diyah's body was on fire. She'd never felt anything so exhilarating before, and she wanted more. She parted his lips, tasting his hot breath. When his hand reached the top of her thigh, Diyah tightened her grip on his neck and let out a sharp gasp. He paused for a moment, but she kissed him again, urging him to continue. His fingers were strong and gentle, sliding between her legs with ease, and his eyes shone as he watched her trembling beneath him.

After a few minutes, Julyán kicked off his boots and pulled

off his breeches. As he climbed up onto the bed, he wrapped her legs around his waist and drew her up so she sat pressed against him. He lifted her dress over her head and tossed it aside, kissing her neck and running his hands down her bare back.

His eyes met hers, and for a moment neither of them dared to breathe.

Then Julyán lifted her hips and guided her back down onto him. Trembling, they moved their bodies together—slowly, at first, but then faster and faster until everything became a hot, sweaty blur.

Later that night, as she lay in his arms, Diyah was pleased to discover she felt safe and comfortable there. She had enjoyed herself even more than she'd expected. As she watched him sleep, she smiled at the thought of doing it all over again tomorrow.

5

THE ORACLE STONE

Catanya sat on the damp forest floor with her eyes closed, trying to focus all her energy on listening. She heard the faint trickle of the stream nearby as it coursed and splashed against the rocks. The gentle morning wind whistled and rustled the leaves on the branches above her.

She collected a handful of soil and pressed it into her palm, the individual grains tickling as they slipped through her fingers. She grabbed another handful and squeezed it into a dense ball, allowing the moisture to hold it together.

"Good, now take a deep breath. What do you notice?" Laylian's gentle, patient voice drifted to her from somewhere ahead.

Catanya inhaled slowly. The air smelled strongly of pine and earth, but there was also a hint of something floral and sweet.

"Hyacinth," she said, opening her eyes and smiling, "mixed with grass and lilacs."

"Good," said Laylian. "And what does that conjure up in your mind?"

Catanya took another deep breath and thought about her answer. "Colours," she whispered. "Violets and blues. Bright green and a gentle pink." Closing her eyes again, she ran her fingers through the soil, imagining brushstrokes and paint. She listened to the sounds of the forest and breathed in the flowery smell.

She didn't know how long she sat like that before Laylian said, "Open your eyes, Catanya. Look."

Catanya did as instructed. To her surprise, a layer of fallen leaves and twigs had lifted off the ground to float around her. As she continued to draw in the soil, they followed the pace of her movements, soaring through the air in perfect arcs.

"So, you see, when you open your senses and actively interact, you can find the connections that exist. You have to experience the world around you, that's the only way to understand it," said Laylian. "Everything grows, Catanya. Everything changes. Change is all around us and you need to learn how to see it flowing through everything. That momentum of change is where your power lies."

"Change," repeated Catanya, nodding. She reached her hand out and touched the nearest leaf. The same strange new exhilaration that she'd experienced by the stream the other night mounted inside her again. This power was beautiful. The power to influence nature and inspire change.

But a familiar tingling sensation itched in her fingertips, branching through her skin like a deceitful web. All at once, the spell was broken. The leaves floated back down to the ground.

Laylian sighed. "I believe that's enough for today," she said, standing up with surprising agility for someone her age.

"Sorry," mumbled Catanya. "I really am trying." It was true. Catanya had spent almost a week working with Laylian, struggling to create a consistent connection to her power. But lately, whenever that new exhilaration mounted inside her, she often panicked and lost focus.

"I know, child. But you've got a lot of interference in that head of yours. It's going to take some time for you to let go."

Catanya deflated, disappointed with herself. They walked back out of the woods towards the glade where everyone gathered to prepare the evening's meal.

"You're doing well," said Laylian. "You've attuned, now you just need to refine it."

Catanya nodded begrudgingly. "I don't understand though, I've used my powers before and it was a lot more instinctual somehow."

"Yes, well, channelling through emotion is easier at first, but it can be destructive, as you know. Better to learn how to resonate from a place of calm. That way, when you are in an emotional situation, you can resist the lure of the Spirits."

"What does that mean?" asked Catanya, a sudden pit forming in her stomach.

"Resonating with the Spirits has always been dangerous," Laylian replied. "It is the most exhilarating, the most potent. But it is also the most intoxicating because, through the Spirits, you also access their Resonance. It is difficult to remain unaffected for long. And for you... with the number of Spirits you're engaging..." She trailed off, shaking her head sadly. "But it isn't your fault."

"What if I can't resist it?" asked Catanya, a hollow dread overtaking her. It was a dread she hadn't experienced in a long time.

"I cannot answer that," said Laylian. "Only you know what strengths and weaknesses you have within yourself. Resonating with the Spirits will amplify them all." She patted Catanya on the arm, then wandered off, humming to herself, apparently unconcerned by the potential danger Catanya could pose.

Catanya felt suddenly miserable. When she arrived back at the glade and found Drayk with a group of people near the forest, it reassured her to see the jaunty grin on his face. His carefree attitude was always hard to resist.

"Well, look at you," he called, beaming as he strode forward to meet her. "Looks like you're making progress." He waved up and down to indicate her hair.

"What?" Catanya pulled the strands in front of her eyes and realized he was right. Where once her hair had been predominantly black, now there was significantly more colour. The iridescence and shimmering quality were dazzling in the blazing midday sunlight. "I don't understand this." Catanya scanned the glade, examining everyone else. It had just occurred to her that no one in Túir-Avlea had any similar physical transformations. But they all used Resonance every day. So why were Catanya and Cadyan different? She turned around, looking for Laylian, and found her standing by the stream. "Is this normal?" she asked, walking back over to her teacher and indicating her hair.

"Normal? Such a dull, uninteresting word." Laylian walked in circles around Catanya, examining her from all angles and humming absentmindedly again.

Catanya and Drayk exchanged long-suffering glances, but they waited patiently. They were used to Laylian's odd behaviour now.

"Hmm, may I?" Laylian raised her hand to touch Catanya's hair. Catanya nodded and waited as she examined the strands, holding them up to the light and turning them back and forth.

To her surprise, Laylian smiled to herself, looking pleased. "I haven't felt this in a long time," she said with an affectionate twinkle in her eye. "Tell me, when your brother drank the elixir and you both received its power, were you by any chance wearing a necklace?"

Catanya frowned. "Yes... how did you know that?"

"Mmm." Laylian nodded knowingly. "A tapered stone with

a luminescent collection of colours that is impossible to describe."

"Yes!" Catanya was surprised. "How do you know about my mother's necklace? Have you seen it before?" Catanya couldn't fathom how that could be possible.

"Oh yes," said Laylian. "I remember it well. It was, after all, one of the three most potent magical relics ever created, known to most people by a memorable, albeit inaccurate, name, The Oracle Stone."

It took a moment for her words to register.

"What?" spluttered Drayk. "You mean the relics really exist? Illayan's relics—or, the Relics of Illayan?" He raised his eyebrows with scepticism, but he looked more than a little intrigued at the idea.

"Relics of Illayan?" repeated Laylian, her expression delighted. "Is that what people call them? Well, isn't that wonderful?" She chortled. "Yes, they exist, but I have only ever referred to them as the Three Relics."

"But they belonged to Illayan right?" Drayk asked.

Laylian smiled broadly. "Oh yes, Illayan made them all right. It was quite an accomplishment, if I do say so myself." She chuckled almost knowingly. "The Oracle Stone used to be here with us in Túir-Avlea. But a long time ago, I gave it away to a young woman by the name of Freihse."

"You... *gave it away*?" repeated Catanya, mortified to think someone would just give away one of Illayan's great relics. "Who was Freihse?"

"Well... For starters, she drew the map that led you to us."

Catanya scrambled to pull the old parchment out of her pocket.

"This map," said Laylian, taking it from her and examining it, "is lightly bonded with Resonance. It calls on whoever holds it to come find us. But, as you may recall, the journey here is difficult."

Catanya snorted. Difficult was an understatement.

Laylian smiled. "Yes, well, the journey was designed to protect us from discovery or attack. It is a series of tests. Only those who are open to Resonance, open to change, can find their way through. And the two of you," she indicated Catanya and Drayk, "together you embrace change." She folded the map and handed it back to Catanya. "That is why you were able to find us."

Catanya and Drayk exchanged looks.

"So, what about the necklace?" asked Catanya, remembering her original question. "Who was Freihse?"

"Ah, yes, Freihse was one of us," said Laylian. "Born and raised in Túir-Avlea. Her mother was a passionate artist—a much better artist than her daughter, if that map is any indication." Laylian chuckled and shook her head, lost in an affectionate memory. "And her father... well..." Laylian scrunched her face, as though trying to find the right words to describe him. "Her father's heart was in the right place, but he was far too preoccupied with his responsibilities as a maílehr in the community. So, Freihse was left alone to daydream. She was always restless. She was so full of energy, and she always had trouble staying still—you both would have liked her." Laylian gave them a warm smile. "And when she told us she wanted to leave the mountain and explore the world beyond, I somehow knew it was the right path for her. No one had ever left before, but I understood this was something that needed to happen. I gave her the necklace so she'd always be connected to us here. So she could always find her way back if she wanted. But we never did see her again. I like to think she found what she was looking for out there."

Catanya couldn't believe what she was hearing. "I was told the necklace belonged to my mother," she said. "That it had been passed down through the generations." She looked eagerly from Laylian to Drayk and saw him staring at her, mouth slightly open in a bewildered expression. "That means —" She broke off, comprehension dawning on her.

Laylian smiled. "This certainly makes sense now." She nodded more to herself than to Catanya. "The stone was a very powerful object. Many believed it held the power of prophecy, but in truth, it was a stone of connection. It was bound with Spirit Resonance so that it forged a connection to the past and the present."

"A connection to the past and the present... Wait, do you mean *visions* of the past?" Catanya remembered all the strange things she'd seen these past few months. The vision of Jémys and his father in Finnua, Drayk at the cottage, Ayr and Fehla in Awnell—were those visions connected to the necklace?

"Yes, that could be one way its power manifests, but it also connects the present through spirit and kinship."

Catanya frowned, trying to make sense of what that meant. "So, it can connect you with another living spirit... or with your kin? How?" Catanya's mouth had gone very dry, and she almost didn't want to know the answer.

"Oh, emotionally, spiritually, mentally—it varies. But in your case, I'd say the connection to your brother was quite strong." She beamed at Catanya, evidently undisturbed by what she'd just said. Then Emra arrived and drew Laylian's attention away.

Catanya was stunned into silence. She barely noticed the movement around her as everyone nearby dispersed to get ready for the fire.

Finally, she understood. The necklace had created the connection that gave her these powers. It had connected her to Cadyan at the moment he drank the elixir.

In a trance, she reached up and pulled the rest of her hair out of its tie, letting it fall across her face. Almost half of her natural black was gone, replaced with the same shimmering colour as her necklace. Soon she would look just like Cadyan.

His ethereal hair gave him such a menacing, ghostly appearance.

"We *are* connected," she said in a blank voice and she stared at Drayk. A chill ran down her spine and she shuddered. She was starting to look more and more like Cadyan with each passing day. Now she knew why.

How long would it be before she resembled him in other ways? Ways beyond the physical?

Catanya's pulse quickened. Heat rose in her neck and her breaths grew shallow and rapid. She didn't want to be connected to Cadyan. She didn't want to become like him.

"Yes," said Drayk, stepping forward and brushing the hair out of her face. "You are connected to him. But that means he's connected to you too, doesn't it?"

Catanya tried to back away. It was just as she'd always feared. She was tainted—dangerous. Everyone was at risk with her around.

"Hey, look at me!" Drayk grabbed her arms and shook her slightly, forcing her to meet his gaze. "This is a good thing. This connection. It means... maybe there's more to him too." He lowered his voice and held her gaze. His bright blue eyes burned with a calm, reassuring clarity. "The things we saw in the Burning Cove—the future of you and him together... Maybe there is reason to hope. Maybe you can have what you want."

Catanya stopped struggling and stared at him, stunned. He really believed what he was saying. No part of him thought she was tainted or corrupted by the connection she shared with her brother. He was still searching for the silver lining, the beauty within the darkness.

"Why aren't you worried?" asked Catanya.

Drayk shrugged. "You know I don't believe in worrying," he said with a playful grin. "Besides... I have faith in you. Always have, always will. You're strong, Catya."

Catanya's pulse settled and her breathing returned to normal. "Thank you," she said in a small voice. Overcome with gratitude and appreciation, she wrapped her arms around him and buried her face in his shoulder.

They stood like that for a moment. The warmth and safety of the embrace reassured Catanya. Drayk pressed his cheek against her head and inhaled. When they pulled apart, their eyes connected, and Catanya remembered another scene the fire had shown them at the cove.

Drayk cleared his throat and dropped his hands. "I'm starving, aren't you? I'll go get us something to eat." And with that, he turned and walked away, leaving Catanya dazed.

Someone chuckled behind her. Catanya turned around, startled to see she wasn't alone. She thought everyone had left.

"You know, you can train all you want," said Laylian, bouncing up and down on her toes. "You can master your powers and discipline your mind, but nothing is as powerful as an open heart." Laylian gestured towards Drayk. "He's a charming young man."

Catanya had to resist the urge to roll her eyes. "Too charming," she said darkly.

"Nonsense!" Laylian chuckled.

Catanya looked back at Drayk, and her stomach did an uncomfortable flip. Still, she wasn't sure she was ready to risk what they had. Catanya needed Drayk. He was the only friend she had left. And after everything that had happened with Jémys, she wasn't sure she even knew how to open her heart anymore, let alone to someone as passionate and unpredictable as Drayk. But then again, they had come to really care about each other, hadn't they?

Catanya sighed and shook her head. "That's a dangerous path," she said.

"Danger! Ha! Fiddle-faddle!" declared Laylian. "That's not

dangerous. No. *Messy*, yes. Confusing, oh, probably. Worth-while, definitely!"

Catanya looked at her, half amused and half exasperated. "This is hardly the most important thing on my mind right now."

Laylian shrugged. "Not every important decision is about life and death, you know. Sometimes the most important decisions are the seemingly insignificant ones." She nudged Catanya with her shoulder.

Catanya laughed feebly and looked at Drayk again. He was by the food table, chatting with Viena and Broinan, the tall, over-stretched teen. From the smiles and blushes on their faces Drayk had obviously been putting on the charm. Catanya suppressed a laugh as Broinan, distracted by Drayk's story, stumbled on the uneven ground and nearly overturned his plate of food. Drayk gave a bark of loud, infectious laughter and clapped the young man on the back before moving over to the other side of the table.

Catanya had to admit Drayk looked very handsome tonight. The loose linen clothes gave him an uncharacteristic buoyancy and gracefulness that was flattering. And she had grown close to him over these last few weeks—closer than she ever would have thought possible given where they'd started. In another lifetime she might have been able to see herself with him, but reality was so much more complicated than that.

"Oh, you know, this isn't how I thought my life was going to go," she said.

Laylian snorted. "Well, I should hope not!" She patted Catanya on the arm. "I've never met anyone whose life is going according to plan. Sounds like an awfully boring way to live, if you ask me."

Catanya smiled despite herself, but didn't respond.

Drayk made his way back towards them, carrying two plates

of food. "What is it?" he asked, looking from one to the other and taking in their sheepish smiles. "What's the joke?"

"Ha!" Laylian raised her eyebrows suggestively before turning and leaving them alone.

Drayk frowned at Catanya as he handed her a plate.

"Don't worry about it," she said, shaking her head and chuckling to herself. She took the plate and beckoned for him to join her. There was a patch of soft grass beneath a nearby ash tree where they could sit together and watch the evening festivities.

Catanya sat down, resting her plate on her knees, and waited for Drayk to sit beside her. They spent the rest of the evening in relative ease, enjoying Laylian's stories, and indulging Viena's insatiable curiosity about the outside world. After Lynor had finished singing three particularly beautiful songs, Catanya's tension had melted away.

She lounged in the grass, watching Lynor rejoin his family, hugging them each. She watched Flian and Heena start clapping their hands together in a rhythmic game, as Lynor and Emra held each other, beaming at their children, and a strange chagrin settled over Catanya. It was hard not to be envious of them in that moment. They were the picture of happiness.

Catanya had never had that kind of family, and she never would. Her time with Jémys was as close as she'd ever get to it. But maybe that was okay. Maybe it was better to leave that perfect memory in the past and move on. Maybe there were other things she should experience.

She turned towards Drayk and was surprised to see him frowning. "What's the matter?" she asked, sitting up straighter so she was level with him.

"How old do you think Laylian is?" he asked, staring at the maílehr across the glade.

The question surprised Catanya. She'd been so lost in her own thoughts, she hadn't realized Drayk's mind was somewhere else. "Oh, um... I don't know. Old, I guess." Admittedly, Catanya had also wondered about the maílehr's age, but there were so many other matters occupying her mind lately. It didn't seem important.

"Mmm..." Drayk nodded but didn't elaborate. "I never really believed they existed until now, you know? The relics," he added, seeing Catanya's confused expression.

"Oh." Catanya frowned, trying to keep up with his jumbled thoughts.

"All these years, the Caerlon royal family has been searching for them in Bratia. But Fehla already had one. The Oracle Stone..."

Catanya mulled over his words for a second. "So, do you think she knew what it was when she gave it to me?" she asked, a pit settling in her stomach. "Do you think she meant for all this to happen?"

"Possibly..." said Drayk. "But that's a pretty big gamble to take, isn't it? And why not use it herself?"

Catanya thought about that for a moment. Drayk was right, if Fehla knew what the necklace was, then why would she take such a big risk with it?

"Do you think it really has the power Laylian described?" asked Drayk. "*Connection*, or whatever?"

"Um..." Catanya hesitated before nodding. "Yeah, I know it does."

Drayk looked surprised. "How?"

Catanya rubbed her forehead. "I've seen things," she said, reluctant to continue. She hadn't told anybody about her visions of the past. She hadn't known what they were, or whether they were even real. Until now. The vision of Jémys, of Fehla, Lia and Ayr... and the vision of Drayk.

"What did you see?" he asked.

Catanya met his gaze and sighed. Then she recounted the visions she'd experienced over the last several months. She described the scene of Jémys with his father. The way his father had taught him to fight, insisting his son should strive to be a good man above all else. Then she recounted the vision of Fehla, Lia, and Ayr before the Midwinter Carnival. The way the young women had seemed—so bright and happy, like a family. But then she faltered, unsure how to continue.

"Those are the only two visions you had?" asked Drayk.

Catanya averted her eyes. "No," she said in a quiet voice. "There was one more... about you."

"You saw *me*?" Drayk raised his eyebrows, then he flashed a grin. "Oh, do tell. What was I doing?" He smirked, obviously hoping for a charming story of his exploits.

Catanya cleared her throat. "Well... I saw the vision while we were at the sea cottage." Catanya worked hard to keep the pity out of her eyes as she met his gaze. "I saw you as a boy."

The grin slid off Drayk's face in an instant.

Catanya took a deep breath and described the vision exactly the way she'd seen it, with as much calm detachment as she could muster. She could still see the images as clearly as the first time. They were burned into her memory forever. The tears in his eyes, the bruises on his little body...

Drayk sat rigid as he listened. When she finished, he just nodded and averted his gaze.

"Drayk," she put her hand on his arm.

"All right," he replied. His voice sounded a little strained, like he was trying not to let his mind go back there. "So the necklace works." He turned to face her again and nodded. "That means the crown probably does too... *immortality*," he breathed the word in a tone that sounded half awed and half afraid.

Catanya understood. A strange mixture of interest and dread mingled inside her, as she thought about what that could mean.

"So... what do you think the third relic is?" Drayk asked,

eyes alight with curiosity and eagerness. "Laylian said there were three. So, there's the necklace." He held up one finger. "And everyone knows about the crown." He held up a second. "But what is the third relic?"

Catanya thought about it for a moment. "I don't know," she replied. The Relics of Illayan were a legend. Great magical objects, created by Illayan before the Quiescence Wars. That was all anyone knew about them. Until recently, Catanya hadn't even known the royal family was still looking for them in the Ruins of Bratia, or that they used slave labour to do it.

"The necklace was never in Bratia," said Catanya, going a little numb at the thought. How long had her family been using labour camps to search the area? And the necklace had never been there, it had been with Fehla and her family all along. Did Fehla know that? Had she stood by and allowed the search to continue, allowing her family to abuse and enslave its people for nothing?

"What if none of the relics are in Bratia?" said Drayk.

Catanya's insides twisted. "Or worse, what if the crown is there and Cadyan finds it?"

Until now, the relics had been mere fantasy. So, she had never really considered it before—never worried about it. But Cadyan, with the power of immortality...

Catanya shuddered. "What if he succeeds? What if he finds the crown of immortality?"

To Catanya's surprise, Drayk smiled. "I don't think he will," he said with a droll tone. Then he turned his attention back to the fire where Laylian sat telling stories like she did every night. "I have another theory about the crown."

6

A REASON TO ESCAPE

Diyah opened her eyes. The soft light of the early morning sun had reached the bed where she lay, giving everything a warm and comforting glow. Her satin dress lay in a heap on the floor next to Julyán's tunic, their wine glasses were still on the mantle where they'd left them, and the fire had burned down to embers behind the grate.

She rolled over to see Julyán lying asleep next to her. He looked peaceful and gentle. His wavy brown hair fell softly on his cheek and she could see the faint stubble of his beard growing along his jawline. His eyelids twitched as he dreamed, and his long lashes brushed against his skin. Here, asleep next to her, Diyah saw the vestige of his stolen youth. He was so much younger than he seemed, but his life had coarsened him, destroying his innocence and replacing it with pain and darkness.

A wave of sadness crashed over her, and she rolled over to face the window so she wouldn't have to look at him. She lay there perfectly still, trying to fight the tears building in her eyes.

But then the bed creaked behind her, and she knew Julyán was awake. He pulled the hair off her neck and ran his hand down her spine, making her shiver. Then, he softly kissed her shoulder blade.

Diyah turned her head and saw him frowning at her. "What is it?" she asked, surprised.

He didn't answer. Instead, he traced his fingers along the scars on her back, the lash marks from her beating in the dungeons. He looked pained, and he leaned in to kiss them.

"Would you really have done it?" asked Diyah in a small voice. She always tried not to think about her time in the dungeons. She tried not to remember Slaedir's laugh or the girls' screams. But this was a question that haunted her every day. "Would you really have tortured them to punish me?"

Julyán rolled over onto his back and, staring up at the ceiling, nodded almost imperceptibly.

It was a blow. Diyah hadn't wanted to believe it, but she supposed she was just being naïve. She turned away from him again and stared out the window, watching the sunrise.

"They're fine," said Julyán after a while. "We promised to release them and we did." Diyah looked at him again and saw him watching her. "The farmers who took them in are good people," he added. "And a few days ago, I went to check on them, to see if... well..." He cleared his throat and stared back at the ceiling. "But they're gone. Somehow, the entire family left the kingdom without anyone knowing, moved somewhere far away, beyond Caerlon's reach. I don't even know where." He gave her a significant look.

Diyah swallowed hard and nodded, trying to convey some surprise. She appreciated what he'd said, but, of course, she already knew the girls were gone. She had asked Lord Zadílar to arrange it. But Julyán didn't know that, and the fact that he seemed to want to reassure her was heartening.

Diyah rolled onto her side to face him and brought her hand up to his chest. She examined the brand above his heart and traced the surrounding area.

"Does it hurt?" she asked, tilting her head.

He shrugged. "No. Not really."

"What about this?" She pulled his arm out from under the blanket and unwound the bandage to examine the long gash Holun had made. It was starting to heal, but it must still be very painful.

"Not anymore," he said, though he winced as she ran her hand along it.

"Sorry," she mumbled, re-binding it and letting go of him.

"Don't be." He shrugged. "You saved my life, I know that." He rested his hand on her head and began absentmindedly twisting his fingers through her hair.

Diyah exhaled heavily. "I shouldn't have had to," she said. "That tournament was ridiculous and barbaric. It's just the king's way of sowing fear and distrust in his people. As if he needed another way."

Julyán gave her an amused look.

"What?" she asked hotly. "You think I'm wrong? You think I'm being foolish?"

"On the contrary," he said with a smile. "And I would never use that word to describe you."

He put his hand on her chin and brought her lips up to his, kissing them gently. Diyah put her hand back on his chest as he wrapped his arm around her. They melted into each other, letting their passions take over.

When Diyah awoke again, the sun was fully in the sky and the room had been tidied. Servants had apparently stoked the fire and brought breakfast without waking her. Diyah found it strangely unsettling to be waited on like some noble or courtier. She was used to taking care of everything herself.

Julyán stood at the end of the bed, dressed in his new

maífirkon uniform. It looked just like the fírkon uniforms, but the purple was the same shade as his ceremonial attire, and there was more gold embroidery. Diyah suppressed a shudder as she remembered the way Slaedir had looked in his maífirkon attire. It would take her a while to get used to seeing Julyán in it.

"I have to go," he said, fastening his belt back on his hips. "I have to meet the king."

"Oh..." Diyah sat up and watched him getting ready. Then before she could stop herself, she blurted, "I don't understand how you can serve Cadyan after what happened to your father. It's all his fault!"

Julyán stopped and stared at her. "No, it's not. Cadyan was just a boy. He didn't know any better. He didn't know what would happen."

Diyah gaped at him. "How can you defend him?"

Julyán stood up straighter, his face hard again. "Cadyan is my king. I swore my allegiance to him." His tone was mild, but there was a definite warning in it. Diyah knew that any more discussion about Cadyan would not go well.

"Fine," she grumbled a little. "How long will you be gone?" She tried to sound nonchalant.

"I have training all day and then I have to meet the new recruits. I'll be back later this evening."

"Okay." Diyah brushed the hair out of her face and wrapped herself in the blanket as she stood up and walked around the bed. The floor was cold beneath her bare feet. She was grateful for the fire now roaring in the grate, and admittedly even more grateful she didn't have to stoke it herself.

"Right," said Julyán, awkwardly casting around for something more to say. "I'll see you later, then." He hesitated before leaning in and kissing her briefly on the cheek. Then he turned and strode out the door.

Diyah watched him go, feeling just as awkward as he had

seemed. She crossed to the wardrobe on the other side of the room and opened it, looking for something to wear. To her surprise, several new dresses hung inside. Julyán must have had them made for her. They weren't as extravagant as the silk monstrosity she'd been forced to wear to the wedding. But they were nicer than what she was used to wearing, with softer wools and brighter colours. She smiled to herself as she began dressing in a hurry.

The servants had left a plate of fresh fruit on the table by the window, along with some hot water and tea. As Diyah ate, she thought over everything that had happened since the tournament ended. Now that the wedding was over and there would be fewer eyes on her, she needed to talk to Jémys and Fehla. She needed to tell them about Catanya.

Diyah was still expected to tend to patients and fulfill her work as court physician, so she wanted to find Jémys before heading to her workroom. Fírkon training would take up most of the day, and she wasn't sure what he would do when faced with life under Julyán's command. He'd seemed increasingly reckless and despondent during the tournament. Now, he was liable to pick a fight with Julyán or get himself killed. But perhaps, if he knew Catanya was alive, he wouldn't do anything rash.

She searched the mess hall and the armoury, but he wasn't there. Then, heading towards the soldiers' barracks, she saw him walking towards her down the hall.

"There you are," she breathed, smiling at him.

But the worried look on his face gave her pause. He grabbed her hand and pulled her around the corner and out of sight.

"Are you all right?" he asked, surveying her.

"What?" But then she realized what he meant. "Oh! Yes. Yes, I'm fine," she said, trying to reassure him, despite her own awkwardness.

"Did he hurt you?" Jémys made a move like he wanted to

comfort her, but then he dropped his hands almost like he was afraid to touch her.

Diyah's face burned with embarrassment. "No. Everything is fine," she said. "Don't worry about me. Honestly, I'm more worried about you." She took his hand and squeezed it. "Julyán said training starts today, are you ready for that?"

Jémys's eyes were still full of concern, but Diyah held his gaze without flinching. After a short pause, he seemed to accept her assertion that she was fine. "Not really," he muttered. "I hate this, Diyah. Honestly, I have half a mind to just walk in there unarmed and let them kill me. I would rather die than fight for Cadyan."

"Well, I think you should reconsider," said Diyah. Then, lowering her voice, she told Jémys everything she'd overheard at the maífírkon ceremony. She told him about Rey and Ayr and about Catanya.

"What? You mean... Catanya's *alive*?" Jémys stumbled backwards and clutched the window frame for support. "I can't believe it." His hands shook as he brushed the hair out of his face. Then his mouth split into a wide grin. "This is amazing!"

"Shh," warned Diyah, glancing around. "We need to be smart and take our cues from Rey. We need to bide our time— make everyone think we're on their side, so we don't arouse suspicion."

"Agreed." Jémys nodded, but he was having trouble wiping the grin from his face.

"And you should just keep your head down and follow orders. If Cadyan finds out, the fírkon will be the first to know about it."

"You haven't told Julyán about any of this, have you?" asked Jémys suddenly.

Diyah was taken aback. "No, of course not. Why would I tell him?"

"Good, that's good. We can't trust him."

Diyah rolled her eyes but didn't respond.

"Should we tell Fehla?" asked Jémys, looking worried.

"Yes, we're going to need her help." Diyah had been thinking about it for days and she knew what they needed to do next. "We need to get into the dungeons," she said. "We need to talk to Ayr."

They agreed to meet again later that night after training ended and after Diyah had spoken with Fehla. The three of them could devise a plan together.

Jémys left to report for training, and Diyah headed off in search of Fehla.

It was early enough that Fehla might still be in her chambers getting ready for the day, so Diyah headed back up to the third floor. The maífirkon's quarters were just down the hall from the royal quarters and though she had never been to either, she knew which room was Cadyan's and which room was Fehla's. As she passed the door to Cadyan's chambers, she heard him laughing within and suddenly remembered who was in there with him. A shiver went down her spine as she pictured Julyán and Cadyan working together and laughing.

She marched up to Fehla's door and stopped in front of the guards. "I am here to see the queen."

"The king says no visitors," said the nearest guard.

Diyah was irritated, but she'd been expecting this. "I'm not a visitor. I'm the court physician and the maífirkon's wife. Now, correct me if I'm wrong, but I believe my husband outranks you, and it would be a shame if I had to tell him your service has been less than pleasing to me." She let the threat dangle in the air, enjoying the tension it created. She was pleased to see that it worked.

"Y-yes, ma'am," stammered the guard, stepping aside so she could knock on the door.

"Fehla, it's me," she called.

"Diyah!" Fehla let her in and closed the door. The queen's

room was larger than the maífirkon's quarters, but it was much cozier, and Fehla's taste was surprisingly decorative. Cut flowers were arranged in vases on the mantle, several paintings of natural landscapes hung on the walls, and the furnishings boasted colourful throws and cushions.

Fehla led Diyah over to the armchairs by the fire. "How are you, dear?"

"At the moment, I'm oddly happy to be the maífirkon's wife," said Diyah as she looked back at the door.

"Really?" Fehla raised her eyebrows.

"Oh... never mind," said Diyah, embarrassment rising in her cheeks again. "I have news."

For the second time that day she recounted what she'd overheard between Rey and his soldier. Fehla was over-whelmed at first. She was so overjoyed to hear that her daughter was alive that it was difficult for her to focus on anything else. But after a few minutes Diyah managed to calm her down.

"I want to confirm with Ayr and find out where Catanya actually is," continued Diyah. We need to get into the dungeons, and that's where you come in."

"Me?"

"Yes. When I was in the dungeons, how did you visit me without anyone finding out?"

"Well, if you recall, someone *did* find out," said Fehla.

"Yes, but now I know where Julyán is going to be at all times, I know how to avoid him," said Diyah, smiling deviously.

"True... But we can't just walk into the dungeons and demand to see the Queen of Awnell. That might have worked when I was visiting you, but no offence, dear, Ayr is a much more conspicuous prisoner. She'll be harder to get to."

"I know," said Diyah. They lapsed into silence, each trying to think of a way into the dungeons.

"Perhaps..." Fehla's face brightened, and she looked at Diyah. "Do you have any of that valerian root sleep tonic left?"

An hour later Diyah walked into the dungeons carrying a tray with a sandwich and a glass of haymead.

"Lunch," she announced, shoving it into the guard's hands.

"Why are you bringing it?" he asked, eyes narrowed. "Where's the usual girl?"

"She's come down with the blistering fever. I sent her home," said Diyah. "But if you'd rather risk it, I can bring her back. Mind you, the blisters on her hands have started to erupt. But if you don't mind, then—" Diyah moved to take back the tray of food.

"No, that's all right ma'am," said the guard, tightening his hold on the tray. "I was just surprised is all. What with you being the maífirkon's wife now. I'd have assumed you'd be done with all that noise."

"That *noise*, as you so eloquently call it, is my profession. If I stop doing it, what do you think will become of the people in this city?"

The guard gawked at her. But then he shrugged and took the tankard off the plate, holding it up in salute. "Well good on ye, then." And he downed the beverage in one gulp.

The effects were almost immediate. His eyes slid out of focus and he slumped back against the wall. Diyah grabbed the tray before it crashed to the ground. Then she waved her hand in front of his face and nudged him hard in the ribs, but he just grunted and remained asleep.

"Fehla!" she called, setting the tray on the ground. "It's safe to come down."

Fehla crept down the stairs and into the light. "How much

did you give him?" she asked, gawking at the unconscious guard.

"Half of it," said Diyah, shrugging. "He'll be fine. Come on, we can't waste time."

They grabbed the keys from his belt and the torch from the wall, and then unlocked the gate into the dungeons. As they walked past the cells, the familiar rancid smell made Diyah's skin crawl. She cringed at the thought of Ayr living down here for almost two months.

"I hate this place," she whispered, looking at Fehla. It surprised her to see that Fehla looked almost sick to her stomach. The colour had drained from her face, and she seemed jittery and nervous. "Are you all right?"

"Oh, she's fine," came a clear, cold voice from deep within the cell on their left. "I'd say that's just guilt on her face."

They squinted into the darkness and watched a woman step into the light. She had a proud face and an imposing presence. It amazed Diyah how strong and impressive she still looked, despite the clear signs of starvation and light deprivation.

"Queen Ayr." Diyah took a step forward to address her.

"I was wondering how long it would take you to come see me." Ayr wasn't looking at Diyah. Her eyes were trained unblinkingly on Fehla. "Incidentally, how long has it been? It's a little difficult to keep track in here." She held up her hand, casually examining her nails like she didn't have a care in the world.

"I want to know the truth, Ayr," said Fehla, speaking in an unusually harsh voice.

"Don't we all," drawled Ayr as she draped her arms through the cell bars. She looked comfortable and at ease, like she was right where she wanted to be.

"What happened to my daughter?"

"Hmm, daughter, you say? I thought you had a son?"

"Don't play with me," snapped Fehla. "I know you know what happened to Catanya."

"Perhaps I do, perhaps I don't." Ayr was clearly enjoying the increasing desperation on Fehla's face.

"Please, Ayr." Fehla took a step closer to the cell. "Please."

"Ah, there it is. The *pleading*." Ayr's face broke into a crooked smile. "I remember a day, many years ago when I was the one pleading. Do you remember what happened next?"

Diyah was so confused. She looked from Ayr back to Fehla and saw pain and anguish on her face.

"I thought so," said Ayr, smiling down at her feet. "You haven't changed at all, Fehla. You're still just as weak as you were then. Just as pathetic. Although..." She scratched her chin thoughtfully. "I must admit, the Jade Moss poison"—she let out a long whistle—"that's a nasty way to die, isn't it? I wouldn't have thought you had it in you. And who in Caerlon would know? Still, I'd have gone for something a little more direct myself..."

Diyah wasn't following the conversation at all anymore. "What—"

"This is a waste of time," said Fehla, turning to leave. "Come on, Diyah. She's not going to tell us anything."

But as Fehla started walking away Ayr called, "If your daughter were here right now, tell me, what would you say to her?"

Fehla turned back to Ayr and sighed. "Everything," she said. "I would tell her everything I've wanted to tell her for these last twenty years."

"That's sweet," said Ayr with a mocking smile. "But what about the things you haven't told *anybody*?"

When Fehla didn't respond, Ayr just snickered and turned her attention towards Diyah. "And what about you," she asked. Her eyes roved over Diyah, taking in her new, high-quality clothes. "What would you say to her?"

Diyah was momentarily caught off guard, but she recovered quickly. "I'd tell her to fight!" she said emphatically. She didn't know what was going on between Ayr and Fehla but right now she didn't care. "I'd tell Catanya that everyone is depending on her and that I believe in her. I always have."

Ayr's face cracked into a wide grin. "I like *her*," she said, jerking her head in Diyah's direction. "She's tough."

"Please, tell *me*, then. Is Catanya really alive?"

Ayr turned back towards Diyah, giving her an appraising look. Then she nodded.

Diyah's heart leapt into her throat. "Where is she?"

"I sent her away. I sent her somewhere to find the answers she needs and learn control." Ayr smirked like she was fighting off a grin. "I had one of my best men go with her."

"Where are they?" asked Diyah, moving to stand in front of the cell.

Ayr seemed to consider her response, but then she shook her head. "The fewer people who know, the safer they'll be."

"But she's alive, and she's learning to control her powers?" asked Diyah. "She's going to come for us?"

Ayr held her gaze for a moment, and then nodded again.

Diyah looked back at Fehla, excitement coursing through her. "Come on, let's go find Jémys and tell him."

"Jémys?" asked Ayr. "Good. I'm happy to know he's still alive."

"You know Jémys?" asked Fehla, frowning.

"I know *of* him... Unlike the rest of her family, Catanya is strong and constant in her affections." She shot Fehla a snide glance and backed away from the bars.

"I did love you," said Fehla in a small, hurt voice.

Comprehension dawned on Diyah.

"I pity the people you love," said Ayr, turning her back and retreating into her cell.

"Come on." Diyah signalled for Fehla to follow her. As they

turned to leave, Ayr called after them.

"But tell me, Fehla, when it comes down to it, you will have another difficult decision to make... Your son or your daughter, who will you choose? There is no way this ends with your family intact. Either way you lose a child. Can you stand by and watch as one of them kills the other?"

Diyah's stomach clenched. She looked at Fehla and saw the devastation written all over her face. With one last critical glance in Ayr's direction, Diyah pulled Fehla back out of the dungeons and closed the gate behind them.

As they walked back down the hall, Diyah watched Fehla closely, lost for words. Diyah didn't know what to make of Queen Ayr. That conversation hadn't gone the way she'd imagined, and she regretted bringing Fehla with her. But how was she supposed to have known?

"Fehla?" She put her hand on the queen's shoulder.

"She's alive, Diyah. That's all that matters," said Fehla. She had regained her composure and her voice sounded more confident.

But Diyah was still troubled. Something about the way Ayr had spoken to Fehla didn't sit right with Diyah. "What was Ayr talking about? I've never heard of the Jade Moss poison."

Fehla made an unusual gesture like she was trying to suppress a shudder. "That's because it is very rare. It only grows in Awnell and only in the most difficult to reach mountains beyond Vonolt."

"But—"

"Don't worry about it, Diyah. Training will be done soon. We need to talk to Jémys."

Diyah had planned for Jémys to meet her in the physician's quarters after training ended. As the sun sank outside the window, Diyah grew nervous. She wasn't entirely sure what time Julyán would be back in their quarters, and she didn't want to risk him becoming suspicious.

Finally, Jémys arrived. Closing the door behind him, he spotted Fehla and said, "Good, you told her." He walked over to join them by the worktable.

"Yes, and we got into the dungeons and saw Ayr. Jémys, it's true! Catanya is alive, she confirmed it."

Jémys's face broke into the widest grin Diyah had ever seen. His eyes crinkled and two large dimples appeared on his cheeks. He rushed forward and grabbed her, hugging her so tightly she thought her ribs might break. Then he let her go and did the same with Fehla.

Diyah laughed at the surprise on Fehla's face.

"This is wonderful," Jémys cried, still smiling from ear to ear. "So, where is she, do we know?"

"Ayr said she sent her somewhere to get answers and learn control. She said she sent one of her best men with her," said Fehla.

Diyah noticed a slight deflation of Jémys's expression.

"One of her men? Surely not... was it Drayk?"

"She didn't give us a name, why?" His dubious tone made Diyah nervous.

Jémys exhaled and strode around the table to sit on the bench. "I don't trust him," he said, brushing the hair out of his face. "I never did. So I don't like the idea of her having to depend on him."

"Well, it might not be him," said Diyah, sitting down on the bench next to Jémys. "Maybe it's someone else."

"Maybe."

Diyah could tell from his tone that he didn't really believe that. She wondered if Jémys had another reason for hating Drayk, but she didn't want to spend time talking about feelings when there were more important issues at hand.

"So, what do we do now?" she asked, looking from Fehla back to Jémys. "We have the upper hand, but sooner or later this information is going to get out."

"I agree. We can't wait for that to happen, we need to act." Fehla paced back and forth.

"We need to go to her." Jémys stood up, wearing an expression of steely resolve. "We need to find her."

Diyah smiled but shook her head. "If it were that easy to escape, I would have done it ages ago."

"We'll just have to find a way," he said, jaw set with determination. "I'm sure if the three of us put our heads together, we can figure it out."

Later that night as Diyah opened the door to her quarters, she found Julyán standing by the window, holding a glass of wine and staring up at the stars. A tray of food sat on the table, waiting for them.

"I'm sorry," she mumbled, closing the door and resting her head on the wood as she watched him. "Have you been waiting long?"

"Not long," said Julyán, still gazing out the window. "What kept you?" His tone was light, but Diyah heard a hint of distrust underneath it.

"I was with Fehla." She walked to join him by the window, then she sighed pointedly. "Her spirits are so low. I think losing her daughter has affected her in ways that will never heal."

She sensed Julyán's eyes on her and she turned to meet his gaze. A sharp pang of guilt reminded her that this escape plan meant leaving him behind. But the excitement of seeing Catanya again overpowered that unpleasant sensation.

"What about your spirits?" asked Julyán, taking her hand and guiding her over to the table. Then he took his seat across from her.

"I'm fine." Diyah lifted her glass off the table and swirled its contents before taking a sip. She sensed his eyes on her again, and it troubled her. She was tired of lying, tired of holding back. "I miss her terribly!" she blurted, putting her glass down hard and splashing some of its amber liquid onto the table. "Catanya was my best friend, my *sister*. When I was just a little girl and I arrived at the lodge, she was the one who befriended me and welcomed me. Ever since I lost my parents, she's been the only person I've ever loved. The only family I've ever had."

The words poured out of her so fast she barely had time to breathe. But when she was done, she felt lighter. She hadn't realized how much she'd been holding in. She had never wanted to admit how much she missed her friend because she couldn't face the thought of never seeing her again. But now that they'd be reunited soon, she could finally acknowledge it.

Julyán watched her curiously. "I cannot say I understand it, but I am sorry for the pain you feel," he said, frowning.

"You *should* understand," said Diyah. "You have a brother."

Julyán shook his head. "Yes, but as you may have noticed, Jémys and I are not very close."

Diyah sighed, torn between sympathy and frustration. "So, all this time, all these years, you've had no one? Not even a friend?"

Julyán smiled wryly. "The firkon do not have the luxury of friendships."

Sadness overwhelmed Diyah anew. "I'm sorry," she mumbled as she watched him rip a chunk of bread off the loaf in the middle of the table. "I hope one day you find someone you can trust... someone you can love."

"Why?" he said with an incredulous half-laugh. "You loved your friend and now she's gone and you're miserable. Why would anyone want that?"

Diyah smiled and shook her head patiently. "Trust me, it's worth it," she said, eyeing him from over the top of her glass.

It will all be worth it if I can see my friend again, she thought to herself as they continued eating their meal in silence.

7

THE MOUNTAINTOP

Catanya awoke with a start. The sky outside the tent was dark, but the moon and the stars filtered some pale light through the thin fabric. She wasn't immediately sure what had woken her, but then she realized someone was standing over her pallet, staring at her.

"Arg!" she yelped and shuffled back from the shadowy face.

"Oh, dear, don't worry. It's only me," came Laylian's voice.

Catanya relaxed, but her heart was still pounding in her chest. "What are you doing?" she asked a little more rudely than she meant to. But really, who in their right mind would wake someone up that way? "Is everything all right?" She cast around nervously. All the instincts she'd developed in her months living on the run had become dulled by her time in Túir-Avlea.

"Oh yes," replied Laylian, but she had a strange distant sound in her voice. "I just want to show you something."

Catanya groaned and rubbed her face, embarrassed by her overreaction. "All right..." She stifled a yawn and nodded as she crawled out of bed, wondering why this couldn't have waited until a decent hour of the day.

"It's a fair hike, so you might want to dress for ease of movement," said Laylian, facing out the open tent door to give Catanya privacy.

Catanya paused. She had been about to throw on one of her long, linen dresses, since she'd grown quite fond of the loose material and the breathable fabric. With another sigh, she nodded and dropped the dress, searching, instead, for the clothes she'd brought from Awnell. The leather was uncomfortably tight on her legs. She cinched the laces on the boots so they gripped her calves, supporting her ankles. It felt odd to be in these clothes again. These were the clothes of a warrior.

"Good, good," said Laylian, when Catanya had finished dressing. "Come along."

Catanya snatched her canteen off the chair and shook it, hearing the contents slosh around. Then she turned and followed Laylian into the forest.

They walked one of the winding paths for a few minutes until they stopped outside another tent. Catanya realized where they were.

Laylian moved to enter and then stopped. "Ah, perhaps, you'd better..." She gestured to the door. "I wouldn't want to startle two people in one morning."

Catanya snorted and shook her head. Then she pushed aside the canopy doors and stepped into the tent. "Drayk," she called. She saw his sleeping frame in bed. "Drayk, wake up." His tent was much the same as hers, with a small sleeping pallet, and several woven rugs and furs covering the ground. However, he had tossed his clothes unceremoniously on the floor so it was impossible to tell what was clean and what was dirty.

He groaned and rolled over to face her. "S'happening?" he asked groggily. He propped himself up on his elbows so the covers slipped off his bare chest. She considered averting her gaze, but he seemed unabashed, and... well, she was curious. She examined him in the moonlight as he rubbed the sleep from his eyes. He really was well built—not as broad as Jémys, but the weeks of rest and food in Túir-Avlea had done him good. He looked healthier than she'd seen him in a long time. And his years of military training in Awnell were certainly visible in his muscles.

Catanya shook her head, a little dazed and discomfited. It had been a while since she'd been with a man. And it would be a lie to say she hadn't thought about it.

"Laylian wants to show us something," she said, glancing at his ribs as he sat up straighter. This was the first time she'd seen the scars and burns on his chest since that time in the woods. She hadn't realized how far they extended down his left side and along his abdomen.

"Apparently it's a long hike." She indicated the outfit she was wearing as an explanation. "So... I'll wait outside, then."

She stepped out of the tent to wait with Laylian. A few minutes later, Drayk joined them in the dark of predawn.

"Where are we going?" he asked, pulling his long jacket over his vest.

Catanya's stomach twisted. It had been weeks since she'd seen him in his usual attire. She'd forgotten how well it suited him.

"Up," replied Laylian. She gestured to the slope of the mountain beyond the plateau where the community was nestled.

"We're going to climb the mountain?" spluttered Catanya, shocked out of her contemplation. She gaped at Laylian a little incredulously. Laylian might be spry, but hiking up a mountain would be a challenge even for Catanya and Drayk.

Laylian chuckled. "Oh, don't worry about me," she said, and she set off along the path, deeper into the forest. "I've done this many times."

Catanya exchanged dubious glances with Drayk. He shrugged and the two of them set off after her.

Laylian moved surprisingly fast as they walked along the path through the forest.

They passed the spot that led to the tranquil bathing pool. Catanya heard the rushing sound of the waterfall and smelled the faint scent of roses in the air. The vines and bushes surrounding the pool would be in full bloom any day now.

She made a mental note to visit it again as soon as possible. The thought of being there while the roses were in bloom sounded wonderful.

As they continued deeper into the forest, the path became wilder and more overgrown. Tree branches dangled overhead, grasping at them as they passed. Squirrels and other wildlife scuttled in the shadows between the trees, and their movement was especially loud against the backdrop of early morning. The lanterns that hung every few feet became farther and farther apart, leaving patches of darkness to swallow them for several minutes.

After a while, the dense darkness bled into the pale light of dawn. They could see where they were going more easily.

A slight ache in Catanya's legs told her they had begun their upward climb. Nobody spoke. Catanya and Drayk were still too groggy from sleep, and Laylian seemed content to walk in silence.

By the time the sun had risen completely, they had reached a point in the forest where the path curved sharply upward. If the walk had been steep before, it was nothing compared to what it was now.

Catanya panted as she tried to keep up with Laylian. But the old woman seemed oddly relaxed and comfortable, like she wasn't tired at all.

Then it dawned on Catanya. "You're using Resonance, aren't you?" she asked, eyeing Laylian.

Laylian beamed at her. "Of course! How else could I walk like this at my age?"

"And what exactly is your age?" asked Drayk, who was also panting from the exertion.

Laylian chortled and wagged her finger at him. "Old," she replied.

Catanya and Drayk exchanged significant looks. Catanya glanced at the wreath on Laylian's head. Drayk had told her his theory, but she wasn't sure she believed it.

"This is a long hike to do on muscles alone. When you're tired enough, you'll use your Resonance too," declared Laylian happily. "And I do hope you'll spare some for Drayk. Otherwise, I'm afraid we might have to carry him back down when we're done."

Catanya gaped at her. If she understood how to use her Resonance like that, she'd be doing it already.

They continued trekking along. The incline grew steeper and steeper until it bent upward so it was more of a wall than a path.

"Great. More stairs," grumbled Drayk. Someone had carved a set of crude steps into the incline to help with the next leg of the journey. The staircase was reminiscent of the one they'd climbed up the mountain from the Dead Wood, but these steps were even narrower, and much steeper. They looked treacherous.

"Come along," called Laylian as she scaled the stairs with enviable ease and speed.

"So... Resonance?" asked Drayk. He doubled over, clutching a stitch in his side and sweating.

Catanya didn't have enough breath to speak. She glanced up at Laylian, wondering which form of Resonance she was using. Then she closed her eyes, trying to reach out with her mind. She was still too nervous to reach out to the Spirits after what Laylian had said about the risks the other day, so she tried to call on the Natures. She reached out to the Earth first, searching for a way to make the journey easier. But there was nothing she could draw on—at least not without risking an earthquake or a landslide. So, instead, she focused on steadying her breathing. As she came back into balance with the air, she let its energy flow through her. Gentle gusts of Wind swirled around her limbs, and a sudden lightness coursed through her body, and she opened her eyes, smiling.

She reached out and took Drayk's hand in hers, allowing the energy to flow through her arm and into his.

Drayk shuddered and recoiled. "Oh, what is that?" he asked. He moved to pull his hand away, but Catanya tightened her grip.

"It's okay," she said. Then she released her grip, making sure the connection she'd created remained.

Drayk's eyes widened, and he looked down at his body, amazed.

"Excellent," called Laylian from a few feet above them. "Now we'll be there in no time."

Catanya laughed, feeling quite literally lighter than ever before. She began climbing the stairs after Laylian. All pain in her legs was gone.

As elated as she was, it didn't take long before the fear and doubt returned, chipping away at her connection. Whenever it did, the heaviness of her body increased. She tried to keep her mind clear, to focus on maintaining the connection without worrying about anything else. But by the time midday rolled around, her legs had a steady dull ache. Her control was slipping.

Drayk struggled slightly as he climbed, but he didn't say anything.

Catanya was frustrated with herself, which didn't help. Whenever she let the agitation take hold she felt the itching, prickling sensation in her fingers. It made her nervous, causing her connection with the Wind to fade even more.

It was well after midday when they stepped off the stairs and onto a plateau. By that time, Catanya's legs were burning again, and sweat poured down her back. The air was thin, making it difficult to breathe, let alone resonate with anything.

They paused for a few minutes as they passed around Catanya's canteen. Laylian had brought a few provisions for them, including some berries and flatbread. So, they ate and drank in silence, examining their new surroundings. They had left most of the forest behind. This area was much rockier, with wiry shrubs poking out at irregular places. It was cold so close to the clouds, and a fine chilly mist clung to the air.

Catanya stood at the edge of the plateau gazing back the way they'd come. Far below, she could just make out the glade. Everyone would be finishing their midday meal now. When she squinted, she thought she could see figures moving. They looked minuscule, no larger than ants.

She wondered how many of them had struggled to invoke Resonance like her. Or had it been easy for them, like instinct? Perhaps when you grew up around it, you didn't need to be taught, perhaps you learned Resonance the same way a child learned to speak.

"We're almost there," said Laylian, repacking the remaining flatbread.

Catanya sighed and strapped her canteen back on her belt. As she followed Laylian along the plateau, she attempted to re-establish her connection with the Wind.

It didn't work.

She reached out again and again, but nothing happened. And the harder she worked, the angrier she got. Why couldn't she do this? What was wrong with her that she struggled so much?

She took slow, calming breaths, trying to centre herself, but she was too frustrated. Too tired. As they continued moving, Catanya's legs weighed heavy like lead, and her irritation mounted.

They walked for another hour at a much slower pace. Catanya sensed Laylian was deliberately taking her time.

Staring down, Catanya noticed the ground had an odd, sparkling quality to it, almost as if there were diamonds embedded in the stone. She didn't think much of it until she realized the shimmer was getting more pronounced the farther they walked.

She stopped and knelt down, running her fingers along the stone.

"Hold on," she muttered, spinning around to look at the ground behind her. It wasn't diamonds. It was something else. A shimmering, luminous collection of colours that danced in the sun's light. "Is this—" She broke off, turning to stare at Laylian.

"It is indeed," she replied, smiling serenely.

The ground was marbled with the same iridescent stone that had been in her necklace. Veins of glinting colour branched beneath her feet.

"It's stunning," said Drayk, looking at the ground in apparent wonder. He had never seen Catanya's necklace, and when he glanced at her next, his eyes roved over her hair, like he hadn't realized how beautiful it was.

"Come along," called Laylian. "We're nearly there now, just over the ridge." She beckoned for them to follow her as she climbed the narrow ridge and disappeared from sight.

Catanya felt strangely nervous as she followed Laylian. When she and Drayk climbed up the final incline and crested the top of the mountain, Catanya's jaw dropped.

The entire area shimmered so brightly with colour that it was nearly blinding in the afternoon sun. A strong, cool breeze stirred the air, rustling their clothes and hair.

Catanya blinked several times as her eyes adjusted to the glare. Then she stepped forward, gazing at the view.

They were standing in some sort of ceremonial gathering place. A dozen iridescent rocks the size of small chairs formed a semicircle around an empty fire pit, facing a solitary yew tree. The tree's broad, contorted trunk stretched at least six feet wide, with rippling burls and knots cloaked in peeling reddish-brown bark. The branches twisted and sprawled above the gathering place, intertwining to form a tangled canopy that littered the ground in a blanket of old berries and needle-like leaves.

Catanya and Drayk revolved slowly on the spot, staring around in awe. As they moved into the centre of the plateau, Catanya's eyes took in the full scene. In the distance beyond the mountain, she saw the outline of the entire island as it gave way to the unending expanse of the sea.

The sheet of brilliant blue water was breathtaking. It reminded her of questions she used to ask back in Faltir, as she'd gazed at the boundless ocean from her secluded little beach—questions about what lay beyond the horizon. And now she knew there was no answer. Here she was in Túir-Avlea, a magical land, far beyond the horizon of Mórceá. She stood at the peak of this mystical place, gazing at yet another unknown horizon.

There would always be some place else, some new horizon. New questions, new mysteries. She could never learn everything, but she could find beauty in wondering.

And this place—this summit of Túir-Avlea—was the single most beautiful thing Catanya had ever seen.

With a broad smile on her face, Laylian perched on one of the iridescent boulders, watching Catanya and Drayk as they gazed around. "Come join me," she said after a while.

Catanya wrenched her gaze away from the view. Laylian beckoned for her to take a seat on one of the boulders, but

Catanya hesitated to sit on something so beautiful.

"Why have you brought us here?" asked Drayk. His incredulous tone told Catanya he felt the same way she did—that this place was somehow sacred, not meant for them.

"For the truth," Laylian replied, waiting for them to sit.

"What is this stone?" Catanya ran her hands along the nearest boulder. It was unnaturally smooth and glossy, almost wet like ice starting to melt. She sat down gingerly and watched Drayk do the same.

"We call it skystone," said Laylian. "I have never seen it anywhere but on this mountain. I have often observed that certain stones can inspire magic, inspire change and movement. The red and black stones found in the east villages of Mórceá—I believe you know the area as Awnell?—those stones were said to inspire passion."

"Flamestones," said Drayk, nodding. He glanced at Catanya.

She remembered the necklace Ayr had lent her for the Midwinter Carnival. At the time, she hadn't fully believed what Drayk had said about the stones inspiring passion. Now she wondered if there was some truth to it.

"Well, just as flamestone is said to inspire passion—or the heart—let's say that skystone inspires the soul, the part of us that exists in ether—the spirit. That is why this place is so sacred, why we chose it to be our home, and, of course, why the stone was used to create a relic."

"How do you know this?" asked Catanya.

Laylian smiled but didn't respond. Instead, she stood up and walked over to stand in front of Catanya.

"The Oracle Stone was hewn from the ground atop this mountain. And it was bonded with Spirit Resonance here many centuries ago," she spoke calmly, but her voice echoed with the years. "I want you to see. Use the power of the stone and take us back to that time."

Catanya gaped at her. "I can't do that," she blurted without thinking. When she'd told Laylian about her previous visions, she'd never imagined the maílehr would ask her to do something like this.

"Of course you can," said Laylian with the same patience she always showed. "Until now you've been passive, allowing the visions to come to you when you forge a connection to a place or an object. But you can also reach out to call the visions forth. Place your hand on the stone and allow your mind to journey back."

Catanya glanced at Drayk for support but he raised his eyebrows with curiosity and nodded encouragingly at her.

"Oh, all right," said Catanya, biting her lip. She wasn't sure why she was nervous. But the farthest back she'd ever seen had been the vision of her mother. It was disturbing to think she might be able to conjure a vision of something that happened centuries ago. A vision from a time that had faded into legend.

But she was curious too. If she really could see that far back, she'd be able to learn things no one else knew...

So, she placed her palms flat on the boulder beneath her and closed her eyes, reaching out with her mind. She vaguely heard Laylian say something to Drayk, but she didn't hear the words. Then a slight pressure on her shoulders told her they had each laid a hand on her in order to join her in the vision.

Catanya cast her mind back, trying to imagine a time centuries ago. A time when the great Maílehr Illayan had stood on this mountain, had touched this stone and bonded it with Resonance.

She opened her eyes again and felt the telltale dizziness sweeping over her, but it was much stronger this time. She was grateful for the support of the boulder beneath her.

Her vision blurred and her head spun. All she could see was a bright patch of swirling colour, blending into fog. A gentle humming sound broke through the din. She followed it, letting it carry her towards its source. Her vision slowly cleared, as the scene in front of her came into focus.

The yew tree was much smaller now, though it still stretched several feet wide. The sky was overcast and bleak, and bright red berries among the needles told her it was nearing winter. A gentle layer of frost coated the ground, but the temperature didn't reach her. Nor the warmth from the blazing fire in the pit. The scene existed as an echo of the past, a mirage. She turned around to see Drayk and Laylian staring at their new surroundings. She had brought them with her to witness the past.

The humming sound started again. Catanya turned back to see someone in a long, flowing robe walk out from behind the tree. Her first thought was that this person was a man, but he had unusually delicate features and he carried himself with a grace that Catanya had never seen in a man before. So, the longer she watched him, the more she thought perhaps he was a woman. Whoever this person was, (Catanya settled on using "he" in her mind) he looked about ten or fifteen years older than Catanya, but his hair was already grey and he wore it short along the nape of his neck. He placed his hands on the tree trunk and closed his eyes, humming gently.

"Maílehr Illayan," came a voice from behind them. They all turned to see a young man emerging over the hill, carrying a wide pail of sloshing water. He looked to be in his late teens, with light brown skin and thick, dark hair. He wore a decorative mauve vest over a pale orange tunic, and the colours clashed flamboyantly like he was trying to make a statement, but hadn't quite succeeded. "Are you sure this will work?" he asked, placing his pail on the ground beside the fire.

"Of course I am," responded Illayan, with an airy voice that sounded strangely familiar. "I have done it many times on smaller scales. And experimentation is the lifeblood of any serious practitioner." The faint admonition was clear. The young man looked appropriately chastened as he nodded. "Your doubt serves no purpose and only hinders your progress," continued Illayan. "Now come over here and watch how this is done."

The young man nodded again and trotted over to stand with his teacher. Catanya looked back at the great Maílehr Illayan, the legendary practitioner who'd trained so many people in the years before the Quiescence Wars. It surprised her how ordinary he looked. How human. In her mind Catanya had always pictured someone more extraordinary. Someone brimming with magical power and solemnity.

"Now, binding is very delicate," said Illayan, "so it should not be attempted without sufficient time and practice. The Spirits have to trust you if they're going to allow themselves to be bound to an object."

"What if they don't trust you?" asked the young man.

"Then you won't be able to resonate with them at all."

Illayan's apprentice sighed. It was obvious he found that response disappointing.

"Steady, Caer, the Spirits are what gives us our superior power, we cannot be disrespectful or impatient. We've been over this."

Caer. Catanya's stomach clenched as she realized who the young man was.

"I know, I just find it a little tedious sometimes. Wouldn't it be better if we could command them at will?"

Illayan shot Caer a sharp, piercing look. "That is not Resonance, that is compulsion and it is reprehensible."

Caer gave a sceptical sniff.

"You disagree?" Illayan looked livid, all benevolent patience evaporating in an instant. "Fine. I'm tired of having this conversation with you. Since words seem incapable of penetrating that skull of yours, then let us try a more practical approach. Fortunately, I have an item perfectly suited for the lesson."

Illayan yanked a plain, iron ring off his finger and placed it on the stone in front of them. Then he held his hands above the stone and closed his eyes.

Thick, menacing clouds rolled across the sky, casting the mountain in oppressive darkness. A violent gale whipped against the branches of the yew tree. Illayan's entire body gave off a faint golden glow that grew brighter and brighter against the increasing darkness of the sky.

A shudder ran down Catanya's spine as she watched Caer struggling to stay on his feet. The nervous awe in his eyes was evident. He had never seen such a display of power before.

Slowly, the golden glow extended from Illayan to encompass the ring. The iron band blazed like a scalding ember, shaking from the force of the Resonance channeling into it.

Then the force abated. The glowing light dimmed and the sky cleared. Illayan relaxed, opening his eyes again to stare at his student.

Without speaking, he slid the ring back on his finger and placed his hand on Caer's shoulder.

"If compulsion is fine, then you won't mind a little exercise." His tone was light but there was a cold edge to it now that Catanya found terrifying. "Just a simple test. How about you break the smallest finger on your left hand? Off you go."

Catanya couldn't believe what she was seeing. She watched in utter shock as Caer gripped his finger in his right hand and yanked. A small pop and a crack told her that the finger had snapped in two.

"Very good," said Illayan, ignoring his student's cries of pain. "Let's think, now, I'd like you to stop breathing."

At once Caer began to splutter and gasp as if his lungs had stopped working. "Good. Now, while you're suffocating to death, let's see if we can't use some of that Resonance of yours. I'd like you to channel your powers into the Earth and lift this entire mountain."

Caer's eyes popped. He collapsed onto his knees, still sputtering and gasping, but also trying to channel his power into the Earth. He heaved and spluttered on empty lungs. His face flushed, and the veins pulsed in his forehead. It was a pitiful and wretched sight to see.

"Have you had enough?" asked Illayan.

Caer gasped and nodded frantically. Illayan laid his hand on Caer's shoulder and spoke, "Breathe. Relax." He released his grip. Caer gasped and choked on the sudden intake of air. Tears in his eyes, he crumpled onto the ground, panting.

"Good." Illayan knelt down, so he was face to face with Caer. "Now, imagine that impotence, that abuse and enslavement—imagine enduring that for every second of your existence throughout all eternity. Really think about that." Illayan stood up and his face relaxed again. "Tell me, would you wish that fate upon another soul?"

Caer glared at Illayan but shook his head. "No," he said dismally, but his eyes darted to the ring on Illayan's hand. Catanya couldn't tell if it was fear or longing she read in his expression.

"Very good," said Illayan, but his eyes narrowed as he surveyed his student one last time. "Now, if you don't mind, I'd like to finish what I came here to do. Go over there and fetch me the stone and the headdress."

Caer scrambled to his feet. He cupped his misshapen finger and stifled a gasp as he straightened the bone again.

Illayan glanced at him with a softer, more compassionate expression, almost like he regretted his actions. "I'll have Heiltúir Imndal set that for you when we return."

Caer nodded, blinking away tears of pain. "So... what power are you planning to bind into these?" He gingerly lifted a small, polished skystone and what looked like a wreath off the nearby boulder and handed them to Illayan.

"Every object has a history which will help to inform its

power. This ring," Illayan waved his hand, "was forged from the chains that once imprisoned me."

"What?" asked Caer, obviously surprised to hear of his teacher's previous fate.

"Yes," replied Illayan with a sour smile. "That was a long time ago, when I was first testing my power and discovering who I was. The people of Tirimsi were not very understanding..." He drifted off into a dark silence for a moment.

"Maílehr," prompted Caer, a look of nervous pity in his eyes.

Illayan seemed to recollect himself. "Never underestimate the power of fear in the hearts of simple people. It can make them cruel, but it can also make them easy to manipulate." The triumphant tone in Illayan's voice sent a chill down Catanya's spine. She had a dark suspicion about what became of the people of Tirimsi.

One of the hands on Catanya's shoulder tightened. She glanced up to see Laylian cringing. Laylian seemed to be watching the scene with profound disappointment.

"So..." Caer sounded intrigued as he prompted Illayan to continue.

"So, I was able to call upon the ring's history and use it to amplify the power I sought to bind into it." Illayan looked down at the ring. "Perhaps a little more power than I ought to have used. Admittedly, the memory of that time is still quite painful..." He looked momentarily ashamed of himself, but Caer didn't seem to notice. "The relationship between the practitioner and the object seals the binding and gives it strength. No two bindings can ever be the same."

"So, what about the stone and the wreath?" asked Caer. "What power will these have?"

Illayan recollected himself and turned to face Caer. An indulgent smile spread across his face. "You will see."

"I believe that is enough," came Laylian's voice. Catanya

turned to see her smiling sadly at the vision. Catanya relaxed her mind, allowing herself to be pulled back into the present. It took a long time for her vision to clear, but when it did, she was back with Laylian and Drayk, squinting into the blinding sunlight.

"That was unbelievable," said Drayk in an awestruck voice. He released his grip on Catanya and stepped back.

Catanya watched Laylian. It was hard to tell under the wrinkles and the unkempt hair, but Catanya thought Laylian must have had fairly epicene features when she was younger. And the timbre of her voice was quite similar to Illayan's.

"That wreath," Catanya pointed to the headpiece Laylian wore, "it looks strikingly similar to the one Illayan had." It was true. The wreath in the vision had been made of evergreen branches, twisted and woven together around a silver circlet. Aside from the patches on Laylian's wreath where the needles had begun to wilt and turn brown, the two wreaths were practically identical.

"Yes, it does, doesn't it?" said Laylian, with an almost sad smile. She held Catanya's gaze for a moment, and Catanya suppressed a sudden urge to laugh out loud.

"What happened to the ring?" asked Drayk after a while.

Laylian turned to look at him. "Alas, the ring was such a wretched thing. It should have been destroyed the minute it was created. But as you saw, even Illayan was not immune to anger and hubris." Laylian shook her head wearily. "The ring was lost in Bratia during the final battle, but recently, ripples of its power have stirred the air for the first time in centuries. I believe it has been found."

Catanya and Drayk exchanged dark looks.

"Cadyan. That's perfect," said Drayk with a heavy voice. He shook his head angrily and turned to face the open ocean, staring at the northern horizon.

Catanya thought back to the last time she'd seen her

brother—the time on the beach. She didn't remember seeing a ring on his finger, but when he'd placed his hand on her shoulder...

Last chance, sister. Come with me to Caerlon.

And Catanya had almost agreed. She'd felt so calm and peaceful, like she would have done anything he'd said.

Catanya shuddered. He had used the ring on her. She was certain of it.

The image of Caer kneeling on the ground flashed before her eyes. The great Maílater Caer hadn't been able to resist the power of the ring. How had she managed to resist it?

Everyone lapsed into silence, lost in their own thoughts for a time. Laylian sat on one of the boulders, while Drayk wandered over to the yew tree, examining it up and down. Catanya stood still, replaying the vision in her head. Before now, she had always viewed Illayan as a noble folk hero, one who stood up to tyranny and injustice. It frightened her a little to discover there had been such a dark edge to the famed maílehr.

"Illayan and Caer," she said after a while, "how did they go from this to the legends we know today?" She couldn't get over how normal Caer had seemed. She had always imagined Maílater Caer as some kind of villain or monster, but in the vision, he had been so ordinary—just a student, eager to learn from his teacher.

Laylian sighed. "How do any of these things happen?" she asked, and leaned forward on her boulder, looking older than Catanya had ever seen her. "Imagine you are Illayan," she spoke slowly. "You are the greatest and most sought-after maílehr ever to live. You're invincible, all-powerful, all-knowing. It is simply impossible that you could do anything wrong. Anyone who doesn't understand your greatness is either too weak to cope or too feebleminded to comprehend. You never even realize that this arrogance of yours is rubbing off on your students. You don't notice the resentment building in them, nor do you notice how you've allowed your own grudges and fears to poison their minds. Years pass and you move on. You teach new students, you grow and learn, and maybe you improve somewhat. But it is too late to undo the damage you inflicted. By the time you realize what's happening, there's nothing you can do to stop it."

Catanya listened to Laylian in stunned silence. "I could see why Illayan might want to disappear after that, to become someone else." She eyed Laylian, a great swell of sympathy spreading through her.

"I believe this experience inspired Caer to create the elixir," continued Laylian after a while. "He was searching for a way to bind Spirit Resonance into a permanently submissive state— something to be wielded as readily as the relics themselves."

"And he succeeded," said Drayk darkly.

"Yes, he did," said Laylian. "But it is unnatural. Every binding fades over time. The ring, the crown, the stone, they will lose their power eventually... But the elixir will not. It is constantly refuelled, so it does not fade. Instead, it grows stronger and more volatile, siphoning more and more from the Spirits until eventually there will be nothing left. No Resonance left in the world."

Catanya was slightly nauseated as she thought about the implications of that. "And that's the power I have inside of me?" She didn't need Laylian to confirm it. She already knew. The tug of its power was strong, connecting her to other people.

Laylian gave her a kind smile. "Yes, I'm sure you've felt it. Your Resonance is drawn to other sources of it, magnified by the effects of the Oracle Stone. The pull is strongest with kin. You must experience it with us here in Túir-Avlea."

Catanya nodded. Even now, it pulled at her, connecting her to Laylian. It had been there from the first moment they'd met.

"The old man in the cabin," said Drayk suddenly. "You said

there was a connection between you. Could he have been related to you somehow?"

Catanya had been wondering the same thing for a while. "I think he was. Remember what he said about wishing he'd ended his bloodline before it got poisoned. He mentioned his daughter and her daughters." Catanya paused as the certainty settled in her head, and her voice caught in her throat. "I think he was talking about Fehla and Lia and about Fehla marrying Casréyan. The sullied bloodline... He meant Cadyan and me." Catanya shuddered and looked at Laylian. "And I killed him— my great grandfather... But it's worse than that, isn't it? I didn't just kill him, I siphoned his spirit into me, fuelling my own power more?"

"Yes," said Laylian with surprising calm. "From what you've said, I believe he had more Resonance than most people in Mórceá. That is why you were drawn to him. It also explains why his mind was affected by the lure of the elixir and the map. The tug of your power and your brother's is too strong. It prevented him from committing to the journey across the shoal. And his Resonance was not strong enough to resist."

"And Fehla and Lia? My mother and my aunt. They don't have Resonance? Is that why I don't feel the same connection to them?"

Laylian shrugged. "Resonance is not a birthright. You could be descended from one of the greatest practitioners in the world, and it wouldn't matter. Resonance is about your own connection to the Natures and the Spirits. Your connection to change."

"But I *am* descended from Maílater Caer," said Catanya in a dead voice. "His spirit is bound to the elixir too, isn't it? And Casréyan, and every king and queen of Caerlon in between them..."

Nausea mounted in her again and she struggled to breathe. It was like she could suddenly feel them inside her. Their darkness twisted and glommed onto her. Like a black smoke, extinguishing every trace of colour and light in her, dragging her into the dark with them.

"Yes, and that is why you've been struggling to control it. Your natural instincts are telling you to reject the power. But you mustn't resist anymore."

"What? Why?" Catanya was surprised to hear it. Now more than ever, she had the urge to resist. Every fibre of her being told her not to use the well of power inside her. She wanted to wash it clean, to scrape the contagion from her soul.

"Because it is too strong. If you continue to resist, it will subsume you. You will lose yourself to it, becoming just another spirit tethered to its power." Laylian gave her a stern look.

Catanya's breath caught in her throat. She stared at her maílehr, consumed with fear and dread.

"However," continued Laylian in a reassuring voice. "If you willingly open yourself up to it now, I can teach you to find balance. I can show you how to redirect it and how to wield it without letting it overwhelm you."

Catanya's heart slowly resumed its normal pace. "All right," she said, nodding. She understood now that she didn't have a choice. She either learned to control the power or else it would control her. There was nothing more to it.

After a few more minutes of silence, Drayk suggested they begin their return journey. Catanya thought she heard a slight edge to his voice. As the three of them made their way back along the mountaintop towards the stone stairs, she thought he seemed unusually taciturn.

"Are you all right?" she asked.

Drayk shrugged. "Fine," he muttered. But he was cold and aloof the rest of the journey back.

Catanya, however, felt a peculiar sense of confidence and reassurance. The vision had been unnerving, but it had given her a lot of answers. She understood what she needed to do, and she could finally see her way forward. She had thought that resisting the power would keep her safe, but she was wrong... All those times when her power had overwhelmed her, it had been draining her... But not anymore.

It was time to embrace it.

8

MURDER AND CHAOS

Diyah awoke with a start to the sound of someone banging on the door. The sky outside the window was pitch black, and the room was completely dark except for the faint glow of the dying fire. Julyán had snapped up beside her in bed. He was holding a blade, poised for a fight.

"Where did you get that?" she blurted, panicked at the sight of so much tension in his body. He didn't respond. He was staring fixedly at the door, waiting for something to happen.

"Maífirkon, sir?" Someone spoke from outside and Julyán relaxed.

"Enter," he called, and the door swung open, pouring torch-light into the room.

Diyah let out a feeble protest as she yanked the covers up around her body. Julyán glanced at her, surprised. Then he leaned forward slightly to block her from view.

"What is it?" he asked as a castle guard came into the room and stopped a few feet from the bed. The torch in his hand cast eerie shadows on the walls.

"Sorry to disturb you, sir." The guard glanced at Diyah and averted his gaze. "But there's been an incident."

"An incident," repeated Julyán. Even in the dark, Diyah saw the muscles in his back tense up again.

"A murder."

"What?" Forgetting her embarrassment, Diyah leaned forward, careful to keep the covers tight around her body. "Who?"

The guard looked uncomfortable and glanced at Julyán as though requesting permission to speak.

"Well?" prompted Julyán impatiently.

"The chaplain, sir."

Diyah gasped and Julyán groaned, swinging his legs off the bed and standing up. "When?" he asked. Diyah was impressed by his apparent lack of inhibition as he stood stark naked in front of one of his guards and began dressing in a hurry.

"We're not sure, sir, it's—well, messy."

"Has the body stiffened?" asked Diyah, her mind snapping into work mode. "Is it still warm?"

The guard just gaped at her, and she rolled her eyes. "I should come with you," she said, wrapping the blankets tightly around her and crawling across the bed to kneel in front of Julyán. "I can examine the body."

Julyán looked at her curiously for a moment and then nodded.

There was a pause as everyone waited, but Diyah didn't move. She stared at the guard, who was eyeing her with curiosity and interest. Diyah glanced back to Julyán and saw comprehension dawn on him.

"Get out," he said to the guard. "Wait for us in the corridor."

The guard gave a start. "Oh... of course, sir." He cast one last sheepish look in Diyah's direction before he scrambled out of the room.

Diyah dressed in a hurry, and she and Julyán left together. They made their way quickly through the dark corridors until they arrived at the chaplain's chambers and pushed open the door.

Someone had lit the candles in the room, and Diyah was not prepared for the sight that met her eyes. It was gruesome. The chaplain lay naked in a pool of blood on his bed. His arms and legs were twisted and contorted at odd angles as though they'd been broken.

"He's been tortured," said Julyán in a quiet voice as he stepped forward for a closer look.

Diyah took a deep breath to calm herself and joined him at the bedside. "It looks that way," she agreed, leaning over to inspect his battered limbs. "His throat has been slit." She pointed at his neck. The slash was carved so deeply that she could see his spine. She shuddered involuntarily, but no one seemed to notice. "Who would do this?" she asked more to herself than to anyone else.

She couldn't think who would want to kill the chaplain of all people. It couldn't have been Cadyan. He would have wanted an audience, and he wouldn't have needed a knife.

"Someone must have snuck into his rooms overnight," said one of the guards matter-of-factly.

"Why wasn't this door being watched?" Julyán's tone was sharp as he turned his attention to the guard.

Diyah glanced back to see the embarrassment on the man's face. "Well, normally it is, sir, but the chaplain... he asked us not to tonight."

"What?" Julyán looked angry now. "You mean you left the old man unprotected all evening?"

The guard fidgeted uncomfortably. The fear in his eyes reminded Diyah how intimidating her new husband really was.

She laid her hand on Julyán's arm in an effort to calm him. "So, he must have known his attacker," she said. "Whoever it was, he trusted them, and didn't want the guards to know about their visit."

Julyán glanced down at her, slightly surprised.

Diyah shrugged and continued her examination of the body. "Was no knife found?" she asked to the room at large.

"We didn't look."

Diyah let out a sigh of exasperation. "Well, you might want to have a quick glance now, then."

"You heard her," snapped Julyán, and the guards spread through the room, searching for a blade. "And has anyone informed the king?"

No one responded, and the guards exchanged nervous looks. Diyah snorted and rolled her eyes. "They're too scared."

Julyán made a sound of frustration. "We don't have time for this. You there," he gestured to the nearest guard, "go wake the king and tell him what has happened. Then alert the rest of the fírkon. There is a murderer somewhere in this castle and we need to find them."

The guard jumped and stammered his apologies as he hurried off to do as instructed.

"Imbeciles," muttered Julyán under his breath. Diyah worked hard to suppress a sudden urge to smile.

The remaining guards continued searching the room for the weapon with no luck. "Nothing, Maífírkon."

Julyán made an irritable sound.

"I might be able to narrow it down," said Diyah. She'd never tried anything like it before, but she was curious to see if she could.

"What do you mean?"

"Well, right now there's no way to tell if it was a sword or a knife or even just a sharp piece of glass. But I can compare the wound to different blades and try to narrow your search."

The guards sniggered. "What good will that do?" asked one of them.

Diyah stood up straight and glared at him. "Because if it was a sword then we know it was likely a soldier. If it was a kitchen knife, then maybe a servant did it... Or perhaps it was the tip of a spear, in which case it seems likely that one of our *fine castle guards* was feeling a mite homicidal and couldn't find anyone under the age of eighty to stab."

There was a long silence as the guard gaped at her. She turned to find Julyán eyeing her with a strange expression on his face, like he was fighting the urge to laugh.

"Like I said," she continued in a calmer voice, "I can try to make a cast of the wound and compare it to different weapons."

Julyán nodded, and she relaxed slightly.

She wasn't sure why she was so intent on helping, but she'd liked the chaplain. He had always been kind to her, and he seemed like such a harmless, sympathetic old man—a bit plodding and foolish, but harmless. She couldn't fathom why anyone would want him dead.

She stood over the corpse, trying to keep her mind detached as she examined his wounds. The bruises didn't look like they'd been made with a weapon, but with fists and legs. Whoever had done this, had beaten an old man senseless. Then, they'd slit his throat with a brutality she'd never seen before.

"It's horrible," she said in a quiet voice. Julyán met her eye but didn't respond.

Diyah wanted to fetch her supplies so she could make a cast of the wound, but Julyán insisted on sending a servant. So, she was forced to remain in the room, trying not to let her mind slip into the territory of emotion as they waited for the servant to return.

After a few minutes, they heard a commotion outside the door. "Where is he?" came Cadyan's voice.

The king burst into the room, looking furious. He halted at the sight of the chaplain's mangled corpse, a look of genuine revulsion on his face. "What happened?" he gasped, averting his gaze and turning to face Julyán.

"We're not sure yet." Diyah heard Julyán explaining about the wounds and the cast she was planning to make.

"I see," said Cadyan, glancing at her. Diyah had expected him to be angry that she was involved, but his expression was strangely blank in that moment.

"I am sorry, my lord," said Julyán in a calm voice. "I know you were close."

"Close," scoffed Cadyan. "We weren't close. The man was an old fool. He was just a... he..." Cadyan seemed to be struggling to remain detached. "He was my teacher," he finished in an oddly strained voice that Diyah had never heard before.

She looked up at him, startled to see something almost like sadness in his eyes. He seemed to have trouble looking at the scene in front of him.

"Of course, there are larger safety concerns at play here," said Julyán, covering up for the king's discomposure. "I think we should discuss them in private, but—" He broke off as another fírkon came into the room. "Ah, excellent, Holun, I need you to remain here with Diyah as she finishes her work, do you understand? Don't let her out of your sight until I return."

Diyah felt a sudden stab of irritation, and she glared at Julyán. What did he think she was going to do, kill the chaplain again?

"Yes, Maífírkon." Holun nodded and gave Diyah a reassuring smile.

Julyán cast Diyah one last look before turning and leaving with the king. She suddenly realized he wasn't worried about what *she* might do. He was worried about what might happen to her if they left her without protection with a murderer on the loose. That thought was oddly comforting. She turned her attention back to the gruesome body in front of her and began working on a more thorough examination.

It was well into the morning when the chaplain's body was

finally removed and they cleared the room of the remaining signs of the murder. Diyah had taken notes about the injuries and she'd made a cast of the wound on his throat.

She was standing by the window, examining the mould in the daylight when Julyán returned. He looked tired and agitated.

"Thank you, Holun," he said, nodding to the other firkon.

"No sign of him?" Holun looked torn between relief and disappointment.

Julyán just shook his head. "Whoever it was, they've covered their tracks well. Any trouble here?" He glanced around at the newly cleaned room.

"No, sir." Holun smiled as he glanced at Diyah. Then he turned and left.

Julyán waited until he was gone before walking over to join Diyah by the window.

"It's not a sword," she said, holding the cast out for him. "The slit is too fine and there's a jagged tear at the end which makes me think there might have been serrations on it."

He took the mould and examined it. "Good," he said, closing his eyes in a momentary sign of relief. "That is good."

Diyah thought she understood. The only people in Caerlon City who carried swords were the firkon, and if a firkon had killed the chaplain, that would have been an enormous problem for him.

"So, what now?" she asked, watching him closely.

Julyán slipped the mould into his pocket. "Leave it with me," he said, and then he took her hand. He laced his fingers through hers and frowned down at them. Diyah followed his gaze. She couldn't help but remember how they'd held hands in this way as the chaplain had sealed them together with wax.

She didn't know how she was supposed to feel about the fact that the man who'd married them was dead. Did that make her more or less sad? Or perhaps it didn't matter...

She found it difficult to think straight whenever she stood this close to Julyán.

"You must be tired," he said after a while. "Do you want to return to the rooms and sleep?"

Diyah thought about it for a moment. She was definitely tired, but she didn't think she'd be able to get the image of the chaplain's body out of her head. "No," she said finally, "I want to work."

Julyán nodded, and they set off together towards the physician's quarters. As they moved through the halls, Diyah noticed a definite tension in the air. Extra guards were stationed at every entrance and the firkon patrolled the corridors, on high alert. It was unnerving to say the least. Diyah was relieved when they reached the physician's quarters and the familiarity of her cluttered workroom.

She pushed open the door and was on the verge of entering when she realized Julyán had stopped. "Aren't you coming?"

Julyán shook his head. "I have work to do. But I'll have two firkon come join the guards." He indicated the two men already positioned outside the door.

"Oh." Diyah was surprised she felt so disappointed. "All right, then. I-I'll see you this evening."

He made an odd gesture like he was going to kiss her but then second-guessed himself. He glanced at the guards and nodded stiffly, then turned and walked away without another word.

Diyah closed the door and stood for a moment, alone in her old chambers and overcome by a peculiar mixture of embarrassment, fatigue, and melancholy. It had been a strange morning.

She sighed and shook her head. Then she strode towards her worktable, determined to find something to distract herself.

Diyah spent the rest of the day mixing and labelling as many tonics and serums as she could. It was all she could think to do at the moment.

Despite the uproar of the morning, she hadn't forgotten her conversation with Jémys and Fehla the week before. Jémys was determined for them to escape Caerlon and reunite with Catanya, and the idea had filled Diyah with a wild kind of hope she hadn't felt in ages. She didn't know how or when they would do it—especially now that the castle was on high alert, looking for an assassin—but they'd find a way soon. Diyah would finally be free, and Caerlon City would have no healer. She couldn't help feeling a little guilty about all the people in the city who still needed her help. So, she planned to leave behind a sizeable store of remedies for the most common ailments. It was the best she could do.

As the sun was setting, she sealed her last vial of tonic for the day, grateful that she'd regained some of her composure. But a sharp knock on the door broke through her calm and set her on edge once again.

"Come in," she called.

The door burst open to reveal a pair of firkon stumbling under the weight of something they were carrying.

"What is it?" she asked, dread settling in her gut.

To her surprise, it was Jémys who responded. "He just started convulsing!" he cried.

Diyah realized they were carrying an unconscious firkon in their arms. The man spluttered and shook uncontrollably, making it difficult for them to carry him.

"Over there." Diyah pointed to the cot by the fire and scrambled into action. "Tell me exactly what happened." She hurried to his side to examine him. She recognized the man from the tournament and felt a rush of relief when she remembered distinctly disliking him. Then shame prickled on her skin, and she forced herself to continue her examination.

"He was off duty today," said the other firkon. Diyah gave a start when she realized it was Rey. "He and a handful of the other men were off in the tavern to have a few drinks... He came back to the barracks and then he just sort of collapsed and started seizing." Rey grabbed the man as he convulsed and started vomiting and choking.

"Roll him over." Diyah watched Rey and Jémys struggle to turn the man onto his side.

"Diyah," said Jémys in a serious voice, "I think I know what this is. I could smell it on him when he returned."

"Smell what?" asked Rey.

"I think he was exposed to delirium."

"Delirium," said Diyah, momentarily surprised. Delirium was illegal in Caerlon. She couldn't imagine Cadyan would take too kindly to his soldiers using it behind his back.

"How would he get his hands on a delirium pouch?" asked Rey. "Maybe it's something else." He glanced at Diyah, but she just shook her head. Now that Jémys pointed it out, all the signs were there. This was delirium sickness.

Diyah swore under her breath and rushed over to her work-table, looking for the ingredients she needed. If she didn't act quickly, the man would die.

"What do you need?" asked Jémys. He appeared by her side, eager to help.

"Top shelf, charcoal powder," she said as she rooted around in the bottom cupboard, looking for the vials of oil she needed. "Masks," she called as Jémys handed her the jar of powder. She pointed to the far corner where she'd stacked some rags made of a dense material that helped block out toxic smells. She had to hope they were thick enough to block what was coming.

Rey tossed the rags to Jémys who held them out for Diyah as she began mixing the oils and charcoal powder together in a bowl. Then she dove under the counter, looking for the resin she'd distilled weeks ago and never used. She said a silent thanks to herself for being prepared for something like this.

"Put on the masks," she said as she wrapped one of the fabric strips around her own face and tied it tightly so it wouldn't slip. Then, without hesitating, she snatched a heating pan, the charcoal mixture, and the resin off the table and ran over to the fire.

She thrust the charcoal mixture into Rey's hand. "See if you can get him to swallow that," she said. Then she turned and began heating a portion of the resin in the pan over the fire. It melted, smoking and giving off a noxious stench.

The man started convulsing again as Rey struggled to pour the oily grey mixture down his throat.

"Oh no," groaned Diyah and she willed the fire to work faster. When the resin began to boil, she whipped the pan out and poured its contents into a sturdy glass vial so the vapour rose in a thin stream out the top. "Hold him steady."

Rey and Jémys each pushed their weight against the man, trying to stop the convulsions as Diyah held the vial up to his face and clamped her hand over his mouth so he was forced to inhale it.

Diyah held her breath and waited, watching for a sign that it was working. Slowly the man's convulsions began to ease, and his breathing settled. After a few more spasms and tremors, he eventually lay still.

Diyah relaxed and stood up. "He should be fine," she said, her voice still muffled by the cloth in front of her face. "He'll sleep now, but when he wakes up, he should feel relatively normal." She sighed and stepped away from the bed.

"That was incredible," said Rey, looking at Diyah like he had never seen her before.

"Yes, well." Diyah wiped the sweat from her brow and shrugged. "I've dealt with delirium sickness once or twice before. It's nasty but if you act quickly, you can often prevent it from being fatal."

"The real question is, who in their right mind would use delirium?" asked Jémys. He exchanged exasperated looks with Diyah.

"I don't know, but let's hope he's the only one," she said.

As it turned out, he wasn't the only one. Before the evening was over, Diyah had received ten more patients with varying levels of delirium sickness—all of them fïrkon from the same barracks. After a search of another barrack revealed another dozen fïrkon who had been dead for several hours, the castle was on high alert again.

"It's a distraction," said Julyán through the fabric wrapped around his face. He paced angrily through the rows of cots, watching his men convulse.

"Well, it's working," called Diyah as she raced around, trying to pour the charcoal mixture down her patients' gullets. She had converted several lanterns into vapour dispensers and distributed them throughout the room but it wasn't enough. Several of these men would be dead before the night was through and she was already running out of materials.

"Someone is creating chaos so the assassin can slip away," said Julyán. Diyah thought he was probably right, but she couldn't worry about that. She had a dozen patients who needed her attention right now.

After a while, Julyán stormed off in search of answers elsewhere, and Diyah was able to concentrate.

"A distraction," repeated Jémys as he walked over to help her. "I suppose that is the only way someone could slip away undetected in Caerlon, isn't it?" He gave her a significant look.

"Jémys, we can't do something like this," she muttered so only he could hear.

"No, of course not," he said. "But there are other kinds of distractions." He nodded thoughtfully and walked away to help Rey on the other side of the room.

When she'd finally finished treating everyone, Diyah was utterly exhausted. Three of the men had died in the night, but most of the others would recover in time. It might take days or weeks, but they would heal eventually.

It was nearing dawn when she made her way back to her chambers. She pushed open the door and found the room empty. Whatever Julyán was doing, he likely wouldn't be getting any sleep tonight.

Diyah stumbled over to the bed and collapsed, fully clothed. She didn't care that her clothes were filthy. She just wanted to sleep.

When the sun had risen enough to drench the room in morning light, she thought she heard the door open, but she was too exhausted to see who it was. She felt the covers drape over her and realized it must be Julyán. She wanted to open her eyes, to sit up and talk to him. Before she could muster the energy, the door opened and closed again, and he was gone.

Overcome with the emotions of the day, Diyah pulled the covers over her head and waited for sleep to come.

9

READY FOR A FIGHT

The Earth rumbled gently beneath Catanya's feet. Slowly, the topsoil parted and the underlying clay stretched and folded in upon itself. Layers and layers of clay stacked in pleats, tucking and gathering together like a mound of folded cloth. Catanya imagined moulding the mass of clay into different shapes. Sprawling tree trunks, castle turrets, horses, flowers. One after another, the clay twisted and smoothed into the different shapes, until finally Catanya stopped, and it resettled into the Earth.

"So, invoking means I can control a force that already exists?" she asked, waving her hand, so the topsoil drifted down and settled back on top of the clay. "Like the Earth now, or the Water—that time I forced the tide back in Awnell, and the time in the pond when I created the whirlpool."

"Exactly," said Laylian. She was crouched on the ground, lifting up rocks as though searching for something.

"What are you doing?" asked Catanya, staring at Laylian in the dappled afternoon sun.

"Oh, just looking," replied Laylian, hopping over to the next closest stone and lifting it up.

"Looking for what?"

Laylian shrugged. "Anything." She put the rock back down and stood up. "There's always something to look for if you open your eyes," she added, humming a disjointed tune.

"Right." Catanya had grown accustomed to Laylian's random comments and distractible nature. They'd spent the last few days together in the forest beside the central glade, working through various exercises in Resonance. And despite the old maílehr's oddities, Catanya's lessons were progressing well. The things she'd once found difficult were now becoming second nature to her.

Since their journey to the top of the mountain and Catanya's decision to embrace her power, something had changed in her. She seemed to have unlocked the door to her Resonance and now she finally understood how to access it completely. It was as though there was a current running through everything and everyone. Now that she was no longer resisting, she could access it and she could use it.

"Now, where were we?" muttered Laylian, scratching her head. "Oh yes, invoking. Good you've got a handle on that, let's try materializing now. Creating something where there is nothing."

Catanya thought about that for a moment. "But if the Spirits are everywhere and the Natures are eternal, doesn't that mean that there is never *nothing*? Wouldn't materializing just be a sort of intensified form of invoking?"

Laylian laughed heartily and beamed at Catanya. "Why, yes, you are quite right. But it is much more difficult to invoke from a place of near stillness, so it sometimes helps to view it as a moment of creation, rather than a moment of change." She chuckled and sat down on an upturned log, gesturing for Catanya to proceed. "Well, off you go, then."

Slightly taken aback, Catanya turned and centred herself in the clearing. She closed her eyes and focused all of her energy on listening to the sound of the breeze passing through the trees.

Every once in a while, a small gust of Wind wafted through the clearing, rustling the leaves and blowing through her thin linen dress. It was cool but not unpleasant. She imagined what would happen if a stronger gust encircled her, if stronger currents passed over and under her body. She imagined swaying with the trees as a heavy gale billowed, sweeping her into the air like a feather...

And to her surprise, her feet lifted off the ground. She opened her eyes and looked down at the forest floor now several feet below her. The familiar prickling sensation ran through her skin. And this time she welcomed it, letting the Resonance course through her body. She concentrated all of her energy on creating a dense cushion between her feet and the forest floor, imagining an invisible barrier of Wind. The barrier held her up, allowing her to glide around the clearing.

It was an incredibly liberating experience, to soar through the trees without a tether. It surprised her to discover how easy it was to stay afloat once she'd started. She rose higher and higher until her head was level with the tallest branches and she could see the entire community stretched out below her.

From below she heard Laylian whooping and cheering as she danced around, watching Catanya.

"Wow," breathed Catanya, lowering herself and letting her feet gently touch back down on the ground. "That was unbelievable!" She laughed along with Laylian.

Catanya spent the rest of the afternoon materializing and invoking the Wind to do different things. She soon discovered that she could generate gales strong enough to tear down branches and uproot trees. As she soared above the forest, she felt something she'd never felt before—she felt truly invincible.

"It's amazing, isn't it?" she called jubilantly when she spotted Drayk standing with Laylian later that afternoon. He was leaning against a tree on the edge of the small clearing, watching Catanya soar through the air like a bird.

"It certainly is something," he responded, but Catanya heard the slight reticence in his voice.

"What's the matter?" she asked as she touched back down beside him. He was once again wearing his old clothes. His leather breeches, vest, and jacket. He had even strapped his sword back onto his waist so he looked startlingly out of place in the tranquillity of Túir-Avlea.

"Nothing," said Drayk. But he looked haughty and disdainful.

Catanya glanced at Laylian. But the old woman just smiled and averted her eyes. "Messy, messy, hmm, hmm, hmm," she mumbled. Then she started humming to herself again and wandered away into the trees, leaving them alone in the clearing.

As soon as she was out of sight, Catanya rounded on Drayk. "All right, are you going to tell me what's wrong with you?" she demanded, putting her hands on her hips and staring at him.

"Wrong? Nothing's wrong." Drayk tried to shrug it off. "Out here, they don't even know what that word means." He kicked a rock and watched it ricochet off the nearest tree.

"You've been acting strangely ever since we got back from the mountaintop. You've been avoiding me," said Catanya. It was true. She had barely seen him all week. At first, she'd assumed he was just tired from the mountain climb, but now it seemed something else was bothering him.

"Why would I be avoiding you?" asked Drayk.

Catanya threw her hands up in frustration. "I don't know, Drayk. You tell me. Possibly because my powers are getting stronger and that scares you?"

"Scares me?" he repeated, smirking. "Believe me, I'm not scared of you, love. Remember, I'm actually quite fond of you."

He winked at her playfully. "Besides, it's not like you can actually hurt me." He cast a sidelong glance at her.

Catanya knew he was trying to goad her and she shouldn't respond. But she was getting frustrated now. "Don't be so sure about that," she said hotly.

"It's all very well and good for you to use your powers in this place where it's peaceful, safe, and calm. But let me ask you, what's going to happen when you need to use them out there?" He gestured beyond the mountain. "You need to be able to react under pressure. You need to be able to fight."

"And I can!" Catanya's annoyance grew stronger. She couldn't understand why he was suddenly acting this way again. He had been so supportive and helpful for weeks, and now that she was finally getting the hang of things, he seemed upset.

"Yeah?" Drayk slowly unsheathed his sword and held it out in front of him, blade pointed towards her. "Prove it," he said with a wide, provocative grin.

"Are you kidding me?" Catanya snickered and stepped backwards, eyeing the blade. "Do you really think you can fight me?"

Drayk shrugged. "Only one way to find out," he said, playfully tapping his sword on the ground.

Catanya rolled her eyes. "Okay, then." He was probably just getting bored and antsy. Maybe she just needed to knock some sense back into him. "Let's go." She smirked and beckoned for him to come at her.

Drayk's face split into a wide grin. He barely had time to raise his sword before Catanya conjured a blast of Wind so strong it knocked him off his feet. To her surprise, Drayk laughed as he pushed himself back up off the ground.

"Had enough?" she asked, a little irritated to see him still smiling.

"Not even close," he said with scorn. Then, without warning, he threw himself to the ground in a somersault and spun around with his sword dangerously close to her stomach. She had less than a second to react and she launched herself up into the air just in time.

Drayk stood up and watched her sail above him and land gracefully a few feet away.

Catanya felt a little less confident having narrowly missed his attack, so she wasted no time once she landed. She focused her energy on the ground beneath Drayk's feet, sending vibrations into the Earth. It began to quake. Drayk's footing was unsteady. When he tried to take a step, the ground opened up beneath him, and he tripped in the crater and tumbled down.

Catanya laughed at the sight of him struggling to stand up again. In her moment of distraction, she lost focus, and the ground steadied beneath his feet. Drayk reacted instantly. He pulled a long dagger out of his belt and hurled it at her.

Catanya just barely deflected it. She watched it soar right past her head and pierce the tree behind her with a dull thud.

"Are you mad?" she asked furiously, staring at the dagger. But as she turned back to look at Drayk, she found him standing right in front of her, with his sword pressed against her throat.

"A flick of the wrist and you'd be dead," he said, giving her a hard look. "Don't let your arrogance cloud your mind."

"Oh, you're one to talk about arrogance," she snapped, swatting his sword away and glaring at him. "I can't believe you!" She looked from Drayk back to the dagger, realizing how narrowly she'd avoided it.

Drayk yanked the blade out of the tree, sliding it back into its sheath. "What? I thought you were all-powerful. I thought you'd found *balance* or whatever you want to call it." He gave her a condescending smile. Catanya felt the prickling in her fingers that always presaged a surge in power.

"I want a re-match," she snarled. She had been going easy

on him. But if he was going to fight like that, then she wasn't going to hold back either.

"A re-match?" Drayk gave her an appraising look. "All right... But do us a favour, love, try to stay focused this time. It's no fun for me if it's too easy."

Catanya scowled at him as they took their places opposite one another. She was determined to win this time, to prove him wrong. The itching started in her fingers, and she breathed it in, letting the power burn through her.

This time, when Drayk advanced, she was ready. Instead of soaring out of the way, she used her powers to lift him off the ground and send him flying into a nearby tree. He crashed to the ground, winded. But Catanya could still hear him laughing as he stood back up. The sound infuriated her.

"A little angry, are we, now?" he taunted. "Good."

"I'm not angry," said Catanya, "I'm determined." She stood poised to fight as she watched him warily.

"Is that so?" He smirked and swaggered forward. "Well, let's see if your determination is enough."

They stood in front of each other. Drayk watched her, wearing a peculiar expression on his face, somewhere between disdain and desire. He made a move as if to raise his sword, but Catanya was too quick. She sent a gust of air at him and he stumbled back a few feet, laughing. He tried to take another step, but she blasted him back again... and again, and again until Drayk had been backed up against the trunk of a large oak. He had nowhere to go.

Catanya smiled and made a gesture with her hand trying to call his sword out of his grasp, but his reflexes were too fast. Before the sword had drifted to his fingertips, he tightened his grip on it, refusing to let go.

"If you want it, you're going to have to come take it," he declared. "Or pry it from my cold, dead hands." He shrugged as if either option would please him. "I wonder what *he* would do in this situation," he added, flashing his eyes at her. "And I wonder if you have what it takes..." He paused, allowing the taunt to dangle in the air.

It was all she needed. Blind rage crashed over her. In that moment, she wanted nothing more than to wipe that condescending grin off Drayk's face.

She closed her eyes and stretched her Resonance out towards him, feeling the bristling warmth of his spirit as it connected. Then she slowly squeezed, drawing his energy into her. She pulled the air out of Drayk's lungs, watching him struggle to breathe as his skin drained of colour. He doubled over, gasping, and let the sword fall to the ground. Catanya picked it up and pointed it towards him. For a wild moment she considered tightening her grip on him, but then she relaxed her hold. His breathing gradually returned to normal.

"Well," he gasped, choking on the air. "I always knew you had *that* in you somewhere." He rubbed his throat, eyeing her triumphantly.

Catanya suddenly realized what she'd done. A hot, stinging shame came over her. It had been a long time since her powers had taken control of her like that, but—

No.

She hadn't lost control this time, it had been a conscious decision. And she still felt strong and powerful, and—

"I could have killed you," she said, horrified. She backed away from him, nauseated by how energized she still was. Every muscle, every fibre of her body still burned with warm, invigorating power.

"Yes," said Drayk, reaching out for his sword. "Rather exhilarating, wasn't it?" His eyes sparkled, and he grinned.

Catanya stared at him blankly. Then his hand touched hers and she dropped his sword to the ground.

"I—"

"Don't say you're sorry," said Drayk, shaking his head.

Catanya was taken aback and she gaped at him. Drayk stared at her intently, wearing a self-satisfied expression on his face. Once again, she was irritated. Drayk moved to bend down and retrieve his sword and before she registered what was happening Catanya shoved him as hard as she could.

He stumbled back, looking at her in surprise. But she was so angry she just shoved him again, so he slammed against the tree behind him.

"Wha—" Drayk tried to protest, but Catanya had lost control. She raged at him, lashing out with her fists, striking every inch of him she could reach.

"Ow, ow!" he cried, trying to block her. "What is the matter with you?" He grabbed her wrists and squeezed them to prevent her from hitting him.

"What's the matter with *me*?" shouted Catanya. "What's the matter with *you*?" She tried to wrench her arms free, but Drayk just tightened his hold. "I don't understand! Do you want me to use these powers to hurt you? To hurt everyone?"

"No! Of course, I—"

"Then what do you want?" she yelled, still trying to hit him.

"I want you to learn how to fight!" he shouted, finally matching her anger.

"No, you want me to learn how to fight like *him*!" She struggled even harder against his grip. "I thought he was the enemy. Why do you want me to be like him?" She tried to knee Drayk, but he blocked her with his leg.

"BECAUSE!" He threw her hands out of his grasp so hard that she stumbled. "Because maybe then you might survive!"

Catanya straightened up, ready to fight, but Drayk's words stopped her in her tracks. She stared at him, lost for words. Her heart pounded in her chest and she heaved great, angry breaths. She was still furious, but as she stood mere inches away from him, she felt something else taking over.

Without thinking, she shoved him back up against the tree

and kissed him hard on the mouth. He hesitated, caught off guard. But before she could pull away, he responded with enthusiasm.

He parted his lips as he wrapped one arm around her back and lifted her leg up with the other, wrapping it around his waist. Spinning her around, he slammed her against the tree and started kissing her neck and running his hands over her body. She brought his face back up to meet hers and pressed her hips into his, drawing him closer, as her hands ran down his back, clutching at his coat.

"Catanya, are you here?" called a voice from behind them.

They broke apart in a hurry and turned to see Viena walking along the path to meet them in the clearing.

"Oh, good you're both here," she said. "I was wondering if you could help me with something."

"Yes. Yes, of course," said Catanya, a little out of breath. She looked sheepishly from Drayk to Viena. "What do you need?"

Drayk shook his head and turned to lean against the tree, facing the forest.

"I have some more questions about Awnell." Viena grinned and held up her notebook.

Drayk snorted. "Catanya can help you. It'll do her good to remember," he muttered, and he walked off without saying another word.

Viena watched him go, frowning. "Is he all right?"

Catanya just sighed and shrugged. "What are your questions, Viena?" she asked, turning her attention back to her friend.

She spent the rest of the afternoon talking with Viena and helping out with odd jobs around the glade while trying not to think about what had happened between her and Drayk. But it was difficult to think of anything else.

Drayk obviously cared about her, but she still thought there was something else going on with him. When she had been with Jémys, she had never questioned her feelings for him or his feelings for her. But with Drayk, it was like teetering on the edge of chaos all the time, never knowing what might happen. He was unpredictable, and he seemed to like it best when things were out of control. Was that why he had come on this journey with her? Was he just in it for the thrill—the danger?

She found herself getting distracted throughout the day as more and more questions popped into her mind. She had come to rely on her friendship with Drayk. Why was he regressing back to the person he'd been before they'd left Awnell? It was almost as if he'd forgotten everything they'd been through, or worse, that he'd suddenly decided he regretted it.

It didn't seem fair that just as she was learning to open herself up, he was deciding to shut down on her. Wasn't this what he had wanted? He had been encouraging her to learn control for weeks—months even. So why, all of a sudden, did he want to provoke her?

After all this time, she couldn't let them revert to their old ways. She was tired of holding back and hiding things. She deserved to know where they stood.

Later that night as everyone gathered for the fire, Catanya headed to Drayk's tent.

"What do you want from me?" she asked as she pulled back the canopy and marched into his tent.

"What?" He whipped around, surprised to see her.

"You heard me," she said. "What do you want from me?" She stopped a few feet away from him, blocking the door.

"Hey, you came to my tent," he said, deflecting the question. He seemed calm and relaxed, more like the Drayk he'd been before the mountaintop. That just made Catanya even angrier.

She strode forward and stared at him. "Why are you here?" she asked. "Why are you helping me? There's got to be something in it for you."

Drayk tried to laugh it off as he turned his back on her,

lifting his coat off the chair and pulling it over his shoulders. "What happened to 'thanks for your support, Drayk', and 'I appreciate you'?" His voice was mocking now, and it grated on Catanya's nerves.

"That was before you nearly goaded me into killing you!" she snapped, fighting the urge to smack him. "I can't figure you out anymore. Sometimes you act like you're my friend and I believe we care about each other, but other times..." She glared at him, waiting for a response.

Drayk just shrugged and tried to walk past her out of the tent but she stopped him.

"I want a real answer," she said. "From the moment we met, you've been holding back. Why did you come after me in the woods in the first place? You said you knew the moment you met me that you'd follow me. You said it wasn't about Ayr or about the old man in the cabin, so what? Why have you been helping me? I deserve the truth!"

Drayk sighed heavily and turned to look at her. "Survival," he said. "I want to survive. It's what I do! I survive, no matter what. I always choose the winning side!" His voice was louder now, like he was losing his temper too.

"That can't be all you care about."

When Drayk just shrugged insolently and didn't respond, Catanya threw her hands up in the air in frustration. "Argh! You drive me insane!" she shouted.

"Well, right back at you!" snapped Drayk.

Catanya was furious. She didn't know why she'd expected to have a serious conversation with him. She turned around and stormed out of the tent, but she had barely gone two feet before he called after her.

"There you go again, running away! You know, sooner or later you're going to have to fight. You can't keep avoiding it."

"What did you say?" she snarled, spinning around to face him.

"You heard me." His voice was suddenly calm. He took slow, measured steps towards her. "All you ever do is run away," he said, shaking his head. "Why are you so afraid of a fight?"

Catanya scoffed. "I'm not afraid," she said. "I'm just not going to waste my time arguing with you. It's pointless."

"I'm not talking about me!" he shouted, giving her a hard look. "We can't stay here, Catya! We need to go back and fight. You have responsibilities. People are counting on you! Or have you forgotten? Maybe in all the flying and visions and 'invoke this' and 'resonate that' you've forgotten why we're really here."

Catanya felt defensive. "What do you know about responsibility?" she snapped, laughing in an unusually high-pitched tone of derision. "You've never taken responsibility for anything in your life. You're just a selfish, dishonourable thief!"

Drayk looked like she had just slapped him in the face. "Yeah, well, maybe I am," he said in a low voice. "But you," he looked her squarely in the eyes with an unapologetic intensity, "you are an uptight, self-righteous coward."

There was a long pause before Catanya responded. "I am not a coward," she said in a deadly calm voice. She was angrier than she had been in a long time, and her power itched at her, begging to be unleashed.

Drayk just let out a small, sceptical sniff.

They glared at each other in defiance, neither one saying a word until the air between them was swollen and close to explosion. Catanya longed to strike him, to hit him harder than ever before. She hated the self-satisfied twinkle in his eyes and the haughty expression tugging at his lips. They stared at one another, each daring the other to move. Drayk swayed slightly, and his gaze roved over her face, resting on her lips. His eyes flashed back towards hers, reflecting the light of the nearby lantern.

And all at once, defiance and anger transformed into fire. They launched themselves into each other's arms. Catanya wrapped her hands around his neck, pulling his face to meet hers.

There was no hesitation this time. Drayk responded immediately, gripping her tightly and drawing her into his body.

She clutched the collar of his coat, breathing in the smell of leather and smoke. Then she tugged it off his shoulders and threw it to the ground. He lifted her up in the air, swinging her legs around his waist as he stumbled forward and crashed up against a nearby tree.

She ran her hands down his chest towards his waist where she unbuckled his belt and let it fall at his feet. Then she unfastened his breeches as he slid his hand up her leg under her dress. She clutched at his shoulders gasping as he began kissing her neck and chest while he pushed himself into her.

He brought his lips back up to hers and kissed her, gently at first, and then more fervently as he rolled his hips over hers.

She was alive with the feeling of him—his body against hers, the taste of his lips, and the strength of his arms around her. Every inch of her seemed to cry out for more. He smiled as she clutched at his arms, tightening her body around him and gasping. Wave after wave came crashing over her. The more she responded, the more he continued, until everything became an ecstatic blur.

Later that night, they made their way back to Drayk's tent. He lowered her down onto the bed where they shed their remaining clothes. Catanya climbed on top of him, relishing each expression he made as she moved her hips back and forth. He traced her breast with his fingers, and her skin tingled at his touch, giving Catanya an idea.

She laid her hands on his chest and paused for a moment, carefully reaching her power out through her fingertips and into him. She felt her energy connect with his and start to build. There was a crackle and a spark of golden light as a jolt shot through them.

Drayk sat bolt upright, pressing his chest into hers. "What was that?" he asked, trembling as he looked at her.

Catanya smiled and brought his mouth up to meet hers. She traced his lips with her tongue allowing the energy to swell between their bodies. Drayk's hands tightened on her back. He closed his eyes as she pulled his head down to her chest, moving her hips faster and faster in a frenetic energy. The light began to build around them again, crackling and flickering as they moved. It was intoxicating. Catanya let the power swirl around her, swirl through her and through him in a chaotic passion. Their bodies tightened together, and Drayk cried out in a mixture of pain and pleasure.

Catanya let out an exultant laugh as she rolled off him and lay still, staring up at the canopy and smiling.

They lay side by side, breathless and sweaty, waiting for their hearts to resume their normal rhythms.

"All right," said Drayk after a while, panting as he turned to look at her, "I take it all back. I don't care if you fight or not, as long as we can keep doing that." He grinned widely and the two of them started to laugh. They laughed until their stomachs hurt and they had tears in their eyes. They laughed until they couldn't laugh anymore. Then they wrapped their arms around each other and drifted off to sleep.

10

THE ESCAPE PLAN

lmost two weeks had passed since the chaplain's murder and the rash of delirium deaths that swept through the ranks of the fīrkon. The castle was only just returning to its normal functions. The last delirium patients had left Diyah's workroom, and everyone seemed resigned that the chaplain's murder might never be solved.

Julyán was working the fīrkon harder than ever, scheduling extra training sessions and springing impromptu weapons tests on them. He seemed to think the recent events exposed a lack of discipline in his men, and he was determined to train it out of them. Jémys was training harder than any other fīrkon. He needed everyone to think he'd become one of them, and he wanted to be ready when it came time to fight.

Diyah spent every spare minute in the physician's quarters, treating patients and gradually packaging up various materials she might want to take with her when she finally escaped Caerlon.

In all the uproar of the last two weeks, Diyah and Jémys hadn't risked discussing their plan to escape. But as the castle settled back into its routines, they could finally talk. All Jémys needed to do was feign an injury that needed her attention and he could meet Diyah without anyone suspecting anything. The only trick was making sure he didn't do it too often.

One afternoon, after a particularly brutal training session, he made a visit to treat his too-real bruised ribs.

"Ow!" he protested as she tightened the bandage around his chest.

"I'm sorry, but really, you should be more careful!" she said, tying the bandage and wiping her hands on her apron.

"You didn't see the size of him, Diyah. He was a giant! But I still beat him." Jémys grinned mischievously.

Diyah rolled her eyes, trying to fight the urge to smile along with him. She tossed the soiled bandages into the fire and watched them go up in flames. Then, trying to sound disinterested, she said, "I'll bet that made Julyán happy."

Jémys frowned and shook his head. "Julyán wasn't there. He left early. He's still meeting with Cadyan in private almost every day."

Diyah sighed a little bitterly. "I know." Julyán often arrived late to their rooms at night, and she felt strangely resentful about it.

"I still can't believe someone killed the chaplain," muttered Jémys. He winced at the pain in his ribs as he hopped down from the worktable.

"I've been thinking about that, actually," said Diyah. "I couldn't understand why Cadyan seemed so worried. I mean, even if he really did care about the chaplain—which isn't likely —I can't imagine he'd devote this much energy into finding out who killed him. What's one more dead person to Cadyan at this point? It certainly wouldn't warrant all these private meetings with Julyán, right? So, that got me thinking... what if this is all about the elixir?"

Jémys frowned. "You think someone is trying to steal it?"

"It's possible, isn't it? I mean, other than Cadyan, the chaplain is the only one who has access to it, right? It's the chaplain's job to safeguard the kingdom's traditions... I can't think of any other reason someone would kill him."

"Hmm..." Jémys trailed off, lost in thought. "Well, as disturbing as that thought is," he said after a minute, "right now, you and I have other things to worry about. I've been thinking..." He pulled his tunic over his new bandages and winced again. "I think we need to talk to Ayr again. We need her to tell us exactly where to go when we get out of here." He limped over to stand with Diyah.

Diyah nodded. This situation with the chaplain was still unsettling her, but Jémys was right. They needed to stay focused. "I agree, but—" She broke off as the door opened and Julyán strode in, looking angry.

"Are you almost done?" he asked, eyes scanning the room with distrust. "You've been up here for ages."

"All done," said Diyah, hastily walking back to her worktable. "A few bruised ribs. He should take it easy for the next few days."

"I'm fine," said Jémys, grabbing his sword and strapping it back onto his waist. "I don't need to rest."

"Jémys!"

"I'm fine, Diyah." He shot Julyán a dirty look. "I'm sure the *maífírkon*"—he pronounced each syllable with ire—"expects me back on the field."

He tried to walk past his brother, but Julyán grabbed his arm and stopped him.

"Why are you doing this?" he demanded, pushing Jémys back a few steps.

The entire energy in the room changed in an instant. Jémys had his hand on his sword hilt. He looked poised for an attack, while Julyán stood glowering at him in anger.

"Doing what?"

"Acting like you want to be here?" Julyán spoke in a deadly

calm voice. "I've been watching you for weeks now. You behave like one of us but you're not, are you?"

"Maybe I am. How would you know?" Jémys chanced a quick glance at Diyah, who was frozen in fear, watching the entire interaction.

"You have no allegiance to the king so what is your reason for fighting alongside us?" Julyán was bearing down on his brother. "The woman you love is dead, your family is gone, you have nothing left to lose so *why*?"

Jémys's face flushed with anger. "Why?" he spat. "*Why*? Because I have no other choice, do I? So, I'm doing what my father did—what *our* father did!" He shoved Julyán and stormed off towards the door. Then, gripping the handle, he turned back to face them. "I'll fight alongside the firkon the way my father did, Julyán, in the hopes that maybe, *just maybe*, I can change the way things work around here. And you're right, the woman I love may be gone, but her memory runs through my veins. I feel her in everything I do! And I fight to honour her just as I fight to honour my father. But I wouldn't expect *you* to understand that. I wouldn't expect you to understand honour or love." And with that, he stormed out of the room, slamming the door behind him so hard it rattled the shelves on the walls.

Diyah stared at the door, not daring to move. Then she heard the sound of metal scraping and turned around to find Julyán stoking the fire with his back to her.

She took a long, slow breath. Then she returned to the dandelion roots she'd been slicing before Jémys arrived. "If you would just tell him the truth, it might help repair the rift between you."

"I have told you before, it won't."

Annoyed, Diyah smacked her free hand on the table. "You don't know that for sure! You're just scared!"

Julyán glared at her and raised his eyebrows. "Excuse me?"

"You heard me," she snapped. "I'm fed up with the lies. If you won't tell him, maybe I will." It came out sounding more like a threat than she'd intended. A long pause stretched between them. Diyah was afraid to look at him so she turned her back and started pulling vials off the shelf. She was standing on her toes, struggling to reach the last box when Julyán appeared at her side and retrieved it for her.

"Thank you," she murmured, taking it and placing it on the table behind her.

She sensed him standing beside her, but she didn't want to look at him. She was angry and a little ashamed of how she felt at the moment. Ashamed that she really hoped he would reach out and touch her.

"I should go," he said after a while. As he walked past her, his hand gently brushed the top of hers.

She watched him go, and a sinking sense of disappointment overcame her.

But Jémys was right, they needed to focus on escaping, and she couldn't let anything (or anyone) distract her from that. So, she spent the rest of the afternoon working on a plan to get into the dungeons to see Ayr. They couldn't risk being seen by one of the guards again, not with all the extra precautions lately. They had to think of a way to slip in undetected. It wouldn't be easy, but Diyah thought she had a way to do it.

When the sun had set, she marched out the door with a vial of valerian root tonic in her pocket. Fírkon training was about to end, and Diyah wanted to be ready.

She waited outside the armoury for Jémys to make his appearance. Then, mustering her most commanding and irritated voice, she shouted, "Jémys, I specifically told you not to over-exert yourself! What's the matter with you? Come with me now so I can check your wounds. You'd better pray they kill you before I get the chance." She turned imperiously and stalked off down the corridor with Jémys in tow.

"In here," she muttered, grabbing him and ducking into an empty room near the stairway that led down to the kitchens.

"What's going on?" Jémys cast around, confused.

"We're getting in to see Ayr tonight," replied Diyah. "Just follow my lead." She pressed her ear up against the door, listening.

After a few minutes, she finally heard what she was waiting for. "Stay here," she whispered, and she scurried out the door.

Laboured footsteps echoed down the corridor—the sound of a kitchen maid carrying a tray of food up the stairs. Diyah waited until the maid was in sight and then—crash!

Diyah walked straight into her, causing half of the tray's contents to clatter onto the floor.

"Oh, I'm so sorry, I didn't see you there," cried Diyah, hurrying to help. She grabbed the tankard before it tipped and carefully poured the vial into it when the maid wasn't looking. "Everything looks okay, though. Nothing is damaged. I'm so sorry, please forgive me." Diyah backed away and allowed the frazzled girl to pass.

When the maid was out of sight, Diyah ducked back into the room where Jémys was hiding.

"What was that about?" he asked.

"That was the dungeon guard's dinner," she said. "He should be sound asleep in less than ten minutes."

Jémys looked impressed, and he grinned. "Excellent."

Ten minutes later, they made their way down into the dungeons. Thankfully, the guard lay sprawled on the ground, fast asleep.

Relief rushed through Diyah. She resisted the urge to kick the guard as she unlocked the gate and held it open for Jémys.

"Ayr—er—Your Majesty?" she called as she hurried down the dark corridor between the cells. "Your Majesty, it's Diyah."

"Please... call me Ayr," said the queen, stepping into the light. "Ayr, Queen of the Rancid Dungeons. Not a bad title." She gave a wry smile. "Hello, Diyah. I'm surprised you came back. What brings you here?" Then her sharp gaze landed on Jémys in his violet uniform. "My, my... it's one of Cadyan's loyal firkon!" She pulled a face of mock alarm and then smirked. "Let me guess... Jémys?"

"Yes," he replied, a little taken aback. He cast a questioning look in Diyah's direction.

"What brings you to my lovely corner of the dungeon?" asked Ayr, gesturing at her dank surroundings.

The sound of dripping water and the distant moans of forgotten prisoners deep in the bowls of the dungeon made Diyah shiver.

"We need your help," she said, ignoring her discomfort. She didn't know how much time they'd have to talk.

"Well, I live to serve." Ayr's voice dripped with irony. "What do you need?"

"We need you to tell us where Catanya is," said Jémys.

Ayr smiled indulgently and nodded. "As I said last time, Diyah. I'm not going to tell you that. It's too risky."

"I know, but this time we have a plan. We're going to escape and find her. We want to help her."

"I see." Ayr looked from Diyah to Jémys. "And you really think you can escape?"

"Yes," said Jémys without flinching. "They won't be expecting it, and we can keep them distracted. By the time they realize what's happened, we'll be long gone."

Diyah was impressed with how sure he sounded. She decided it was best to just nod along.

There was a short pause. Ayr tilted her head and stared at Jémys. "Do you love her?" she asked brazenly.

Jémys blinked. "Excuse me?"

"Catanya. Do you love her?" repeated Ayr with an expectant smile. She stepped forward and leaned against the bars, eyeing Jémys.

Jémys looked affronted, but he quickly regained his composure. He stood up tall and stared through the bars. "With everything that I am, I do," he said emphatically.

"Hmm... And do you think she loves you too?"

"What does—" Diyah tried to interject, but Ayr held up her hand to silence her.

"I want to hear what he thinks," she insisted.

Jémys frowned, but he looked her in the eye and said, "Yes, I do. Or—I believe she does."

"I see... Well, let me tell you what I believe." Ayr suddenly straightened up and gave Jémys a hard look. "I believe the last time you saw her, you left Catya uncertain about your love. And I'm afraid I had to watch as that doubt ate away at her, undermining the strength of her own feelings." She gave him a pitying look.

"Catya?" repeated Jémys, eyebrows raised.

"Oh, sorry, just a little term of endearment—Catanya, then," said Ayr, giving him a sly glance.

There was a pause. Jémys clenched his jaw and shook his head. "Well, it doesn't matter," he said, exhaling as though trying to calm himself down. "I love her more than anything in this entire world. That's all that matters to me. I love her more than life, and I will lay my life on the line for her, regardless of how her feelings may or may not have changed."

"That is very *gallant* of you," said Ayr.

Jémys's eyes narrowed. "Now are you going to tell us where to go or do you want to toy with us some more?"

Ayr's face broke into a wide grin. "You caught me," she said, holding her hands out in the air. "I confess I've grown a little mischievous in my solitude down here. Do forgive me?"

Jémys kept his eyes locked on her, but he nodded curtly.

"Let me give you some advice, Jémys," said Ayr, and her face grew serious. "Take it from me, if you love someone, you should never leave them in any doubt. Because that doubt can destroy everything you thought was secure." She had a far-off, almost regretful look in her eye.

But in that moment, a faint crunching sound drew Diyah's attention, and she suddenly had the sense someone was watching them. She glanced over her shoulder, but there was nothing out of the ordinary.

"So will you help us?" she asked, lowering her voice just in case.

Ayr turned her attention towards Diyah and surveyed her momentarily before nodding. "Catanya has gone to Túir-Avlea," she said in a voice like a whisper.

"Túir-Avlea?" said Jémys, frowning. "But that's a myth."

Ayr made an impatient sound. "It's not," she snapped. "It is as real as Caerlon or Awnell, and Catya is there now."

"How do we get there?" asked Diyah, brushing away the absurd notion that Túir-Avlea was a real place and trying to focus on the tangible.

"You can't get there," said Ayr bluntly. "But you can get to Awnell. Catya will return there. I'm sure of it."

"How can you be sure?" asked Jémys.

Ayr turned slowly to rest her gaze on him. "Because this is war, and wars require armies."

Diyah shivered at the cold look on Ayr's face, suddenly very aware of who this woman really was. Ayr might seem flippant and easy-going, but she was also a queen, a military commander. A warrior.

As ruthless as the Awnadh warriors had been during the tournament, Ayr was their leader. How many people had this woman killed in her lifetime? Whether directly or indirectly.

Diyah suppressed another shiver. She didn't think she wanted to see Queen Ayr on the battlefield.

"You need to get to Awnell," continued Ayr. "There's a man who docks at the city here, Osrin. He's a smuggler. Among other things, he smuggles people in and out of Caerlon on his ship."

"Osrin?" Diyah looked at Jémys uncertainly.

"He's a good-for-nothing bastard," said Ayr, shrugging. "He also transports prisoners for Cadyan."

"Transports prisoners?" A hollowness spread through Diyah, draining her energy and leaving her light-headed. The last place she'd ever imagined herself wanting to be was on one of those ships.

"Yes," said Ayr with obvious distaste, "but he'll get you where you need to go, for a price. Make sure you can pay it." She looked at them significantly.

"What if he won't help us?" asked Jémys.

Ayr sighed. "Tell him if he helps you, I'll make sure he gets what he wants."

Diyah didn't like the sound of that. "What does he want?" she asked, not sure she really wanted to hear the answer.

"Nothing you need to worry about," said Ayr. "He wants access to something I have—something he hasn't seen in a very long time."

Jémys and Diyah exchanged uneasy glances. It was clear Jémys found the idea of working with Osrin as unappealing as she did, but they had no other choice.

"Okay, supposing we find him and he can take us to Awnell... then what?" asked Jémys.

"Go to The Fairweather. It's the inn near the port. Find a woman named Isa and tell her I sent you. She can help you with the rest."

"Fairweather. Isa. Got it," repeated Diyah, nodding.

"Good luck," said Ayr as she retreated into the shadows.

"Oh, and Diyah," she called, "you should ask Fehla what she knows about Túir-Avlea. Her answer might surprise you." She grinned widely. "I suspect there are more than a few things my old friend has forgotten to mention."

Diyah bit her lip and looked back at Queen Ayr. Other than Jémys, Fehla was the only friend Diyah had in this place. They cared about each other. But Ayr had struck a nerve. Diyah knew Fehla had been hiding things from her, but Ayr seemed to imply it was worse than she'd imagined. Surely Fehla wouldn't have kept anything really important from her. If she'd known anything that might have helped her or helped Catanya, she would have told Diyah...

Yes. Diyah had to believe that whatever secrets Fehla was keeping, she was keeping them for a good reason.

But as Diyah and Jémys exited the dungeons, she couldn't stop her mind from dwelling on all the other possible reasons Fehla might be lying to her.

Later that evening, Diyah sat across from Julyán, eating her dinner and trying to conceal her thoughts. She couldn't help noticing that Julyán also seemed especially distant and reserved. This was the first time they'd eaten together all week, and he'd barely spoken two words to her. And she couldn't be sure, but she thought he was avoiding eye contact with her.

"Is everything all right?" she asked, setting her glass down on the table and leaning forward to get his attention.

Julyán seemed to come out of a reverie as he looked at her. "Yes, everything is fine."

"I know the situation with the chaplain is worrying you. And the delirium... I'm sure the king is angry."

"Mmm," was all Julyán said as he slipped back into his taciturn state, allowing his eyes to glaze over.

When they'd finished their meal, the maidservant came and took the dishes away.

"Bring us some more spiced wine, will you?" said Julyán as the servant backed out of the room.

"Of course, Maífírkon," she said, inclining her head.

Diyah looked at him quizzically, but Julyán didn't respond. Instead, he held out his hand for her. Diyah stood up and walked over to meet him, placing her palm on his. She looked up into his face, trying to make sense of his expression but she couldn't figure it out.

"Wha—" she started to ask, but he cut her off by closing his mouth firmly around hers. He pulled her into his arms with more force than he'd ever done before and squeezed her against his body so tightly it almost hurt.

But Diyah didn't mind. Whatever it was about his touch that set her body on fire was taking over again. She responded in kind, grabbing him by the neck and arching her back as she pressed herself into his embrace. Every inch of her ached for him. All thought of escape fled from her mind. In this moment, all that mattered was him—the strength of his body and the taste of his lips.

She couldn't explain it, but since her first night with him, something had changed in her. Whenever he was around, she had trouble focusing on anything else. She counted the minutes between touches, eagerly awaiting the evenings when she could have him all to herself.

"Ahem," came the sound of someone clearing their throat.

Diyah and Julyán broke apart. An embarrassed-looking maidservant stood in the entrance, holding a carafe of wine.

"Excuse me, sir. I didn't mean to intrude. But I've brought the spiced wine you requested."

"Thank you, Eva," said Julyán, straightening his tunic and flashing his eyes in Diyah's direction. "You can put it over there." He gestured to the table.

Diyah smiled sheepishly at the young girl. It was the same servant who'd helped her on the night of the wedding. She had also assisted Diyah in the infirmary during the tournament.

Diyah walked over to sit in the chair by the fire. The door opened and closed as the servant exited. She was alone with Julyán once more, and already the desire was building again.

"Here." Julyán handed her a glass of wine and sat down in the chair next to her. He smiled at her before turning his gaze to the fire. Before long, his eyes had glazed over again like they had at the dinner table.

"What's on your mind?" she attempted again, reaching out to take his hand.

"My brother," said Julyán, "he really loves her, doesn't he? The king's sister?"

Whatever Diyah had been expecting, this wasn't it. "I—yes, I believe he does," she said, letting go of his hand and sitting back in her chair.

"And she loves him too?"

Diyah looked at him warily and hesitated before saying, "I think she *did*, yes."

"But not anymore?" Julyán was still staring at the fire, transfixed.

Diyah frowned. "Catanya is dead…"

"Yes, of course." Julyán shook his head and waved away the comment. "But if she were alive, what do you think Jémys would do?"

This is getting very peculiar, thought Diyah. "I think he would do whatever it takes to be with her," she answered honestly.

"And what about you?" Julyán finally turned to look at her. "Would you do the same?"

Diyah took a large sip of her wine to delay responding. "Yes, I would," she said calmly. There was no point in denying it.

Julyán nodded. "And I would have to stop you." He ran his

hand through his hair and leaned back in his chair, looking weary.

"Would you?" asked Diyah after a short pause.

"I wouldn't have a choice."

"You always have a choice," said Diyah, taking his hand again and squeezing it. "You can choose to help the people you love—choose to help your brother."

"I don't love him," said Julyán as he stared at their interlocked hands. "I don't love anyone. I don't know how."

Diyah rubbed the back of his hand with her thumb. "I don't believe that," she said. "I know you loved your father."

Julyán sighed, suddenly looking like a much older man. "I don't want to love anyone," he muttered, shaking his head.

Diyah chuckled and stood up, walking towards the fire. "You don't *decide* to love someone," she said, like a parent explaining something to their child. "You don't have a choice. It just happens. Gradually over time you start to ache for that person. You need them and they need you, and suddenly you realize you would do anything to make them happy."

Julyán stared at her, looking perplexed. Then he placed his glass on the table and stood up. "Are you happy?" he asked, walking towards her.

Diyah flushed and averted her eyes. She didn't know how to answer that question. His hand took her hers, and he traced the tops of her fingers with his thumb. She looked at him again and found his vivid green eyes tinged with an ardent, almost tender intensity.

"Are *you*?" she asked. The heat of the fire warmed her back as they stood staring at each other, tension building between them. Both waiting for the other to move.

Then he reached out and pulled her into his arms, kissing her hard on the mouth. She laced her fingers through his hair, squeezing him tighter as he pressed her up against the mantle. The hot stones stung her skin through her dress. She heard his sword fall to the floor as he unfastened his breeches and hoisted her up into the air, slamming her back into the wall.

They spent the night consumed by a fierce and unrelenting passion, clinging desperately together and clawing at every inch of each other's bodies as if they'd never be able to get enough.

As the sun rose and they finally pulled apart, Diyah found herself wondering how much more time they would have before everything changed.

11

A FOND FAREWELL

I t was late in the morning when Catanya awoke. The sun had fully risen, and the tent was pleasantly warm and bright. She rolled over to see Drayk lying on his stomach beside her, fast asleep. The events of the previous night came rushing back to her. Then she leaned over and kissed him softly on the cheek, waiting as he opened his eyes.

"Good morning," she said with a cheerful smile.

"Morning..." He sat up and eyed her apprehensively.

The nervous look on his face made her self-conscious. "What is it?"

"Nothing," he said, shrugging. "I'm just a little surprised... I was sure you were going to say last night was a mistake." He ran his hands through his hair, giving it a jaunty, ruffled look.

"I don't regret it," she said, leaning in and pressing her lips against his just for a moment. "I'm tired of living with regret."

His face cracked into a wide grin. "Finally!" He pulled her into his arms and they sank back into the bed.

It was near midday when they ultimately dressed and left the tent. It took them a while to find all their clothes, which they'd strewn across the tent in their evening of passion.

As they dressed, Catanya remembered their argument from the night before. She wasn't angry with Drayk anymore. In fact, now that she thought about it, she had to admit there was some truth in what he'd been trying to say to her.

"You were right," she said as she watched him pull on his boots.

"I usually am," he quipped with a grin. "But what about this time?"

Catanya sighed in resignation. "I can't stay here," she said, squinting out the tent door, towards the glade.

Drayk stopped lacing his boots and looked at her.

"I can't stay here and hide anymore. Cadyan needs to be stopped. I have to stop him."

"I agree," said Drayk, waiting for her to continue.

"When I think about everything he's done..." Shame prickled down Catanya's spine. "When I think of how long this has been going on—how I could have stopped him..."

"You weren't ready. He would have killed you," said Drayk.

Catanya shook her head. "I keep telling myself that I didn't have a choice. I had to run. But we both know that's not true." She met Drayk's gaze. "If I hadn't been so afraid to be who I am, to use these powers, I might have been able to stop him long before now. Think about all the lives I could have saved if only I'd—"

"Don't think like that," said Drayk, standing up. "That's not helpful. You just got through saying you don't want to live with regrets, well," he raised his eyebrows impatiently, "you can't focus on what might have been. It's too late for that."

"I know." Catanya pressed her face into her palms and groaned, then she dropped her hands. "All right." She stood up, adopting a steely resolve. "I'm done running and I'm done hiding. It's time to take this fight to him."

When they arrived in the central glade that afternoon, they found everyone busily preparing what looked like a celebratory feast.

Lynor and his family stood at a table, chopping vegetables and kneading breads. Viena and a group of her friends were draping additional garlands from the trees. Musicians gathered near the stream, setting up drums and lyres. And everyone else laughed and chatted as they brought out stores of candied fruits, honeyed wines, and cured meats to arrange in platters around the central fire.

Catanya spotted Laylian carrying a small bucket of water from the stream to the food preparation table.

"What's going on?" she asked, hurrying to join her.

"Oho!" Laylian set down the bucket and beamed at Catanya and Drayk. "We're preparing the goodbye feast."

"Goodbye feast? Who's leaving?" Drayk looked around, evidently surprised at the notion of someone leaving the mountain.

"Why, *you* are, of course," said Laylian, chortling.

Catanya and Drayk stared at her. "How did you know that?" asked Catanya.

"Well, I didn't *know*, but I still knew, you know?"

Drayk laughed out loud and shook his head in disbelief.

"Well, I'm right, aren't I?" said Laylian, ignoring Drayk's amusement and addressing Catanya. "You're leaving?"

Catanya hesitated, suddenly not sure if it was the right decision. "It's time, don't you think?" she asked.

"Oh yes!" said Laylian. "Time, time, time..." She lifted the bucket and continued towards the bench where Lynor waited. "We'll miss you, of course," she said, handing the bucket to Lynor and turning to address them again. "But we always knew your story would not end here."

"We knew you were only here with us for a short time," said Lynor, smiling at them. "But soon it will all be over!" He turned and grinned at his daughter, Heena, who was standing next to him.

"Soon you will stop the bad king, and the Resonance will return!" said Heena eagerly.

Lynor smiled at her and nodded. "Yes, indeed. And then we'll be able to emerge from the mountain."

"Right." Catanya wasn't sure what else to say. All of these people were counting on her. And despite everything she'd said to Drayk, she still wasn't sure she was strong enough to defeat Cadyan—assuming she could even get to him. After all, he would be in the most heavily guarded fortress in all Mórceá, and he would have the command of an entire army.

"Well, actually..." Catanya looked at Drayk for support.

"We were hoping some of you might join us," he said.

"Fight with us." Catanya nodded and looked around at them all. She and Drayk had discussed it this morning and he'd suggested they ask. "We'll need help to get through Cadyan's army. And more Resonance would be a significant advantage."

"Us? Fight?" Lynor stared at them blankly. He didn't seem to understand what they were saying.

Laylian placed her hand on Catanya's shoulder. "I'm afraid we cannot help you," she said gently. "We are not fighters. It's not in our nature."

"No, nor mine, but—"

Laylian held up her hand to cut Catanya off. "I'm sorry. We can't be a part of this fight."

"I don't understand," said Drayk. "I thought you wanted to help us. You have Resonance too. You could use it to—"

"We do want to help," said Laylian as she began slicing carrots and tossing them into a large pot. "But this is your story, and our part in it is almost over. Our journey is a different one." She smiled sadly. "Whatever the outcome of this fight, it will determine our future as well."

"Yes, we know. That's why we want you to come with us," insisted Drayk.

Laylian just shook her head. "We cannot leave this mountain yet. If we leave, the magic here will die. And our Resonance, out there with you... it would be a distraction—a temptation for you, and for Cadyan."

"What do you mean?" asked Catanya, her pulse quickening slightly.

Laylian sighed. "Here in this mountain, we have balance. Until there is balance out there, my people cannot leave. We are the only free source of Resonance left in this world. But out there... You and your brother are too powerful. The pull would be too strong. It would drive my people mad. Why do you think we sealed this mountain off in the first place?"

"But... I've been here with you all this time, and you're fine. Aren't you?" asked Catanya. She glanced around, suddenly nervous that her presence here had affected these people.

Laylian chuckled, her cheeks flushing a bit. "That is because *I* am here," she said. "At the risk of sounding self-important, I must tell you my power is... stronger than most. I have been protecting the others from the draw while you've been here."

Catanya and Drayk exchanged surprised looks.

Laylian smiled. "But my protection will not last forever. In fact, I can feel it coming soon—much sooner than I had anticipated..." She trailed off, a glazed look in her eyes. She raised her hand absentmindedly to the wreath on her head. To Catanya's surprise, the woven branches, which, until now, had been predominantly green with spots of yellow, had turned almost completely brown. "Soon I will plant my tree in the wood."

"What?" Catanya spluttered, gaping at her.

"Oh yes," said Laylian, coming out of her trance and chuckling at the expression on Catanya's face. "I have been blessed with more time than most, but soon I shall lay myself down for a long overdue nap. And then, the time of Túir-Avlea will be at its end."

"You can't!" protested Catanya.

"Nothing is meant to last forever. Everything ends," said Laylian matter-of-factly. "It has to, otherwise nothing would ever get started. Resonance is in the momentum of change, remember? We have to move forward. Pain and loss, they define us as much as happiness or love. Whether it's a world or a relationship... Everything has its time, and everything ends. If you are successful, Catanya, there will be no reason for my people to hide anymore. They can emerge from the mountain and take their places in the world. Become maílehrs in their own right."

"And if I fail?" asked Catanya, dreading the answer. What would happen to the people here? Her eyes roved over the glade, over Lynor and his family, Viena and her friends. The children playing in the grass and the young couples holding hands or working together.

Catanya stared back at Laylian, hoping for some reassurance that they would all be okay.

Laylian just smiled sadly. "Everything ends, Catanya," she said once more. Then she turned and walked away, humming happily as though they hadn't discussed anything more serious than the weather.

Catanya's insides twisted. The fate of these people—this entire community—rested with her. And she had no army, no help. How was she supposed to succeed?

"We'll figure it out," said Drayk calmly, as if he'd read her mind. "We can stop in Awnell and regroup. Maybe some of the kingdom survived. There might be people in the city who can join us. Besides... It's probably for the best that this lot stays here. Laylian might have been a fighter in her youth, but now..." He shook his head, watching her meander around.

"And I can't imagine the rest of this lot would be much use in a fight."

"No, you're right." Catanya glanced back at Heena and Lynor and saw that they'd started singing together as they worked. Her heart ached at the sight. "These people are too peaceful. They wouldn't stand a chance in a war. And without Laylian, I don't want to think what will happen to them. We'll have to come up with another idea."

"The good news is that we have the entire journey back to Awnell to figure it out," said Drayk, half amused, half exasperated.

Catanya thought about the long journey ahead of them. The Shrouded Caves, the Reflecting Channel, the Windy Shoal... She shuddered at the idea of experiencing it all again. Would this journey be just as difficult as the first time?

"You're right," she said, shoving aside her fears. She couldn't be that person anymore. Consumed with fear and dread. She needed to take control if she wanted to succeed and save everyone.

"I could get used to hearing you say that," said Drayk with a smirk.

Catanya smacked him on the arm and shook her head. "Let's just enjoy our last night here... together," she said, meeting his eyes. This was her last chance to experience a tranquil, simple life. After tonight, she couldn't afford to be distracted or to put her own needs first. Not anymore. "I don't know what lies ahead of us. This may be the last night of peace we get for some time. So, just for tonight, I want to pretend we're free. I want to enjoy it with you."

"That's an idea I can get behind." Drayk took Catanya's hand and leaned over to kiss her.

That evening's fire celebration was a bittersweet affair, but Catanya was determined to enjoy every minute of it. There was more food than ever before, and the singing and dancing continued throughout the night. Everyone wanted a chance to talk to Catanya and Drayk, to wish them luck and thank them. Several of the young children had even prepared parting gifts for them.

"For you," said Flian, Lynor's youngest son. It was the first he'd ever spoken to Catanya. He had one hand on his face and he squirmed nervously as he handed Catanya a woven crown made of flowers and twigs to match the one that Laylian always wore.

"Thank you." Catanya smiled as she placed it on her head where it seemed to float atop her long, shimmering hair. It had been weeks since she'd lost the last strand of her natural black. It had taken her some time, but she had slowly learned to appreciate her new hair. She no longer feared what it represented. And although there would be no hiding her identity once she arrived back on the mainland, she wasn't worried. She meant what she'd said to Drayk. She was done hiding.

"How do I look," she asked, turning to face him.

"Like a princess," he said with a playful smile.

Catanya chuckled and kissed him. His hand cupped her cheek, and his fingers twisted through her hair.

Flian gave an embarrassed squeak and ran away, leaving them alone.

Hand in hand, Catanya and Drayk watched the festivities.

Despite her newfound resolution, Catanya really didn't want to leave the mountain. These last months had been the only time in ages that she'd truly felt safe. It was difficult to walk away knowing what was waiting for her on the other side. And what was at stake if she failed.

"I can't believe you're leaving," said a voice she recognized.

They turned to see Viena walking to join them, a look of mingled envy and sadness in her eyes. "I'm going to miss you."

"Nonsense," said Drayk, patting her on the shoulder. "You're going to come find us when this is all done, and tell us about your own adventures."

Catanya's heart swelled at the confidence in Drayk's voice. She squeezed his hand in silent thanks for his continued confidence in her.

"Yes, of course," she said, smiling. "And actually"—she reached into her pocket and pulled out her drawings and the old tattered map that had led her and Drayk to Túir-Avlea— "you should keep these pictures for your stories, and this map... well, we don't need it anymore. I think the journey is burned into our memories."

Drayk laughed grimly and nodded.

"Thanks," said Viena, tucking the pictures into her notebook. Then she took the map and unfolded it to examine the images. She traced the parchment with her fingers. "It's so old," she muttered under her breath.

Catanya frowned. Viena was right. Catanya had noticed it the first time she'd held the parchment too, but she hadn't thought about it since then. She looked up at Drayk curiously. Then she noticed Laylian walk by, humming to herself. "Laylian," she called, grabbing Drayk's hand again and walking over to join her. "How long ago did you say Freihse left the mountain?"

Laylian scrunched her face in thought, so her wrinkled cheeks bunched beneath her eyes. "Oh, a long time ago now... a long time," she replied.

"But that map must be a century old at least," said Drayk, catching on to what Catanya had seen.

"Is it?" Laylian chuckled. "Well, isn't that something?" She smiled at them expectantly, her bushy eyebrows raised so high they disappeared into her feathery hair.

"And you said *you* gave Freihse the necklace..." said Drayk.

"Mmm, yes, I did say that."

"And you said Freihse's father was a maílehr in the community..."

"Oh yes, a very important one, if I may say so myself."

Catanya and Drayk exchanged glances. "So... we're right, aren't we?" asked Catanya in a low voice. She'd been nervous to ask before, but she couldn't keep pretending.

"Right?" asked Laylian. "About what?"

Drayk cleared his throat. "That crown," he gestured to the wreath on her head, "the necklace, the ring..." He trailed off awkwardly.

"*Illayan.*" Catanya breathed the name as quietly as she could and held Laylian's gaze.

"Mmm..." Laylian grinned from ear to ear, watching them stumble their way around the questions.

"They say the crown of immortality is what Maílater Caer was really after when he went looking for Illayan in Bratia," said Drayk.

Laylian chuckled heartily. "Yes, well, I'm afraid he always was a little short-sighted." She scratched her head absent-mindedly, causing the yew wreath to move up and down.

"But every king of Caerlon has continued searching for it. For centuries, they've looked and they've never found it," continued Drayk. He was eyeing Laylian.

"Is that so?" asked Laylian innocently. "Hmm, well sounds like an awful great waste of time to me. After all, there's no such thing as forever. Only time. And a great deal of time may seem like forever, but it's like I said before, everything ends."

"It's easy to see why someone might want more time though," said Catanya. Laylian would never admit it, but Catanya was certain now.

"Oh yes, quite!" Laylian nodded, beaming at them. "But

time is like a rare jewel, it's only precious because it is rare. If you have too much, you forget to admire it."

Catanya thought about this for a second. "I agree," she said, deciding in that moment that it really didn't matter if they were right or wrong. She grabbed Drayk's hand, and, laughing, dragged him off towards the dance area, determined to enjoy these last few hours of merriment.

Later that night, when the celebration was winding down, they walked together through the labyrinth of trees towards their tents.

Tomorrow they would leave the safety of the mountain and head back towards the pain and misery they'd left behind in Awnell. It was time to wake up. But Catanya wasn't quite ready. She wanted to live in the fantasy a little longer.

When they arrived outside the entrance to her tent, Catanya pulled Drayk in for a tight embrace. She pressed her body against his and felt the warmth and freedom she had come to associate with him. They stumbled half-blind into the tent and crashed down on the bed where they spent the rest of the night entwined together, avoiding the thought of what the morning would bring.

Altogether too soon, the morning arrived. Catanya and Drayk dressed in silence, donning their swords and leather clothes from Awnell. Then they packed their bags with everything they'd need for the journey: weapons, cloaks, canteens, and a large sack full of rations Lynor had given them the night before.

"Are you ready?" asked Catanya, wrapping the cloak around her shoulders and looking at him.

Drayk nodded. "Are you?"

Catanya shrugged and smiled. As she turned to walk past

KATHRYN KNOWLES

him out of the tent, she felt his hand grab her arm. She stared into his face, surprised to see an unusually serious expression.

"Catya, I mean it. Are you ready to do what needs to be done?"

"Of course, I am," she said, a little surprised.

"No." Drayk shook his head. "I mean, are you *really* ready? If it comes down to it, will you be able to kill him?"

A lump rose in Catanya's throat, and she averted her gaze. "I don't want to kill him," she mumbled in a small voice. "I want him to see reason. Laylian has taught me so much. I really think if I can just get him to understand..."

"I know that, but..." Drayk sighed and gave her an apologetic look. "What if he doesn't?" he pressed, and Catanya saw the concern in his eyes.

Drayk watched patiently as Catanya worked through her thoughts. Then she exhaled and closed her eyes. "Then, yes," she said. "If it comes down to it and I have no other choice. I'll do it." It was true, but she hated herself for saying it.

Drayk squeezed her hand. "Okay," he said, looking relieved. He leaned in and kissed her forehead.

"But what about you?" asked Catanya. "You don't need to fight, you know? You could just return to Awnell and stay there." She hesitated before saying what came next. She didn't want to upset him, but she needed to be clear. "You don't owe me anything, Drayk."

She watched him apprehensively, hoping she hadn't injured him with her bluntness. But as usual, Drayk seemed to take everything in stride.

"I know I don't owe you anything," he said. "And believe me, I've considered it—staying in Awnell, I mean. It would be safer..." He exhaled heavily and then flashed his eyes in her direction. "But where's the fun in that?" Then he swooped down and hoisted his bag onto his shoulder, looking primed for an adventure.

202

Catanya laughed and shook her head. "All right, then. Let's go."

They emerged into the glade, ready to depart with little fuss. But to their surprise, the entire community had gathered to wait for them in the early morning mist, standing together in silent vigil. Catanya scanned the group, exchanging silent looks with her friends. Lynor and Emra nodded and smiled, holding their sleepy kids in their arms. Viena and her friends were bunched together at one side, positively glowing with admiration and respect. Laylian stood at the front of the group, and as Catanya and Drayk approached, she stepped forward to greet them.

"My dears," she raised her arms out and embraced them each in turn, "it has been my privilege to know you both."

"Thank you for everything," said Catanya. "I don't think I can ever express how grateful I am for everything you've taught me."

"Just promise me one thing," said Laylian. "Promise me you will remember what you are fighting for."

Catanya thought this was rather odd. "Of course," she replied, a little perplexed.

"Fighting *for* something is far more powerful than fighting *against* something." Laylian gave her a piercing look. "Remember that. Focus on what you want, and the rest should become clear."

"I will," said Catanya, thinking about what she'd just promised Drayk. She hadn't told anyone else what she'd told him. Nobody but Drayk knew the truth of what she hoped would happen with her brother. But in this moment, she couldn't help wondering if somehow Laylian knew as well.

Laylian smiled at her and pulled her in for another hug. Then she whispered in Catanya's ear, "You are powerful in more ways than one, Catanya. Your strongest gifts lie within your heart. You have the power to shape the future." She pulled away and held Catanya at arm's length. "Trust in that, and trust yourself."

"Thank you," murmured Catanya, overwhelmed with the emotion of the farewell.

Now that it was time to leave, she found it more difficult than she could have imagined. She cared deeply for these people, and she felt a strong connection to the place—stronger than she'd ever felt for anywhere else. She didn't want to part from them. But she was grateful that, for the first time in her life, she wasn't leaving devastation in her wake. These people, this place—her presence hadn't ruined anything. And that was an encouraging thought.

As she and Drayk began walking away, Catanya turned back and called, "I will carry this place with me, you know?" She looked around, taking a deep breath and closing her eyes momentarily. "Always."

"Farewell," called Laylian. "Our thoughts go with you."

Catanya nodded and smiled, then she turned and joined Drayk on the long walk back through the Dead Wood.

12

THE ESCAPE

"Tomorrow?" Diyah was shocked. A blistering headache had been pounding against her skull all day. It made it difficult for her to concentrate on anything else. "Tomorrow," she repeated in a hollow voice. She smashed her knuckles into her forehead, trying to push away the pain, but it didn't work.

"Yes, tomorrow—are you all right?"

"I'm just surprised, is all," said Diyah, opening her eyes and looking at Fehla. "I didn't think we'd have an opportunity so soon."

"Well, we do," said Fehla in a hurried voice.

"What makes you think we can get out undetected tomorrow night?" asked Jémys.

"Tomorrow is the Royal Offering. It's the perfect distraction. Once the ceremony starts, you two can slip away undetected."

"Wait." Diyah dropped her hands and gaped at Fehla. "Us two? What about you?"

Fehla sighed and shrugged apologetically. "I'm not coming," she said. Then, ignoring their protests, she continued, "No, listen, I've thought a lot about this. Not only is it safer for you if

I don't go. But"—she cleared her throat gruffly—"my place is here with my son. I made my choice years ago, and it's time I accept it. My son is my responsibility."

"Fehla—" Diyah tried to interject, but Fehla held up her hand to silence her.

"I have made my decision. Don't argue with me," she said in an authoritative voice. "Just promise me you'll find her, and you'll make sure she's safe. That's all I ask."

Diyah and Jémys exchanged looks.

"Promise," said Jémys, and Diyah nodded.

"Good. Then all that's left is for us to go over the plan..."

They spent the next hour discussing their plan in excruciating detail, making sure they had contingencies in case something went wrong.

"I don't like it," said Diyah after Fehla had left, and she was alone with Jémys. "There are too many things that can go wrong. What if someone sees?"

"Nobody will see us. Fehla's right. The entire castle and the entire city will be preoccupied. The guards will be worrying about who's coming in, not who's going out. No one is going to notice two people slipping away in the middle of the chaos. And if they do, well, that's what this is for," he added, patting the sword at his side.

Diyah bit her lip. She didn't like the idea of having to fight. But, if it came down to it, she would do whatever it took to save herself, and to save Jémys.

"Okay," she said, nodding. "But... what about Julyán?"

She had avoided broaching the topic because she didn't want to upset Jémys. He had a tendency to lose his temper whenever he talked about his brother.

Jémys's body stiffened and his face flushed. "What about him?"

"Well..." Diyah chose her words carefully. "I'm wondering if we should consider... possibly... telling him the truth," she said, avoiding his eye.

"Are you mad?" Jémys stared at her like she'd lost her mind. "Why would we tell him?"

"I don't feel right leaving him here," said Diyah, finally voicing the concern that had been growing stronger inside her for weeks. "He's my—I mean, he's your brother! I don't think you should leave him here."

"That won't matter to him, Diyah." Jémys shook his head and gave her a pitying look. "You know what he's like. He's Cadyan's right-hand man now. He'll sell us out without batting an eye. We can't trust him."

"But what if we can? Jémys, I think he might help us."

"He's not our friend Diyah." Jémys's tone was firm. "His allegiance is to the king and to the king alone. Not us. He doesn't care about us."

Diyah's face flushed. "I think you're wrong," she said, ignoring the sting from his harsh words.

Jémys placed his hands on the table, looking weary. "It doesn't matter if I'm wrong or I'm right. Julyán won't have a choice. If he helps us, they'll call him a traitor and he'll be killed. He won't risk it."

"Why not? We are!" exclaimed Diyah.

"Yeah, we are. But you and I, we're doing it for Catanya. She's worth the risk to us," said Jémys. "But she's not worth it to him."

Diyah wanted to protest, but she couldn't. Jémys was right. Julyán had no reason to care about Catanya. He didn't even know she was alive. If they risked telling him, and it didn't work, they'd lose their only advantage—Cadyan would know she was alive.

"Okay," said Diyah. "We won't tell Julyán."

Jémys breathed a sigh of relief. "Thank you," he said. Then, seeing the dejected look on her face, he walked around the worktable and pulled her into his arms. "This is going to work, Diyah. I know it will. And we're going to see her again. We're going to be with her." His voice shook with emotion, and he squeezed her tighter.

Later that night, as Diyah sat in bed, unable to quiet her mind, she turned her attention to Julyán's sleeping silhouette. She watched his chest gently rise and fall as he breathed. He had one arm lying over the blankets and the other bent up underneath his head. She liked watching him sleep. It was the only time he ever looked truly at ease.

She wondered what he would do when he realized she and Jémys were gone. She liked to think a small part of him would be sad—sad for his own loss and not just angry on behalf of his king. But the truth was, she didn't really know how he felt about her or his brother. And Jémys was right. They couldn't take a chance that Julyán would betray Cadyan for them.

She leaned down and kissed him on the forehead, trying not to think about the next night when she would be sleeping alone—alone on a ship in the middle of the ocean, surrounded by sailors and smugglers, travelling into the unknown.

As she pulled away, Julyán's eyelids flickered and opened, and he looked at her with something close to tenderness in his eyes. He brought his hand up to her face and brushed her cheek. Then he ran his fingers across her lips and pulled her head back down to meet his. He kissed her softly as he ran his hand through her long blonde hair. Pulling her into his body, he let out a soft sigh and drew the blankets up around them.

As they dressed the next morning, Julyán and Diyah barely spoke two words. Diyah was terrified if she spoke to him, he'd be able to tell something was wrong. So, she kept to herself, blaming her taciturn behaviour on the headache that still lingered from the day before.

Julyán left early to prepare for the Offering. Diyah headed straight for her old chambers to gather supplies and meet Fehla.

Most of the essentials had been ready for weeks. Spare clothes, food and water, blankets... And Diyah had been gathering a small supply of bandages and basic remedies to take with her. But she wanted to double check everything and replace the herbs in her satchel.

When she was rummaging around in the cupboards, she found a familiar vial lying in one of the far corners. She had completely forgotten about it until now. She held up the sickly green liquid and examined it under the light of the nearest candle.

Could it be? She wondered, remembering her first encounter with Ayr.

I must admit, the Jade Moss poison... that's a nasty way to die, isn't it? I wouldn't have thought you had it in you. And who in Caerlon would know?

Just then, the door opened and Fehla came bustling in, looking harried. "Are you ready?" she asked.

Diyah reacted instinctively, slipping the vial into her bag before Fehla could see it. "Yes, I think so," she said, not looking Fehla in the eye. "Here." She handed her the bag, trying to push away the uncomfortable thoughts seeping into her mind.

"It will be waiting for you in the large urn by the door to the kitchens. Now, don't forget, you need to leave within the first hour of the Offering, that's when—"

"That's when Cadyan will be most preoccupied. I know," said Diyah, nodding. They had been over the plan so many times she could hardly forget.

"Good." Fehla opened her mouth to continue but Diyah cut her off.

"I have to ask you something," she blurted. She had so many questions burning inside her. If she didn't get at least one answer, she thought she might explode. "Why did Ayr think you would know about Túir-Avlea?"

Fehla looked surprised by the question, but she shrugged. "Well, I have been searching for it for a long time, actually... But it seems Ayr has beaten me to it."

Diyah was genuinely stunned. "What do you mean you've been searching for it? Everyone thought Túir-Avlea was just a legend."

"It's not a legend," she said. "There have been rumours for a long time about a map to find it. Apparently, several generations ago someone left the mountain—a woman, so they say. And when she came to the mainland, she brought a map so one day her children could find their way back if they wanted to."

Diyah frowned. "How do you know about this?" she asked, trying to keep the accusation out of her voice. "Does Cadyan know?"

"No! I promise you, he doesn't. It was a story my mother used to tell me before she died. I don't even think she told Falia about it. I was so young when my mother died but I never forgot."

"And you told Ayr," said Diyah, nodding. She suspected the two women had been close, close enough to share stories and secrets.

"I did. But at the time, I thought it was just a story. I had no idea Ayr would remember it after all these years."

Diyah snorted. Ayr seemed like the kind of person who never forgot anything once she'd heard it. The kind of person who acted on valuable information, no matter how absurd it seemed. She had probably started looking for the map the minute Fehla told her about it.

"Wait a second..." A memory suddenly came back to Diyah. Almost a year ago, when she'd first started working as the court physician in Caerlon, Diyah had overheard Fehla talking with one of the fírkon. It was right after the fírkon had returned from decimating Finnua. "You said you were looking for a map..." Diyah looked at Fehla, comprehension dawning on her. "So that's what you were doing. You had one of the fírkon out there looking for it."

"How did you know that?" asked Fehla, astonished.

"I overheard you talking ages ago with someone. I had hoped you'd tell me about it, but..." Diyah shrugged. It was hard to keep the resentment out of her voice.

"Diyah." Fehla reached out and took her hand, smiling sadly. "I didn't tell you because it wasn't safe—not for any of us. If they'd caught Holun, they would have killed him. And if Cadyan had gotten his hands on the map..." She shook her head darkly.

"Holun?" asked Diyah, genuinely surprised.

"Yes. Holun is one of the few good fírkon left. He wanted to help me, but it became too dangerous for him with Slaedir and the others watching. I never told him what the map was for, only that it was important to help Caerlon."

Diyah's head was spinning. "All right, but why were you looking for it?" she asked, trying to make sense of everything. "Were you trying to help Catanya?"

Fehla rubbed her forehead. "I was trying to help everyone. I just wanted answers, Diyah. It was naïve, but I thought if I could find Túir-Avlea, maybe the people there could help me understand. Tell me what to do, but..." She trailed off, shrugging. "I can only hope they've helped Catanya because this magic—the elixir... It's too powerful. I don't think any of us quite understand what the cost of using it is. Cadyan wasn't ready. If I had known Catanya would get the powers too I never would have—" She broke off, looking miserable. "Well, I would have done things differently is all."

A pit formed in Diyah's stomach. She wanted to ask the

other question—the one upsetting her the most. But she didn't have the nerve.

They lapsed into silence, each silently worrying about different things.

Fehla cleared her throat abruptly. "Now, I'd better go before Cadyan realizes I'm not in my chambers." She turned to leave. Before she'd taken two steps, she froze and turned around.

They stared at each other, lost for words. Then Diyah rushed forward and wrapped her arms around Fehla. "Thank you for everything," she mumbled, fighting back her tears. "I don't know what I would have done without you."

"Nor I, you," said Fehla, embracing her. Then she held her out at arm's length and looked her over, frowning. "You look pale, are you all right?"

"I'm just nervous," said Diyah.

Fehla squeezed Diyah's arms before letting go. "Well, it has been a true privilege getting to know you, Diyah. I hope we meet again."

Diyah tried to blink the tears out of her eyes. She laughed in embarrassment and wiped them away with her sleeve.

"Come on. Brave faces," said Fehla. She straightened out her dress and gave Diyah one last motherly smile before turning and walking out the door.

Diyah spent the rest of the day absentmindedly tending to patients and counting the minutes until the ceremony began. Twice she realized almost too late that her patients were about to drink from the wrong bottles.

"Oh, sorry, not that blue liquid, this one," she said, hurrying to swap the vials.

She would have been ashamed of herself had she not been too preoccupied with worry.

Finally, the sun set, and it was almost time. She washed her hands and walked slowly back to her quarters where she changed out of her work dress and into something more formal.

She ate alone that night since Julyán was busy with Cadyan. Though she was hungry, her stomach was tied up in knots, making it difficult for her to swallow anything. Eventually, she gave up, wrapping the rest of the food in a handkerchief and putting it in her pocket to add to their travel rations. After all, she didn't know how long it would be before her next meal.

Then she sat on the edge of the bed, her legs trembling restlessly as she waited for the minutes to tick by. Thick, hazy clouds rolled through the darkening sky outside her window, blackening the stars. When the full moon had risen, shimmering through the streaks of fog, she stood up, took a deep breath, and made her way down to the throne room.

As she approached the side door, she heard the unmistakable sound of hundreds of people talking as they crammed into the nearby entrance hall, waiting for their turn to see the king. She nodded at the guard, who pushed open the door. Then Diyah walked into the room.

The front doors hadn't been opened yet, so the room was almost empty save for a few fírkon. Cadyan was leaning over the arm of his throne talking animatedly with Julyán, who looked up as Diyah entered.

Fehla sat in her chair a few feet away from Cadyan. She gave Diyah a reassuring smile as Diyah made her way to stand beside Julyán.

"Ah, good, there you are," said Cadyan, nodding. "Julyán here was getting worried."

Diyah glanced quickly at Julyán, but he seemed not to notice.

"But I told him not to worry, didn't I?" continued Cadyan,

smacking Julyán on the arm. "She knows better than to disobey her king, and her husband. Don't you?" He smirked at her.

Diyah forced her face into a false smile and said, "Of course, Your Majesty." Hatred surged through her, coursing along familiar, callused paths as she looked into his cold, haughty face. Whatever goodness or kindness she thought she'd seen in this man on the night the chaplain had died, she knew now it had all been in her head.

"Let's get this started, shall we? Open the doors!" Cadyan called to the guards at the other end of the room. "Oh, I do love this part," he whispered, rubbing his hands together and grinning.

The doors opened, and Diyah watched the crowd push and shove at each other as the guards tried to force them into an orderly line. She craned her neck searching for any sign of Jémys, but she couldn't see him. *He must be farther down the line,* she thought. But that was okay, he knew the plan. He would meet her there.

Diyah stood and watched as dozens of people pleaded their cases with Cadyan, offering him treasures in exchange for his help. Before long, a pile of gifts teetered in the corner of the room, with everything ranging from sacks of grain to boxes of jewellery. And all the while, Cadyan sat there offering empty promises and occasionally using his powers to dazzle them.

When one man towards the back of the line started getting impatient and tried to force his way forward, an all-out brawl erupted in the middle of the room.

Cadyan sighed dramatically and looked back at Julyán, shaking his head. With one casual wave of his hand, everyone in line before the dais collapsed on the ground, unable to move. An invisible barricade held them down. "Take care of *that* will you?" he said, pointing at the man who had instigated the fight. The man looked to be in his forties, with long greying hair and weathered skin. He wore a long, worn-out coat, and tattered fisherman's boots above stained breeches. Blood trickled from a gash above his right eye.

Julyán jumped off the dais and strode over to the man, hauling him onto his feet.

"No, please! I must speak with the king, I must!"

"Get up," said Julyán.

"Animals." Cadyan curled his lip in disgust. "Who's next?" he called, releasing his hold on the room. A young woman clambered to her feet and hurried forward, trembling. "Ah, yes, and what have you brought for me?"

Diyah stood frozen in her spot, staring at the scene in front of her. The firkon were all preoccupied with re-establishing order, Julyán was still wrestling with the desperate fisherman, and Cadyan was engrossed with the hand-carved sculpture the girl was holding out to him.

It was now or never.

She looked over at Fehla. The queen nodded almost imperceptibly without taking her eyes off the throne. Without a second glance, Diyah turned and walked resolutely back through the side door and out into the corridor. She took a deep breath and strode down the hall with purpose, ignoring the guards as she passed. When she turned the corner out of sight, she broke into a sprint, hurtling down the hallway towards the kitchens. She barrelled down the stairs and stopped just before she reached the door to the kitchens.

There was a small alcove beside the stairs with a large urn big enough to fit a whole person. She ducked behind it and found herself face to face with Jémys.

"You're here!" she whispered, grabbing his arms in relief.

"Yeah, I've only just got away, but we're cutting it close."

"Did you get my bag?"

"Yes, it was in the urn," he said. "Along with these." He handed her a thick old cloak and a second, lumpy bag. "You need to change, there are extra clothes in there."

Diyah whipped open the bag and pulled out a pair of old breeches and a ragged shirt. She changed in a hurry and stuffed her dress back into the bag, along with her satchel and the food from her pocket.

"I'm ready," she said, pulling the cloak's hood over her head.

"Okay, let's go." Jémys drew his sword and steered her back up the stairs towards the entrance hall.

Diyah kept her head down and allowed Jémys to push her down the hallway, past the guards.

"Found this one trying to hide away in the kitchens," he announced, jostling her. "I'm going to escort him out to the southern gate and show him our king's *best hospitality*."

Diyah heard someone laugh. Jémys shoved her forward, and she stumbled. His firm grip on her arm kept her from falling.

"*Our king's hospitality?*" she muttered when they were out the door and descending the steps into the courtyard.

"It worked, didn't it?" he whispered.

They pushed their way through the hordes of people all bumping and shoving each other. All the while Diyah kept her head down, staring at her feet as they navigated the uneven cobblestones. Jémys kept his hand tightly on her arm so they wouldn't get separated.

After a few minutes, the noise faded and the air seemed to clear, and Diyah realized they'd made it through the crowd. A dense fog rolled through the streets from the ocean. The full moon illuminated the grey stones, mixing with the pools of yellow torchlight that dotted the streets. They hurried along the narrow lanes of the commercial district and then ducked into a dark alley, littered with debris from the nearby shops.

"Okay, I think we're far enough." Jémys released his grip and looked back at her. "How do we get to the port?"

"It's just on the other side of the western gate," said Diyah. "If we follow the outer wall, we should get there." She looked up at the stone buildings around her. They were just outside the millinery shop, at the border of the fashion district. "This way." She grabbed his hand and pulled him off in the direction of the wall, away from the finery of the central city.

They hurried along, not daring to stop until the surrounding buildings took on a new style. They were shabbier and more run down. Rotted wooden slats dangled haphazardly from the roofs, paint peeled from the shutters, and several walls were cracked and crumbling.

"They call this Beggar's Lane," said Diyah bitterly. "This leads down to the gate."

"It's so quiet." Jémys looked around nervously. Fewer torches lined this street, giving the impression that darkness was creeping from the corners, slowly swallowing it entirely. And the fog blanketing the streets grew thicker as they neared the port.

"That's because everyone who lives here is up at the castle, giving away what little they have in the hopes that Cadyan will help their loved ones, or give them food and shelter—ease their troubles."

"But he doesn't," said Jémys.

"Sometimes he does," muttered Diyah, shrugging. "But only when it suits him. He wants to be feared, but he also wants to be worshipped. He has them all convinced that this time they might be the lucky ones. This time he might choose them."

They walked another few minutes in silence.

"I hate him more and more with every passing day," said Jémys through clenched teeth. His eyes roved over the decrepit streets, the tattered clothes hanging from windows, and the heaps of festering garbage in piles next to broken down carts.

"So do I," said Diyah. Her insides twisted as she thought about these people. She was their healer. How could she abandon them to Cadyan's neglect?

I'm not abandoning them, she told herself. *I'll come back with Catanya. We'll help them together.*

"Oh, good, we're almost at the gate," said Jémys as they turned the corner and it came into view, a wide arch leading through the enormous inner wall of Caerlon. The heavy stone door had been cranked open, and the spiked portcullis dangled warningly above the entry.

"Yeah, but prepare yourself... It gets even worse on the other side," said Diyah with a grimace. "That's the slum."

Through the gate stood row upon row of dilapidated, half-ruined buildings stacked on top of each other like cordwood. The makeshift roofs were sloped and sunken with leaking cracks and holes. Decades of filth clung to the walls with a slimy, sticky sheen that glistened in the moonlight. Rats and other mangy animals scuttled over the crumbling walls. It reeked of urine and stale barkbeer, and they could hear a baby crying somewhere in the distance.

Diyah felt dizzy. She had to work hard not to throw up as she stared at the dank, decrepit slums.

A sudden gust of wind tore through the gate, whipping Diyah's cloak and extinguishing the nearest torch. Dense clouds rolled in, shrouding the moon and momentarily dampening its light. The night grew eerily still as the street fell into darkness.

Diyah shivered and snatched at her cloak, pulling it tighter around her arms, trying to ignore her apprehension.

"Where's the guard?" whispered Jémys, pulling her attention back to the wall.

She cast around, searching for a sign of someone, but the street appeared deserted.

"There's always a guard stationed at the gate," she muttered, her uneasiness mounting inside her.

The scraping of metal against a scabbard told Diyah Jémys had drawn his sword.

"Stay close," he muttered, inching towards the gate.

Diyah crept after him, hand hovering above his arm as she resisted the fear urging her to grab onto him.

Jémys stepped through the gate and examined the area on the other side.

"There's no one here," he said, beckoning for Diyah to follow him.

Diyah stepped through and glanced at the wall where the guards usually stood. There was no sign of anyone.

"I don't like this," she said, exchanging glances with Jémys in the dark. "It feels like a trap."

"I know... But we can't turn back, Diyah." A beam of moonlight broke through the cloud cover to illuminate his face. He was staring at Diyah with nervous resolve. "We need to keep going."

Diyah swallowed hard and nodded.

Together they continued along the street. Jémys kept his sword drawn, poised to react, but nothing happened.

When bright spots began to form in Diyah's vision, she realized she'd been instinctively holding her breath, trying to make as little noise as possible. She forced herself to breathe deeply and collect herself.

With each step they took, more moonlight leached through the clouds, lighting the streets. And still nothing happened.

They reached the end of the lane, where it branched in opposite directions.

Jémys glanced at Diyah, and she nodded. They cast around one more time, searching for any sign of movement, but there was nothing. Then they turned right, towards the western edge of the city.

"So, it's true," came a voice from behind them.

Jémys reacted so fast. He pushed Diyah behind him and brought his sword around before Diyah even had time to turn.

A figure was visible in the darkness, leaning against the

dilapidated wall of the nearest building. A long, gilded sword dangled from his arm at his side, gleaming in the moonlight.

Julyán emerged from the shadows, disappointment etched on his face. "One of my men saw you leaving with a peasant," he said, striding forward and smacking Jémys's sword out of his way. Jémys seemed momentarily stunned, he stumbled sideways and turned back, looking terrified.

Julyán smirked. He stepped up to Diyah and pulled the hood off her head. "When you didn't come back, I knew something was wrong," he said, shaking his head. Then he crossed behind her and blocked their path through the slums.

"Get out of the way," said Jémys, holding out his sword again. He had regained his calm, but anger burned in his eyes as he glared at his brother.

"No," replied Julyán with a hint of amusement in his voice. "Where do you think you're going to go, anyway? Hmm? How far do you think you'll get?"

"We know what we're doing," said Diyah. "We know it's a risk, but we can't stay here!" She took a step towards Julyán, but Jémys held out his hand to hold her back, shaking his head in warning.

"If you leave, you'll die," said Julyán in a slow, measured voice. "Catanya is no match for him. If she tries to fight him, she will die and you will die along with her."

"Wait a second..." Jémys dropped his outstretched hand and stared at Julyán.

"You *know*?" gasped Diyah. "You know Catanya is alive?"

Julyán locked eyes with her. A flurry of emotions seemed to pass through his eyes but his well-trained face remained impassive. He nodded.

There was a long pause when no one said anything until—

"How long have you known?" demanded Jémys.

Julyán turned his gaze towards his brother. "Since the tournament," he said. "Slaedir's last words were his confession. He wanted my first act as maífirkon to be something that would infuriate the king. He seemed to find it rather amusing to saddle me with his guilt."

Jémys swore and kicked a nearby stone.

"Jémys," said Diyah reproachfully.

"What? He knows!" shouted Jémys, gesturing manically at his brother. "Which means Cadyan knows! And Catanya is still in danger!" He advanced on Julyán, brandishing his sword, but now it was Diyah's turn to hold him back.

She had been watching Julyán and noticed the discomfort on his face. He averted his eyes.

"You haven't told him yet, have you?" she asked in a low voice. "You haven't told Cadyan she's alive?"

Julyán gave her a pained expression. "No."

"Why not?" Diyah pushed past Jémys to stand in front of Julyán. When he didn't respond she threw caution to the wind and grabbed his hand in hers. "Come with us," she urged.

"What?" said Jémys and Julyán in unison.

"Come with us. Help us fight. Catanya can end this, I know she can! And we can help. Come with us now. Let's go. *Please.*" Diyah squeezed his hand and tried to pull him forward.

Jémys stood off to the side, gaping at her. But Julyán stared down at her face, looking confused and torn.

"Don't you want to be free?" asked Diyah in a voice like a whisper. "To be happy again?"

Julyán frowned and for a moment he seemed to be debating his options. Then he smiled to himself and shook his head. He let out a short, irreverent sigh and turned his eyes back on her. "I want *you* to be happy," he said pointedly, giving her a pained smile.

There was a pause like an eternity. Diyah's heart raced faster and faster inside her chest. Then Julyán grabbed her and pulled her into his arms, locking his mouth over hers in a passionate and urgent kiss that set her entire soul on fire.

"What's happening?" asked Jémys in a weak voice.

Diyah and Julyán broke apart. Diyah teetered, slightly light-headed, and turned to look at Jémys.

"Go," commanded Julyán, pulling away, but keeping his hands on her waist. "I'll delay Cadyan as long as I can." He looked down at Diyah and kissed her one more time on the lips.

Jémys was still having trouble understanding. "So... you won't tell him she's alive?" he asked sceptically.

"No." Julyán shook his head and took his hands off Diyah. "But I can't promise he won't find out. Now go," he said again. Then he pulled a dagger out of his belt and flipped it around in his hand. "Here." He held it out for her.

Diyah reached out and wrapped her fingers around the cool steel handle. It was the same blade he'd handed her all those months ago in the training field. Before she could respond, Julyán turned and walked past them, back towards the gate.

"Wait," called Jémys, and Julyán paused, looking back at them. Jémys frowned and took a step forward. "Thank you, brother," he said, holding out his hand.

Julyán stared at it blankly for a second, and then he brought his hand out and grasped it firmly. "Yes, well. Good luck," he replied. Then he strode back up the street towards the gate without a second glance.

INTERLUDE

CADYAN

THE CHOICE

The carriage jostled and jerked along the dark, dry roads, finally coming to a halt. They had been travelling for days nonstop. Cadyan's body was stiff and aching from being cramped in the small space for so long, not to mention struggling to contain his nerves. He hated travelling with his father.

The door opened, and a footman hurried to lower the steps onto the ground.

"Out," snapped Casréyan. He grabbed Cadyan's arm and shoved him towards the door.

"I can walk by myself," said Cadyan. He yanked his arm out of his father's grip and clambered down the stairs into the chilly night air.

The ground was dusty beneath his feet, and the dry breeze was uncomfortable on his skin. He hated being this far away from the city, so close to the desert. Out here everything was desiccated and lifeless. It was depressing. He glanced behind him, wondering how far away the southern coastline was. The docks couldn't be far, but he saw no sign of water. Just arid, burnt desert.

The royal guard dismounted their horses, lighting additional torches and scanning the area for threats. Cadyan shook his head and suppressed the urge to roll his eyes.

As if anyone would be stupid enough to attack the king.

One of the fírkon broke away from the group and walked to join them. Even in the dark, Cadyan recognized Slaedir. His uniform was a darker colour, and his gilded sword was a stark contrast to the dull steel of the others.

"Your Majesty." He inclined his head towards Casréyan and tossed Cadyan a small sneer. He wore the same self-important smirk that he always wore, and he carried himself with an arrogant swagger.

Cadyan longed to hit the maífírkon, but he forced himself not to react. Slaedir made his skin crawl, but he knew better than to do something that might provoke his father. The journey had been bad enough as it was.

"My reports say the ship should arrive before the night is out," said Slaedir.

"Good." Casréyan turned and started walking north along the raised and uneven terrain. Faint lights were visible, emanating from the compound ahead. "I'm pleased at how quickly Osrin seems to find replacements."

"Indeed." Slaedir hurried to keep up with him.

Cadyan took a deep breath and followed them. He wasn't entirely sure why his father had insisted on bringing him along on this journey. Whatever the reason, it wouldn't be pleasant.

Years had passed since he'd been forced to join the king on business outside the city. The last time they'd been anywhere together, Cadyan had been fourteen and they'd gone to Sidina. Cadyan had snuck off to try one of Sidina's famous healing pools, and Casréyan had rewarded him with a broken arm and three cracked ribs.

At least then, Zadílar had managed to intervene before

Casréyan went too far. But there would be no one to help on this trip.

Cadyan followed the king and his firkon farther inland along the rough dirt path. They passed overturned carts, crumbled walls, and old, dilapidated fencing until they emerged into what looked like a semi-permanent war camp. Dozens of buildings surrounded a series of makeshift streets, and the place was crawling with firkon. Some seemed to be off duty, relaxing for the evening. They gathered around campfires, drinking and eating. Others patrolled the streets, shouting orders and marshalling lines of slave workers.

At the end of the street, Cadyan saw a series of tunnels set into the massive outline of an old foundation. The jagged rise and fall of the landscape beyond it was irregular and unnatural. The remnants of the city were buried beneath centuries of overgrowth, detritus, and sand.

"Your Majesty," called one of the firkon near the tunnels. He rushed forward to greet them. "Maífirkon, sir. Your Highness," he addressed Cadyan last and inclined his head to all of them in turn. He looked strained and nervous.

"Explain to me what happened," commanded Casréyan. He marched through the camp, ignoring the other firkon as they snapped to attention when he passed.

"Well, one of the shafts collapsed, my lord," spluttered the man as he hurried to keep up with his king. "The support beams were weak and the more we carved away, the less they could support the ceiling."

Casréyan came to a halt at the entrance to the nearest tunnel. A single lantern dangled on a post beside the entrance, lighting the narrow, cramped passage. The passage seemed to extend deep below the ground and out of sight into darkness.

Casréyan glanced down the shaft with a grimace. "How much is this going to delay you?"

The firkon fidgeted. "Well, it'll take years to re-excavate

the area, and with the number of workers we lost..." He gestured to a hill a few feet away and Cadyan realized with a jolt, that it wasn't a hill at all. It was a mound of human bodies. Fresh corpses, broken and bent into grotesque positions.

"These are just the ones we've cleared out so far," said the firkon.

Casréyan brushed away the comment. "That is no matter," he said without emotion. "A new shipment should arrive by the morning. You'll have plenty of new labourers."

"Ah, yes, good," said the firkon, but Cadyan noticed a shadow in the man's eyes. This firkon didn't relish the idea of more workers, more bodies to sacrifice to the search. And Cadyan couldn't blame him. He was having trouble taking his own eyes off the sickening heap of bodies.

"What about the other tunnels?" asked Casréyan.

"Well, if you'll follow me." The firkon turned and led the way forward. Cadyan made a move to follow but his father put out his arm to stop him. "You," he barked at one of the other men, "take the prince and show him around the rest of the site. He needs to learn."

"Yes, of course, Your Majesty," replied the firkon, and there was a definite note of relief in his voice. Cadyan thought he understood. None of these men wanted to be around Casréyan while he assessed the site's damage.

Come to think of it, neither did Cadyan.

"What's your name?" asked Cadyan as the firkon came to join him.

"Lundril, Your Highness."

Cadyan nodded and motioned for him to lead the way.

Lundril led Cadyan through the camp, pointing out the various sights. He showed Cadyan the tools first. Pickaxes and shovels, pans and carts. Some carts were pulled by animals—oxen and horses. But most were pulled by people. Pairs of slaves struggled to remove carts of debris from the tunnels, emptying them for other workers to sort.

The workers paused to watch their prince pass. Cadyan averted his eyes.

"And here come the barracks," said Lundril, leading Cadyan to a series of stone buildings along the western side of the camp.

As they entered the first building, Cadyan had to suppress a gasp. The barracks were revolting—nothing like the barracks in the city. These were cramped, and they smelled like decades of sweat, piss, and grime. The roof leaked, and the walls were mouldy. If this was how the firkon slept, he didn't want to know where the slaves spent their evenings.

But Lundril took him to the slave lodgings next, and they were even worse than Cadyan expected. The buildings were half the size of the soldier barracks and filled with rickety hammocks instead of beds. Little black bugs scuttled along the musty ropes.

"It's two to a hammock," announced Lundril, as if Cadyan should be pleased with how economical they were being. "And they sleep in shifts so there's never an hour wasted."

Cadyan coughed and recoiled as an enormous rat darted past his feet. "It smells like death in here," he said, choking on the air. His eyes burned with the sting of it.

"Yeah." Lundril shrugged like it didn't bother him. "Well, the ones who don't die in the tunnels usually die in here. We try to rinse them down once every couple of months, but it's an awful waste of water if you ask me."

Cadyan stifled a gag as they turned and left the building. The stench seemed to follow them out into the lane. It took several minutes before he could breathe normally again.

"I know what'll make you feel better," said Lundril, grinning as they approached another building. "You ever been to a brothel before?"

Cadyan was taken aback. He shook his head, suddenly nervous.

"Come on," said Lundril, and he pushed open the door.

Cadyan was momentarily stunned as he stood in the doorway, gaping at the scene in front of him. He had never seen anything like this before. The small, smoky room was packed with half-naked people in various indecent positions. They were entwined in pairs and groups, lounging on various pieces of mismatched furniture, laughing, groaning, and grunting. The torches on the walls cast a dim, orange glow over the room. A sultry voice drifted from somewhere towards the back of the room as someone sang along with a steady drum pulse.

Cadyan was embarrassed and uncomfortable, gazing at the unseemly display of bodies. He saw the depraved pleasure on the firkon's faces, and the masks of resignation on the others.

"There are private rooms too," said Lundril, indicating the staircase at the back of the building. "If you want to..." He trailed off as one of the women approached them. She was at least a decade older than Cadyan, but very petite, with long brown hair cascading over her shoulders, and dull, sunken eyes. She wore nothing but a thin robe, laced at the front, exposing strips of bare flesh.

"Special price for two," she said, stepping forward and smiling expectantly at them. Then she recognized Cadyan and her smile widened, though it still didn't reach her eyes. "I'll give you the *royal* treatment."

Cadyan just gaped at her, unsure how to respond. She smiled indulgently. "I tell you what, first time is free." She reached her hand out towards him, but Cadyan recoiled, shaking his head.

"No," he said, repulsed. He didn't want any of these people to touch him.

The woman looked offended. She muttered under her

breath as she stalked off to join a group of people in the far corner.

Lundril was eyeing Cadyan with an almost pitying expression.

The heat of embarrassment rose in Cadyan's neck. "What?" he snapped.

"Well... um... There are boys if you'd prefer..." He trailed off, looking awkward.

Cadyan's face flushed, and he shook his head. "I'm fine," he said. A part of him felt ashamed that he didn't want to partake, but the thought of doing what these people were doing made him queasy. He hated being touched at the best of times. Physical intimacy made him nauseous. He'd never been interested in it, and certainly not like this.

"There's also the back rooms," continued Lundril. He seemed eager to find an option that would appeal to Cadyan. "That's where we bring the new arrivals. First arrival of a new group of slaves always means unspoiled goods. A lot of the men like that better, you know? They like the ones who put up a fight..." He shrugged. "You want to see?"

Cadyan was torn between a morbid curiosity and an urge to run screaming from the place. He just shook his head and didn't speak.

Lundril eyed him closely. "All right, then. Suit yourself." He sounded disappointed and more than a little concerned, like he feared for Cadyan's sanity. This made Cadyan even more embarrassed and angry.

They made their way through the rest of the camp, stopping to explore each of the other buildings, including the cookhouse, and the excavation pavilion, where all the rubble from the tunnels was sorted and examined to assess its worth.

"And last but not least, the discipline cabins," announced Lundril. He stopped in front of a series of small stone structures, each the size of a closet. Each cabin was locked from the outside, and the doors had one small slit of a window to let in air. "That's where we keep the really unruly ones. The ones who don't seem to break with pain. We leave them there for days or weeks depending on what they need. Sometimes even a few of the junior firkon need some tuning up." The man snorted. "Once, we even forgot one in there and by the time we remembered, well..." He grimaced at Cadyan. "Oy!" He banged on the door and Cadyan heard a sudden yelp and a scuffling sound inside. "Still moving, that's good." The firkon grinned at him.

Cadyan's queasiness returned with force. He tried to ignore it, but his legs trembled as they made their way back to the main camp and the entrance to the collapsed tunnel.

When they arrived, Casréyan and Slaedir had already returned. They were talking with a group of men, and Casréyan looked even more irritable than earlier.

"Is this really as fast as they can work?" he snapped. He was watching a train of emaciated slaves make their way out of the tunnel, stumbling under the weight of the rubble they carried.

Halfway down the line, a young boy of about seven or eight tripped and fell to the ground, slicing open his knees on the hard stones.

"Useless brat," shouted one of the firkon. He grabbed the boy by the arm and yanked him back up to his feet.

The boy had tears in his eyes, but he wasn't making a sound, as if he were afraid to draw attention to his sadness. Cadyan remembered that feeling all too well.

The firkon shoved the boy back into the line, but he just stumbled and tripped again, yelping as he hit the ground. The firkon was livid. He shouted something as he raised his crop preparing to snap it against the boy's back.

Before Cadyan registered what he was doing, he'd stepped forward. "Don't," he said, taking himself by surprise, "I mean, just leave him. He's fine, he can..." Cadyan trailed off at the expressions of surprise and indignation on everyone's faces.

Then a sharp pain twisted up his arm as his father grabbed him with a vice grip and spun him around. "What's the matter with you, boy?" he snarled.

Cadyan's heart raced. "No-nothing, Father, sorry, I didn't mean—" But his father backhanded him before he could finish his sentence. Casréyan's knuckles collided with Cadyan's lips and teeth. Cadyan spun around, clutching at his mouth and tasting the blood now trickling from the wound.

"How many times must I tell you not to call me that?" shouted Casréyan. "You never listen. I am the *king*. And don't you dare give orders to my firkon, boy. You don't defend vermin. You don't tell me what to do with my property."

Cadyan straightened himself up, wiping the blood away from his mouth. He caught sight of Slaedir's delighted expression over the king's shoulder, and he felt a flash of hatred for the man. He knew Slaedir always enjoyed watching Casréyan abuse his son.

Cadyan took a deep breath, trying to compose himself.

"I'm sorry, *Your Majesty*," he corrected, struggling to keep his voice even. "It won't happen again." It took every ounce of control he had to remain calm in that moment. He had learned the hard way many times that showing emotion only made his father worse.

"Really?" Casréyan snarled at him, then his eyes darted to the left. "You there, child. Come here." He beckoned for the slave boy to approach, and a pit formed in Cadyan's stomach.

If the boy had been terrified before, it was nothing compared to how he looked now. He stumbled towards them, trembling from head to toe, tears still streaming down his cheeks.

"Clearly the prince was not satisfied with the punishment being offered," jeered Casréyan to the crowd of onlookers. "He wants to take charge of it himself." Casréyan snatched the crop out of the fírkon's hand and held it out towards Cadyan.

There was a pause as Cadyan just stared at the crop in his father's hand. "W-what?"

Casréyan's nostrils flared, and he leaned in so only Cadyan could hear him. "Let me put it this way," he said in a deadly whisper, "you either punish the boy, or I punish you both. And I will not use the whip."

Cadyan saw the unbridled hatred in his father's expression. As terrified as he was, a part of him still wanted to refuse. He longed to stand up to the man and prove he wasn't afraid. He seriously considered it for a few seconds. But his moment of hesitation made Casréyan's anger even more intense. The king's eyes flashed gold in the moonlight.

A burning sensation exploded beneath Cadyan's skin, like his blood was on fire. He gasped and nearly dropped to the ground in agony. "All right," he spluttered, holding up his hand in surrender. The pain mounted towards a sharp peak, then it stopped.

Casréyan glared at him with a ferocious look in his eye.

Cadyan glanced at the surrounding fírkon and saw the cruel grins on their faces. As he stood up straight again, trying to regain his composure, his face burned with humiliation.

"I'll do it," he said, snatching the crop out of his father's hand and ignoring the urge to use it on the man himself.

He took a step towards the trembling boy. The boy was crying even harder now. He stared at Cadyan with imploring eyes and backed away slightly.

A tremble ran through Cadyan's body. He hated himself for being weak.

Why didn't I keep my mouth shut?

He closed his eyes momentarily and took a deep breath. Then, before he could lose his nerve, he raised his arm over his head and brought it back down in a quick motion. There was a swish and a crack, and a strong vibration ran through his arm.

The boy yelped and fell to the ground, crying even harder as he curled up into a ball. The sight of it churned Cadyan's already upset stomach.

"Again," commanded Casréyan.

Cadyan's arm shook as he raised it up and slashed out again. The vibration was more intense this time, and the boy was sobbing now.

"Again."

Cadyan closed his eyes and repeated the gesture. Again, and again, and again. His entire body reacted to the movement. Where at first there had been a strained discomfort, now there was a sick rush.

The more the boy cried, the more exhilarated Cadyan felt.

He opened his eyes to stare at the boy as he repeated the gesture. For a moment, he saw Casréyan at his feet, weak and whimpering. In his mind, Cadyan broke the whip against his father, instead of the boy. And the blood now spraying back at him was Casréyan's blood, the cries were Casréyan's cries.

Faster and harder, Cadayn brought the crop down several more times, enjoying the sensation in his muscles.

"All right," said Casréyan, and he sounded almost bored now.

Cadyan started and looked up. He had almost forgotten where he was. Glancing around, he saw the firkon and the slaves staring at him with an expression he'd never seen before. Was that fear in their eyes? They averted their gazes, and muttered to each other.

Reluctantly, Cadyan looked down at the crumpled body at his feet. The boy was unconscious now. His shirt was ripped to shreds and soaked in blood. Long gashes lined his fragile, little back.

Cadayn stumbled back and dropped the crop. Casréyan and

Slaedir were talking, but he didn't know what they were saying. He didn't care. He stood frozen as one of the firkon hurried forward and dragged the boy's limp frame out of sight. The other slaves stared at him with hatred and revulsion.

Cadyan teetered, light-headed and weakened. "I have to..." he muttered, taking a shaky step back as his stomach churned and the bile rose in his throat. He didn't want these people to see him throw up. "I just..." He gestured behind him and turned to walk away as quickly as he could.

When no one tried to stop him, he broke into a jog, stumbling away towards the nearest barrack. He skidded to a halt, nearly colliding with the wall, and scrambled around the back and out of sight. Then he doubled over, hot and nauseated as he tried not to think about what he'd just done. And then he retched.

He heaved and vomited until his throat was sore and his stomach was empty. Then he gagged and spluttered on the hollow air. It took a few minutes before he regained control. He leaned against the barrack wall, panting and sweating. His mouth tasted foul. He rubbed the spit away and closed his eyes.

"Here," said a voice from the shadows, and he nearly jumped out of his skin. He hadn't realized anyone was there.

A young man dressed in a firkon uniform emerged into the pale moonlight. He held a canteen out towards Cadyan, a look of calm understanding on his face.

Cadyan glanced around reflexively, making sure no one else was with them. Then he relaxed. "Thanks," he muttered, embarrassed. Sweat beaded on his forehead as he took the canteen and rinsed his mouth.

He handed it back to the firkon and surveyed him for a moment. The boy looked only a few years older than Cadyan, but he was already a man. His facial hair was coming in evenly and he didn't have any youthful air about him at all.

"I'm not upset, I just..." But he trailed off, unable to finish the sentence.

"Yeah, I know," said the firkon. He squinted at the dark horizon as though remembering some distant memory.

Cadyan watched him for a moment, strangely calmed by his presence. "How long have you been here?" he asked. He didn't know why he asked it, but he was curious.

The firkon paused before responding. "It's hard to remember."

Cadyan stood up straighter and looked at the man more closely. "You look sort of familiar. Did you fight in the last tournament?"

The firkon nodded.

"Okay, that must be why I recognize you."

The young soldier paused, straightening his sword belt. "Must be," he replied without looking at Cadyan.

"So, you ranked low in the tournament, then? My father doesn't send men out here unless they place low in the tournament." It was true. Casréyan used this place as a sort-of punishment for the firkon. Cadyan had never understood why until now.

"He has other reasons."

Cadyan frowned, feeling strangely uncomfortable, like he should feel guilty for something, but he didn't know what. "How old are you?" he asked. The last tournament was almost four years ago. This boy didn't look old enough to have fought in it.

The firkon looked at him with a strange expression on his face. "I don't know," he replied.

Cadyan would have laughed if he weren't so miserable. But then he caught sight of the expression on the firkon's face. "You... you're serious?" he asked a little nervously. "You really don't know how old you are?"

The firkon shrugged. "Does it matter?"

Cadyan thought about that for a second. He didn't know how to respond, but he couldn't help feeling like it did matter. What could have happened to this man that he didn't remember his own age?

"What's your name?" he asked.

The firkon frowned as though struggling to remember. "Julyán," he replied finally, and he looked almost relieved.

"And have you ever had to... have you..." He gestured feebly in the direction of the tunnels. He felt like an infant asking it.

Julyán looked at him with a dark expression. "Yes," he replied, "many times."

Cadyan felt a sick admiration for how calm he sounded.

Then he groaned and pushed the hair out of his face. "I feel so... I..." Cadyan trailed off, unable to continue. His hands shook and his heart pounded.

Julyán nodded like he understood. "It doesn't matter," he said, turning to face Cadyan with a hard expression. "You have two choices. You either learn to enjoy that feeling, or you learn to *stop* feeling."

Cadyan's stomach clenched. He wanted to disagree, but he couldn't. This man was right. "S-so which option did you choose?"

Julyán didn't respond. Instead, he just turned his eyes back to the dark horizon. Cadyan thought he knew what the answer would be.

"I have to return to my post," said Julyán after a few more minutes of silence. He inclined his head before turning to walk away.

Cadyan sighed and turned to follow him. His father would be looking for him soon.

He and Julyán made their way along the back of the barrack until they reached the edge of the wall. Julyán moved to turn the corner but Cadyan reached out and grabbed his arm to stop him. Voices sounded in the dark passageway ahead.

"I don't know why you brought him, frankly," came Slaedir's unmistakable oily voice. "He's too weak, too much like his mother…"

Cadyan thought he noticed Julyán tense up beside him. The young firkon must recognize his leader's voice.

"I know. So, the sooner we find that crown the better," said Casréyan in an irritable tone. "Then I can finally be rid of him."

"Why not just take care of him now?" asked Slaedir. "I'd be happy to do it for you."

"Because, as the chaplain delights in reminding me, I still need an heir," said Casréyan with an edge. "At least for now. But once I find that crown, I'll slit the brat's throat myself."

Their voices trailed off as they moved away in the other direction.

All sensation drained from Cadyan's body, leaving him hollow and weak. He couldn't believe what he'd just heard. He'd always known his father hated him, but he'd never imagined that hatred could be so strong. Was his father really planning to murder him? His own son?

Cadyan glanced at Julyán and saw a strange expression on the firkon's face, almost like he wanted to sympathize but didn't know how.

Neither of them spoke as they started walking again. When they arrived back at the central camp, Cadyan turned to leave but Julyán called after him.

"Hey!" He lowered his voice and glanced around to make sure no one was listening. "You want to survive? Figure out what his weaknesses are and use them against him. Make sure his weaknesses are your strengths."

He gave Cadyan a meaningful look and then nodded stiffly before turning and walking away.

Cadyan watched him go, feeling exhausted and miserable. Part of him wasn't sure he wanted to survive anymore. What was the point of living when no one cared about him? What was the point of continuing? So he could visit brothels, and learn to enjoy whipping slaves? So he could spend his days waiting and wondering when his father would finally crack?

"We're leaving," said Casréyan as he arrived back at the central camp with Slaedir in tow. He beckoned for Cadyan to follow, but Cadyan found himself unable to move.

"Move it!" snarled Casréyan. "Or I'll leave you here to join the slaves. Then you might at least be useful for a change."

This comment finally broke through Cadayn's stupor. A white-hot rage blazed through him. It was a rage unlike anything he'd ever experienced. Blinding, burning, all-consuming. He glared at his father, finally realizing something he should have realized years ago.

He hated the man as much or more than the man hated him.

Gone was the last vestige of childish hope that he could earn his father's respect or love. All there was now, was a cold determination.

A determination to be better than him. To take everything his father ever wanted and leave him powerless and pitiful. To usurp him in every possible way.

And when his father was broken and begging to die, Cadyan would finally take his life. He'd use his father's power to fuel his own. And Casréyan's soul would be trapped forever, enslaved by the son he loathed so much.

PART II

13

SEASICK

Diyah groaned and kept her forehead planted firmly against her knees, trying not to be sick. She closed her eyes and wrapped her arms around her legs as the world around her rocked with the movement of the waves. The stench of rotten seaweed and musty cedarwood filled her nostrils, threatening to overpower her.

She supposed there was something ironic about a healer suffering from seasickness with no way to treat it or make it stop.

"We're nearly there," said Jémys.

"You keep saying that," she groaned, tilting her head to look at him. "I'm beginning to think you've been lying to make me feel better."

"What, me?" Jémys pulled a face of mock offence.

Diyah smiled and sat up, resting her head on the back of the cabin wall. Despite their current circumstances, Jémys seemed to have developed a positive attitude that was impossible to resist. Now that they'd left Caerlon City and were on their way to find Catanya, he seemed to have trouble containing his excitement.

"I hope you're right," said Diyah in a weak voice. "I will be so grateful to stand on dry land again."

It had been days since they'd arrived at the port, looking for the smuggler that Ayr had told them about. They'd managed to find his ship quite easily, and, to Diyah's surprise, Jémys had recognized it almost immediately.

"I've seen this ship before," he whispered to her. Something in his voice told Diyah he had expected this.

"What? Where?"

Diyah hadn't seen many ships in her life, and never one this close. It loomed over the port with a sort of audacious grandeur, its wood so dark it was nearly black, but with an ominous ruddy tinge. Diyah had to crane her neck to see the top of the hull, not to mention the three enormous masts stretching into the sky.

"Months ago, with Catanya and Drayk near Glorna. They're marauders—pirates," he added.

Diyah didn't like the sound of that. "I thought this smuggler was someone Ayr knew..." But then she remembered what Ayr had said about him transporting prisoners for Caerlon.

"Yes, but his crew doesn't fly under Ayr's flag or Cadyan's. They have no allegiance. They can't be trusted."

Diyah bit her lip. Under normal circumstances, she wouldn't dream of doing business with people like this. But these were anything but normal circumstances.

"Well... I don't think we have any other choice," she muttered, ignoring the fact that every instinct in her body told her to turn around.

"No, I suppose we don't," said Jémys. He beckoned for her to follow him as he stepped forward and made his way towards the ship.

They stopped near the edge of the dock and watched the men on deck. They were busy loading crates of cargo and barrels of supplies for the voyage. Now that she was closer,

The Age of Resonance

Diyah noticed the figurehead adorning the front of the vessel. It depicted a creature with large fangs and horns on either side of its head. It looked like a cross between an enormous, scaly serpent and a shark, with deep, dark eye holes that seemed to follow her movements. Its twisted body coiled around the fore of the ship, disappearing into the water.

Diyah shuddered, struggling to wrench her gaze away. Then something creaked and she craned her neck up. Three men dangled precariously from ropes at least thirty feet in the air. Two more were climbing the swaying shroud lines to unfurl the masts and get ready to set sail. A momentary dizziness overcame Diyah at the sight.

"Oy! You there," called one of the men, pointing at them and making them jump. His face was weather-beaten and tanned, and he wore a large tricorn hat and a whale skin jacket. The compass, sword, and spyglass strapped to his belt told Diyah he was likely an important member of the crew. "What are yous two lookin' at?"

Diyah and Jémys exchanged nervous glances. "We're looking for a man called Osrin," said Diyah.

The man surveyed them for a moment. "Oy, Captain," he called, louder than Diyah would have liked. "This lot 'ere want a word with ye."

A tall man with severe features pushed past his men and stopped a few feet away, staring down at them appraisingly. The lines on the captain's face and the greying sides of his thick, dark hair betrayed his age, but they did nothing to lessen the ferocity of his presence. He looked wild and dangerous.

"What do you want?" he asked in a gruff voice.

Jémys tilted his head and frowned at the man. "Captain Osrin?" he asked with a hint of surprise.

"Depends who's asking," replied the captain. "Who're you, then?"

Jémys cast Diyah a furtive glance. "Our names aren't important," he called.

Osrin narrowed his eyes and jumped off the ship onto the dock. "You know who says things like that?" he asked in a low voice. "People whose names are worth knowing."

Diyah rolled her eyes and brushed past Jémys. They couldn't afford to waste time. "Fine, my name is Genna, and this is my brother Grante," she lied smoothly. "We were told you could help us."

Osrin leered at her. "Is that so?" he said, looking back at his men with a lecherous grin. They had all stopped working to watch the exchange. "Help you with what, gorgeous?"

Jémys stiffened. "Safe passage," he said, taking a half-step forward. "Out of Caerlon and into Awnell."

Osrin turned his attention back towards Jémys. "Really? And what makes you think I can help you with that?"

"Well, it's true, isn't it?" said Jémys.

Osrin smiled. "Possibly. But my help doesn't come cheap." He picked at a spot on his chin and watched them out of the corner of his eye.

Jémys clenched his jaw like he was fighting the urge to retort. "We can pay you. We have gold."

Osrin nodded. "And what if I'd rather have a different form of payment?" he asked, staring at Diyah with hunger and delight.

Diyah's skin crawled but she held his gaze. "You'll take the gold or we'll take our business elsewhere," she declared. She'd had enough experience dealing with degenerate men like this, and she wasn't about to let him intimidate them or get in their way. Not after everything they'd been through to get here.

"Oho!" He snickered and clapped his hands together. "Feisty. I like that." Then he turned his attention back to Jémys. "Ten gold pieces each and you mop the decks with the rest of the swabbies, boy," he added, holding out his filthy hand for the money.

"Fine," muttered Jémys, reaching into his pocket and pulling out the coins Fehla had given them. "But we get a private cabin," he added, before handing over the gold. He cast an apprehensive look in Diyah's direction.

Osrin looked disgruntled, but he nodded begrudgingly. "Welcome aboard," he said, closing his fist around the money and grinning at them.

The first few days had been uncomfortable at best. But once Diyah's seasickness had arrived, the trip had become almost unbearable for her. Jémys was doing his best to take care of her, but he also had to make good on his promise to help the crew. So Diyah found herself alone a lot of the time in their cramped, mildewy cabin, with nothing but her dizziness and upset stomach to keep her company.

Jémys joined her in the evenings whenever he could, and he tried to distract her. He spent a good deal of time trying to convince her to eat something, but she struggled to keep anything down.

"Try this." He handed her a loaf of plain bread. "Come on, you need to eat something," he said when she tried to push his hand away.

"Ugh, I can't," whimpered Diyah, shaking her head. "I'll eat when we're back on land."

Jémys sighed and nodded reluctantly. Then he returned the bread to the bag without eating any himself.

"I hate sailing," he said, sliding down to sit next to her. He closed his eyes and rested his head against the wall.

Diyah suspected Jémys was a little nervous around the sea, but he was putting on a brave face for her.

"Did you see anything else today?" she asked after a while.

Jémys had been using his time with the crew to explore the ship and try to learn as much as he could about the pirates.

They both agreed that these men couldn't be trusted and the more they learned about them, the better.

"Well, the hold is full of barrels of liquor—most likely stolen from Caerlon. But there were also several large crates. A few of them were empty but there were two that I couldn't see into."

"Crates?" asked Diyah. "You mean for cargo?"

"Could be," said Jémys. "But if he's transporting cargo for Caerlon, why hide it?"

"Hmm... maybe he's bringing something back for Ayr?"

Diyah considered the possibilities of smuggled goods that could be lying in those crates. Jewels, weapons, silks... She remembered all the stories about pirates she'd heard growing up. Whatever was in there, it was probably valuable.

"Did you get into the brig?" she asked.

"No, not yet."

Before they'd even set foot on the ship, Jémys and Diyah had agreed that if they found any prisoners being transported for Cadyan, they would use their remaining gold to purchase their freedom. Neither of them could stomach the thought of standing by as these smugglers sold people into slavery.

Jémys had been trying for days to get into the ship's prison and see if anyone was down there. But it was the most heavily guarded area of the ship. He hadn't been able to get near it.

"It's okay," said Diyah. "We should be past the Tirimsi coast by now. He would have stopped if he had anyone to deliver in Bratia." She turned to look at Jémys, hoping to hear him agree with her. Instead, she saw him staring at the door with a glazed look in his eye. "What is it?" she asked.

Jémys shook his head, frowning. "Osrin... There's something familiar about him, but I can't quite place it."

"You think you've met him before?" she asked, sitting up straighter.

"Possibly." Jémys's forehead creased as he thought about it.

"I have worked all over the kingdom. It's possible I met him on one of those jobs, but if so…" He looked at her nervously.

If Jémys had met the captain in his travels, there was every possibility Osrin would recognize him now. Diyah expressed her concerns, but Jémys seemed to think it was unlikely.

"Besides, even if he recognizes me—so what? I'm nobody. Just a villager from Finnua, right?"

Diyah thought about it. "I suppose you're right," she said, nodding. "And, if anything, he's more likely to recognize me, isn't he? I mean, everyone in the city seems to know who I am now that the tournament is over."

"Mmm, the maífirkon's wife," mumbled Jémys, staring at the wall.

Diyah felt a sudden wave of sadness. She had been trying not to think about Julyán because every time she did, she felt wracked with guilt for leaving him behind. She was terrified for him. What if Cadyan found out that he had let them escape?

"I'm sure he's fine, Diyah," said Jémys, interpreting her silence.

"I hope so," she said, fiddling with the sleeve of her dress.

Jémys rested his hand on her arm. "It's better this way," he said. "I know he helped us, but Julyán is one of them. He has been for a long time. I'm not sure he knows how to be anything else. I know you think he can be different, and I hope you're right, I really do," he added hastily. "But it will never be enough. It will never change the things he's done… Diyah, he's the reason my father is dead."

Diyah sighed heavily. Jémys was right, Julyán had done a lot of terrible things, but it bothered her to hear Jémys blame him for their father. She had never understood why Julyán wouldn't tell Jémys the truth. And now they might never see him again… Surely it couldn't hurt to tell Jémys now. She couldn't stand the thought of him living the rest of his life, still hating his brother.

"He's not," she said quietly.

"Not what?" asked Jémys, raising his eyebrows.

"He's not the reason." Diyah took a deep breath and looked Jémys in the eye. Then she recounted the entire story, everything Julyán had told her about his family and his time with the fírkon. She told him about her encounter with Cadyan in the woods and how Julyán had intervened, how that altercation had led Casréyan to target their family. She knew there was a chance this could make everything worse—Jémys might blame *her* for what had happened—but it was a chance she needed to take. Both Julyán and Jémys deserved better.

"I don't understand." Jémys looked stunned when Diyah finished talking. "You mean to tell me that Julyán never betrayed my father? And all this time, he's been... I can't believe it," he muttered, rubbing his face with his hands. "And he told you this, Julyán told you this?"

"Yes," said Diyah. "But he didn't want you to know."

"Why?" Jémys climbed to his feet, but he was too tall. He had to stoop to avoid the low ceiling.

Diyah shook her head sadly. "He said it would be easier for you to hate him. But honestly, I think it was easier for *him*, easier than the risk of losing you all over again. He's damaged, Jémys, but he's not gone. And he loves you. I know he does."

Tears formed in Jémys's eyes, and she reached out and took his hand.

"All this time..." Jémys's voice was disjointed and heavy with emotion. "They were punishing him! Of course, my father was trying to protect him... I just wish I'd known. I... I could have— I should have done something!"

"What could you have done, Jémys? You were just a boy when it all happened."

Jémys jerked his shoulders as if he were trying to shake off the unpleasant truth. "Still... so was Julyán, though, wasn't he? I never thought... He must have been so scared. Forced to live with them all this time. Forced to do what they do... Competing in that tournament. Obeying Slaedir and Casréyan, even after..."

"It's okay," said Diyah, squeezing his hand. "You'll see him again and you can tell him... We both can." It pained her to see Jémys so upset, but she was also relieved. Relieved that he didn't seem to blame her for what happened, and relieved he was finally letting go of the anger he'd been harbouring towards Julyán. She had hated being caught between the two of them.

Jémys nodded and averted his eyes. He rubbed the tears out of them and cleared his throat, trying to regain composure. Then he slumped back down onto the floor beside her.

They sat together in silence for a while, each lost in their thoughts about what lay behind them and what lay ahead. Although she was eager to reunite with Catanya, Diyah had never been thrilled about the idea of leaving Julyán. It had seemed like the right thing to do when she'd thought he was still loyal to Cadyan, but now... She couldn't stop replaying their last conversation in her head.

I want you to be happy.

Those words made her ache. The look on his face as he'd said them, like he couldn't believe his own feelings.

He loved her—she knew that now. And he was willing to lie to Cadyan for her. But he'd been lying to Cadyan for weeks. He'd known Catanya was alive, and he hadn't told anyone. Why?

She still had so many unanswered questions. Now that she finally had what she wanted—she was finally free—she felt an uncontrollable desire to turn back. The only thing keeping her moving forward was the excitement of being reunited with Catanya.

A patch of moonlight streamed through the tiny window on the cabin wall. Diyah watched the specks of dust floating in the air, wondering where her friend was—whether she was standing under that same moonlight. "What do you think Catanya is doing right now?" she asked.

Jémys closed his eyes, thinking. "Hopefully she's somewhere safe."

Diyah nodded and rested her head on the wall again, trying to picture her friend.

"To tell you the truth," he continued in a low voice. "I'm a little nervous to see her again." Jémys rubbed his neck in obvious discomfort. "I mean, what if Ayr is right?" he asked, frowning. "What if Catanya thinks I don't love her? We didn't exactly part on the best of terms. What if she doesn't love me anymore?"

Diyah shook her head. "People don't just fall out of love that easily," she said with a kind smile. A tightness settled in her chest as she privately hoped her words applied to Julyán just as much as Catanya.

Jémys sighed and nodded. "Yeah, but what if she has moved on?"

Diyah shrugged. "We probably can't fathom what she's been through these past few months. Are you the same person you were when you last saw her?"

"No."

"Right, me neither. I imagine she's changed a lot too, but that doesn't mean she doesn't love us. I think we just have to trust that, despite everything, the connections we share are strong enough to withstand anything."

"Yeah, you're right."

"Besides, it could be nice to start again, don't you think? Sometimes a fresh start is the best thing that can happen."

"Yeah," muttered Jémys. "I guess I'll be making fresh starts with a lot of people."

Sympathy swelled in Diyah's chest, and she took his hand in hers. "We all will be."

Later that evening, after Jémys had fallen asleep, Diyah was pleased to find she felt better. After being cooped up in that room for so long, she yearned to stretch her legs and breathe the fresh air above deck before trying to sleep. So, she stood up, bracing her hand on the ceiling, and crept out of the room.

It was a calm night, and the wind was cool. She stared out at the water, listening to the waves break against the hull. For a moment, she appreciated the appeal of living a life at sea—the freedom of having a ship and being untethered to any kingdom. Yes, she could understand wanting to have that.

"Careful on the deck," said a voice behind her.

She turned to see Osrin emerging from the captain's quarters. A shiver ran down her spine that had nothing to do with the temperature.

"I was just heading in," she said, turning to walk away from him.

"What's the rush?" he called after her. "You left your husband back in Caerlon, didn't you? I imagine your nights are rather lonely now, aren't they? Or is that why you ran off with *him*?" He gestured below deck.

"Excuse me?" Diyah turned around and glared at him.

"Oh, come on," his voice dripped with delight, and he sauntered over to her. "I recognized you the minute I set eyes on you. Your face isn't the kind that goes unnoticed. The whole city's been going on and on about the beautiful girl that was sold off to that man—that statue of a man. He looks good, I'll give you that, but he doesn't say much, now does he? Of course, once you're married, you do most of your talking with your hands, don't you?" He laughed. Then he clicked his tongue and moved to grab her by the waist, but she smacked him away.

"Keep your hands off me," she said in a low, threatening voice.

"Hmm..." Osrin twisted his face into a mocking frown. "I don't think I will, thanks."

He tried to grab her again, but Diyah was ready for it. She kicked him hard between the legs and watched him crumple to the floor in agony. Then she grabbed him by the hair, drew her dagger from her pocket, and held it against his throat.

"Now listen closely," she said. "I have spent the last eight months of my life living in constant fear of the men around me. Believe me when I say that you pale in comparison to them. So, if you so much as think about touching me again, I will not hesitate to slit your throat. I won't think twice about it either. In fact, I might even enjoy it. Do I make myself clear?"

"This is my ship, you can't just—"

"I can and I will," said Diyah, jerking the knife so it made a small slit just underneath his chin. "Between my husband in Caerlon, and the people waiting for me in Awnell..." She whistled. "You should think twice before doing anything that might upset me. And once I tell Cadyan what you're really smuggling in those crates..." She laughed out loud. "Well, I can guarantee he won't be happy with you."

She stood perfectly still, hoping against all hope that her bluff had worked.

Osrin looked momentarily nervous, but then he grinned. "We're heading to Awnell, not Caerlon. You won't be telling Cadyan nothing."

Diyah frowned. "Maybe not yet," she said, twisting her dagger to press deeper into his skin. "But Cadyan's not the only ruler with an interest in your business. In fact, I have a message for you from Queen Ayr. She and I had a nice little chat about you... And, well, I have the power to make sure you get what you *really* want. You know what I'm talking about, don't you? The thing you want most in this world?"

Osrin's eyes widened. "How do you—"

Diyah jerked the knife. "Continue to harass me, on the

other hand," she said with a growl, "and I'll burn it all to the ground, do you hear me? Everything you hold dear, everything you've ever wanted. I'll reduce it to ash along with you and your little ship. Do I make myself clear?"

"All right," said Osrin, holding his hands up in surrender.

Diyah stepped back and lowered her knife.

Osrin stood up, wincing as he rubbed his neck where she'd cut him. "I tell you, after everything I heard about you, I was picturing someone a little more downtrodden. But you... you're just as ruthless as the rest of them."

"And I trust you won't forget it," declared Diyah. She hardly dared to believe how well her threat had worked.

"Aye, I won't forget," grumbled Osrin, but his eyes still gleamed in the moonlight.

"Good." Diyah turned and strode back to her chambers, working hard to keep her pace even and resist the urge to run. When she had locked the door behind her, she stood for a moment trying to steady her breathing. She looked down at the dagger in her shaky hand. All those months ago, when Julyán had handed it to her outside the armoury, he had told her to channel her anger into it.

I don't have any anger, she had said.

Diyah snorted at the memory. *Julyán would be proud of you,* she thought.

A strange sense of satisfaction warmed her from the inside out. Now, she realized how much she'd changed over the last few months. She could barely remember the innocent, carefree girl she used to be. Her time in Caerlon had changed her forever. It had forged her into someone who knew what she wanted. Someone who wouldn't let anyone get in her way.

Nobody would ever make her feel weak again.

14

A REUNION

The journey out of Túir-Avlea proved to be much smoother than the journey in had been. Now that they knew what to expect, Drayk and Catanya were able to pass through the various phases of the trip without much incident. And now Catanya could use her powers to make it even easier.

A small flame in Catanya's hands illuminated the Shrouded Caves and showed them the way through. The boat rowed itself down the Reflecting Channel, leaving Catanya and Drayk to rest. Thankfully, no ice appeared this time to freeze their passage. They soared out of the Burning Cove without incident. And the journey across the Windy Shoal was nothing more than a pleasant walk, with Catanya directing the Wind away from them.

When they reached the mainland, they made their way carefully back towards the city in order to assess the damage from the battle. Drayk was positive there would be survivors, but Catanya wasn't nearly so optimistic.

"Trust me, Catya," he said confidently. "You don't know these people like I do. They're strong."

Catanya didn't say anything. She hoped Drayk was right.

As they arrived at the eastern escarpment, they caught their first glimpse of Awnell City. Once a beacon of resilience and strength, the kingdom's capital was now a cadaverous wreck of its former glory. Catanya remembered the first time she'd seen it—how its shape had filled her with awe, its presence both splendid and terrifying.

Now the city lay in ruins. The enormous fortress had been shattered, its front torn asunder and scattered through the streets like massive shards of black glass. The open face of the fortress snarled like a wounded beast, its frame exposed to the elements like a skull without its flesh. Small dots of people moved through its unprotected corridors, risking the sheer plummet down to the city below.

It surprised Catanya to see any signs of life in the city at all. She wrenched her gaze from the decimated fortress and scanned the streets. Despite the destruction, Drayk was right. There was a surprising number of people down there, and a handful of ships docked at the port.

Drayk let out a low whistle, a look of horror on his face, but he still managed a small, triumphant smile. He made a move to climb down the embankment, towards the dock and the workers.

"Wait." Catanya grabbed him and held him back. "How do we know they aren't spies for Caerlon?"

Drayk looked back down at the people and took a deep breath. "We have to assume they are. But I tell you what—"

Drayk broke off mid thought, his body rigid. A crunching sound and a sudden pressure against Catanya's back halted her. The pressure increased, and the unmistakable sharp point of a sword dug into her shoulder blade.

"Don't move," said a menacing voice behind them. "Put your hands up where I can see them."

Catanya chanced a half-glance at Drayk as she raised her

hands above her head. Her heart pounded frantically in her chest.

"Turn around slowly and take off your hoods." There was something familiar about that voice.

"Isa?" asked Drayk, frowning. "Is that you?"

"Drayk?"

Catanya turned around. Isa and another young woman she recognized from the court of Awnell stood behind them with outstretched shortswords.

"And Catya—whoa, look at you!" Isa gaped at Catanya. "You look just like him." A shadow of fear flickered in her eyes as she took in Catanya's new appearance. But then her face cracked into a wide grin. "Finally!" she said, grasping arms with each of them. "What took you so long?" She looked at Drayk. "We expected you back weeks ago."

"Oh, well, the journey took longer than expected," muttered Drayk, waving her comment away.

Catanya gave Drayk a searching look. *Longer than expected?*

"Well, come on, then. We've been waiting for you." Isa sheathed her blade, hiding it inside her vest. "Take off your swords and hide them in your cloaks. We don't want to draw any attention from the city's new *wardens*."

They did as she instructed. Then she beckoned for them to follow her, as she led the way down the escarpment, towards the port.

Awnell City had become a labyrinth of broken buildings and dead-end streets. Grey water pooled in holes gouged in the black cobblestones, and everywhere she looked, Catanya saw buildings in ruins and old landmarks destroyed.

"So... wardens? You mean the firkon?" she asked, racing to catch up with Isa. "They're still here?"

"Some," said Isa, nodding. "Most of them are holed up at the fortress, and the others patrol in shifts that are easy to predict. It helps that Cadyan doesn't think we're a threat anymore—nothing but old men, invalids, civilians, children, and... oh yeah, weak, little women." Her lips twisted into a triumphant smile. "As long as we don't look like warriors, they seem unconcerned with us." She indicated the hidden blade in her vest.

As they passed the harbour, Catanya stared out at the waves. Once, the harbour had been grand enough to house dozens of ships. Now it barely had enough docks for the three vessels floating in it.

Distracted by all the destruction she witnessed, it took Catanya a while to realize where Isa was leading them. Then she saw the crooked old sign for *The Fairweather*. It hung more lopsided than ever, dangling above the door. But the rest of the building seemed miraculously unscathed. Even the barnacles latching onto the outer walls looked undisturbed.

"Really?" she asked.

Drayk tossed her a wink as she crossed the threshold into the old battered inn. The familiar smell of stale barkbeer and sweat greeted her nostrils, and she was surprised to find the place full of people talking in overly loud, boisterous voices. But the atmosphere seemed off, like the entire scene had been staged to look like it had on her first night in Awnell. "What's going on here?" she asked.

"We have to keep up appearances," whispered Isa. She nodded curtly at the bartender. Then she crossed the floor towards the stairs at the back without a second glance at the other people in the room. "Follow me." She led the way up to the top floor of the inn.

Isa steered them towards a simple parlour room at the end of the corridor. The room was old and dusty. Several faded armchairs were tucked into corners, and one long table filled the centre of the room. Isa walked straight past the table to the far wall, pulled out her sword and struck the ceiling with it four times in quick succession. Then, giving no indication that she recognized her behaviour as strange, she paused briefly before knocking two more times.

With a faint click and a creak, a trapdoor opened in the ceiling, revealing a well-worn ladder.

"After you," said Drayk, smiling at the surprise on Catanya's face.

Isa pulled the ladder down and proceeded to climb the rungs. Catanya, Drayk, and the other Awnadh followed.

As she stepped off the ladder into the hidden attic, Catanya's jaw dropped. The cramped space had been transformed into a full-blown war room. It was packed with people, strategizing and arguing as they hunched over tables laden with maps and documents. There were no windows, so dozens of lamps were scattered through the room, flooding it with warm, yellow light.

And in the centre of the room, looking as imposing as ever, stood Lia. She turned to stare at them as they emerged. "So, you have come," she said, stepping towards them. "It appears our queen was right. And your time away seems to have taught you a thing or two." Lia gestured towards Catanya's hair.

"It did," said Catanya warily, ducking to avoid the sloped ceilings and low rafters as she stepped forward. She looked at all the soldiers in the room and realized what they all had in common. "Where are all the men?" she asked.

Lia tilted her head to the side as she examined Catanya. "Dead," she said with her usual bluntness. "Dead or captured. The only people left in the city were the women and children, and the men who were too old or untrained, and those too injured to be of any threat."

Hollow grief filled Catanya as she took in what Lia said, but she forced herself to push it aside. "But..." She frowned. "Isn't everyone in Awnell trained to be a warrior?"

"We are," smirked Isa. "When Ayr became queen, she made minimum training mandatory. Everyone has to complete a year of training once they come of age. But Cadyan doesn't know that. He thinks his precious firkon are the best fighters in Mórceá."

"Caerlon's elitism and biases blind it to its own potential," said Lia with a sneer. "In Caerlon, you scoop up your first-born sons to train them as sycophantic prigs. In Awnell, we hone our blades from all types of metal. We work in secret, training real warriors, using Caerlon's ignorance and naïveté to our advantage."

A gentle murmur of amusement went through the room.

"Okay..." Catanya frowned as she worked through the information, struggling to remain composed. "But what about Ayr?"

"The queen was taken prisoner," said Lia without feeling. "As expected."

"As *expected*?" repeated Catanya.

"Yes. And I must say I had my doubts, but as usual, Ayr was right. Her plan is working perfectly."

Catanya raised her eyebrows. "What plan?"

Lia was still staring at Catanya's hair, wearing a dubious expression, but she responded without hesitation. "During the siege of Awnell, when it became clear we would not prevail, Ayr enacted retreat protocols, giving us all a very specific set of instructions." Lia turned and walked back towards the largest table in the attic.

"The priority was to get you out, Catya," said Isa. "Drayk was supposed to go with you somewhere you could learn how to master your powers. Then, when you were ready, make sure you came back here."

"Is that so?" Catanya turned towards Drayk and watched him shift uncomfortably under her gaze. "Then what?" she asked, looking back at Isa, feeling more and more humiliated.

"Then Rey would betray us all and join the fight with Caerlon."

"What?" blurted Catanya, shocked and appalled.

Drayk stifled a laugh. "That sounds perfect for Rey," he muttered, earning himself a slight scowl from Isa.

"He took a great risk for us," she said with a warning edge. "And the ruse allowed him to join the firkon and secure the safety of our men—or at least most of our men. Then, Lia and I instructed the women to fall back, to take shelter and let Awnell fall."

Catanya gaped at them all.

"It was the best way," said Lia, shrugging. "It has allowed us to remain here, away from Cadyan's watchful eye where we can plan our attack. Meanwhile, our men have infiltrated Caerlon City from the inside."

"And what about all the people who died?" asked Catanya, horrified.

Lia shrugged again. "Collateral damage. We all understood the risks. That is the price we pay for freedom."

Catanya scoffed and turned her back on Lia, anger swelling inside her. She clenched her fists, trying to hold back the outburst.

"We don't have time for your sentimentality," said Lia. "Now that you have finally returned, we need to act."

"My *sentimentality*?" spat Catanya, spinning around and glaring at Lia. "You've been lying to me from the beginning. How am I supposed to trust you—any of you?" she added, glaring at Drayk. She was furious now, making it difficult to ignore the power swelling inside her. She inhaled deeply and the temperature in the room plummeted.

Drayk shivered and took a step forward, eying her hands. "Listen, Catya," he said in a calm voice. "You can be angry later. Right now, all that matters is that we have access to an army. We have what we need. This is it."

Catanya was by no means ready to let this go, but she bit her tongue. "Fine," she said through gritted teeth. "What happens next, *Commander*?"

Lia spent the next half an hour explaining the basic outline of the attack plan so far. Eventually Catanya's anger subsided enough for her to concentrate. It surprised her to discover that a large part of the plan hinged on Ayr being able to convince Cadyan that Catanya had died during the siege of Awnell.

"So he won't be expecting you," said Isa, grinning.

"I don't know..." Catanya shook her head. "How do we know he hasn't discovered the truth?"

"Because we get updates from Rey." It was clear from Isa's tone that these updates meant more to her than pure strategic value. It pleased Catanya to know at least someone in Awnell still displayed some emotion.

"How does he manage to get information out to you?" she asked.

"Please," scoffed Lia. "That is child's play for a soldier of Rey's calibre. And Ayr has spies and messengers scattered all over Caerlon."

"Letters, runners, coded messages left in cargo shipments—it varies." Isa shrugged. "So far, Cadyan has no idea you're still alive. But if we want to keep it that way, we need to keep you concealed until the very last moment. You don't exactly blend in anymore," she added, gesturing to Catanya's hair.

"You don't say," muttered Catanya in a weary voice, closing her eyes in frustration.

"Speaking of Rey," said Lia, "I should send word to him. He should know that you're back. The last shipments of armour will be arriving any day now. We'll be riding by this time next week."

"A week?" spluttered Catanya, gaping at her.

"We need to move quickly," said Lia, rolling up maps and clearing away their notes. "There's no time to waste. Hopefully he'll get the message with enough time to prepare." And with that she turned and climbed down the ladder out of the room.

As she was leaving, the old barman appeared. He'd

somehow managed to climb the ladder while carrying a jug of barkbeer and a precarious-looking platter of food. "Thought you lot might be hungry," he said, placing the platter on the nearest table.

"Thank you, Reg." Isa smiled as she took a mug off the platter and poured a generous amount of the dark liquid into it.

"Oy, Drayk, been up to no good, I take it?" said Reg, smiling as he cuffed Drayk on the shoulder. "Good to see you, mate,"

"And you, Reg. Glad to see you made it out of the battle unscathed."

Reg smiled. Then he turned to address Isa again. "Lieutenant, there's a couple of folks down in the main room asking for you."

"Who are they?" asked Isa, suddenly serious.

"A young man and a woman. They wouldn't give me names, but they said they'd only talk to you. Should I tell them to shove off?"

"No," responded Isa. "No, I'll handle it." Then she turned and followed Reg back down the ladder, closing the trapdoor behind her.

Silence filled the space she left behind. Catanya looked around, surprised to discover she and Drayk were alone in the attic. Everyone else had filtered out during the last hour while Lia explained the plan.

Drayk was looking at Catanya, wearing an apprehensive expression. "Look, love," he ventured, moving towards her.

"I'm not interested in any more of your lies, Drayk," said Catanya, cutting him off.

"Lies?" Drayk sounded slightly outraged. "No, no, no. I never lied to you."

Catanya rounded on him. "Well, you never told me the whole truth either, did you?"

"Well..." Drayk grinned sheepishly.

"Ugh!" Catanya threw her hands up in the air and turned away from him.

"Look, I didn't keep this from you for some malicious reason, I was just following orders. Ayr told me not to tell you about the entire plan, not until you absolutely needed to know. She didn't even tell me everything. I just knew Awnell was going to fall and we were supposed to go to Túir-Avlea. Then when we were finished, we'd return here and Lia would give us our next orders."

"That's ridiculous," muttered Catanya.

"Well, it's the truth," said Drayk.

"Why didn't she want me to know? What, she didn't think I could handle it?" Catanya was incensed. She was sick and tired of being underestimated and used like a pawn in Ayr's game.

"No, I think she just didn't want to burden you with it, Catya. You had enough on your mind already."

Catanya snorted. "You have a kinder opinion of her than I do."

"I've known Ayr for most of my life," he said. "I stopped questioning her decisions a long time ago. She has good instincts, and trusting her has kept me alive this far. Besides... she was right, wasn't she? I mean, be honest here, Catya, you wouldn't have left the city if you'd known the whole plan—if you'd known how many people were going to die. You would have stayed, and you would have died in Awnell along with our only hope to stop Cadyan. Ayr made a judgement call. That's what it means to be a leader, to be a queen."

Catanya sniffed but didn't respond.

Drayk gave a weary sigh. Then he placed his hand gently on Catanya's shoulder, turning her around to face him. "Look, love, you can be mad at her and you can be mad at me, but Ayr is counting on you. We all are. You are the only one who can do this. Ayr knows that, I know that, even you know that. And we are all willing to do whatever it takes to help you get there."

"Yes, I know," said Catanya, nodding, "but I can't shake the sense that there's something they're still not telling us. I don't trust them and I'm going to keep a close eye on them from now on. It's like you said, this is my fight, and it's going to be on my terms."

"Okay." Drayk nodded and held his hands up in surrender. Then, adopting a hard expression, he continued, "But I'm tired of proving to you again and again that you can trust me. In case you haven't noticed, I'm on your side. I'm in this with you and I'll follow your lead. As much as I trust Ayr's instincts, it's you I'm betting on, love. But if I haven't earned your trust by now, then..." He trailed off, looking exasperated.

"No, you're right," said Catanya in a quiet voice. Her anger subsided almost immediately, replaced by a slight sense of shame. "I do trust you." She reached out and took his hands in hers. "But no more secrets, agreed?"

"I think I can manage that." Drayk smiled at her.

"I need to know that you'll be watching my back."

"Oh, believe me, I'll be watching every bit of you," he said with a playful grin.

Catanya had to suppress the urge to grin back. "I'm serious," she said.

"So am I," said Drayk, dropping his facetious manner. Then, grabbing her waist, he pulled her into his body for a passionate kiss.

They stood there together, locked at the lips, ignoring the sound of the trapdoor opening again.

"Oh!" Isa looked startled as she climbed back into the room, followed by two other people in long, dark cloaks. "Sorry," she muttered, as Catanya and Drayk broke apart, grinning.

"Great timing," said Drayk, laughing as he wrapped his arm around Catanya's waist and kissed her on the cheek. "What is it, Isa?"

But Catanya didn't hear the reply. Her attention had been

drawn to the two people now stepping off the ladder into the room behind Isa. She couldn't believe her eyes.

"Catanya!" shouted the woman in front, flinging herself forward and pulling Catanya into a side-splitting hug.

"Diyah?" Catanya was in shock. She stood frozen, holding the friend she'd thought was dead. The last time she'd seen Diyah, her friend had launched herself into the fray at Camlee Lodge, sacrificing herself to give Catanya time to escape. Memories of that night still haunted Catanya's dreams, memories of the fires and the screams. Diyah's panicked face as she'd urged Catanya to run. All this time, Catanya had believed her friend was dead. But now, here she was. "I don't believe it," she whispered, hot tears forming in her eyes.

Then she turned her attention to the man behind Diyah. He wore an expression of mingled pain and joy.

"Jémys?" she croaked, overwhelmed with emotion.

"Hello, Catanya," he said, smiling as his eyes roved over her face. "Drayk." He nodded curtly in Drayk's direction. "It's been a while."

"I can't believe it!" Catanya let go of Diyah and hugged Jémys. "I can't believe it!" she repeated. She was so surprised that this seemed to be all she could say.

"I know, I can hardly believe it myself," he replied, his gaze lingering on her hair as he let go of her.

"I never thought I would see either of you again!" She kept one hand on Jémys's arm while she grabbed Diyah's and squeezed her. "How? How are you here? And together!"

"It's a long story," said Diyah. She had tears in her eyes and she was beaming at Catanya. "But I want to hear everything about you." She reached forward and touched Catanya's hair, frowning slightly as she did it. "I want to know everything that's happened since we last saw each other. I've missed you so much!"

Catanya wrapped her arms around her friend again. "I've missed you too."

She was so overjoyed to be reunited with Diyah and with Jémys that for a moment Catanya forgot where she was.

But then Isa cleared her throat. "It seems we all have a lot to discuss. I'll have Reg prepare a private dining room. Tonight, we celebrate the return of lost friends."

That night, Catanya found herself sitting between Jémys and Diyah at a long table that creaked ominously under the weight of all the plates. Isa and Drayk sat on the other side along with a handful of other people. Lia—much to Catanya's delight—had still not returned from her earlier excursion.

The first half of the evening was spent filling everyone in on what Catanya and Drayk had been doing since they'd left Caerlon. Diyah seemed particularly curious to learn about Túir-Avlea, having heard all the same stories Catanya heard growing up.

"It sounds incredible," she said in a hushed voice as Catanya finished telling them about their time with Laylian and the others in Túir-Avlea.

"It was." Catanya took a sip of her wine, thinking for a second. "There was something otherworldly about it. You could feel the magic in the air. It was as if... as if anything was possible in there..." She trailed off, remembering it fondly.

"Yes, but that's a dangerous sensation, isn't it?" asked Drayk, giving Catanya a pointed look.

Catanya felt her face flush. She shot him a dirty look across the table.

"I have to admit," said Jémys, cutting through the tension. "I'm surprised you're still here, Drayk."

Drayk leaned back, balancing on the rear legs of his chair,

looking carefree. "I can't think why," he replied. "I can be very useful can't I, love?" He winked at Catanya.

Catanya just shook her head and turned her attention back to Diyah. "But what about you? Where have you been?" She was eager to change the subject before Drayk had an opportunity to tell anyone what had happened between them in Túir-Avlea. She wasn't ashamed of it, but she didn't want to deal with the uncomfortable questions. As far as she was concerned, her experiences with Drayk were her business.

"Well..." Diyah put her cup down and looked at Jémys. "We've been in Caerlon City, at court. That's where I've been this entire time."

"What?" gasped Catanya, surprised. She couldn't fathom how they could have survived this long living under Cadyan's nose.

Then Diyah recounted everything that had happened to her since that fateful night in Faltir almost a year ago.

It pained Catanya to hear confirmation of Lady Genna's death. She'd always known her guardian must have died, but it still wasn't easy to hear. She closed her eyes, holding back the tide of emotion swelling inside her.

"I tried to stop them," said Diyah, her voice pained. "But they knocked me unconscious. There was nothing I could do. I—"

Catanya rested her hand on Diyah's arm to stop her from spiralling. "It's okay, Diyah. It's not your fault. And Lady Genna wouldn't want you to blame yourself."

Diyah took a deep, shaky breath and nodded. It took her a moment to collect herself before she was able to continue. "I woke up on a horse miles away from Faltir..." she said. "They brought me to the city, along with three of the girls. Meya, Hahney, and Gréys."

Catanya swallowed hard.

Three. Only three of the girls survived.

She wrestled back her rage and chagrin, trying not to picture the girls who didn't survive, their bodies crumpled and broken... the way Olly's had been. Catanya fought the urge to look at Jémys. She didn't think she could bear to see the pain in his eyes right now.

Diyah continued her story uninterrupted for a few minutes. As she recounted her time in Caerlon's dungeons, and her torture at the hands of Slaedir, Diyah's voice hardened, like she was refusing to let her mind revisit it. Catanya struggled to remain calm and she found herself squeezing Diyah's arm harder and harder.

"But Fehla helped us," continued Diyah. "She brought us food and water."

"Fehla?" asked Drayk with surprise. Murmurs broke out among the Awnadh at the table. "You mean the queen?"

Catanya's swirling emotions stilled, momentarily overcome by curiosity. "What's she like?" she asked in a voice like a whisper.

Diyah paused, thinking about her answer. "She's... well, she's not at all what I expected." Diyah frowned and glanced at Jémys for help.

Jémys tilted his head. "She's an odd mixture of contradictions," he said, nodding. "Gentle and strong, accessible and reserved. And well... she has this overwhelming sense of sadness about her. Like she hasn't been happy in years."

Diyah nodded, but then her face suddenly brightened. "Oh! But Catanya," she said, turning eagerly to face her. "She still wears it, you know? The bracelet she bought from you all those years ago. She wears it every day."

Catanya blinked. This was the last thing she'd expected to hear.

"Bracelet?" asked Drayk with a curious frown.

"Yeah." Catanya shrugged. "I used to make them and sell them in the village, along with my art... A child's hobby really, but I always enjoyed it. I never thought..." She trailed off, remembering the day ten years ago. The royal family had been touring the kingdom as part of Cadyan's first rite of manhood. When they'd stopped in Faltir, the queen had visited all the local vendors, and she'd stopped to talk with the young girl she must have known was her daughter.

Before I go, Catanya, I should very much like to buy one of your bracelets. Fehla had selected one of Catanya's pink coral bracelets with the white shells. *This one is quite beautiful, and something about it reminds me of that necklace you are wearing.*

A stab of anger broke through Catanya's pleasant reminiscence.

Fehla's necklace. The Oracle Stone.

Once again, Catanya found herself wondering just how much Fehla had known about the family heirloom she'd given her daughter. If she'd known the necklace was one of Illayan's relics, then she must have known what would happen. Had she intended for Catanya to get these powers—had she intended for all of this to happen?

Or perhaps she hadn't known what it was at all. Perhaps she'd believed it was just a nice family heirloom, and she'd wanted her daughter to have it... But if that were the case, it meant Fehla was just a naïve, sentimental fool who'd made one reckless decision after another.

Catanya didn't know which was worse.

"Sorry, Diyah," she said, shaking away her pessimistic thoughts. "I derailed your story. What happened next?" She motioned for her friend to continue.

Diyah seemed momentarily caught off guard, but she cleared her throat and continued with her story.

She explained how Cadyan had discovered her Heiltúir ancestry and decided to exploit her skills as the court physician —and how she'd negotiated the release of the girls in exchange for her cooperation. But as Diyah started describing a man named Julyán, her entire tone shifted. Catanya could tell there was something special about him. Then Diyah described the Maífirkon Tournament, and the story skewed more towards her concern for Julyán's welfare than anything else.

"And, of course, Jémys was angry at his brother," said Diyah in passing, causing him to choke, spluttering wine all down his chin.

"Brother?" repeated Catanya.

"Yes. Julyán," said Diyah matter-of-factly. "Didn't you know Jémys had a brother?"

"No. I didn't." Catanya frowned at Jémys, who flushed and averted his eyes, taking a deeper sip of wine.

"Oh. Well..." stammered Diyah, looking back and forth between Catanya and Jémys.

"Well, I can understand why," interjected Drayk with a wide grin. "Who would admit to being related to some firkon scum?"

The rest of the table roared and cheered their support. Catanya caught sight of the pained expression, not only on Jémys's face, but on Diyah's. She was on the verge of asking her friend about it when Diyah launched back into her story.

"Anyway, they held the Maífirkon Tournament and Julyán won," she continued, casting a furtive glance in Jémys's direction that did not go unnoticed by Catanya. "And not long after that, Jémys and I escaped during the chaos of the Royal Offering. Ayr told us to come here and look for you," she added, nodding at Isa. "And so here we are..."

"Reunited at last!" said Jémys, raising his glass in salute to cover for Diyah's hurried conclusion.

As everyone raised their glasses, laughing and cheering, Catanya noticed Jémys and Diyah exchanging silent looks. There was more to the story than they were letting on.

As the meal was winding down, Reg reappeared to let them know he'd arranged rooms for them all. Everyone filed out, looking forward to a good night's sleep. As Catanya moved to follow them out the door, someone touched her arm. Turning around, she saw Jémys.

"Can we talk?" he asked.

Catanya nodded. As she followed him back into the dining room, she caught sight of Drayk's expression. Their eyes met briefly and he tossed her a mordant smirk before disappearing through the door. She suddenly felt very uncomfortable.

Jémys took Catanya's hand and led her back over to the chairs. They sat down, facing each other, and she leaned forward, causing several strands of hair to fall across her face.

Jémys hesitated before lifting his hand to brush the strands back. His gaze lingered on the new colour and Catanya thought she noticed a shadow pass through his eyes. For the first time in weeks, she felt slightly self-conscious about her new appearance—her resemblance to her brother.

She tossed her hair back and straightened in her seat, leaning away from Jémys, but he seemed to notice her sudden discomfort. "Catanya, I owe you an apology," he said quickly. "For the way I reacted when I found out the truth."

Catanya exhaled and shook her head. "No, Jémys. You don't need to apologize. You had every right to hate me."

"But I don't hate you," he said, looking slightly alarmed. "I never hated you, Catanya. You must know that." He held Catanya's gaze for a moment, as if urging her to believe him. "You have no idea how much I regret the way I acted," he groaned, burying his face in his hands. "I never meant to leave, I was just so upset and I wasn't thinking clearly. As soon as I calmed down, I turned back to join you at the cottage but it was too late."

"You turned back?" repeated Catanya, a swirl of emotions tangling inside her. All this time, she thought he'd chosen to leave, and she'd accepted that. After everything he'd endured because of her, he deserved the chance to move on.

"Yes! Catanya, not a single day has gone by that I haven't

thought about you—that I haven't wished I could do it differently. And when I thought you were dead—" He broke off, fighting back tears. "I couldn't stand the thought of never getting to tell you..."

Catanya's breath caught in her throat and she found herself leaning in again. "Tell me what?" she asked in a hushed voice.

"Tell you how much I love you," he said, making eye contact with her. "And I do. I love you so much, Catanya. I never should have let you think otherwise."

He put his hand on her cheek, and his teary eyes searched her face. That deep green colour, like a forest after a rainfall... He hesitated slightly, but then he pulled her lips over to meet his. He kissed her gently at first, almost like he was afraid to move. But then the dam broke, and he laced his fingers through her hair, kissing her with an intense, affectionate passion that she'd never felt before.

Catanya reacted instinctively. The strength of everything she felt for Jémys took over in that moment and she allowed herself to be swept away in it. She wrapped her arms around his neck and breathed him in, recalling the smell of cider and wild flowers in a meadow.

Warm tears poured down her face as she remembered every other moment they'd shared. She was so overwhelmed and overjoyed that he'd forgiven her—that he still loved her—that for a moment it was like they'd never been separated. And the future she'd always wanted with him was still within reach.

All at once, harsh reality doused the fire burning inside her.

"Wait," she said, pulling away and looking at him. Tears streaked down his cheeks. Catanya smiled sadly and took his hands in hers again. "I've missed you so much," she breathed, trying to calm her racing heart. "And I love you too. More than I ever would have thought possible." She laughed feebly. A part of her longed to stop talking and just kiss him again, to feel his lips against hers and abandon herself to the sensations she hadn't felt in months. "But... now is not the right time," she forced the words out, struggling not to let the bitterness consume her.

"What do you mean?"

She shook her head and took a deep breath. "When I first met you and we fell in love, all I wanted was to escape. To live a quiet, happy life with you. But now... well, now I know that's never going to be possible. That's not my life. And I've accepted that."

"I know that, and I'm okay with it. I want to be with you. We can still—"

"Jémys." She spoke his name with a mixture of tenderness and regret. "It has taken me ages to come to terms with who I am, to accept my responsibilities, and I need to focus on what lies ahead. I can't afford to have any distractions or any weaknesses going into this. There's too much at stake, and I love you too much—" She broke off, emotion rising in her throat. She averted her gaze momentarily as she collected herself. When she'd regained control, she turned back to face him. "Jémys, the way I feel about you... it scares me sometimes. I already did this once—I put my feelings for you first, and look what happened." She met his gaze and saw her own pain reflected back at her. "Everything that happened to Finnua, to Nelle and Olly... I can't take any of that back," she said. "And the guilt... it's crippling. If I open myself back up now, I don't know if I can trust myself to stay focused on what lies ahead and do what needs to be done. The person I need to be in order to succeed... I'm not sure she can have the things she wants."

Jémys looked heartbroken, but he nodded. "I understand," he said in a deflated voice. "But when this is over, I promise you I'll fight for this. For us. Whatever it takes. You and me together, that's my future. I know that now more than ever."

Catanya smiled sadly. "Jémys, we've both already changed so much—I've changed so much. This war is only going to change me more. I don't know who I'll be when this is over, or what future I'll be able to have."

"It doesn't matter," he said firmly. "Whatever *has* happened, whatever *will* happen. When this is over, we'll pick up the pieces and move forward together. No matter how much work it takes. I promise."

But a part of Catanya knew... She might not survive this coming war, and she couldn't bear to think what that would do to him. She couldn't let him back in, and risk breaking his heart all over again. It was better for everyone if she kept her mind clear and her priorities straight. She'd sworn to herself before leaving Túir-Avlea that she was done putting her own needs first. If that meant she couldn't be with the man she loved, then so be it.

Catanya sighed as she stood up. She kissed Jémys on his forehead, and walked out of the room, not daring to look back at him.

15

BLOOD OR FAMILY

When Diyah awoke the next day, it took her a while to remember where she was. She looked around the dank room, breathing in the faint fishy smell of the port. And everything came flooding back to her.

She was in Awnell, reunited with Catanya and safe. She had everything she'd wanted for the past several months. Yet for some reason, she still felt miserable.

Diyah sat up and swung her legs off the bed. She stayed there for a minute, trying to slow her breathing as she listened to the sounds of the inn waking around her.

After a while, there was a gentle knock on the door. A barmaid came in carrying a tray of breakfast.

"Thank you," said Diyah, wrapping herself in a shawl and looking at the food. It smelled delicious. Diyah was ravenous, but her stomach had been in knots since she'd boarded that ship leaving Caerlon. The idea of eating still made her queasy.

Instead, Diyah dressed and left the room to find Catanya. She needed to tell her the rest of the story. She needed her friend's advice.

Diyah didn't know why she hadn't told Catanya about

Julyán the previous night. But she hadn't wanted to discuss her personal feelings around a group of strangers. And Julyán wasn't what these people thought he was. Catanya would understand.

Diyah headed down the narrow corridor towards the room with the trapdoor. As she turned the corner, she nearly collided with Jémys.

"Ah, sorry," he said. "Are you looking for Catanya too?" He looked a little morose and pale this morning.

Diyah nodded, straightening up. "I need to tell her... I'm not sure why I didn't before..." She trailed off, looking at him apologetically.

"You don't owe me an explanation," said Jémys, shaking his head. "These people... they can't understand what it was like for you living in Caerlon this whole time. What you had to do to survive. And I guess we can't understand what it was like for them either."

"I don't regret any of it," said Diyah.

"I know." He patted her on the arm. "Now, come on." He jerked his head for her to follow and the two of them set off to find Catanya.

Diyah wanted to ask Jémys how his conversation with Catanya had gone the night before, but his mood told her it hadn't gone well. And after what they'd seen yesterday emerging from the trapdoor, it seemed Catanya and Drayk were more than travel companions.

But Diyah knew her friend well, and she'd been watching her closely last night. Whenever Catanya had looked at Jémys, Diyah had seen it in her eyes. Underneath the bittersweet happiness and guilt, there was something else—something she'd never seen there before.

If it wasn't love, Diyah didn't know what it was.

When they emerged into the attic a few minutes later, they found the place teeming with people.

Catanya, Drayk, and Isa were all hunched over a map in one corner talking in animated voices. It sounded like a disagreement.

"I'm telling you, if we approach from the east, he'll know. There are informants everywhere in those forests," said Drayk, shaking his head. "No, our only chance is if we approach from the south."

"We need to surround them," said Isa. "With fighters on the east and riders on the south, we can—"

"We don't have enough fighters," said Catanya.

"It's not about the number, it's about the strategy. And don't forget we have an entire army lying in wait inside the castle. This will work."

Catanya sighed and nodded. "Let's hope it does." She turned away from the table and noticed Jémys and Diyah. "Oh, I didn't hear you come in." Her entire demeanour changed as she smiled at them, looking more like her usual, relaxed self. Diyah noticed Isa mark the change as well, then exchange dubious glances with the others behind Catanya's back.

"We—" started Diyah, but Jémys cut her off.

"I want to fight with you," he said, looking serious. "If you'll have me…"

There was a brief pause before Catanya smiled and nodded. But Isa snickered and exchanged amused looks with Drayk.

"What?" asked Jémys a little defensively.

Drayk cleared his throat, grinning. "No offence, mate, but this isn't a place for farmers." He cast a sidelong glance at Isa. "It's going to be a brutal, merciless fight. It's not for amateurs."

"Jémys is an amazing fighter," said Diyah. "Trust me, he's not an amateur. He held his own in the tournament."

Isa snorted. "That tournament is nothing compared to what we're facing now."

"I can fight," said Jémys. "And I know my way around the castle, I can help you."

"He's right," said Catanya, before anyone else could say anything. She glanced over her shoulder at Isa. "Jémys should be there with us."

Isa sighed. "Fine, have it your way." Then, muttering under her breath she added, "Oh, the commander is going to love this."

"I don't really care what she does or doesn't like," said Catanya in a loud voice. "This fight hinges on me and *my* powers. It's my fight, and it will be on my terms."

Isa looked affronted. She turned and stared at Drayk, but Drayk just laughed. "Hey, don't look at me," he said. "I agree with her." He winked at Catanya, and Diyah noticed a small smile on her friend's face.

"Good, then that's settled," said Catanya. After a tense pause, she added, "But I still think we need more fighters." She looked weary and a little nervous as she glanced down at the map before her.

"What about the Awnadh interned at Bratia?" asked Diyah, remembering all the soldiers Cadyan had sent there after the battle. "I know Cadyan sent at least half of them there."

Isa nodded. "I know, but we have no way to reach them. We can't afford a detour."

Jémys took a step forward and looked down at the papers. He ran his finger along the map. "You know," he said, tapping the drawing of the ocean, "the ship that brought us here could get us all the way into the city port." He turned to look at Diyah for support. "And it passes through Bratia."

"That's true," she said begrudgingly. She had no desire to step foot on that ship again. "They're smugglers. That's what they do."

Drayk's attention snapped towards them. "Smugglers? What smugglers?"

"Ayr told us about them," said Diyah. "That's how we got out of Caerlon. We bartered a ride on his ship."

"Bartered with what?" Drayk's voice was loud, almost panicked. He looked at Diyah with wide eyes.

"With gold," said Jémys, surveying Drayk like he'd lost his mind.

"Gold," repeated Drayk. "That's all? You're sure?" He glanced again in Diyah's direction.

"Yes, that's all... And, well, maybe a few threats..." she muttered.

"Wait a minute," said Catanya, turning towards Drayk. The two of them exchanged meaningful glances.

"What's going on here?" asked Jémys. "Do you know him, then? That Captain Osrin?"

Drayk seemed to suppress a shudder as he heard the name. His face flushed with anger. Then he strode to the trap door, wrenched it open, and disappeared without a second glance.

"Drayk, wait," called Catanya, but he was already gone. Catanya swore under her breath. "I can't go after him and risk being seen!"

"I knew this was going to happen," said Isa in a low voice. "That's why I didn't mention it before."

"You knew he was here?" snapped Catanya.

Isa just shrugged. "How else do you think we've been getting our shipments? You think we can just trade openly across the border while our city is under Caerlon's control?"

"You mean you've been work—"

"We don't have time for this right now," interjected Isa. "We need to focus."

Catanya still looked furious. Her hands were balled into fists and she glowered at Isa. But then she gave a resigned sigh and cast one longing glance at the trap door before turning back to the map.

Diyah didn't understand what had just happened. Then someone tugged on her sleeve and she turned to see Jémys beckoning for her to follow him.

"What is it?" she whispered as she followed him back down the trapdoor.

"Drayk," he said. "I've never trusted him, but now..." He trailed off, lost in thought and didn't elaborate.

They made their way out of the inn and back down the winding streets towards the port. Jémys walked so fast that Diyah had to jog to keep up with him.

"Jémys, what are we doing?" she asked, exasperated. But then she saw Drayk walking a few feet ahead of them. "Are you *serious*? We're following him?"

"Yes," said Jémys, brushing away the question.

She had never seen Jémys acting like this before. She was starting to worry he might do something he regretted.

They watched as Drayk stopped outside Osrin's ship and drew his sword.

"Oh no," whispered Diyah. Jémys pulled her behind some large barrels and out of sight.

"Shh," he said, craning his neck to listen.

"Where is he?" they heard Drayk say, and he sounded angry.

Diyah glanced out from behind the barrel to watch. She saw the smugglers all milling about, loading and unloading supplies. Then she saw him. Captain Osrin stepped off his ship and onto the dock in front of Drayk. A wide grin stretched across his face.

"Well, well," he drawled, and his crew snickered. "It seems the little girl was telling the truth."

"So," said Drayk in a low, venomous voice. "You accept gold for payment now. Funny how things change."

"I've always accepted gold," said Osrin, showing no sign he noticed the sword in Drayk's hand. "Doesn't mean I won't take other things when the occasion arises."

Without warning, Drayk pulled back his arm and struck Osrin hard in the face with his fist. The rest of the crew reacted instantly. They drew their blades and advanced on him. But Osrin just laughed and held up his hand to stop them.

"S'all right," he said, spitting blood onto the dock. He grinned as he turned back to face Drayk. "It's been a long time, Drayk. And that's how you greet me?"

"Not long enough, if you ask me. Still trading in stolen goods, I see. What is it this time?" he asked, kicking the nearest crate.

"Oh, a little of this, a little of that... Awnell pays me well to keep my mouth shut. Caerlon pays me well to keep shipments coming from Bratia. And Sidina, well," he shrugged, and a greedy sneer curled his lip, "Sidina just pays well for everything. So, you see, it's good business, isn't it? And no one cares to look too closely at what may or may not get skimmed off the top, or what may get a little... *worn out* in the journey."

Drayk just scowled at him.

"Why do you look at me like that?" asked Osrin. "So much hate in your eyes! When really you should be thanking me. After all, without me you wouldn't exist, now, would you?"

The rest of the crew snickered and exchanged complicit glances.

Drayk's body went rigid. "Believe me, it is not hate that you see," he said coolly. "It's shame."

Osrin laughed. "Oh, come on, Drayk. It's not so bad. I keep telling you I've changed, haven't I? Come and join us. Look around you! Awnell is dying. There's nothing left for you here. Come join me on my ship. Father and son, it'll be great."

"I am not your son," snarled Drayk.

"Oh, come on, just give me a chance," said Osrin. The sneer in his voice was enough to make Diyah's skin crawl. "We could be unstoppable. Think of the glory, the freedom."

Drayk snorted. "Freedom? Yeah, freedom you get by trading other people into slavery! And what do you know about glory, anyway? You've never done anything worth remembering.

You've led a disgraceful, meaningless existence. What do you have to be proud of?"

Osrin seemed to think about that for a second. "I can be proud of my son," he said with a smile.

Drayk's entire posture changed. He looked as if he was going to attack him again. "You have not earned the right to that pride." He stepped forward, raising his sword. "I am not your son," he repeated, punctuating every word with spite.

"Oh, come on," said Osrin, laughing. "You do hold a grudge, that's for sure. But honestly, boy, you'd have done the same thing if you were in my place. And it's not like that whore mother of yours ever deserved any better. Slaves like her exist for other men's pleasure. What do you think the firkon were doing with her before they sold her to me?"

Diyah felt sick again. She watched as Drayk completely lost control and attacked Osrin. This time, he showed no sign of stopping. He pummelled Osrin with his fist over and over, lashing out at every inch of the man he could find.

"Stop," said Jémys, jumping out from behind the barrels. "Drayk, stop!" He tried to restrain him before the other crew members joined the fight.

"Let go of me," snarled Drayk, trying to wrestle himself free. Jémys just tightened his grip and wrenched him back a few steps.

"You've got a powerful arm, boy," said Osrin, staggering back up to his feet and wiping blood from his mouth. "Just like your father."

Drayk cried out in rage and tried even harder to break free from Jémys's grip.

"Oy, it's you," said Osrin, looking at Jémys and ignoring Drayk's incoherent grumbling. "Come to join the crew again?" he asked with scorn. "Oh, don't tell me you need another ride?"

"Well, actually." Jémys loosened his grip on Drayk and gave him a warning look. "When do you sail for Caerlon?"

Osrin narrowed his eyes and didn't respond.

"No," said Drayk, turning to address Jémys. "No. We're not using his ship. I can't believe you even set foot on it to begin with. You know what he does with it, don't you?" He looked at Jémys with disgust in his eyes.

"It's the best way in," muttered Jémys. He gave Drayk an apologetic look. "We'd be fools not to use him."

Diyah stood up and walked over to join them. "Drayk," she said quietly. "Jémys is right."

"Oho, and the girlie!" Osrin clapped his hands together. "Will you be coming back aboard, then?" he asked, leering at her.

Drayk's face contorted in rage again. He broke free from Jémys. In one swift movement, he had his sword pressed against Osrin's throat. The crew lurched forward but Drayk jerked his blade, glaring at them. "Make one more move, and I will kill him without hesitation."

Osrin let out a low whistle. "All right, what's really going on here? So many people threatening to kill me." He smiled at Diyah, his teeth smeared with blood. "I'm beginning to feel special."

Diyah had a sudden urge to put this man in his place. She took several measured steps forward and stopped next to Drayk. "You're not special," she said, trying to channel as much haughtiness and disdain as she could muster. "You are merely a tool to be used by more intelligent people—a pawn in a game that you will never understand."

Drayk kept his blade planted firmly against Osrin's neck, but he stared at Diyah in open surprise. He looked impressed.

"Now, the way I see it, you have two options," continued Diyah. She sauntered forward and lifted an oil lamp off the nearest crate, swinging it casually through the air. "One, we can kill you. I'll set fire to your ship before you have the chance to go running back to Cadyan." She let that option dangle in the air, pleased to see the alarm on Osrin's face. "Or two, you can take us where we want to go and live to breathe another day."

Diyah wasn't surprised to hear the authority in her voice. She had spent so long living with the enemy that she'd learned a thing or two about coercion and intimidation. She knew where to apply pressure to get what they needed.

"Well?" she snapped. "What will it be? Those barrels of liquor will make a quick job of it." She swung the lamp towards the stack of barrels waiting on deck to be unloaded.

Osrin looked from Diyah to Jémys and then back to Drayk, with his sword still poised to strike. And the captain seemed to read the resolve written on their faces.

"All right, all right," he said, holding his hands up in surrender. "There's no need for threats. I'm always happy to play my part. Now, who all am I transporting and where are we going?"

Diyah smiled triumphantly. "Oh, we'll be making a few stops, actually."

A short while later, as Diyah, Drayk, and Jémys made their way back up to the inn, Diyah felt the tension building between them. She and Jémys walked a few feet behind Drayk, exchanging silent looks. They were each trying to convince the other to say something.

"Spit it out," said Drayk. He stopped dead in his tracks and rounded on them. "Say what you have to say."

Jémys cleared his throat and looked at Diyah uncomfortably. "So, that's your father, then?" he asked rather lamely.

"Oh, you're perceptive," said Drayk, rolling his eyes.

"Drayk, I'm so sorry," said Diyah. She didn't know him well, but she wanted to say something. She reached out to touch his arm, but he brushed it away.

"Don't be. I don't want your pity."

"It's not pity," said Jémys. "It's just. I never realized. I mean, I loved my father more than anything—"

"Look, mate," said Drayk, rounding on him again. "You and I have led very different lives. Don't assume we want the same things. I like my life and I wouldn't have it any other way, understand?"

"Still," said Diyah, trying to sound compassionate. "Surely you want more, don't you?"

"No," said Drayk. "Trust me, love, the only thing I want from that man is to see him get what's coming to him."

They walked the rest of the way without saying a word. As they climbed the stairs back up through the inn, Diyah thought about her parents. It had been a long time since she'd thought about them, and she found herself wondering how they'd feel about all of this. What they would think of their daughter, living at the centre of a war, with her thoughts half a world away, still stuck in the enemy's camp? What would they tell her to do?

Lost in her thoughts, Diyah hadn't noticed that they'd reached the attic already. She had climbed the ladder without even realizing it. The sound of noisy voices brought her out of her trance. Catanya and Drayk were arguing, but it was the expression on Jémys's face that really drew her attention.

"What is it?" she asked.

Jémys didn't respond, instead he gestured to the older woman now standing with Catanya and Drayk.

The woman was instantly recognizable. She was tall with proud features and choppy grey hair. She bore a striking resemblance to her sister, Fehla.

The energy in the room seemed to dissipate as everyone noticed Jémys and Diyah gawking at the woman.

"What?" snapped the woman, glaring at them.

"Y-you look just like her," spluttered Jémys.

She gave him a questioning look.

"He means Fehla," said Diyah, walking forward to greet her. "She's your sister, isn't she? We spent time with her in Caerlon and she told us about you. You must be Falia—"

"Lia," she corrected with a touch of irritation. "And I take it you two are the *friends* we've heard so much about." She sneered at Catanya and then turned her attention back towards them. "Tell me, how did you enjoy your time in Caerlon?" Mistrust and suspicion were clear in her voice.

Diyah frowned. "*Enjoy*? We didn't enjoy it. We were prisoners, we weren't there by choice."

"Right... And how did you manage to escape? No prisoner has ever escaped the city before."

Diyah was taken aback. She hadn't expected Fehla's sister to be so standoffish.

"Fehla helped us," said Jémys. "And Julyán."

"Julyán?" Lia's eyes flashed. "The new maífirkon? He's supposedly very skilled, very brutal." She cast a glance in Isa's direction. "Possibly even worse than Slaedir."

Anger shot through Diyah. "Julyán is *nothing* like Slaedir," she said before she could stop herself.

Lia snorted. "What do you know about it, little girl? He's a firkon—he's their leader. They are the enemy and he is their master. Every horrible thing that they do, they do on his command."

"What? No, it's not that simple!"

"Diyah," said Jémys, putting his hand on her arm and giving her a warning glance.

"No!" She jerked her arm away. "I'm serious. What do *they* know about Julyán? He's your brother, he's *my* husband. We're the ones that know him!"

Silence followed this declaration. It took Diyah a minute to realize everyone was staring at her, wearing expressions of utter shock.

"Your *husband*?" repeated Lia.

Diyah stood perfectly still. She had surprised even herself with her outburst. But then she turned to address Lia again. "That's right," she said. The heat rose in her face, but she was determined to stand her ground.

"You mean to tell me we have allowed the wife of a firkon to walk straight into our midst?" she asked, glaring at Isa. "What is the meaning of this?"

"She's my friend," said Catanya with a warning tone. "I trust her with my life."

It relieved Diyah to hear Catanya say that. They made eye contact and Diyah saw the understanding and sympathy on her friend's face.

"*Friend*," scoffed Lia. "There's that sentimentality again. I'm beginning to question your resolve here. If you put your faith in people like this..." She let out a long whistle. "We may as well give up now and save ourselves the trouble."

"Come on, Lia," muttered Drayk.

"Oh, wake up, Drayk! Haven't I always taught you that the mission comes first? You can't have attachments because then you have something to lose. *Weaknesses*. Well, I made my choice. I chose the mission. And I would make the same decision again without hesitating. As should you," she added, nodding in Catanya's direction.

Drayk opened his mouth to retort, but Catanya cut him off.

"All right, that's enough!" she declared, glaring at Lia. Diyah had never seen such hatred in her friend's eyes before. "We don't have time for this. We need to work together if we're going to have any chance of winning. Like it or not, we are all going to have to trust each other. Family, or not, *sentimentality* or not, it doesn't matter."

"Well, that's not true," sneered Lia. "You, at least, will have to decide before the end. Family or the mission, which one will you choose? You can't have both."

Catanya glared at her, stony-faced. Diyah shivered as she noticed the resemblance to Cadyan in her friend's features.

"If you are suggesting that I would even consider choosing my brother over the people in this room, then you don't know the first thing about family," said Catanya in a clear, ringing voice. "I'd die before I let anything happen to these people." She gestured towards Diyah, Drayk, and Jémys. "Can you say the same?"

Lia let out a hard sniff. "I would certainly die for the mission."

"Good," said Catanya coldly, turning her back on Lia. "Then let's get to work."

16

POISONED AND ALTERED

Diyah had dedicated her entire life towards helping people and saving lives. So, as she sat in the attic at The Fairweather the next day, listening to everyone plan a war, discussing the potential casualties with nothing short of indifference, she felt all of her most important values being challenged. And the more uncomfortable she became, the more she needed to find a way to resist.

"We have to rescue all of them, not just the soldiers. We have to rescue *everyone* from the Ruins of Bratia," she said for the hundredth time that day. She was sure that if they could just do this one thing—this one purely good thing—then she would feel better about the entire plan.

"I agree," said Jémys. "And I owe it to my people to help them."

Diyah had told him that after the firkon destroyed Finnua, Slaedir had brought all the survivors back to the Caerlon City dungeons. And a few weeks later, they had all been taken to the work camps. Since learning of their fates, Jémys had been determined to free them.

"Please, Catanya," he implored, and Diyah saw the shadow

of pain on his face, and on Catanya's.

"We don't have the capacity for this, and we don't have time for distractions," snapped Lia. The commander had taken an instant dislike towards Diyah. She didn't seem to think Diyah had any place in their conversations.

"It's not a distraction," said Diyah. "It's what's right! If we stand by and allow this to continue, how are we any better than Cadyan?"

"Diyah's right," said Catanya. "We owe it to the people there to try." She smiled at Jémys, and he reached out and squeezed her arm gratefully.

"And besides," Catanya cast a sidelong glance in Drayk's direction, "if I'm going to set foot on that man's ship, I'm going to make sure it's the last time he profits from human cargo... I'm going to raze those camps to the ground."

Diyah was a little surprised by the hardness of her tone. She'd never heard Catanya speak like that before, and she wasn't sure if she was impressed or frightened.

Lia just snorted. "Oh, really?" she scoffed. "Everyone knows the royal family is obsessed with finding the relics. You're no different. I'll bet on that."

"The relics aren't there. They don't exist," said Jémys, sounding irritable. "The firkon know it, they talk about it behind Cadyan's back. But Cadyan's deluded. He thinks if he finds the crown, he'll be able to rule forever. But even if some immortal crown did exist, Catanya wouldn't want it." He sounded confident and he stared at Catanya with pride.

To Diyah's surprise, Catanya exchanged meaningful smirks with Drayk. "What is it?" asked Diyah.

Drayk shook his head and grinned knowingly.

"Nothing," said Catanya. "Jémys is right. The relics definitely aren't there. But he's also right that even if they were there, I wouldn't want them."

Lia closed her eyes in frustration. "Very well," she said

through gritted teeth. "We save everyone, but then what? We can't exactly stroll into Caerlon with a shipload of unarmed soldiers and battered slaves?"

Silence fell in the room.

Unarmed soldiers... unarmed. *Armour.*

"What about Sidina?" asked Diyah.

Everyone turned to look at her.

"I think... well... maybe Lord Zadílar would help us."

"Zad has already helped us," said Lia, indicating the armour piled against the wall behind her. "But he's not an idiot. He won't risk openly taking sides in this, he'll be hedging his bets until the end."

Diyah bit her lip. "This is different," she said, "I know he'll help us this time."

"How do you know?" asked Catanya.

"I can't explain it," she said. "But I know him, and he seems... well, he seems genuinely concerned about me. He'll help us if I ask him to. I'm sure of it."

Lia snorted. "*You?* Why would Zadílar, Lord Steward of Sidina, care about helping you?"

Diyah was more than a little irritated now. She put her hands on her hips obstinately. "Well, aside from the fact that he already *has* helped me and he continues to offer his support every time he sees me, there's also the fact that I'm the last of the Heiltúir—which, incidentally, makes me infinitely more valuable than you. And you're right, Zadílar isn't an idiot. If nothing else, he knows what a Heiltúir is worth. He'll help me."

Beside her, Jémys made an odd noise like he was trying to stifle a snort. She could see the look of amusement on Drayk's face from the corner of her eye.

Catanya seemed to weigh her options. "It's not a bad plan, but we don't have time to contact him..." She trailed off, looking at Diyah with an apprehensive expression.

"I'll come with you," said Diyah. She had always intended

to join them. Now she had an excuse. "I can talk with Zadílar."

Catanya stared at Diyah, her expression oddly inscrutable. But then she nodded.

"Great," said Drayk, clapping his hands together. "I've always wanted to meet ol' Zaddy. I hear he throws wonderful parties."

They spent the next several hours planning and strategizing, and it wasn't long before Diyah felt overwhelmed. She was surprised, however, to see how easily Catanya slid into this life. All that time on the run and living amongst the Awnadh must have taught her a great deal about how to survive and how to fight.

As the strategy session wound down and everyone filtered out for the evening, exhaustion weighed on Diyah's mind and body. She was looking forward to a good night's sleep, and maybe something to eat.

She had been hoping for a moment alone with Catanya before retiring for the night, but her friend was busy talking with Jémys and a few Awnadh. Diyah didn't want to interrupt. So instead, she walked over to Isa, who stood alone in the far corner, sorting through various pieces of armour. Diyah had a question, and Isa seemed slightly more approachable than Lia. "Are there any healers left in the city?" she asked, stopping next to the lieutenant.

Isa glanced up at her. "Some," she said, placing a gleaming breastplate on the nearest pile. "After the battle, the firkon captured a few and brought them up to the fortress to heal their soldiers—the ones Cadyan left behind to die." Isa smirked. "From what I understand, our healers are... struggling to make progress."

Diyah felt lightheaded. Isa seemed to imply that the

Awnadh healers were deliberately failing to heal the firkon. They were allowing them to die, possibly even hastening it.

We do not mete out death, nor do we fear it.

Diyah couldn't condone it. A healer was meant to heal, to help. Not to injure. But she supposed she couldn't judge. This was war, and the Awnadh needed to do whatever it took to protect their people.

But Diyah felt a twinge for the dying firkon. Most of them were young men, forced into a life of brutality and cruelty. Their own king had sacrificed them without a second thought. Did they really deserve to die?

She thought about Julyán and everything he'd gone through. It could have been him lying on the streets of Awnell, forsaken by his army and discarded by his enemies.

Diyah cleared her throat, pushing the unpleasant thoughts aside. "And what about the injured Awnadh?"

"The other healers work in secret, trying to restore as many Awnadh as possible. But it's challenging."

"I'd like to help," said Diyah. "And I can speed their work." She needed to keep busy and these people could use a good healer.

Isa surveyed her for a moment, then nodded. "I'll take you to join them tomorrow."

Diyah nodded and turned away. She wanted to talk to Catanya, but her friend was still deep in conversation with Jémys, so she decided it could wait. Jémys seemed happier than he had the day before. Maybe it was just the energy of preparing for battle, but she hoped his brightened mood meant he and Catanya were working things out together.

Diyah stifled a yawn and decided to return to her room. Some alone time would do her good, and maybe Reg would bring her some food. She climbed out of the attic and headed towards the corridor. As she pushed open the door, she walked headlong into Drayk, who was coming back into the parlour.

"Oh sorry, love," he muttered, grabbing her arm to stop her from falling.

Diyah steadied herself and looked up at him. They'd never been alone together, and she welcomed the opportunity to study him. He was much taller than her, but not as towering as Jémys or Julyán. His thick dark hair was neatly styled, and he had a bright, animated energy that was certainly intoxicating. But something about him unnerved Diyah. The way his eyes flashed in the dim candlelight... He seemed unpredictable.

"Where's Catya?" he asked, glancing around the room.

"She's still upstairs talking to Jémys."

"Oh, right." He seemed mildly irritated. "Well, I think I'll go get a drink." He waved and turned away, but Diyah caught his arm and stopped him.

"Drayk, your hand!" The back of his hand was purple and blue, and fresh blood smeared across his scabbed knuckles.

"What?" he asked, looking down. Then he gave a crooked smile. "Oh yeah, Osrin's got a tough jaw." He shrugged. "I'm fine though."

He tried to take his hand back, but Diyah tightened her grip. "Let me help," she said, directing him to sit in one of the dusty parlour chairs. Diyah knelt on the floor in front of him and pulled off her Heiltúir satchel.

"I haven't seen one of those in years," said Drayk, awed as he watched her.

"You've met another Heiltúir?" she asked, surprised.

Drayk frowned. "Ah, no," he muttered. "But I've had my hands on all kinds of valuable objects over the years. Some more valuable than others." He trailed off, watching her as she treated his wounds. "I always wondered about the Heiltúir, though. I thought they sounded like true heroes."

"Heroes?" repeated Diyah, surprised, and a little flattered.

Drayk shrugged. "I haven't known many people in my life who would willingly dedicate themselves to helping others. I know I could never do it." He winced as she tightened the bandages on his hand. "How does the old saying go? *'A sacred knowledge used, not for glory or for fame, but for peace.'* It's hard to imagine people like that really exist."

"How do you know those words?" she asked.

Drayk shrugged. "Growing up on the streets, I used to read a lot of books, trying to learn as much as possible about the world. I liked the stories about the Heiltúir, with their enhanced memory and instincts bordering on the supernatural." He grinned at her. "I always wanted to believe they were still out there somewhere."

His level of knowledge amazed Diyah. But it saddened her to hear him speak with such wistful reverence for the Heiltúir, like he'd never encountered kindness or sympathy before. He must have lived a very difficult life.

"Can I ask you something?" she ventured somewhat hesitantly. "Have you ever heard of the Jade Moss poison?"

Drayk looked taken aback, and he frowned at her. "Yes, it's extremely rare and toxic. It causes painful paralysis until you can't breathe and you suffocate inside your own body. It's a horrible way to die." He shuddered. "Why do you ask?"

Diyah finished tying off his bandage and sighed. She didn't know who else to talk to about this. She didn't want to tell Catanya until she was sure.

Diyah reached into her pocket and withdrew the vial of green liquid. "Is that what this is?" she asked in a voice so low it was barely audible.

"Where did you get that?" asked Drayk, wide-eyed. He took it from her and examined it under the light of the nearby candle. "Ayr banned it years ago."

"I found it... in Caerlon," she whispered, glancing around to make sure they were still alone. "It's been opened and I think half of it is gone. And..." She took a deep breath, trying to muster the nerve to share her suspicions. "You know, they say

Casréyan's body just shut down. They say he couldn't move in the end..."

Drayk let out a low whistle. "You think that's how Cadyan did it?" he asked, and his expression was an odd mixture of revulsion and respect.

Diyah cleared her throat. "That's just it. I... um... I don't think Cadyan did it..."

Drayk raised his eyebrows. "Then who?"

Diyah just stared at him without responding, and he seemed to understand.

"You think... the queen?" he whispered.

Diyah nodded slowly. "It makes sense. Fehla grew up in Awnell. She knew about the Jade Moss poison and she hated Casréyan more than anyone—certainly enough to want him dead... And after everything he did to her..." She shrugged. Oddly enough, the thought of Fehla killing her husband wasn't what bothered Diyah the most about this.

Drayk eyed her. "What's the matter?" he asked. "So Fehla killed him? She probably did it to protect Catya, didn't she?"

Diyah bit her lip and averted her eyes. "I'm not so sure," she muttered. Then, seeing the confusion on Drayk's face, she continued, "If Fehla wanted to protect Catanya, then why wait so long? Why not kill Casréyan before any of this had happened? No... I don't think she did it for Catanya. I think she did it for Cadyan. To protect him or... Possibly to help him get the throne."

There was a long pause as Drayk took in what she said. "You think Fehla is on his side?" He stared at Diyah warily.

"I'm not sure, but whatever her reason, I know she loves her son. She seems... I don't know..." Diyah shook her head, trying to find the words. "She seems worried about him."

Drayk frowned as he twirled the vial between his fingers. "Worried about him..." He repeated her words in a blank voice. His expression was hard to read, and it made Diyah nervous.

"Well, she is his mother, after all," she said, not sure why she felt the urge to defend Fehla's actions.

"Yes..." Drayk's voice sounded strained. "And despite everything he's done, she loves her son... That's what a mother does, isn't it? She loves and protects her son, no matter what." He looked up at her, a dark glint in his eyes. "And Casréyan was evil. He got what he deserved."

Diyah frowned. "Well... I don't know... I don't think anyone really deserves to die like that, do they?"

"Of course, you don't. You're a Heiltúir—a *hero*." Drayk gave her a warm smile before he turned his attention back to the vial. Then his expression twisted again. "But you can't expect the rest of the world to share your sense of honour. Most people will do whatever it takes to protect themselves above everything else. A lot of us aren't strong enough to resist the temptation for revenge."

Diyah was deeply alarmed by this. She opened her mouth to respond, but before she could say anything, the attic door opened. Catanya and Jémys were coming down the ladder.

"Oh, there you are," said Jémys, hopping off the ladder onto the parlour floor.

Diyah and Drayk stood up, and Drayk slipped the vial into his pocket before anyone could see it. "Here we are," he said, holding his hands out in mock presentation. Then he clapped them together and grinned. "Reunited and about to set off on another grand adventure." He cuffed Jémys on the shoulder playfully. "You missed some good ones though, mate."

Diyah observed his eyes twinkling in Catanya's direction. Taken aback by the sudden return of his jaunty attitude, she didn't know how to react.

Jémys closed his eyes, evidently holding back his frustration. Then he shook his head. "Same old Drayk. You still can't take anything seriously, can you?"

"Well, I *could*... but I don't think I will, thanks." Drayk grinned from ear to ear. There was a long pause while everyone stared at him. "Well, I think I'm off to bed now if anyone wants to join me? Work out some of this awkward tension... I bet the four of us could mix things up nicely. No?" He looked at each of them and laughed at the disbelief on their faces. Then he turned and swept out of the room.

Catanya sighed and shook her head, watching him leave.

Diyah wasn't sure if it was disappointment or pity she read on Catanya's face. Either way, Catanya was obviously upset.

She thought she understood what was going on. After all, Catanya and Jémys had been apart for a long time now, and Drayk was certainly charming. But Diyah was still wary of him. He had a darkness about him that unsettled her.

Her instincts about people were rarely wrong. When she'd first met Jémys, she'd known immediately what kind of person he was. Kind, honest, loyal... And she could tell how much he loved Catanya. It was visible in his eyes whenever he looked at her.

But Drayk was harder to read. She wasn't sure it was love she saw in his eyes when he looked at Catanya. He obviously cared about her, but there was something else underneath it as well—something she couldn't quite figure out.

The way he had attacked Osrin yesterday had disturbed her. She knew Osrin deserved it, but—and perhaps she was just used to it because of Julyán—she had come to respect people who showed restraint in emotional situations. Drayk seemed to be the complete opposite. He seemed driven by his emotions, letting them control him rather than the other way around. She supposed it must be liberating to live like that. But he obviously spent a great deal of energy ignoring the darkness and pain inside him, toying with people and playing games to distract himself.

The attic door opened again and Lia climbed down the ladder towards them.

"So, tell me," she said, walking towards Catanya. "After you've rescued all your precious slaves in Bratia, what do you expect will happen to them?"

There was a brief pause in which no one said anything.

"No, really," insisted Lia. "Most of them won't be fit for anything after the camps. The merciful act would be to kill them and have done with it."

"What's the matter with you?" snapped Jémys. "Those are human beings you're talking about."

"Not anymore," she declared in a dark voice.

Diyah was momentarily frozen in shock. She couldn't believe this woman was Fehla's sister. No two women could be less alike. Fehla may well have killed Casréyan, but if that was the case, she'd done it with the intention of saving lives. Diyah was sure of it. But this woman...

"At the very least, they deserve to die as free people," said Jémys.

"Exactly," said Diyah, finding her voice. "And besides, I'm a healer. I'll be there and I can help the ones who need it most. We can save them."

Lia gave her a disdainful look. "You have an over-inflated opinion of yourself," she said. "I suppose we shouldn't expect any better from some jumped up little whore who's spent the last few months in bed with the firkon."

Diyah and Jémys made sounds of outrage. Before either of them could respond, however, the temperature in the room plummeted. All the candles extinguished, leaving only the pale light of the crescent moon to shine eerily through the window.

"Don't you dare speak to her like that," snarled Catanya as she advanced on Lia. Her hair seemed to glow in the darkness. It crackled and billowed like it was alive with energy.

The expression on Catanya's face was something Diyah had never seen before. It was blind rage—wrath—and it sent a shiver down Diyah's spine.

Lia's posture stiffened, and she braced her hand on her hidden weapon.

"Catanya, it's okay," said Diyah, not surprised to hear herself whispering. She glanced at Jémys, and he seemed to be thinking along the same lines she was. Neither of them had ever seen Catanya look so dangerous before, so much like her brother.

"Catanya?" Jémys reached out and touched her arm.

The candles flickered back to life, and the temperature returned to normal. Catanya looked around to face her friends.

Lia relaxed as the danger seemed to pass. "Like father like daughter," she muttered as she turned and strode out of the room, slamming the door behind her.

A heavy silence settled in the room. Catanya averted her gaze and walked away from them to stand near the window. Diyah didn't really know what to say. Catanya had never been prone to fits of rage like that. This wasn't like her at all.

"Catanya, what just happened?" she asked.

"Sorry," she said. "Lia brings out the worst in me." She turned around to face her friends, wearing a strained smile.

In that moment, Diyah remembered the things Fehla had tried to tell her about Cadyan.

He's becoming something I hardly recognize—something vicious and cruel... this isn't who Cadyan really is.

Diyah had never really taken her seriously before. She struggled to imagine Cadyan as anything other than the monster he was now. Even as a child he'd been a mean, impetuous brat... But maybe he *had* changed. Maybe he had gotten worse.

Diyah exchanged nervous glances with Jémys that, unfortunately, did not go unnoticed by Catanya.

"Well," said Catanya in an unusually high-pitched voice, "I think I will go get some sleep." She smiled halfheartedly again and turned to leave. Before she reached the door, Jémys hurried after her.

"Catanya, wait." He grabbed her arm and leaned in. He spoke in a low whisper, but Diyah still heard everything he said. "It's okay, you don't have to pretend. You don't have to hide it from us. We're not afraid of you. We love you. You know that. There's nothing you could do that could scare us away."

Catanya gave a pained smile and kissed him on the cheek. Diyah wanted to echo his sentiments, but before she could find the right words, Catanya turned and left without saying anything.

Later that night, as Diyah climbed into bed, her mind reeled over everything that had happened that day. She was frustrated with herself for not knowing how to respond after Catanya's display of magic. Catanya was like a sister to her, and she needed Diyah's support now more than ever.

Diyah longed for an opportunity to talk alone with her friend, like they used to do before all this had happened. But she recognized Catanya's desire to be alone—she always sought solitude whenever she was overwrought and overwhelmed.

And in all honesty, Diyah wasn't sure what she could say that would be of any help. Perhaps she'd spent too much time around Cadyan, but magic unnerved her. She wasn't afraid of Catanya, but she was definitely worried about her. Catanya might have learned to wield her powers, but Diyah was beginning to wonder what the cost of using them would be. And would it be worth paying?

As Diyah drifted off to sleep, her thoughts strayed back to Caerlon City, to where Fehla remained, stuck watching her son unleash his powers on others. And for the first time, Diyah thought she understood the full weight of fear and helplessness that had been consuming Fehla since her son had taken the throne.

17

A REBELLION

As preparations for the upcoming invasion continued, Catanya grew increasingly restless. When she'd left Túir-Avlea, she'd been determined, focused. It had been easy to feel confident from the safety of the mountain. But here, on the other side of the shoal, everything seemed more precarious.

She didn't like working with Lia. Her aunt had a knack for drawing out Catanya's anger. But, as Drayk reminded her daily, they needed an army, and they needed a plan. Lia provided both.

But the more the plan unfolded, the more disempowered Catanya felt. Lia was the one with the experience, with the strategy. Catanya might dress like a warrior and associate with warriors, but at the end of the day, what was she?

Catanya felt like nothing more than a wayward orphan. The Awnadh talked of battles and armies, but her mind was on something else.

Family.

One way or another, this entire war depended on her and

Cadyan. A brother and a sister, separated their entire lives, endowed with powers beyond their control.

Could she convince him to listen to her? To stop the fighting?

She clung to her hope like a life raft, keeping her from drowning in despair. But it was difficult to imagine this conflict ending with a peaceful resolution.

At best, she hoped she could find the strength to draw his Resonance into her, leaving him powerless. She'd done it once before, hadn't she? The old man in the cabin—the man she suspected to be her great grandfather—she'd drained his power, pulling it into herself.

If she could do the same to Cadyan, this would all be over. And now that she'd trained with Laylian, perhaps she could manage it without killing him.

The army was almost ready to move. For the last few days, Diyah had been helping the Awnadh healers, and she'd rehabilitated almost a hundred soldiers. Some were still too damaged to march, but most of them were back on their feet.

Catanya and Diyah hadn't found much opportunity to talk since being reunited, and Catanya longed to enjoy some peace and quiet with her friend, to reminisce and speak openly like they used to do. But there was too much at stake right now, and they needed to prioritize their strategizing and planning. Part of Catanya yearned to run away with Diyah, to return to Faltir and forget this entire war. But she wasn't the same person she used to be, and neither was Diyah. Catanya noticed it in the way her friend held herself, the way she moved and talked. She was still the same stubborn, clever, and generous person she'd always been, but there was a new edge to her. Catanya wondered if Diyah recognized it. This last year had changed them both. They weren't carefree, innocent girls anymore, and they never would be again.

It was a little over a week's journey from Awnell to Caerlon on foot. Isa would lead the core army by land, while Catanya, Lia, and a small group of warriors sailed with Osrin and his crew. The army would depart first, which meant Catanya's party would have a week to rescue everyone in Bratia, stop in Sidina, and then sneak into Caerlon's port unnoticed with however many able soldiers they found in Bratia. All without alerting Cadyan to their plans.

Nothing about this would be easy.

Catanya worked hard to conceal from everyone how terrified she actually was. But as nervous as she felt, she was also a little impatient to get started. Standing on the cusp of battle was more stressful than anything she'd ever done. She just wanted it to be over...

The night of their departure arrived. Isa and her army had already departed, leaving a trail of dead firkon behind them. At a word, the remaining Awnadh civilians had risen up to reclaim their home with ease, ensuring no Caerlon loyalists escaped the city to warn their king. It was the quietest takeover Catanya could ever imagine. But Lia had had months to prepare the Awnadh in secret. Catanya may not like the commander, but she couldn't deny Lia was effective, and efficient.

Supplies had been loaded and everything was moving smoothly so far. Catanya stood on the dock with the others, staring at a ship she'd seen once before in passing. The ship looked even more massive than it had at sea all those months ago. Its three gigantic masts towered into the sky, creaking in the wind. The serpent figurehead seemed to stare at Catanya, its hollow eyes menacing in the moonlight.

She still remembered Drayk's warning about the marauders, and the fear in his eyes when he thought they'd seen him hiding at the cottage.

Now she understood, of course. She understood the real reason he'd been so upset, and she couldn't blame him. When Catanya had first heard the story about Drayk's father, she never imagined that one day she'd meet him, let alone be forced to rely on him in any way. She felt unbelievably uncomfortable, like somehow she was betraying Drayk by accepting this man's help.

It felt wrong to be working with him when all she wanted to do was make him pay for the things he'd done. So, she promised herself, if she got the chance, she would do just that.

"You're mad!" exclaimed Osrin when they'd boarded his ship and told him about their plan for the rebellion at Bratia. "Cadyan will kill you all."

His arrogant tone irritated Catanya, but she did her best to contain her displeasure. She stood off to the side of the group with her face hidden underneath her cloak so no one would recognize her. Everyone seemed to think it best to conceal her identity for as long as possible. But she found it difficult not to intervene in the conversation.

"No, he won't," said Diyah. Catanya smiled at the familiar obstinate and rebellious tone Diyah always used when she disliked someone.

"And besides, we weren't asking for your opinion," said Drayk.

"No way. You told me you needed to get into Caerlon. That's fine. But this..." Osrin shook his head. "I won't be a part of this. You can count me out. I'm not risking my life for a bunch of filthy slaves."

There were shouts of outrage from the rest of the group but he didn't listen. "No!" he called over the noise. "I'm not going to risk pissing off the most powerful man in Mórceá for a fool's errand. Not a chance."

Silence fell over the group, and Catanya sensed everyone trying to think of a way to force his hand. She was growing impatient, and she was admittedly a little annoyed to hear how scared he was to upset Cadyan... Osrin should be frightened of her too.

"You don't have a choice," she said, stepping into the lamp-light and allowing him to see her face. Her vision flared with golden light and she stretched her mind out to the Water beneath the ship. The vessel pulled away from the dock of its own accord, tearing the planks free from the port and letting them splash into the bay.

Everyone on deck stumbled as the ship jerked.

"Excellent," said Drayk under his breath.

Osrin gaped at her in shock. "That-that's not possible," he spluttered, stumbling backwards away from Catanya.

"You understand who I am?" she asked in a low voice as the sails unfurled, ballooning and snapping angrily in the Wind. The mooring anchor burst into the air above the bay and thudded onto the deck. The ship cruised forward effortlessly into the open sea.

Osrin nodded.

"Good. Then you understand that this ship no longer belongs to you. You no longer dictate where it goes and what its passengers do." Her voice grew deeper and more threatening with every word. "In fact, the only reason you are still breathing is because you know how to get into the camps and into Caerlon undetected. Is that clear?"

Osrin nodded begrudgingly without taking his eyes off her.

"Very well, then it's settled. You will take us where we need to go with no further objections," she finished. "How long until we reach Bratia?"

Osrin hesitated. Catanya relished the sight of him quivering before her—this terrible, cruel, self-serving man finally experiencing a dose of the fear he so loved to inflict. "We should be there by sundown three days from now," he said, casting uneasy glances at the rest of the group.

"Hmm..." Catanya squinted at the horizon. "Let's make it two days, shall we?"

Osrin looked outraged. "Listen, lady, this ship can only go so fast. You can't just expect—"

Catanya held up her hand to cut him off. Her eyes flashed again and the Wind speeds increased around them, pushing the ship forward even faster.

"Like I said, sundown tomorrow." Then she marched past him towards the officer's quarters, tingling with the thrill of using her powers, and ignoring the temptation to push them further.

Catanya spent the better part of the next day locked in her quarters, avoiding the others. Her mind overflowed with worries and concerns. She didn't think she could bear to talk to anyone.

Time crept by interminably slowly. She had gone over the plan dozens of times in her head. Now there was nothing to do but wait. But she was eager to get the rebellion over with and prove herself in some way. She had begun to tie the thought of success at Bratia together with her hopes of success in Caerlon. The rebellion would be easy compared to what came after, but still... She had never done anything like this before, and she needed to know she could handle herself.

So, when the ship finally docked on the southern coast, outside the Tirimsi desert, she felt ready.

She stood on deck, baking in the blazing sun as it set beyond the sandy horizon, its orange glow burning across the sky. It reminded her momentarily of her younger self—the girl who'd longed to see that skyline.

"I still think you should let me come with you," grumbled Diyah, watching from the deck as Catanya, Drayk, Jémys, Lia, and the others descended the ship to head inland towards the mountains.

Catanya had agreed that Diyah should join them on the journey—they would need her help in Sidina—but she was adamant that Diyah stay behind while they infiltrated the camps. She wasn't sure what they were walking into, and she'd never forgive herself if something happened to Diyah.

"It's not safe," said Catanya. "You're not a fighter, you're a healer. And besides, we need someone to keep an eye on Osrin."

"I know that," said Diyah. "But, Catanya, please be careful."

Catanya smiled at her friend. "We'll be back soon," she promised as she climbed down the ladder and landed beside the others. "Okay, let's go."

Lia gave the signal for the soldiers to move.

It took over an hour for their group to make their way in from the coast. The sun had set, and the clouds had rolled in, making it a particularly dark night. But Catanya was grateful for the added cover.

As they trudged on together, they came upon the first vestiges of abandoned excavation territories. Old carts with broken wheels, scraps of metal, and shards of rotted wood decorated the poorly reconstructed land. The path was treacherous. They stumbled forward, eyes and ears straining to detect any signs of movement.

Tension tore at Catanya's nerves, making it more difficult for her to keep her powers restrained. They itched beneath the surface almost like they knew what was about to happen. She had never experienced this strange combination of excitement and unease before.

They walked on through the arid desert, navigating the dilapidated landscape as best they could. Finally, the Ruins of Bratia appeared on the horizon, cast against the dark night sky like the desiccated skeleton of an enormous beast.

Catanya had heard stories of Bratia. In her youth, she'd longed to gaze upon its ruins, upon this artifact of a bygone era.

Thousands of years ago, Bratia had been the greatest city ever built. It was a paragon of innovation and peace. Its people had lived together in prosperity and safety for generations, each contributing to its grandeur with new creations and works of art. It had stretched along the coast with a myriad of structures including lyceums, amphitheatres, and temples of the old religion. And the great labyrinth of tunnels below the city had once served as both the sacred treasury and the hallowed tomb.

Now, it was nothing more than the haunted echo of a time long past and a people long dead. The last and bloodiest casualty of the Quiescence Wars. City ruins lay scattered and scorched across the now parched land. Centuries of overgrowth and sand blanketed the rubble of once glorious buildings. Its tunnels had been transformed into mines, with hordes of people trampling through them, disturbing the bodies and pilfering treasures.

As Catanya and the others approached the ruins, they saw the pale glow of light up ahead. Distinct outlines of several makeshift camps were scattered across the landscape, and voices echoed in the distance.

Then came a shout, and the unmistakable crack of a whip burst through the air. Catanya swallowed back her sudden nausea.

"We should split up now," whispered Drayk.

"Agreed."

The others broke off into pairs and crept along the outer fence of the compound. Catanya's gaze lingered on the outline of Jémys and Lia as they headed east. Uneasiness ate at her, as she watched them go. Catanya had only just gotten Jémys back in her life. Watching him walk away brought up uncomfortable feelings.

And then there was Lia. The commander would do whatever it took to rescue the Awnadh, but what about everyone else? Catanya wasn't sure she could trust Lia to do the right thing where the other prisoners were concerned. She would have preferred if Lia had stayed behind on the ship, but they needed her help.

So Catanya had asked Jémys to go with Lia and keep an eye on her. She knew Jémys would make sure everyone was safe, but it still felt wrong letting him go off without her.

"Are you ready?" asked Drayk.

Catanya took a deep breath and nodded. "Yes," she said, forcing her worries aside to concentrate on the task at hand.

Drayk drew his sword and the two of them continued towards the largest camp at the south edge of the ruins. From a distance they saw the enormous iron fence drawn around the perimeter like bars on a prison. The camp was bigger than Catanya had expected. Beyond the fence stood row after row of stone buildings. Haphazard lanes and streets connected them all together like a small, shabby town. Several watchtowers were visible at regular intervals, and they could just make out the faint outlines of the firkon patrolling the area.

"We need something to conceal our approach," whispered Catanya. She glanced around until her gaze landed on the dry and dusty path ahead. "I have an idea..." She reached out to the Wind, conjuring a powerful gust that carried layers of sand into the air in billowing clouds. She repeated the gesture, channelling it towards the firkon posted outside the gate.

As Catanya and Drayk approached the fence, she heard the firkon coughing and spluttering on the sandy air.

"Oh, I hate windstorms out here," said one of them. "I can't see anything."

"Me neither, but it's not like there's ever anything to see, now, is there?" said a second, gruffer voice.

Catanya and Drayk hurried along, keeping low behind the sand storm. They crept up to the gate and ducked behind the wall of the watchtower.

"That's true." The man coughed again and then groaned. "How'd we get stuck here, eh?"

"You know how," replied the second voice.

Catanya and Drayk exchanged glances. She let the wind-storm abate so they could see through to the backs of the two men now standing in front of them. One looked surprisingly young—too young to be guarding a prison camp—and the other looked much older, perhaps in his fifties.

"That vile tournament. I swear next year I'm going to make it past the first round," said the young man.

"You don't really want that, trust me. We've got it easy here. Keeping a few hundred slaves in check. Not to mention wide open skies, fresh breezes, and an endless supply of girls and other entertainment. Nah, you couldn't pay me to work in the city."

"You can't mean that! The city's where all the real excitement is."

The older man mumbled something incoherent and the young boy laughed. "I suppose you're right," he said. "Even so, I reckon I'd make a fine maífirkon one day."

"That's the last thing you should wish for," muttered the old man, sounding serious. "Just you trust me on this, boy. You're better off far away from all that."

The young man sat down on an overturned barrel, looking glum. "Yeah, all right," he muttered.

Catanya peeked her head around the wall. Both men still had their backs to her. Their weapons leaned against the fence a few feet away, and no one was manning the watchtower. It was almost too easy. She nodded towards Drayk, and he smiled as he stepped out from their hiding spot. He moved quickly, grabbing the first man and locking his arms behind his back. Drayk slapped his hand over the firkon's mouth to stop him screaming.

"Wha—"

Catanya bashed the younger man on the head with the hilt of her sword. He collapsed on the ground in a heap.

"Listen closely and do as I say, then maybe we'll let you live," hissed Drayk into the older firkon's ear as Catanya retreated to the shadows so she wouldn't be recognized. "How many firkon are stationed at the camps?" He relaxed his hand so the man could respond.

"Who are you?" asked the firkon, wrestling against Drayk's hold.

Drayk kneed him in the back, and he let out a cry of pain. "Don't make me repeat myself."

The firkon grunted and swore under his breath as Drayk tightened his grip. "Three battalions," he grumbled.

"And where are they now?"

The firkon hesitated, so Drayk wrenched on his arms.

"Ow—all right!" he protested. "One on watch at the tunnels, one off duty, and one patrolling the camps. Who are you, then?" He struggled against Drayk's grip, trying to see.

"Where are the Awnadh?" asked Catanya. The man tried to turn his head to see her, but Drayk forced him back in the other direction.

"Down the lane," he grumbled. "Some of 'em'll be in the tunnels and some'll be off shift, sleepin'... So you one of them, then, eh?" The man tried again to turn his head. Drayk released his hold and smashed him on the side of the head, knocking the man unconscious. Then, straightening out his coat, he turned towards Catanya. "Right, onwards?" he asked playfully.

Catanya struggled to keep her face serious. "Onwards," she said, leading the way through the gate and into the camp. "Now we need to create a distraction that draws the firkon to us so the others can get in, clear the tunnels, and find the Awnadh."

"Oh, is that all?" asked Drayk with blithe cheerfulness. "Then I say we—"

A shout rang out in the distance followed by the sound of crashing and banging.

Catanya raced forward and emerged onto what appeared to be a central lane connecting all the buildings. The area was conspicuously deserted. She looked around for a sign of the disturbance.

More people shouted in the distance. Something was drawing the firkon in the other direction. Panic seized Catanya, driving her thoughts towards the others, towards Jémys. What if something happened to him? She picked up the pace as she and Drayk hurried down the lane towards the noise.

As they approached a nearby building, the door swung open and a horde of people poured onto the street. Catanya recognized the violet uniforms. Half a dozen firkon were locked in a fight with a group of men in tattered brown clothes. Catanya braced for an attack, but then she heard a voice she recognized.

"Drayk, is that ye?"

They turned to see who it was.

A lanky man stood in the doorway, grinning at them.

"Niq?" asked Catanya and Drayk in unison.

Catanya couldn't believe it. He looked thinner and droopier than ever, with several bruises and cuts on his face. But other than that, he seemed fine.

"Whoa, Catya, look at ye," he said, grinning at her altered appearance. "I always thought there was somethin' different about ye." He chuckled knowingly and shook his head.

He barely reacted to the brawl happening around him, but when one firkon broke free and lunged at him, Niq punched the man squarely in the face so he toppled over.

"We heard a disturbance and figured we'd join the ruckus, ye know. Anythin' to pass the time and piss off a few firkon... Had no idea it was ye lot here to rescue us—" He paused, frowning at them. "Tha's why yer here, right?"

"Yes, Niq," replied Catanya. "We're here to save everyone."

Just then, one of the firkon spotted her. His eyes popped as he saw her hair and realized who she was. He raised his sword and took a step forward, but Catanya shoved him back with another gust of Wind.

"Niq," she called over to him, as Drayk jumped into the fray, yanking one of the firkon off a fallen Awnadh. "Drayk and I can handle this. Can you find the rest of the Awnadh? We need your help to clear everyone out of the camps and meet us on the southern fields."

Niq nodded and snatched a sword off an unconscious firkon. He sliced through two others as he rallied the Awnadh and took off down the lane. There were only a few firkon left. They seemed to be debating whether to follow Niq and the other Awnadh when a new pair of firkon careened around the corner and lunged at Catanya and Drayk.

Catanya reacted instinctively. She raised her hands in the air and lifted the new men off the ground before hurling them backwards so they crumpled into the others and fell in a heap.

She heard a strangled yelp behind her. Turning around, she found Drayk grappling with yet another man, who must have snuck up from behind. She watched the firkon wrestle Drayk onto the ground and draw his sword.

"No!" she shouted. Without thinking, she threw out her hands.

A flash of blinding gold light obscured her vision, illuminating the entire sky. The man gave a sharp cry before collapsing, his face slack and his eyes glazed. He stared up at the stars without seeing them. The man was dead.

Drayk scrambled to his feet and glanced down at the man, shocked. Then he turned and stared at Catanya.

"H-he was going to kill you," she stammered. She'd only wanted to incapacitate the man, not kill him. But as she stared down at his lifeless body, she felt strange—oddly unmoved by what she'd done. It had been easy. Too easy.

"Hey, I'm not complaining," said Drayk, shrugging and rubbing a spot on his arm.

They stared at each other for a second until they heard running footsteps. The flash of light had drawn the attention of still more guards. And the other fallen firkon were climbing back to their feet.

"I think we found the distraction we were looking for," said Drayk with a wry smile.

Catanya nodded. A horde of firkon emerged onto the lane ahead of them and came to an immediate halt.

Catanya took a deep breath to settle her nerves. "Evening, fellas," she called. If she hadn't been so focused on remaining calm, she might have laughed at the expressions on their faces.

"You!" shouted one man, dramatically pointing his finger at her.

"Me," she replied, clasping her hands behind her back, waiting for them to attack. But none of the men seemed inclined to make the first move.

Then one of them spotted their dead companion on the ground. "She killed Bordlun!" he shouted, outraged.

Catanya pursed her lips. "Yes, but in my defence, he didn't really give me a choice," she said offhand, looking down at him and shrugging. "But I'll give *you* one," she continued, keeping her voice calm. "You see, this little operation of yours is over." She gestured around the compound. "I'm here to put an end to it."

As if on cue, a series of rally cries echoed somewhere in the distance. Niq had reunited with the other Awnadh.

She smiled serenely at the apprehension on the firkon's faces. "As I was saying," she continued, "your work here is done. Now, you can either leave this place and never come back, or you can try to stop me, and die."

There was a stunned silence and nobody moved. In her peripheral vision, she saw Drayk raise his sword.

The power surged in Catanya's fingertips, begging to be unleashed, but she kept it contained. Though she had to admit... She liked seeing the fear in these men's eyes. These were the kind of men who spent their life intimidating others. She wanted them to be on the receiving end of that for a change. She wanted them to know how dangerous she could be.

Still, nobody moved. Suddenly, Catanya realized they were all waiting for something. She heard a crunch behind her and turned around. One of the unconscious firkon had returned to his feet. He advanced on her with his sword outstretched, hands trembling with fear.

He let out a cry and charged. Catanya sprang up into the air and floated down gracefully on the other side of him. Then she tossed her arm out lazily, sending a blast of Wind at him. He half stumbled, half soared forward, crashing clumsily into the line of other firkon, slicing one of their arms with his sword.

Catanya snorted. "Not the top tier firkon here, are we?" she said, eyeing the stupid looks on their faces.

There was a pause while everyone stared at her. Then all at once the firkon charged. Drayk braced for the attack, but Catanya just shook her head and held up her hands. The firkon collided with an invisible barrier. Unable to advance further, they stumbled over each other in a heap.

"Really?" she asked with droll scepticism. Then she clapped her hands together, and the sound echoed through the air. Right on cue, the men all fell to the ground, gasping as she forced her power down upon them.

"I gave you a choice," she said, tightening her grip so the men spluttered and gasped. "Why are you so eager to fight me? Do you *want* to die?" She stepped over the nearest soldier and stood in the middle where she could glare down at them all.

The true terror on their faces was almost comedic. These men had obviously never seen magic like this. They had probably never experienced her brother's wrath, so they had no idea what she was capable of doing to them.

She sighed, a little disappointed. She'd been hoping for a bit more of a fight. "All right, fine," she said. "I won't kill you." She gave one last heave, lifting the men off the ground and then slamming them back down, where they lay unconscious and unmoving.

"That was impressive," said Drayk, re-sheathing his sword and nodding. "But you know, you could have left a few for me." He flashed her a playful grin.

"Sorry, I just thought time was a factor, you understand." She grinned back at him. Despite her earlier fears, everything seemed to be going well, and she had to admit it was rather exhilarating to fight alongside Drayk like this.

"Come on," she beckoned for him to follow her farther down the lane, towards the entrance to the tunnels.

A faint commotion came from inside the widest tunnel. They arrived just in time to see Niq emerge, leading a group of bedraggled people dressed in rags and covered in dirt and grime.

"Good work," said Catanya, beaming at him. She and Drayk stood back to let the people pass.

She recognized a lot of faces from Awnell, but there were also a lot of faces she didn't know. The people were emaciated, their withered bodies covered in patterns of purple bruises and half-healed wounds. Some bore clear signs of repeated beatings and lashings. And every single one of them had a hollow, sunken look in their eyes.

A sudden flash of white-hot rage blasted through Catanya, as she thought about everything these people had suffered.

"Catya," said Drayk, laying his hand on her arm and glancing around at the sand storm forming around them.

Catanya hadn't realized that, in her anger, she'd been channelling the Natures.

"Sorry," she muttered, taking a deep breath to relax. It
wasn't easy to keep her emotions in check when she was
surrounded by so much pain.

"Right tha's everyone from down there," said Niq, peering
down the tunnel and nodding. "We'll head to the outskirts and
wait for ye and the others."

He turned to leave, but Catanya stopped him, holding out
her arm in the Awnadh fashion. He smiled faintly and
grasped her arm. "Thanks for comin' to get us," he said.
Despite his affected gaiety, she saw the hollow look in his eyes
now too.

She watched him lead his rescues away from the tunnels
and towards the outer boundary of the camp, then she stared
up at the sky.

"It's time," she said, turning her gaze back to the ground.
But a creeping doubt began to take heart inside her, and she
turned to stare at Drayk.

"It's okay, love," he said, grabbing her shoulder. "You can do
this."

Catanya swallowed hard. "Yeah... I just hope the others
have cleared the area—that they're safe."

"They are," said Drayk. "They have to be."

Catanya nodded, allowing his conviction to sweep away her
concerns. Then she knelt down at the entrance to the tunnel,
where she placed her hands on the ground. Closing her eyes,
she reached out to the Earth and felt it vibrate beneath her
fingers. Deep underground, she heard a resounding crash. The
tunnel walls were caving in. As the entire ground began to
shake, Catanya heard Drayk stumbling behind her, but she
carried on. The outline of the ruins quivered dangerously, and
rocks came loose, crashing to the ground in the distance. She
forced her mind to pass through every tunnel, pulling them

each down in turn, blocking every access point until there was nothing left.

When she'd finished, she released her hold and stood up, turning around to face Drayk. "It's done," she said, a little breathless. "We did it."

Drayk smiled widely and clapped her on the shoulder. "Come on, let's go find the others." He beamed at her and turned to lead the way back down the lane and out of the camp.

Catanya couldn't help but smile too as she turned to follow him.

As she was walking away from the tunnels, something caught her eye at the side of the compound. She hadn't noticed it before, but there was a large mound of earth blocking her view to the west.

"What's that?" she asked more to herself than to Drayk. She jogged over to the mound and hiked up the hill. Panting slightly, she reached the top and stared down the other side.

In an instant, her good mood vanished. She heard Drayk gasp as he crested the hill and stood next to her, staring down at the enormous trench below them.

The trench was filled with bodies.

Broken and twisted corpses of the recent dead were scattered unceremoniously across a mound of skeletons in various stages of decomposition. The mass grave was enormous, stretching the entire length of the nearest building and at least twenty feet wide. Catanya couldn't tell how deep it was, but judging by the size of the earth mound where she and Drayk stood, she guessed it was at least as deep as it was wide.

The stench was overwhelming. She gazed down at the lifeless faces of the abused and discarded. There were men and women and children all smashed together in contorted positions like they'd been heaved over the hill without a care in the world.

All sense of calm was suddenly gone, and Catanya's body

trembled with rage. The prickling, burning itch coursed through her body like fire.

She breathed that anger in, allowing it to consume her as she closed her eyes. When she opened them again, the world burned with the energy she was channelling. She vaguely heard Drayk saying something, but she didn't listen.

The ground began to vibrate again. The screeching, crashing groan of rock on rock told her she was pulling the entire place down. She glared at the camp, watching the buildings crumble.

Something grabbed her arm and she looked down to see Drayk's hand enclosed around her forearm. The whites of his knuckles shone in the moonlight as he strained to hold on, trying to stabilize himself as the ground shook uncontrollably.

Catanya pushed off with her feet, bringing him with her as they soared above the compound.

She heard shouts and screams coming from the streets below. The unconscious firkon had woken up. She concentrated on those sounds, drawing herself towards them. The buildings continued to crumble, and the men came into view, desperately scrambling over each other, trying to escape the earthquake. Catanya held out her hands, blocking them in an invisible cage.

She closed her eyes and imagined it—pain unlike anything these men had ever endured. Dehydration, starvation, whippings, rape, suffocation, torture, death. She imagined everything the people in the mass grave must have suffered, and more. She reached out to the Spirits around her and twisted, wringing them until she heard them scream. All around her the firkon cried out, shrieking from their souls as the surrounding air quivered and they dropped to the ground, writhing.

They deserved this. Each and every one of them. They deserved this and so much more.

"Enough!" she called, and her voice echoed through the

night air. Her vision flared gold once again, and in an instant, they were dead. Every single firkon in the compound.

She lowered herself and Drayk down into their midst and relaxed her hold on the world.

Slowly the Earth stilled and the darkness of night returned.

"Shall we go?" she asked after a while, glancing over at Drayk. He stood beside her, gaping at the dead bodies scattered across the ground.

He wrenched his gaze away and turned to face her, plastering on a blank expression. Then he nodded and the two of them made their way out of the camp.

18

REPERCUSSIONS

"What's taking them so long?" asked Catanya. She was pacing back and forth along the deck of the ship, waiting for the others to return.

The blackness of the evening had given way to the pale light of dawn. The eerie blue tint of the sky did nothing to ease her nerves.

"What if they didn't make it out of the tunnels before I collapsed them?" she asked, whipping around to look at Drayk and Diyah. "Or what if—" She broke off, glancing nervously at Drayk.

"They're fine, Catya," he said. "They'll be back soon. We still have time, try not to worry."

"Right," mumbled Catanya as she resumed pacing.

She and Drayk had reunited with Niq and the other Awnadh hours ago. Then they'd made their way back to the ship, only to discover that no one else had returned.

As the night wore on, all the other groups had returned with their rescues. But there was still no sign of Jémys and Lia.

"What if she did something to him?" muttered Catanya

under her breath. "If I find out something happened to him because of her..." She trailed off, feeling helpless and hostile.

Before they had stormed the ruins, they'd agreed that no matter what happened, the ship would depart promptly at daybreak. They needed to be fast if they were going to have time to stop in Sidina and still arrive in Caerlon before Isa and her army.

But Catanya hadn't thought through the realities of that agreement. She'd never imagined someone wouldn't make it back in time.

A shout and a thud drew Catanya's attention, and she spun around to face the hull. Jémys and Lia appeared, climbing awkwardly back onto the ship. A group of rescued prisoners was visible behind them.

Relief washed over Catanya, and she hurried forward. But she stopped when she realized something was wrong.

"Help!" gasped Jémys. He and Lia were carrying someone unconscious between them. Their faces bore several noticeable bruises and cuts.

"Oh no!" Diyah rushed forward to help. "What's wrong with her?"

"I don't know." Jémys's voice shook, as they lowered the unconscious girl to the ground. "We found her like this."

Catanya inched forward to see who it was. Her heart sank when she realized she recognized the woman. "Roslin," she whispered, kneeling down beside the unconscious girl and gaping at her bruised and shrunken frame.

The last time Catanya had seen Roslin was during the attack at Finnua. Jémys had told her to run and hide at the manor house. Roslin had been so gentle, so innocent. Catanya remembered how sweet she'd been at the Harvest Festival, modeling her hairstyle after Catanya's, becoming abashed and flustered whenever Jémys approached.

Catanya locked eyes with Jémys and felt his anguish pour into her.

"Can you help her?" he asked Diyah.

Diyah bit her lip, but she nodded. "Bring her through to the officer's quarters and lay her down on the bed."

Jémys beckoned for Drayk to help him, and Drayk hurried forward to grab Roslin's legs. He and Jémys lifted her gently off the ground and carried her through the door and out of sight.

"What happened?" asked Diyah, watching them go.

"The boy is a sentimental fool! That's what happened," hissed Lia, turning her head and spitting blood onto the deck. "After barely surviving an ambush by two full battalions, we were almost finished our sweep when we found that girl moaning, half-dead in the back room of a ruined brothel on the edge of the compound. I told him she wasn't going to make it, but he wouldn't listen to me. And then..." She let out a mirthless laugh. "Once we made it out of the camp, the stupid girl woke up and starting panicking, lashing out at us. We had to keep stopping, trying to get her under control. She's deranged. I told him we should put her out of her misery, but"—she shrugged and rolled her eyes—"here we are."

Fury blazed through Catanya. "You can't—" She started, but the sudden sound of screaming below deck halted her.

Diyah raced off towards the officer's quarters.

"Tell Osrin to set sail," called Catanya as she rushed after her.

"What's going on?" asked Diyah when they'd arrived outside the room. Roslin was crouched on the bed, shrieking at the top of her lungs. Jémys and Drayk appeared to be trying to calm her, but she lashed out at them, attacking them like a wounded animal.

"She just went mad!" cried Drayk, shielding his face from her blows.

"Rosy! Rosy, it's me," called Jémys, trying desperately to reason with her. "Rosy, stop!"

"Don't touch me!" she shouted, trying to push him away. "I can't take any more!" She was sobbing violently and trying to retreat farther into the corner.

"Stop!" shouted Catanya, reaching her power out to everyone in the room, latching on, and immobilizing them where they stood. Diyah and Jémys looked startled and a little frightened to feel the effects of her power for the first time, but Catanya ignored them. "Roslin," she said in a kinder voice, "I need you to calm down, please. It's me, Catanya, and Jémys." She gestured over to him and relaxed her powers enough so that he could move. "You remember us, don't you?"

Jémys cast an uneasy glance at Catanya, then took a slow step forward and smiled reassuringly. "Rosy, you know me," he whispered, kneeling down beside the bed.

Roslin stared at him blankly with a haunted look in her eyes. "Jémys?" she repeated.

"That's right," he said.

Roslin looked around the room, taking in her surroundings. To Catanya's horror she started sobbing even more violently. "Oh no," she moaned, hugging her knees into her chest. "No, no, no, no! Not again. I can't be back here!" She spotted Catanya and Diyah near the entrance, and her eyes popped. She jumped towards them. "Please don't let them hurt me. Don't let them take me, please." She pointed towards Drayk and Jémys.

"Nobody is going to hurt you, Roslin." Catanya tried to sound reassuring.

Roslin grasped at Catanya and Diyah's clothes and sobbed all over them. Whenever they tried to touch her, she flinched and cried out like they were hurting her.

"I think Jémys and I should leave," murmured Drayk. "She might feel safer without us here."

"You!" cried Roslin, staring at Drayk and recoiling again.

"It's you! No wait... No, not quite." She chewed on her finger-nails as she started crying again. "Please don't!" she pleaded, staring at Drayk with tears in her eyes.

Drayk looked like someone had punched him in the gut. "Excuse me," he muttered in a dead voice. Then he turned and stalked out of the room without another glance.

"What's going on?" asked Jémys, looking to Diyah for help.

Diyah shook her head sadly. "I don't know, Jémys, but I think Drayk is right, I think you should go. Let us try talking to her."

Jémys cast one last regretful look at Roslin and sighed before turning and following Drayk.

"It's okay, Rosy," said Catanya, holding her hands up in a gesture of goodwill. "You're safe with us."

"You won't let them hurt me?" she asked, trembling.

"Never. Nobody is going to hurt you ever again," said Diyah. "Now, Rosy, my name is Diyah and I'm a healer. Would it be okay if I came over there to look at some of your wounds?"

Roslin seemed to calm down a vast deal after the men left the room. She even let Diyah examine her and let Catanya help her into some clean clothes. As they dressed her, they noted all the scars and bruises on her fragile body.

An all-too-familiar anger flared inside Catanya.

After a while, she and Diyah left the room so Roslin could rest. Diyah headed off to check on the other new arrivals. She had spent the entire evening treating and dressing wounds, and she was clearly exhausted. But Catanya knew her friend wouldn't stop until she'd seen to everyone.

Catanya, however, needed a place to be alone with her thoughts for a while. It wasn't easy now that the ship was over-flowing with people. She wandered the deck, weaving through groups of refugees, until she found a quiet place at the stern. She leaned over the railing and stared at the waves splashing below.

KATHRYN KNOWLES

The sun was high in the sky now. It was hot, beating down on them, but the breeze was strong and refreshing as it brushed against Catanya's face, whipping at her hair. Catanya closed her eyes and reached out to it, directing it towards the sails and urging the ship to move faster. The sooner they could get these people off the ship and somewhere safe, the better.

The rebellion hadn't gone exactly how Catanya had hoped or imagined it would. She supposed it was naïve of her, but she hadn't fully comprehended all the possible forms of abuse that could exist in a place like Bratia. Just when she thought she'd seen the worst, something new presented itself and she had to fight to contain her emotions. She couldn't afford to give into them again.

"Do you regret it?" said a voice behind her, causing her to jump. She turned around to see Drayk watching her with a hard expression.

"I'm not sure," she muttered, turning back to face the water. She didn't need to ask what he meant. She'd been trying not to think about what she'd done at the camp. But seeing Roslin had brought it all back. The blind rage and urge for retribution. "I don't know what came over me, Drayk. I've never felt that violent before..."

Drayk stood next to her and rested his hands on the railing, gazing at the horizon. "They deserved to be punished," he said.

Catanya sighed and nodded. "Still... Not like that," she whispered, watching the water glitter in the sun. The weight of her actions pressed down on her.

"There were always going to be casualties in this fight, Catya. You knew that from the beginning."

Catanya put her face in her hands. "I've killed before but this was different... I wasn't out of control this time. No one was trying to hurt me or you... I just..."

"Wanted to do it," Drayk finished the sentence for her.

Catanya glanced over at him. The understanding on his

332

face made her feel somehow better and worse all at the same time. "Everyone thinks I'm better than him, but I'm not... am I?" she asked in a quiet voice.

Drayk frowned. "I don't know," he said, squinting out at the sun, "I don't think we *can* be better than him—not really. All we can do is make decisions in the moment and live with the consequences. I don't know if what you did was good or bad, but I know those men deserved to be punished, and I'm glad they were."

Catanya watched Drayk for a moment. His expression hardened, almost like he was steeling himself to do something. "Some men don't deserve to live," he said.

They lapsed into silence together until Drayk spoke again and his voice sounded different. "She thought I was him," he whispered. "That girl, Roslin. She thought I was Osrin, and she was terrified." He shook his head, lips pursed like he'd tasted something sour. "We can't let people like him get away with the things they've done. Osrin is every bit as bad as the firkon in that camp. Just as guilty."

"I know, Drayk," said Catanya, putting her hand on his. "But we need him to get us into Sidina and Caerlon. We need him for now but..." She trailed off, shrugging. "When this is over, we'll stop him too, I promise."

Drayk nodded. "And what if we don't survive?" he asked, turning to face her again.

They held each other's gaze, and Catanya thought about all the times they'd narrowly escaped death, all the times they'd barely survived together. Then she shook her head. "I don't know," she replied in a small voice.

After a while, Catanya left Drayk to his silent contemplation. She returned below deck where Lia and the others were discussing plans for the next few days. Catanya didn't have time to waste dwelling on what she'd done in Bratia. Whether it was good or bad didn't matter at the moment. Drayk was right.

She'd made her choice and she would have to live with the consequences. But for now, she needed to speak with the other Awnadh and regroup before arriving in Sidina.

Catanya spent the next several hours talking with Niq. He recounted his experience in Bratia, describing all the different horrors he and the others had endured. The more Catanya heard, the more she felt slightly vindicated for her actions.

The Awnadh had endured especially awful treatment. They'd spent their time alternating between sixteen-hour shifts underground, four hours of work detail in either the cookhouse or the sorting rooms, and four hours of sleep. And they'd slept cramped in rotten hammocks inside dilapidated buildings that were infested with vermin and caked in grime.

All slaves had been expected to live by the same schedule. However, the firkon had devised an additional punishment for the interred Awnadh warriors: fighting rings. Nearly every Awnadh had been forced to fight in grotesque rings while the firkon placed bets on them for entertainment. Anyone who'd refused had been confined to the discipline cabins until they'd changed their minds.

"It's all right," said Niq when Catanya expressed her revulsion about their treatment. "We're trained to handle this sort of thing. I'm not sayin' it was easy, but we coped. And we tried to help the other prisoners as best we could, ye know? Some of 'em had been there fer years, though. Got used to it... thought they were comfortable." Niq shook his head.

"Do you think you and the others will be able to fight with us?" Catanya had explained her plan to invade Caerlon to Niq and the other Awnadh, but a part of her hoped they wouldn't be well enough to join her. She couldn't bear the thought of dragging them through any more pain.

"Most of us, yeah," he said, nodding. "But there's a few... the ones who had it worst... Them discipline cabins are rough, ye know?" He indicated a pair of Awnadh who were sitting mute in the corner, staring at the wall. They hadn't moved since they'd first sat there the night before. "They'll be okay in time," he said. "We all have differen' strategies. Some people shut down. But most of us fix on somethin'—one thing, like a charm to protect us. For me, it's Bir. I think about him and it gives me strength to live. I had to survive so I could see him again. Yer healer friend tells me he's alive in Caerlon. So, I'll keep fightin' till I find him. That's what matters to me. I'd endure Bratia a thousand times over if it meant I could see Bir again."

Catanya's eyes burned a bit at the emotion in his voice. "Thank you, Niq," she said, patting his arm as she stood up.

"Honestly," he said in a lighter tone. "The worst part was the food. No flavour or creativity. Just mush." He grinned and pretended to gag.

At this, a genuine smile finally cracked through Catanya's overwhelming dolour, and she gave Niq an affectionate hug. It heartened her to hear him joking the way he'd done all those months ago in Awnell. For a moment, it was like nothing had changed.

The presence of the rescued slaves was affecting everyone. It was difficult not to feel the weight of the damage that had been done.

Jémys seemed especially disturbed by it all. Catanya observed him closely over the next few days and his anguish was obvious. It tortured him to think about the people from Finnua—his people—wasting away in the ruins for months.

"Look at her," he groaned as he and Catanya watched Roslin walk around the deck, supported by Diyah. She was still terrified of almost everyone, but she had taken a liking to Diyah, allowing her to lead the way on short walks. As long as no one else approached them, she was fine.

"I can't believe that's the Roslin I remember. She was so young and gentle…" He trailed off, looking miserable.

Catanya could hardly bear to look at Roslin at all. Every time she did, she felt overcome with guilt and shame. Diyah had managed to get the story from her about what had happened after Catanya and Jémys left Finnua. Of the dozen people who had been taken prisoner, she was the only one left. The others had all died slow, pitiful deaths, starving and succumbing to untreated wounds. And from what Catanya understood, Roslin's experience had been especially brutal. After everything she'd gone through, it would be a long time before Roslin would ever heal enough to move on with her life.

"I'm sorry," said Catanya, turning and walking away from Jémys. But he grabbed her hand to stop her.

"I don't blame you," he said with slight urgency. "What happened to Finnua, to everyone… it wasn't your fault." He held her gaze and squeezed her hand. "None of this is your fault. It's all *him*." He pronounced the word with contempt.

Catanya just nodded, somehow feeling even guiltier than she had before.

The time was coming soon when she'd have to face her brother, and she still wasn't ready. And now that they'd left Bratia, Caerlon and its king seemed a lot closer.

They still needed to stop in Sidina, but Catanya estimated they'd be in Caerlon by nightfall four days from now. Catanya didn't know what she was going to do when she finally came face to face with her brother. Laylian had told her to fight for what she wanted, but Catanya found it increasingly difficult to remain focused on that. And after everything that had happened these last few days, she was beginning to worry she wouldn't be able to control herself.

19

SIDINA

The movement of the ship still made Diyah sick. She had managed to distract herself as long as she was tending patients, but now that she'd finished most of the work, her nausea was harder to ignore. They were set to arrive in Sidina later today, and she was eager to stand on dry land again, at least for a little while.

It was midday when the cloudy sky began to clear, giving way to another brilliantly sunny day. A strip of land was visible in the distance. The ship cut through the water with ease, slowing down as the city came into view.

Diyah had never seen a more breathtaking place in her life. Sidina was as big or bigger than Caerlon. It stretched along the coast with sandstone buildings and red-soil streets. The land had been carved away in layers stretching out from the centre, so it rippled outwards with different levels and heights. The area bloomed with lush plant life. Crystalline pools of water sparkled across the landscape like shards of glass sprinkled down from the sky.

The closer to shore the ship sailed, the more the ocean glittered. Here at the southwest coast of Mórceá, the water was a brilliant shade of turquoise. Diyah leaned over the deck, watching schools of multi-coloured fish swim amidst the tapestries of coral plant life.

It was the most vibrant and colourful place Diyah had ever seen. The warmth of the sun on her skin was inviting after months of living in the cold and damp of Caerlon.

"Do you think word has gotten to Sidina about our escape?" asked Diyah, looking at Jémys. He was standing with her on deck, watching the distant outline of the city grow larger as the ship carved its path forward.

"I don't think we can rule it out," he said. "It's been almost a month since we left. That's plenty of time for Cadyan to send his firkon out looking for us."

"Has it really been that long?" Diyah was momentarily saddened as she counted back the days and realized he was right.

Jémys nodded. Then he turned and climbed the short set of stairs up to the quarterdeck, where Catanya, Drayk, Lia, and Osrin were discussing plans for entering the city.

Diyah moved to follow him, but then another thought occurred to her.

A month.

She nearly tripped on the stairs.

"What's the matter?" asked Jémys. He stood on the deck, staring down at her and frowning.

"No-nothing," she said, feeling lightheaded. She tried to brush the thought aside for now. There would be time to think about it later. She took a few steadying breaths as she climbed the stairs after him. "So, anyone looking for me will be looking for the two of us together," she said, forcing her attention back to the matter at hand as she crossed to stand beside Catanya. "I should go alone."

"You can't go alone," said Catanya. "It's not safe."

Diyah opened her mouth to object but Drayk interjected.

"I'll go with her," he said, shrugging. "No one will recognize me and I have a lot of experience sneaking in and out of places unnoticed. I'll get us in." He nodded at Diyah.

"I'm coming too," said Catanya suddenly. There was a pause while everyone exchanged looks.

"That is idiotic," said Lia. "You are the most conspicuous of all of us." She gestured at Catanya's appearance, her ethereal hair billowing in the wind.

"I don't care," said Catanya. "We don't have time to play it safe here. They might need me or my powers. If Diyah can't convince Zadílar to help us, we'll have to find a different way to persuade him."

Diyah's stomach clenched, and she exchanged nervous looks with Jémys. "You wouldn't... hurt Zadílar though, would you?" asked Diyah.

Catanya's face flushed, and she averted her eyes. "No, I just... It's just in case—"

"It won't come to that," said Drayk in a calm, steady voice. He and Catanya stared at each other for a moment, and then Catanya nodded.

Diyah suspected there was something else going on between them, but she didn't want to ask Catanya in front of everyone. Catanya had been acting strangely ever since she'd returned from the ruins. Diyah suspected something bad had happened out there that her friend didn't want to discuss.

"Lovely," said Osrin, chiming in for the first time. "Then you lot can scamper off on your own business while me and the boys take a little break for some rest and relaxation. It's been a while since the ship's been this crowded..." He trailed off, his mouth twisting into a lecherous smile.

"Absolutely not," snapped Drayk, glaring at him. Diyah was a little frightened by the anger she saw in his eyes at that moment. "You're not doing anything or going anywhere without supervision."

"I'll watch him," said Jémys with a hard expression. He and Drayk exchanged brief glances before Drayk nodded. The two of them seemed to be on the same page about Osrin and his crew.

Osrin rolled his eyes. "You know, I'm getting mighty tired of being bossed around on my own ship."

"Nobody cares," said Catanya. "Or do I need to remind you what will happen if you refuse to cooperate?"

Everyone waited with bated breath.

Finally, Osrin shrugged. "Whatever," he muttered, scowling as he returned to his helm, but Diyah noticed him shiver.

The afternoon sun was bright and hot as the ship finally came into port. As it turned out, their discussions on how to get in to see Zadílar were unnecessary. As the ship slowed to a stop, he was already waiting for them on the dock. He looked surprisingly underdressed, wearing a simple grey vest over a powder blue tunic with the sleeves rolled up over his elbows, exposing his dark skin to the sun. It was almost like he'd deliberately dressed down to avoid drawing attention to himself, which, Diyah thought, seemed rather uncharacteristic of the Lord Zadílar she knew.

Most of the ship's passengers waited below deck and out of sight. Lia had returned to her work with the rescued Awnadh, preparing for the coming battle, and Jémys was watching over the injured people and monitoring the rest of the crew.

Diyah and Catanya retreated to the shadows behind the rigging while Drayk and Osrin stepped forward to greet Zadílar.

"Captain," called Zadílar. "I wasn't expecting you again so soon." His tone was light but Diyah heard an edge to it. She smiled, realizing Zadílar didn't like Osrin.

"Aye," called Osrin. "We just need a place to make port for the night. A few repairs and whatnot..."

Catanya and Diyah exchanged glances. Diyah was pleased to hear Osrin lying so well. It seemed Catanya's warning had been enough to remind him of his place.

They watched through the rigging as several crew members jumped off the ship onto the dock where they began roping it in place. When the ship was secured, they lowered a ramp.

Zadílar strolled onto the deck.

"I see," he said, glancing around the ship. "Well, you are most welcome, of course. But, as usual, if you intend to disembark, I will require you to keep me informed as to your activities, and one of my stewards will accompany you at all times."

Diyah smiled again at the warning in Zadílar's voice.

It surprised her to see that he had come alone. She would have thought a man like Zadílar would bring guards with him when inspecting ships at the port. But then again, Osrin was a smuggler... Perhaps Zadílar didn't want anyone to know what he was doing.

"'Course," replied Osrin a little bitterly. "But actually—" He held out his arm to indicate Drayk.

"Lord Zadílar," said Drayk, stepping forward and extending his hand. "I was hoping I might have a word with you."

"Really?" asked Zadílar, ignoring the hand in front of him. "And who might you be?" His tone was bright, but his manner conveyed distrust.

Drayk faltered and dropped his hand.

"This isn't going to work," muttered Catanya.

Diyah nodded. Zadílar obviously didn't trust Osrin, and anyone who appeared to be working for him would not be welcomed into the city. "Come on," she said, grabbing Catanya's arm and pulling her out of the shadows. They needed to show Zadílar who he was really dealing with.

"Diyah, what—"

"Trust me," she said, steering Catanya out onto the deck beside her.

Diyah stepped into the light. Zadílar's eyes came to rest on her, and then on Catanya. He blinked in surprise.

"Ah," he said, his entire demeanour changing as he smiled at her. "Well, this is unexpected." He chuckled lightly, turning back to Diyah. "Lovely to see you again, my dear. Can I take it that Jémys is here somewhere as well?" He glanced around as if hoping to see him somewhere.

"Yes," replied Diyah. She didn't see any point in lying.

Zadílar's eyes rested on Catanya again and he tilted his head, like he was surveying her. "Perhaps we should talk in private?" He gestured for them to follow him.

Diyah stepped forward but paused when she noticed Drayk and Catanya exchanging silent glances. Diyah was momentarily worried that they might do something rash, but after a brief hesitation they came to join her.

The three of them followed Zadílar off the ship and onto the dock, where Catanya quickly lifted her hood to conceal her appearance. Drayk rested his hand on the hilt of his sword as though preparing for a fight at any moment. His eyes darted around so fast it looked dizzying.

Diyah supposed it was wise to be cautious, but their tension made her more anxious than she would have been otherwise.

Zadílar led them through the docks towards a shabby row of buildings at one side of the street. Diyah thought they were going to enter the nearest one, but Zadílar curved sharply and led them down a narrow alley she hadn't noticed before. He turned and zigzagged through the streets, leading them down several more alleys and hidden passages.

Diyah felt slightly nervous now herself. Where was Zadílar taking them?

They emerged from a tight passage into a small redbrick courtyard between buildings. Zadílar crossed to the far corner where he stopped in front of a large wooden door. He paused before knocking three times in quick succession. Then he waited.

With a click, the door unlocked, opening only a crack. Zadílar beckoned for the others to follow him through.

The area inside was dark. The light from a few measly candles along the hall struggled to penetrate the dingy, dusty air. Diyah noticed a small, stooped figure moving ahead of them. It was an elderly woman, but she was brawny and strong-looking, like she'd spent her life doing hard labour.

"This way," croaked the woman, leading Zad and the others deeper into the building. The corridor seemed to angle downwards, into the ground. The farther they walked, the more Diyah became aware of the noise coming from above. Thumps and bangs shook the ceiling, showering them in clouds of dust. Muffled voices shouted orders Diyah couldn't understand.

"Any trouble?" asked Zad in a low voice as they came to a halt outside a small door in the building's basement.

"None," replied the woman. "A few inspections as usual, but nothing we couldn't handle."

"Excellent," said Zad, patting the woman's arm. Then he opened the door in front of him and led the way through.

The room on the other side was surprisingly warm. It appeared to be a makeshift study of sorts. Several bookcases lined the walls, a heavy desk stood in one corner, and a pair of squishy armchairs sat by the fire.

"What is this place?" asked Drayk, looking around. He glanced up at the ceiling and Diyah knew he was also wondering about the commotion upstairs.

"One of my many hidden cabinets," replied Zadílar. "Places I can conduct business in private without anyone in my estate knowing about it. Thank you, Mionra. Do let me know if you spot anyone out there looking for me."

"'Course, my lord." The woman inclined her head and left, shutting the door behind her.

Zadílar turned to face the others. "Most of the staff employed at my estate are chosen by the king, so you can't expect me to trust them now, can you?" he asked. "No, I put my trust in the common people. The people who depend on me to secure their safety." He nodded towards the door where Mionra had disappeared. "To the public eye, this building is simply another scrap metal collection site. Someplace where workers can exchange their iron for gold. The noise and traffic make it an excellent cover for my work."

The others nodded. Catanya lowered her hood as she walked to examine the books on the nearest shelf. Zadílar's eyes followed her as she moved through the room. He seemed to be waiting for her to speak.

When Catanya didn't say anything, Zadílar turned his attention back to Diyah. "It is wonderful to see you again, my dear," he spoke as if just making conversation. "When I heard you had escaped, I was quite delighted."

"Do you know what happened after I left?" asked Diyah, thinking of Julyán.

"Ah, yes." Zadílar nodded soberly. "The king was furious. I believe he has branded you a traitor, and Jémys. But there is a fair bit of public opinion on your side. I believe the rumours say that you and Jémys... er... ran off to be together..." Zadílar watched her, wearing an amused expression. "It's quite the tale of forbidden love."

"What?" asked Diyah, startled.

Zadílar chuckled. "Yes, the king and the maífirkon seem inclined to believe those stories as well. Admittedly, I was even hoping they were true. I liked thinking of you, removed from all of this... But it seems I was mistaken." He turned to smile at Catanya. "I take it you're not here to enjoy Sidina's hot springs and baths."

Drayk wagged his eyebrows and grinned at Diyah as if to imply he liked the idea of exploring a few hot springs.

"No," said Catanya, turning around to face Zadílar again. "We're here to ask for your help."

"My help," repeated Zadílar, looking politely curious.

Catanya nodded. "There's going to be a fight," she said in a forced calm voice Diyah recognized. Catanya was trying to act more confident than she felt. Her posture was rigid, and her hands were clenched in fists at her side. "We're on our way to Caerlon now and we're going to put an end to Cadyan's reign."

"I see," replied Zadílar. "And what do you need from me?"

"Weapons," said Drayk. "We need you to outfit our soldiers." He leaned against the back of one of the armchairs, looking comfortable and at ease. He had his usual playful twinkle in his eyes and a smile on his face as though he found everything amusing. Diyah felt strangely envious of him in that moment.

"Soldiers? What soldiers?" Zadílar seemed surprised by this news. "Unless..." He glanced at Drayk and Catanya, finally taking in their attires. "Ah, yes, you're working with the Awnadh." He nodded, smiling. "Well, this certainly explains Ayr's overconfidence." He chuckled and shook his head. "But the Awnadh already have weapons—some of my best designs, I might add."

"Not the ones who were interned at Bratia," said Diyah. "We freed them. We freed everyone from the camps."

Zadílar looked impressed. "Did you really?" he asked, glancing at Catanya, who nodded. "Well, you've been busy, haven't you?"

"We need all the help we can get if we're going to win this fight," she said, holding his gaze.

Zadílar nodded and rocked back and forth on his heels in his characteristic manner. "Well, I suppose there would be no harm in providing a few extra weapons. It just so happens I have a store of blades in an old Awnadh design I wasn't sure what to do with."

Diyah exhaled in relief. She hadn't realized how nervous she'd been that Zadílar might not help them.

"Thank you," said Catanya. "But also..." She exchanged quick glances with Drayk before turning her attention back to Zad. "We know you've developed explosives to break through bedrock in your mines."

"My, my," said Zadílar, grinning now. "You want to blast a hole through Caerlon City? How remarkably callous of you."

"No!" interjected Diyah, horrified by that idea. "We don't want to hurt anyone. We just need to tear down the outer walls... right?" She glanced at Drayk and Catanya for support.

"But surely someone with your power," Zad gestured to Catanya, "could simply tear them down with a wave of your hand."

Catanya shrugged. "Maybe I could. But I can't be everywhere at once in this battle. And I need the distraction."

Zadílar and Catanya stared at each other like they were sizing each other up.

"I see..." said Zadílar, stroking his chin. "Well, I suppose I *could* give you a few of our explosives. But I'm afraid Cadyan would be rather... ah... *retaliatory* if this does not go your way. He will know I helped you."

Catanya pursed her lips and nodded. "I understand. I don't want to put you or your city at risk." She seemed to debate her options for a moment, and then she sighed. "Very well," she said, "just the weapons, then."

Zadílar smiled gratefully. He looked at Catanya with a slightly more favourable expression.

"There is one last thing we *do* need though," said Diyah. "You told me when we first met that you were building a hospital... Did you finish it?"

Zadílar beamed at her. "Yes, I did."

When they'd finished making the arrangements to collect the armour and move the injured people off the ship and into Sidina's new hospital, Catanya, Drayk, and Diyah prepared to leave.

"Wait," said Zadílar, frowning at Diyah. "You're not staying? I assumed you'd want to see the hospital and stay with your patients. I could use someone with your talent to lead and train the other healers."

Diyah was taken aback. She hadn't once considered the possibility of staying in Sidina. Now that she thought about it, she realized how strange it was that she hadn't. When Zadílar had first told her about his idea for the hospital, she'd been impressed and intrigued. In another lifetime, she would have given anything to work at a place like that—somewhere she could make a significant difference, helping people and training new healers.

"You should stay," said Catanya. "You always dreamed of doing something like this. And where we're headed..." She exchanged dark looks with Drayk. "Well, it's going to be dangerous."

"I know that," said Diyah. She understood the risks but she couldn't abandon her friend now. Catanya might think she was hiding her emotions, but Diyah saw through her act. Catanya was terrified and barely holding it together. "I'm not letting you go without me," she said. "We're in this together."

Catanya opened her mouth to protest but Diyah cut her off. "Don't argue with me," she snapped. "I'm coming with you. I spent the better part of a year thinking I'd lost you just like I lost my parents. Now I have you back and I won't lose you again. We're family and whatever happens, we're in this together, Catanya. We always have been. I don't know what's going to happen next but we'll face it together."

There was a long silence as Catanya and Diyah stared at

each other. Then Catanya smiled and visibly relaxed. "I had to try," she said, shrugging.

Diyah smiled. But then an unexpected wave of nausea passed through her, and she remembered the other reason she was so eager to return to Caerlon.

"Very well," said Zadílar, sighing. He eyed Diyah with a knowing gleam in his eye. Did he suspect there was more to her motivation than she'd let on? Zadílar always seemed so perceptive, like he could see through her.

Diyah averted her gaze. She heard Catanya and Drayk discussing a few more logistics, and then there was a general movement in the room as they prepared to leave.

"Thank you, Lord Zadílar," said Catanya, extending her arm.

"Of course, my dear. I wish you the best of luck. If you succeed, all of Mórceá will forever be in your debt."

Catanya nodded and turned to leave. In her haste, she accidentally bumped one of the towering bookcases protruding from the wall. She paused, shaking her head like she was suddenly dizzy. Then she frowned.

"What is it?" asked Diyah.

"I'm not sure. I just..." Catanya looked from Diyah to Zadílar for a moment, wearing a curious expression. She placed her right hand flat on the side of the bookcase, frowning. Then she grabbed Diyah's hand with her left. Without taking her eyes off the bookcase, she spoke, "Drayk, can you—" She jerked her head in Zadílar's direction.

"'Course, love," he said, and he grabbed Zadílar's arm before placing his hand on Catanya's shoulder.

"What are you—" Diyah started to ask, but all of a sudden, the world was spinning around her. Diyah almost let go of Catanya's hand in shock, but Catanya tightened her grip. All Diyah could see now was Catanya, Drayk, and Zadílar, flying through a swirl of shadow and blended shapes.

Zadílar looked astonished. But Drayk's carefree expression told Diyah he knew what was happening and he wasn't alarmed.

Diyah closed her eyes. The spinning room aggravated her already nauseated stomach. Then she heard a voice she didn't recognize drifting to her as if through a thick fog. She opened her eyes again just as the room stopped moving. To her surprise, three new people stood before them in the study.

A young man with a dark complexion leaned against the desk, dressed in a fine blue dinner jacket. Another man in a long travelling cloak stood by the door, holding a little girl's hand. The girl looked to be about six years old with blonde hair and brown eyes. She was carrying a travel bag and staring at the bookcase beside her. Her eyes were red and puffy, like she'd been crying.

Diyah heard Zadílar gasp. She turned to see him watching the scene with wide eyes.

"Lord Zadílar, everything is ready," said the man in the travel cloak, but he wasn't addressing Zadílar, he was addressing the man by the desk. Diyah realized with a start that the man in the blue jacket was, in fact, a younger version of Zadílar. He had the same boyish face, and the same keen eyes. But his hair had no grey in it, and he wore it neatly shorn, instead of threaded.

"Thank you," replied the young Zadílar with a weary sigh. He lifted a glass of auburn liquid off the desk behind him and drank deeply, his eyes closed. "You didn't have any difficulty getting through the barricades?"

"No, sir," replied the other man. "I made it out before the firkon got in place."

Zadílar nodded and rubbed his forehead. "And Dyanyn... was he..." Zadílar trailed off, evidently unable to continue.

"He is gone, my lord."

The young Zadílar nodded again, eyes trained on the wall.

"I owe that man my life," he said in a small voice. "And now I'll never be able to repay him..."

The man by the door cleared his throat, and Zadílar seemed to regain some of his composure. He stood up straighter and put aside his drink. "That's why I have to do everything in my power to protect his daughter," he said. "It's the only thing left I can do for him."

But Diyah was barely paying attention now. *Dyanyn*. "Wait a second," she said, scrutinising the little girl by the door.

"So," said the young Zadílar, grabbing a letter and a small sack off his desk. "I've made arrangements already. It should be about six days' travel to get there by horse. Give Genna this." He handed the man the letter and the sack, which clinked as if it were full of coins. "I'll send more when I can."

"Of course, my lord," replied the other man, stowing the items away inside his cloak.

Then Zadílar took a step forward and knelt down in front of the girl. "Diyah," he said in a quiet, reassuring voice. "Everything is going to be all right, I promise. You're going somewhere safe now. Somewhere far away from here where you'll be cared for and loved."

The young Diyah nodded nervously. "Who are you?" she asked in her little voice.

Zadílar smiled sadly and stood up again. "I'm no one, my dear." He patted her on the head once and turned to walk back to his desk.

The vision blurred and Diyah felt herself being tugged back to the present. They soared through a dizzying haze together, leaving the past behind. Catanya's grip on her hand slackened as the room came back into focus, and everything stopped.

"That," said Zadílar, staggering towards where his younger self had been only a moment before, "was a very unusual experience." He waved his hand through the air as though searching for some sign of the vision.

"That was the past, wasn't it?" asked Diyah, glancing at Catanya for confirmation.

"Yes," she replied. "I can conjure visions sometimes, but I wasn't expecting one to come to me here..." She trailed off, staring at Zadílar expectantly.

There was a long pause as Diyah, Catanya, and Drayk waited for him to explain what they'd just seen. He didn't seem to notice.

"You knew my father?" asked Diyah, breaking the silence.

Zadílar turned around. He looked surprised to find the three of them staring at him. "I did not know him well," he replied. "But he was a very gifted healer. He saved my life many years ago."

"That's why you've been trying to help me," said Diyah, nodding. "You got me out of Murina and arranged for me to go to Camlee Lodge. You sent Lady Geena money to help, you..." But she trailed off, grappling with her emotions.

"Yes. And when I learned what happened in Faltir, I thought you must have died. I was furious with myself for letting you down—letting Dyanyn down again. But then I heard rumours about a Heiltúir working in Caerlon, and I knew it had to be you. So, I set out to meet you. I had no way to get you out of there without arousing suspicion. The king trusts me, but not completely. It would have been dangerous to admit that I knew you, given your connection to his sister." He inclined his head towards Catanya. "I could not risk the king turning on me. There was too much at stake for Sidina."

He smiled almost apologetically before continuing, "So I did what I could from afar. I spread the word about your incredible healing talents, trying to encourage Cadyan to keep you alive. And then the tournament... Well, you know I tried to get you out then, but it didn't work... and as it turns out," he gestured to her and smiled, "you didn't need my help to escape, did you?"

"No," replied Diyah, but she was barely listening. "You knew my father," she repeated. "That's how you know so much about the Heiltúir."

"Yes. He and I spent a great deal of time talking as I recovered, he was..." Zadílar broke off as though looking for the right words. "He was, quite simply, an *excellent* man. And you are cut from the exact same cloth. I saw it the first time we met. The world needs more people like you in it, my dear," he added. Diyah thought she detected a slight quirk of his lips as he stared at her, almost like he knew.

"Real heroes," said Drayk in a quiet voice beside her. Diyah turned to look at him, surprised to see him staring at her with a strange mixture of sadness and respect.

"Thank you," said Diyah, looking at Drayk. Then she turned back to address Zadílar. "Thank you for helping me and for helping us now." She felt overwhelmed to realize how much she owed this man already. "When this is all over, I'll find a way to repay you."

Zadílar smiled broadly. "You can repay me by counting me your friend, and allowing me to count you as mine."

20

REDEMPTION

When they arrived back at the ship, one of Zadílar's stewards was already waiting for them with a crate full of new armour.

"This is for you," he said in a low voice, stepping forward and handing Catanya a smaller box. There was a note fastened to the front that read: *If Diyah trusts you, then so do I. Long live the Queen.*

She lifted the lid to reveal a small collection of powders and other substances in a variety of different bottles. A slip of parchment beneath the bottles contained instructions on how to mix them into an explosive concoction.

Catanya closed the lid again, taking a shaky breath to calm her racing heart.

It was the middle of the night by the time they'd finished unloading all the injured people and escorting them to the newly completed hospital at the east end of the city. They hauled the crates of armour below deck where the Awnadh happily reacquainted themselves with the feel of a weapon in their hands.

"Look at this," said Jémys, gesturing to a second, smaller crate. "He included a few firkon uniforms."

"That's brilliant," said Drayk, grinning as he stepped forward to inspect them. "We can send a few people ahead in these to clear the way for the rest of us."

Before the night was through, they had set sail again, this time towards Caerlon. There was nothing left between Catanya and her brother now. The next time she disembarked, she needed to be sure of herself.

Other than Drayk, nobody knew what she'd done to the firkon in Bratia. She had managed to avoid telling that part of the story. She didn't know what scared her more, that her friends would be horrified to discover what she'd done, or that they'd find a way to rationalize it. Because Catanya realized now that she hadn't been thinking clearly that night when she'd slaughtered all those people, and it terrified her to think it might happen again.

Nobody seemed inclined to give Cadyan a second chance. Other than Drayk, nobody knew how much it pained Catanya to think about killing him. She had never had the chance to know her brother and there was an overwhelming part of her that still wished she could. It was foolish to expect him to change, to expect him to care about her, but she couldn't help it. And she didn't think she could make the others understand.

Drayk knew what she really wanted. He had been there when she'd realized it for the first time herself. He knew she didn't want to kill her brother. She saw the uneasiness in his eyes whenever the others mentioned the plan. But to his credit, he never spoke his uncertainties aloud, and he never mentioned what happened in Bratia. He had sworn he was on her side, and so far, he had kept his word. Catanya was grateful for that.

The reunion with Jémys and Diyah had been uncomfortable enough without adding any more complications to the mix. After everything Cadyan had put them through, Catanya didn't think she could expect them to accept her feelings... Or to accept that she was capable of being just as brutal as him.

But then something happened that gave Catanya hope her friends would understand more than she'd anticipated.

"Catanya?" asked Diyah one afternoon as they all crammed into the navigation room, pouring over maps of the city and running over the plan again. "Will you promise me something?"

"Anything," said Catanya instinctively, looking up at her.

"Will you promise me that no matter what happens out there... No one will harm Julyán?"

Everyone turned to look at Diyah in disbelief, but Diyah ignored them. She kept her eyes trained on Catanya.

"Don't be absurd," said Lia before Catanya had a chance to answer. "Of course we can't promise that. There won't be any time for mercy, trust me. We strike down anyone who stands against us. That's war. If he is foolish enough to ally himself with Caerlon, then he deserves to die alongside them."

"That's my brother," said Jémys in warning.

"You're not the only one whose sibling chose the wrong side," snapped Lia, smacking her fist on the table in frustration. "If you go in there with your head half in it, you might as well surrender now. We can't afford to be distracted."

"Since when is saving someone's life a distraction?" asked Diyah.

"This is not a rescue mission!" declared Lia, getting angrier and angrier. "You've had your rescue mission already, but this is war! Your naïveté has no place in this conversation. So, if you will excuse us, we have actual work to do." Lia turned her back on Diyah. She continued doling out instructions to her soldiers as if there had been no interruption.

Diyah stormed out of the room, and Catanya thought she saw tears glistening on her cheeks.

Catanya waited a moment before deciding to follow her. "Excuse me," she muttered, turning and leaving the room. The ship swayed beneath her feet and she had to stoop to avoid hitting the ceiling. She climbed the ladder up to the main deck and emerged into the windy air.

It was a hot day, but the ocean spray misted her clothes, cutting through the heat. The sun tilted towards the west, glittering against the unending horizon of water. Diyah stood by the side of the ship, gazing out at the ocean.

"Diyah?" Catanya called as she approached. "Are you all right?"

Diyah shrugged and kept her gaze trained in the opposite direction.

Catanya placed her hand on Diyah's arm. "Do you love him?" She'd wanted to ask it for a while, but it had never seemed like a good time.

"I-I don't know," said Diyah. "I think... maybe—" She broke off, biting her lip like she was wrestling with her emotions. "I just need to see him again," she continued, turning glistening eyes towards Catanya. "He's not our enemy, Catanya, I promise. He's just lost. But we can save him, I know we can."

"How can you be sure?" asked Catanya, her stomach clenching.

"Because he's already different," said Diyah. "He's not the same man he was when I first met him. He deserves a second chance."

"I hope you're right," said Catanya. "Believe me, you have no idea how much I hope you're right."

Diyah frowned. "What do you mean?"

Catanya just shook her head and gazed into the water. "I'll do my best, Diyah. If I can save him, I give you my word that I will."

Diyah beamed at her. "Thank you," she said, pulling her into a tight embrace.

"But you have to promise me something now too," said Catanya as they broke apart. "Promise me you won't get your hopes up that he can change. Redemption is a long journey. I'm not sure people really change as much as we'd like to think they do. And it's easy to lose your way again..."

"But this is different," insisted Diyah. "Julyán has always been a good man at his core. He doesn't need to change. He needs to heal—to remember who he used to be and find his way back to that."

Affection swelled inside Catanya, and she smiled. It was just like Diyah to see it this way, to see a problem that could be fixed instead of an inherent defect. "And you believe he can do that?" she asked.

"I know he can."

Catanya nodded and lapsed into silence, listening to the waves splashing against the hull and the rigging creaking in the wind. She thought about what Diyah had said, wondering if it applied to her own situation. She didn't know Julyán, but if he was anything like Jémys, then she supposed Diyah's faith in him was just.

But Cadyan was a different story.

"Now, can I ask *you* something," said Diyah.

"Mmm." Catanya's thoughts were still far away in Caerlon.

Diyah took a deep breath as though preparing herself to ask something difficult. "Do you love *him*?"

Catanya leaned back, frowning. "Love who?" she asked, thinking about her brother and suddenly nervous that Diyah had guessed her thoughts.

"Jémys," said Diyah.

"Oh!" Catanya gave an involuntary laugh and relaxed. "Yes, of course I do. Jémys is the best man I've ever known..." She trailed off, thinking about him for a moment—about the days of laughter and joy they'd spent together, about dances in an orchard and stolen kisses in a barn... "Yes," she continued, her heart aching for those happier times, "I love Jémys so much, but things are... complicated with him right now."

Diyah nodded and squinted at the horizon. "Complicated because of Drayk?" she asked in a forced casual tone.

Catanya frowned. "Yes. And no," she said with a sigh. "Drayk's not the problem, I am. Everything that happened with Jémys, and then after he left... I can't dwell on any of that right now. There is so much more at stake here than my own happiness."

"Does Drayk make you happy?" asked Diyah, and Catanya wondered if a small part of her disapproved. "Do you love him too?"

"No. Or, well... I don't know." Catanya rubbed her forehead, struggling to sort through her thoughts. "I care about Drayk, I really do. And after everything we went through together... I don't know how to explain it." She grabbed the rail, casting around for the right words. "We have a connection—we always have—but I wouldn't call it love. At least, not in the way you mean. It's something more than love, and somehow less at the same time. He's... well... I don't know what he is to be honest." She trailed off, frowning. She wished she could describe what Drayk meant to her. It felt like an insult to him that she couldn't articulate it. It was something about the partnership they shared. His freedom and optimism were attractive. He inspired her to live with more purpose, more conviction. Part of her longed to be like him.

Diyah nodded. "I think I understand what you mean," she said. "It seems like he pushes you, challenges you. And he keeps you moving forward."

Catanya thought about that for a moment. "Yes, he does..." she said, realizing how many times Drayk had been the one to keep her going, to pick her up when she fell. "I wouldn't be here if it weren't for him." Catanya looked at Diyah and smiled wryly. "Not that this is really someplace I ever *wanted* to be."

Diyah laughed. "I know what you mean," she said. "If we could have chosen our own fates, neither of us would have chosen this, would we?"

"No, I'd say not." A smile tugged at Catanya's lips. "But if I could go back, I honestly don't know what I would choose anymore."

"No, me neither."

"Makes you miss the simpler days a bit, doesn't it?"

Diyah laughed again and grinned at Catanya. "Just a bit," she said.

They spent the rest of the morning reminiscing about happier times and remembering what it was like to feel young and free. Their life in Faltir was like a distant memory. Catanya had almost forgotten who that girl used to be—that orphan girl with the soul of an artist and the dreams of something more. She had changed in so many ways. It was nice to stand there with Diyah and realize that girl wasn't gone, not completely.

After a while, Diyah's seasickness returned, so she went below deck to rest, leaving Catanya alone.

Catanya knew she should probably try to rest too, but her mind was racing. When she wasn't consumed with the dread and panic of what lay ahead, she was replaying the unbelievable events of the past few days.

Time seemed to be running away from her. Everything was happening much faster than she'd ever imagined. She felt like she was being forced to make decisions she wasn't ready to make.

"May I join you?" asked Jémys, stepping up next to her. His sudden appearance pulled her out of her private contemplation.

"Please." Catanya smiled and motioned towards the empty space beside her. "I could use the company."

"I can imagine that's true," said Jémys, leaning over the rail.

They stood together in silence for a few minutes, watching

the waves splash below. Then Jémys said, "I'm sorry I never told you about Julyán."

Catanya frowned. "Yes, why didn't you? I've been wondering. Nelle never mentioned him either."

Jémys sighed heavily and started picking at a loose nail on the rail. "I don't know, I guess it was too painful. We never talked about him at all, actually." He took a deep breath and closed his eyes momentarily. "We were ashamed," he said in a strained voice. Then he turned to face her, eyes pinched in sorrow. "You have to understand, until recently I thought Julyán was the reason my father died. I thought he had betrayed my family and sold my father out to Casréyan."

"What?" Catanya couldn't imagine Diyah speaking so highly of someone who would do such a thing.

"It was easier to pretend I never had a brother. Easier than accepting the idea that the brother I had loved and admired so much could do something so horrible. I was a coward," said Jémys. "And now that I know the truth, it's too late to change anything. Julyán never betrayed my father. He didn't deserve what happened to him... What they put him through. If only I'd known... I never would have left my brother to rot in that place for all these years if I'd known what I know now. I spent so much of my life hating him. But he's my *brother*," he repeated, emotion breaking his voice. "I should have..."

Catanya felt a pit forming in her stomach and she looked back at the water, trying to ignore it. She couldn't help her mind straying, making the connection to her own situation.

He's my brother.

"You can't blame yourself," she said. "How were you supposed to know? You did what you had to do, and no one could blame you for that." She could hear herself panicking to rationalize it.

"Catanya?" There was a note of concern in his voice.

"And besides, it's not all on you," she continued, speaking

faster now. "He could have put in some effort, couldn't he? It's not like he ever gave you any sign that he was a good man. It's not like he ever reached out to you either."

Jémys stared at her with his eyes wide in shock, which only made Catanya even more flustered.

"And even if he did?" she spluttered. "Then what were you supposed to do? Join him in Caerlon?" She laughed hysterically. "I mean that's just absurd!"

"Catanya." Jémys, put his hands on her upper arms and turned her around to face him.

"Totally understandable," muttered Catanya, trying to avoid his gaze.

"Catanya," he repeated more sternly, squeezing her arms and urging her to look at him.

"Yes? Yes." She took a deep breath, trying to relax.

"Everything is okay." He spoke slowly, rubbing her arms to calm her down. "Everything is going to be okay."

"No." Catanya shook her head. "No, I don't want to kill him," she whispered, looking Jémys in the eye. "I don't want to."

"I know," said Jémys, and the calm sincerity in his voice surprised Catanya. "I've known all along and I understand. It's a horrible decision to make, and I wouldn't wish it upon anyone."

Catanya suddenly realized Jémys was the only other person who was likely to understand the way she felt. Overwhelmed with gratitude, she wrapped her arms around him and closed her eyes. "Could you do it?" she asked in a small, pitiful voice, with her head pressed into his shoulder. "If it were you and Julyán, do you think you could kill him?"

Jémys took a deep breath and put his hand on the back of her head. "I thought about it, Catanya, I seriously thought about it. I even came close during the tournament, but... I don't think I could have done it. Not really."

Catanya groaned and pulled away from him, looking down at her feet. "Maybe he can change the way Julyán did," she said, taking a step back. "When I talked to him that night outside the cottage, he offered me a chance to join him, you know? It's like he was reaching out to me."

Come with me to Caerlon. Let me show you what it means to be part of this family.

Catanya remembered his words as if it were yesterday, and the power of the ring as he'd tried to force her to give in.

We're brother and sister.

Catanya rubbed her forehead, a slight ache throbbing above her eyes. "Why would he do that if he wasn't trying to connect somehow?" she asked, more to herself than to Jémys. "I don't know, I think there might still be hope for him."

"Maybe," said Jémys, but Catanya heard the doubt in his voice.

"No, I know," she mumbled, recollecting herself and standing up straighter. She closed her eyes momentarily. "But I have to give him a chance, don't I? I have to try talking to him first..."

"I agree," said Jémys. "You have to give him a choice."

Catanya opened her eyes to look at him again, and he nodded. She felt better knowing he agreed with her. For a moment she considered telling him what she'd done in Bratia, but then she saw a faint echo of the smile she loved so much. She couldn't bear to cause him any more pain or bring him into the darkness with her. He deserved so much better that what she had to offer. So, instead, she reached out and took his hand in hers. It felt warm and familiar. It felt safe. She stood like that, allowing herself to feel safe, for just a few minutes before letting go and turning to walk back to her room.

As she climbed down the ladder below deck, she spotted Lia exiting the navigation room. Lia stopped in the corridor and folded her arms, waiting for Catanya.

"What is it?" Catanya asked, jumping off the last rung onto

the platform with a little more force than she'd intended. Her legs protested the impact.

"I need to know if those two are going to be a problem," said Lia in a low voice.

"Excuse me?" Catanya whipped her ethereal hair out of her face and glared at Lia.

"You heard me. From the minute they showed up, your head has been all over the place."

"Is that so?" Catanya's calm mood vanished, and her irritation bubbled up inside her again.

"Yes," said Lia. "That boy is obviously in love with you. I need to know if your affections for him are going to jeopardize everything we've been working for here."

"They won't," said Catanya, her irritation giving way to anger. An unbidden surge of power coursed through her suddenly. The ship rocked back and forth dangerously, as the Water outside stirred in response. She closed her eyes, trying to regulate her breathing and keep her powers from pouring out of her.

"I wish I could believe you," said Lia. "But you're a Caerlon royal. Treachery and duplicitousness are in your blood."

Catanya's eyes snapped open. She strode forward and pulled herself up to her full height so she towered over Lia. "You know nothing about me." She spoke in a deadly calm whisper. "Just because you've turned this fight into your own personal vendetta does not give you the right to question my motivations. I suggest you stop wasting your time and mine with these senseless accusations and focus your attention where it matters."

Before Lia could respond, Catanya turned on her heel and marched down the corridor towards her cabin. She slammed the door and turned around to face the room. Then she opened her hands and examined her palms. Deep indents were visible where she'd clenched her fists so hard that her nails had punctured the skin.

"Get a hold of yourself," she muttered, terrified by how close she'd come to giving in to the violence again. "You are stronger than this. You have to be."

But every day it was getting harder to resist.

21

ON THE VERGE

Before she'd left Túir-Avlea, Catanya had come to a good place with her magic. She had finally learned how to control it and she'd even begun to appreciate and enjoy it. But now that she'd left the sanctuary of the mountain, she was starting to feel a shift in energy. She realized now that it had started almost the minute she'd stepped off the shoal back into Awnell. At the time, she had been too preoccupied to notice the subtle differences.

It was as if her powers were waking up from a long and restless sleep. They were itching to be unleashed. She had to work very hard to keep them from pouring out of her, which was especially difficult whenever she became stressed or upset. Laylian had told her that channelling through emotion was easier, but much more dangerous. Now Catanya knew that was true. However, after experiencing the potency of resonating that way, she wasn't sure she could resist it.

It seemed like the farther she got from the mountain, the more volatile she became. Her emotions were already strained, but being cooped up on a ship with a dozen pirates and a collection of soldiers and uncomfortable allies made her especially tense.

After six days adrift at sea with an ever-increasing sense of dread weighing on her, Catanya was beginning to doubt herself. Whenever she was around the others, she felt overwhelmed and overstimulated—on the verge of exploding. So, she sought private corners of the ship where she could be alone with her thoughts.

She wondered if this instability had something to do with her growing proximity to Cadyan. It was as if her powers were reaching out to his, longing to be reunited. She wondered if he felt it too. And if so, would he understand what was happening and realize she was alive?

Even if he did, it wouldn't change anything. Nothing could prevent her from confronting him. Not anymore. She just had to hope that whatever was going on with their powers wouldn't get in the way.

She thought back over every lesson she'd had with Laylian, trying to remember if the maílehr had mentioned anything that could help now. But the more she thought about it, the more Catanya believed this instability was a sign of something worse to come. She was beginning to understand now... No matter the outcome of the coming fight, the amount of power she and Cadyan had was not sustainable.

She tried to remember Laylian's teachings, she tried to think about balance and harmony... But that was the problem, wasn't it? The Resonance wasn't balanced. It hadn't been for a very long time.

On the eve of their arrival in Caerlon, Catanya stood alone on deck, watching the sun set beyond the horizon. She heard footsteps behind her. Already reluctant to have any company, she turned to see Osrin walking towards her, and her mood worsened.

"What is it?" she asked. His gait seemed laboured, and he

was rubbing his forearm as if it were stiff and painful.

"Now, now," he said, holding up his hands. "I just want to talk." His speech was a little slurred and his breathing was heavy.

"Having a little trouble there, are we?" she asked, irritated by his presence. "Tolerance just isn't what it used to be?" She eyed the open bottle of sourwood rum in his hand.

Osrin frowned and peered into the bottle, as though surprised by her suggestion.

Catanya snorted and shook her head before turning to leave.

She hadn't taken more than two steps when he called after her, "Look, I know what you all are fixing to do here."

"Do you, now?" said Catanya without turning back.

"Yes, I do," he continued. "And I'm not going to interfere. You have my word. I'm just thinkin' well..." He seemed to be grasping around for something to say. "I'm concerned about my... my son. Yeah, that's right."

Catanya turned around and stared at him. "You expect me to believe you care what happens to Drayk?"

Osrin frowned. "Well, yeah, he's my son, isn't he?" He tried to take a step forward and winced, as though his legs were too stiff to move. "It's my job to look out for him," he added with pride.

Catanya just laughed in his face and shook her head. "You're pathetic," she said, turning her back on him again. She didn't know what he wanted from her, but Catanya would never believe for one second that he cared about Drayk.

She tried to walk away again, but a blinding pain erupted on the side of her head, knocking her down. Catanya rolled over to see Osrin bearing down on her, his hand clenched in a fist. He had struck her.

"What did you say to me?" he growled, throwing the bottle away. It smashed on the deck, splattering its contents everywhere. He looked outraged. His eyes bulged, and one side of his face twitched. "You dare speak to me like that on my ship, woman?" His arms jerked, and he winced as he clenched both fists.

Catanya stared up at him and laughed even louder. "And you're an idiot," she cried, jumping up to her feet. His affected indignation was pitiful. "You're just a small, useless man who's spent his life trying to convince himself and everyone else around him that he's important." She gave him a mock sympathetic expression. "You think, because Cadyan pays you to do his dirty work, that makes you important? Or because you can intimidate your men and abuse your passengers, that makes you powerful? You have no *idea* what real power is!" Her anger burst out of her, and a torrent of power flooded in its place.

Osrin looked incensed. He tried to take another step, but Catanya blocked him. An invisible force slowly pushed him backwards, towards the edge of the ship.

Catanya had been working so hard to keep her emotions in check, to resist the urge to use her powers... But he had asked for this. "How did you think this was going to go for you?" she asked, straining to keep herself from going too far.

"You dare—" Osrin spluttered and struggled against his invisible barrier. "You stupid, foul—you *bitch!*" He spat the last word at her.

Catanya's increasingly volatile temper flared again, and she finally stopped trying to control herself. She was tired of holding back, tired of pretending she wasn't dangerous. After all, she was one of the most powerful beings alive. Scum like Osrin should be forced to pay for their crimes. They should be forced to kneel at her feet.

She raised her arms up into the air, and the sky above filled with thick, dark clouds. Lightning cracked through the darkness like tongues of silver flame, and the entire ship rumbled with the sound of thunder.

"Just give me a reason," she said, her voice deep and menacing. Another whip of lightning cut through the sky. She longed to make him suffer, to be the one to punish him. She hated him for the things he had done to Drayk's mother, to Drayk, Roslin, and to everyone else.

What was the point of having all this power if not to use it to punish evil?

Catanya sent a blast of energy towards Osrin. He careened backwards, crashing against the side of the ship. He struggled to breathe as Catanya's invisible force threatened to force him over the edge. She smiled at the thought of watching him fall overboard, cast into the depths of the ocean where he couldn't hurt anyone ever again. Killed by the very thing he'd always exploited to support his life of cruelty and selfishness.

Suddenly the deck was full of people. Strident voices called out in an unintelligible jumble, and Catanya realized what she was doing. Dazed, and a little mortified, she dropped her hands. The sky cleared and Osrin collapsed onto his knees.

"What is happening up here?" asked Diyah, looking around in alarm.

"Nothing," said Catanya, backing away from the group and trying to steady her breathing. She shouldn't have given in to it, the emotions and the raw power. She was supposed to be better than that. But exhilaration still coursed through her body, itching to be used.

"I'll tell you what's happening," said Drayk with a wide grin. "Finally, something entertaining." He jumped up on a nearby crate and sat there watching. "Carry on." He gestured for Catanya to continue.

The sheer delight on his face unravelled some of Catanya's tension. She actually had to suppress a grin. Everyone else stared at her with mingled expressions of horror and fear, but, as always, Drayk seemed to find it all amusing.

"She's insane," spat Osrin as he scrambled back to his feet. "She nearly killed me."

"Pity she stopped," muttered Jémys under his breath. Drayk laughed, and they exchanged congenial smiles.

Catanya was surprised, and a little gratified to see how quickly everyone brushed off what they'd seen. She had been sure they wouldn't understand.

"You're *all* insane!" shouted Osrin, staring from one to the other and struggling to stand upright. His breathing still hadn't returned to normal.

"Well, you're the one who thought it was a good idea to antagonize the most powerful person here," said Drayk, winking at Catanya.

"Son," Osrin took a laboured step towards Drayk and lowered his voice, "you can't seriously be considering joining these people."

"I'm not considering anything," replied Drayk. "I've already decided."

"But this is suicide." Osrin looked at them all like he was seeing them for the first time. "There's no way you'll survive. Even if she does win, then what? It's only a matter of time before she becomes as bad as him? Look at her!" he shouted, pointing at her in accusation.

Catanya's face burned hot. Osrin had struck a nerve.

"Nah, she won't," said Drayk. "She can handle it." He met Catanya's eye and nodded at her.

Catanya's remaining tension dissipated. She breathed in deeply, letting Drayk's continued confidence in her dispel her anger.

"You don't know that! Son, it's not worth the risk," Osrin croaked in a scratchy voice. Then he started coughing. He grabbed hold of the shrouds to steady himself.

Drayk's eyes darted over to the broken bottle in the corner.

Then he shrugged. "Maybe... But me, I like taking risks," he replied, grinning even wider.

Osrin shook his head in disbelief. "Don't be stupid, Drayk. Just let's forget this whole thing. Let them do what they want, but you were meant for so much more. Stay here with me."

Drayk scowled at him. "Why would I *ever* do that?" he asked, losing his joking attitude.

Osrin stiffened as though Drayk had hit him. "Mark my words, if you go with them tomorrow, you will die," he declared in what he clearly hoped was an ominous voice.

Drayk snorted. "So what?" He leapt off the crate and bounded towards Osrin, eyebrows raised expectantly.

Everyone stood perfectly still, watching the exchange with bated breath.

"You don't mean that," said Osrin, shaking his head. "I know you don't—"

"You don't know anything about me," Drayk cut him off.

"Look," Osrin lowered his voice and gave Drayk a patronizing, knowing expression, "I'm sure she's a good time in bed, but that's no reason to risk your life for her. You've had your fun, now enough is enough. There's plenty of other, *easier* ladies who'll do just fine for you."

Everybody was outraged. Jémys took an angry step forward, but one of the crew blocked him. Niq and several of the Awnadh made angry gestures, and Diyah shouted something— but nobody was more infuriated than Drayk.

"Is that what you think this is?" he asked, advancing on his father until they were nose to nose.

"She's got her own motives, son. It doesn't matter to her if you live or die!" Osrin was desperately trying to connect with Drayk.

"Maybe not," said Drayk, throwing his hands up in frustration. "But I would rather die than live a thousand lives like you.

I'm not doing this for her or for anybody else! I'm doing this for the same reason I do everything. *Me.*" Drayk turned to walk away from Osrin but then he stopped abruptly and looked back. "I may well die tomorrow," he continued. "But at least I'll go out fighting, and I'll take as many of my enemies as I can along the way. The price for justice and freedom is worth paying... and so is the price for revenge... No matter what happens tomorrow, at least I'll be remembered. Immortalized in battle for pride and glory. But you"—he pointed at his father, wearing an expression of deepest loathing—"it's too late for you. No one will remember you when you're gone. No one will even care. But I refuse to be forgotten. I refuse to live an unimportant life, to stand by and watch as the world falls into chaos. Not when I have a chance to do something about it. I want a legacy."

Drayk turned to leave again.

Osrin gave a petulant scoff. "Well, *you* are my legacy," he said.

Drayk froze in his tracks. "No, I'm not," he said in a deadly quiet voice. He turned to glare at Osrin. "I am not your legacy, and you will never have any part in mine."

With that, Drayk turned on his heel and strode away, leaving a stunned silence in his wake.

Catanya spent the rest of the evening running over what Drayk had said in her mind. She had never thought about death in terms of legacy before. She knew what was at stake in this battle, and there was a good chance she might die—she had made her peace with that. But what if she failed? Would history forget her the way it had done Maílerier Ana? Would she become a legend, whispered about in secret that nobody really believed anymore?

Then again... Perhaps Maílerier Ana wasn't a hero worth

remembering. After all, she'd worked *with* Maílater Caer, helping him slaughter hundreds of thousands of people. Was she any better than him?

Maybe the true heroes were the ones forgotten by history. The maílehrs who fought tyranny during the Quiescence Wars, and still lost. The Heiltúir who dedicated their lives to healing and helping others. Farmers who shared their food with starving families. Communities who took in orphans and refugees.

Ordinary people, living quiet, honourable lives. People like Lady Genna, Grante, Nelle, Olly...

Casualties of lesser people's cruelty and greed.

Those were the people worth remembering.

How many more people would die tomorrow, fighting this battle with Catanya? How many more people would history attempt to erase?

It doesn't matter to her if you live or die! Osrin's words echoed in her head. Was that what Catanya was destined to become if she won tomorrow? Another leader whose power was earned through other people's sacrifice?

It was late when Catanya crept out of the cabin she shared with Diyah and made her way down the corridor to find Drayk.

"It's only me," she said, knocking and opening the door. "I wanted to check that you were all right." His cabin was much smaller than hers. It was dark and dingy and smelled vaguely like mould, but Catanya was grateful to find him alone.

"'Course, love, why wouldn't I be?" He was sitting at a small desk with his feet up, twirling an empty vial in his hand. He looked oddly calm.

She walked into the room and stopped in front of the desk. "He's wrong you know," she said, shifting awkwardly.

Drayk just raised his eyebrows and waited for her to continue.

"I will care." She fidgeted with her sleeve, avoiding looking him in the eye. "I care what happens to you. I don't want you to die."

Drayk gave her an indulgent smirk. "That's kind of you to say, love, but honestly, I meant what I said. I'm not doing this for you."

Ignoring his glib tone, Catanya plowed on. "But you know I care about you, right?" she asked. It was important that he understand. Whatever happened tomorrow, Drayk needed to know how much he mattered.

Drayk smiled. He tossed the empty vial away and dropped his feet off the desk with a thump. "It doesn't matter," he said, giving her a hard look. "It doesn't matter how you feel, it matters how well you fight. Just make sure you're thinking clearly tomorrow. You can't second-guess your decisions. You need to know they're the right ones before you make them. Trust me." He glanced at the vial on his desk and nodded.

Catanya was taken aback, offended by the insinuation. "I will be thinking clearly. That's not what this is about."

"Then what's it about?" he asked.

Catanya gaped at him. "It's about recognizing what matters," she said. Already, her temper was rising again. "I know where *my* priorities lie. It may have taken me a long time to figure it out, but I know now. I've made peace with it. What about you? I'm not convinced you know where your priorities are."

Drayk stood up abruptly and started pacing around the room in anger. "Why does nobody seem to believe me when I say I have my own reasons for doing this?" he asked, whipping around to face her. "I've been honest with you from the beginning, love. I'm in this for the fight, end of story. What more do you want from me?" He stopped dead in his tracks, glaring at her. "Do you want me to tell you I love you?" he asked in a mocking voice. "Well, forget it! It's not going to happen. I mean, don't get me wrong, I've enjoyed our time together, but this isn't about our feelings! It never was. It's about doing what needs to be done."

"I agree!" shouted Catanya. Her fingertips itched to fight, and she tried to rein it in.

"Good, because when this is all over, I'm gone," he declared, circling the desk to stand in front of her. "I'm never going to be someone who wants to stay still, you know that. I'll be off on the next adventure without you. It's like you said, I don't owe you anything. And guess what, you don't owe me either. So, stop tiptoeing around me like you've got something to apologize for. Stop forcing your shame on me."

Catanya was furious. "Fine," she said through gritted teeth. But as she turned to go, she paused briefly and looked back at him. "You know, we may not owe each other anything, but I still care. You're important to me, Drayk. And I thought—or hoped—that, after everything we've been through, you might have the courage to admit you care too. Maybe we could go into this war with no regrets. But I guess I was wrong."

As she placed her hand on the door handle, she heard his angry footsteps behind her. When he grabbed her and yanked her away from the door, she instinctively tensed up for a fight. But to her surprise, he put his hand on the back of her head and kissed her firmly on the mouth.

Catanya pushed him away, and he backed off, panting slightly and searching her face. As they locked eyes, a burning passion scorched through her, tangling into her anger and overwhelming her, banishing every other thought from her mind except the thought of him, his body against hers one more time. She clutched his coat and yanked him back, smashing her lips into his and wrapping her legs around him as he hoisted her up and slammed her down onto the desk. They tore each other's clothes off, grasping and kissing every inch of skin they could find. The muscles in his back twisted and contracted as he wrapped his arms around her.

Catanya's heart pounded inside her chest like it was trying to escape. She could barely breathe as she squeezed his body tighter against hers. It was as though everything she'd been holding back for days was finally unleashed and matched with Drayk's own intensity.

They clung to each other in desperation, thriving off their frantic, wild energy.

It was the most liberated Catanya had felt in days. She wanted to live in that moment forever.

But she couldn't.

When it was over and Drayk had fallen asleep, she lay awake thinking about what the morning would bring. She looked over at his sleeping silhouette and thought back on everything they'd been through together. She remembered the images they'd seen in the Burning Cove, and she realized with a jolt that almost everything she wanted was now within her reach. Yet somehow, she still wasn't happy.

She watched Drayk's chest gently rise and fall in time with his breathing. She thought about the images the fire had shown him—the things *he* wanted. The image of him as a child with a loving mother. The image of Osrin's punishment. And the one of Drayk riding through battle, triumphant.

Finally, after all this time, Catanya thought she understood Drayk.

Neglected and abused as a child, he had spent his life chasing thrills, chasing purpose, and embracing chaos. But it was more than that. It was a reverence for the world that drove him. An exalted joy of living.

Drayk took nothing for granted. That was what Catanya admired so much about him, what she needed to emulate.

Before the sun had risen completely, Catanya got up and dressed without making a sound. She crept out the door and walked back to her room with a clear head, ready for battle.

22

THE BATTLE BEGINS

"I t's out of the question," said Lia. "You'll be a liability out there."

"I'm coming," insisted Diyah, suppressing a shudder. She looked out at the cityscape and felt a familiar otherworldly energy bearing down on her.

It was nearing nightfall. The ship had been docked at the port of Caerlon for over an hour as they waited for the cover of darkness to make their approach into the city. Cadyan had been expecting Osrin's return, so the guards on the outer wall had waved the ship into the port without inspection. The port officials had logged its arrival and spoken with the first mate briefly, while everyone else had remained hidden below deck.

Over the next hour, the Awnadh had slowly filed off the ship. Disguised as labourers with cloaks and tattered work clothes covering their warrior attire, they had split off into pairs to avoid attracting attention. Then they'd spread through the outer districts, awaiting the signal to begin their attack. Catanya, Jémys, and Drayk were planning to infiltrate the inner city while Lia and the remaining Awnadh proceeded to the eastern boundaries to reunite with Isa and the rest of the army.

"I know these streets better than any of you," said Diyah. "You need me." She had been thinking about it for days. The closer they'd gotten to Caerlon, the more certain she had become.

"Diyah, it's going to be dangerous," said Jémys, eyeing her.

"I don't care!" she said. "I'm going, and you can't stop me."

Lia opened her mouth to argue, but Catanya interjected, "Okay, that's enough. We don't have time to debate this. Diyah, you can come. But I need you to stay close to me, and do everything I say, understood?"

"Yes." She smiled triumphantly. She knew Catanya would take her side.

As everyone resumed their discussion, someone grabbed Diyah's elbow and steered her away from the group.

"Fine." Lia's voice was so low that nobody else could hear what she said. "If you insist on being reckless, I can't stop you. But think twice before you come with us. It's not just your own life you're risking. Not anymore." She gave Diyah a significant look.

"How?" spluttered Diyah, gaping at her. She had only just realized it herself—the reason behind her seasickness and her headaches.

"Oh, please." Lia rolled her eyes. "I've trained hundreds of young women in Awnell. I know. But listen closely. You won't be able to protect your child out there, so choose now. Choose between the child and the fight."

Diyah felt a stab of guilt, but she had made up her mind. "Don't you understand, that's why I have to fight?" It wasn't just that she wanted to help Catanya, or that she wanted to find Julyán. She needed to be out there, fighting for a future where she could live in peace and safety with her family. It was worth the risk.

"Very well," said Lia. Then she gave Diyah a nod of reluctant approbation. "If the fight is more important to you than your child's safety, then perhaps we are more alike than I first realized. I have never put my family above my mission."

Her eyes seemed to glaze over. Then she shook her head and walked away, leaving Diyah feeling extremely uncomfortable.

Diyah didn't like to have her motivations compared to Lia's. She didn't think it was fair to say the fight was more important than her child's safety. But she couldn't just stand by and watch if there was something she could do to help. She needed to go with them. If she didn't join the fight now, what kind of person did that make her? How could she live with herself if something went wrong? She would never be able to explain to her child why she had stood idly by and allowed all her friends to fight.

She rested her hands on her stomach and looked out at the cityscape, hoping against all hope that she could find Julyán before it was too late. Diyah didn't know why, but she thought if she could just find him, then everything would be all right.

She brought her hands down to her Heiltúir satchel and pulled out the dagger he'd given her. Lately she had taken to holding it in her hand and watching the light dance off the blade as she turned it around. She'd even practiced throwing it a few times alone in her cabin, just to keep herself distracted. She found its weight comforting. It reminded her of everything she'd been through already, and it made her feel strong. She liked to think that was why Julyán had given it to her, not just to defend herself with it, but to use it as a reminder of everything she was capable of doing, given the right motivation.

And her motivation had never been stronger than it was now.

"All right, it's time." Catanya looked up at the night sky with an expression of steely resolve. "Let's go."

Diyah took a deep breath and returned the dagger to her satchel, but she kept her hand on it just in case. One of the

Awnadh women had given Diyah a spare set of clothes. They were much too big for her, and she felt oddly exposed without the layers of her usual kirtle. But she had to admit, the leather breeches made it easier to move.

Jémys was once again wearing his firkon uniform. But he, along with the rest of the group, had donned a long, battered cloak to conceal his attire as long as possible.

Together, they all descended the boat, disappearing into the crowded port and leaving the crew and its captain behind— although nobody had actually seen Osrin that day. The first mate had told Catanya he was ill, and she had been too preoccupied to care. But Diyah had her own suspicions about what was wrong with him. If she got a chance, she planned to ask Drayk about it.

But that would have to wait. They had much bigger things to worry about right now.

They crept through the port, trying to remain inconspicuous. Keeping their hoods up and their heads low, they wended through the throngs of people still busily loading and unloading cargo. When they finally arrived in the fishing district, Lia and her soldiers broke into two groups. One group headed east, and the other turned south towards the main city gates.

"Hey, I'll see ye when this is over," said the Awnadh named Niq. He grinned at Catanya and Drayk. "We'll have a feast."

Drayk gave a quiet chuckle. "If we survive this, mate, I promise I'll eat everything you make from now on. No complaints."

Niq grinned. "I'll hold ye to that." He grabbed arms with Catanya and Drayk. "Now if ye'll excuse me. I have a handsome, one-handed firkon to find," he said in a low voice so Lia wouldn't hear. Then he turned to follow his commander.

Diyah had learned that Niq's husband was one of the firkon who'd been forced to fight in the tournament. She remembered

Bir—she remembered cauterizing his severed arm as he screamed in pain. The memory still bothered her. But as she watched Bir's lanky husband set off into Caerlon City, excited to reunite with him, it lifted her spirits.

This was what they were fighting for.

She smiled and followed Catanya, Drayk, and Jémys deeper into the city.

"This way," Jémys said, beckoning for Catanya and the others to follow him.

"No, Jémys." Diyah shook her head. "This way is faster." She pointed up the street that would lead them to the western gate. She had walked these streets many times before, making rounds to help patients living in the poorer districts and the slums. Most of these people struggled with illnesses brought on by their horrid living conditions. Needless to say, Diyah had learned this area well.

They proceeded down the winding road, careful not to move too quickly or to linger anywhere and risk drawing attention to themselves.

"See," Diyah muttered to Catanya, "I told you I would be useful."

Catanya shook her head, grinning, and followed Diyah along the uneven cobblestones.

They made their way through the fishing district, wrinkling their noses at the smell of rotten chum and old bait. The streets were littered with debris of the trade: crates and old, worn-out cages filled with dead fish of all different varieties; nets with dried seaweed and lone crab claws still dangling from their ropes; and countless barrels overflowing with broken bones and tattered skins.

"Ugh," said Catanya, unable to contain her revulsion after stepping in a pile of fish guts.

Jémys and Drayk looked equally repulsed.

Diyah had to remind herself how she'd felt when she first

came to this area of town. It hadn't taken her long to get over her first impression, however. She had quickly learned to respect the people living in this area of the city. They spent their lives working in horrible conditions. Every day was a struggle for them.

But soon these people would be free. If everything went according to plan, these people would have the leader they deserved.

Diyah cast a sidelong glance at her friend, a sudden burst of pride swelling in her chest.

As they progressed through the district away from the coastline, the buildings changed. The smell of stale barkbeer and urine met their nostrils. They had arrived in the slums. A vivid memory came to Diyah—a memory of the last time she was here with Jémys... and Julyán.

Diyah almost laughed when she realized she was reminiscing about a romantic encounter. It seemed ludicrous to associate such a horrible place with such a beautiful thing. But after all, this was where she'd learned that Julyán loved her.

She must have replayed that moment a thousand times in her head since that night.

I want you to be happy. She could still hear his voice, still see the look on his face as if it were yesterday.

If only he'd left with them that night. Julyán could have escaped with her and Jémys, but he'd chosen to stay behind in order to protect them. He had chosen to lie to Cadayn for them, knowing full well what Catanya was planning to do. He had put himself in danger for them.

It didn't matter what anyone else thought about him, Diyah knew he was on their side and she was determined to find him. She needed to make sure he was all right, and she needed to tell him... Tell him so many things.

As they approached the gate in the city's inner wall, they

slowed their pace, keeping their heads down so no one saw their faces.

As Diyah suspected, the guard had been doubled since she and Jémys had escaped. Evidently, Cadyan did not want any more people getting in or out without his permission.

She tried to take this as a good sign—a sign that he hadn't learned of Julyán's involvement.

Catanya motioned for the others to stop and they all ducked behind the wall and out of sight.

"Keep watch," she mouthed as she crept ahead. She kept her head down as she passed through the gate, towards the castle.

"Oy, you there," shouted a guard, lurching forward from his post. "Where do you think you're going?"

Diyah craned her neck around the corner so she could watch. She could see the thin smile on Catanya's face, barely visible underneath her cloak.

"Oh, I have a long overdue appointment to see the king," Catanya responded, turning around so they could see her face.

"What—" The guard stumbled backwards, trying to pull out his sword. A second guard rushed forward.

But Catanya was too quick for him. With a wave of her hand, she summoned both men's spears. Then she threw the guards against the hard stone wall, knocking them out cold.

"Nicely done." Drayk hopped through the gate, looking cheerful.

"You really have learned a lot," said Jémys, leaning over the guards and wincing at the sight of the wounds on their heads.

Diyah scowled at the unconscious men. She might have been more compassionate if she hadn't recognized them. These were two of the guards who used to watch her chambers day in and day out.

"Tie that one up." Drayk tossed a length of rope over to Jémys and proceeded to wrap the other guard's hands and feet.

"We should keep going," said Catanya. "Isa and the others will arrive soon. We need to be in position when they do."

The four of them continued their progress through the streets and towards the commercial district. It was late enough that most of the shops were closing, but the streets were still surprisingly busy.

"Fírkon," muttered Jémys, grabbing Catanya's arm to stop her.

Diyah looked up to see a mass of purple uniforms moving in their direction. They were chatting and walking with a relaxed energy, likely off-duty for the evening. But Diyah didn't want to risk getting caught.

"Come on." She beckoned for the others to follow her through a narrow, cluttered alley. They squeezed between the boxes and crates lining the buildings and crouched down behind a rickety cart filled with old globs of wax and charred wood.

Diyah peeked between the wheels, waiting until the fírkon passed the alley.

"We're close to the barracks now," she whispered. "There will be more fírkon."

"How far is the entrance to the castle?" asked Drayk, leaning forward.

"Not far. It's straight up this road."

Catanya nodded. "Then we wait here," she said, leaning her head against the wall. "It shouldn't be long now."

They sat in silence together, waiting for the sound that would signal the army's arrival. Diyah's stomach was in knots. She had never been more nervous before in her life. Everyone else's controlled calm was unsettling. Drayk seemed to be as relaxed and cheerful as ever. Jémys and Catanya seemed focused and determined. But Diyah's heart was pounding in her chest. Every small sound she heard seemed enormous in the dark, and her muscles were seizing from the cramped position and tension in her body.

They waited for what felt like ages. All the while, Diyah kept one eye on the entrance to the alley, counting the people as they passed in order to keep her mind occupied. Every time she saw a firkon uniform, her heart skipped a beat, but they were always the standard colours, never the darker violet of the maífirkon uniform.

Of course, she thought bitterly. *Of course, it wouldn't be that easy.*

A sharp stabbing pain burned in her leg, and she longed to stand up and stretch. She winced and grabbed her calf, kneading the muscle and trying to take calming breaths. Nothing had happened yet. There was still plenty of time for her to find Julyán.

"Do you feel that?" asked Jémys in a whisper, and everyone turned to look at him.

But then Diyah realized what he was talking about. The ground shuddered gently beneath her feet. Then again, even harder.

The items in the cart beside her rattled. The earth shook violently as a thunderous boom echoed through the air. Then, somewhere to the south came the unmistakable, resounding crash of stones grinding against each other. The enormous outer wall of Caerlon exploded with enough force it catapulted rubble into the air high enough for Diyah to see.

Diyah gave an involuntary start as someone nearby screamed. "Attack! We're under attack!" Hysterical people suddenly rampaged up and down the street.

"Someone alert the king!" cried a shrill woman's voice.

"But who in their right mind would want to attack us?" came another voice, calling into the darkness. "They must be mad!"

More hysterical voices and sounds of doors slamming and people running.

"Oh good, here come the firkon!"

And sure enough, they heard the distinctive sound of hooves barrelling down the street.

"Get out of the way!" shouted a voice Diyah vaguely recognized.

"Where is the maífirkon?" said another voice. This one was instantly recognizable to Diyah. It was Holun.

"I don't know," came the first voice again. It was unnervingly cool and steady, like a seasoned soldier with experience reacting in a crisis. "I'll return to the palace to find him and the king. You get down to the wall and see what's going on."

"All right," replied Holun, and Diyah heard him gallop off towards the southern wall.

There was a brief pause before the other firkon spoke again. "Well, what are you lot waiting for?" he shouted. "Go with him!"

"Yes, of course," chorused a group of other voices. Diyah heard their horses follow quickly after Holun.

With a slight pang, she remembered Fehla telling her that Holun had been her friend. He had been willing to help her despite the danger to himself... and Julyán had told Diyah that Holun was a good man, hadn't he?

She crossed her fingers, hoping he would make it through this battle without too much harm. But then she remembered the way he'd handled himself in the tournament—he'd fought so well that he'd almost defeated Julyán. Perhaps she ought to be more concerned about the Awnadh than about him.

Diyah rubbed her temples in frustration. It was too exhausting trying to worry about everyone involved in this conflict. She couldn't think like that, she needed to focus on what was right in front of her.

She heard a smattering of shouts and cries nearby.

"Out of my way, I must find the maífirkon!" shouted the first fírkon, making Diyah nearly jump out of her skin. He was standing directly outside the alley where they were hiding.

"That's Rey," she whispered, realizing why she recognized his voice.

The others nodded to show that they recognized him too, but suddenly Diyah was panicking again.

"Oh no! Rey is going after Julyán, he doesn't know!" Rey thought Julyán was the enemy. He probably wanted to find Julyán to take him out before the battle really started. Julyán was the best fighter in the kingdom, with him out of the way it would be a direct line to Cadyan. Nobody knew that his allegiances had wavered.

"Diyah..." said Drayk in a slow, cautioning voice. "Stay calm. Stick to the plan."

"No..." She looked around at them frantically. Didn't they understand? Rey was going to try to kill Julyán. "No, we can't let him—I can't let him." She tried to stand up but Catanya grabbed her arm to stop her.

"Diyah, you can't."

But Diyah wrenched her arm out of Catanya's grasp and jumped to her feet before anyone could pull her back. "I have to stop him!" she shouted. She cast them one apologetic glance before taking off after Rey.

23

INTO THE CASTLE

C atanya swore under her breath as she watched Diyah disappear around the corner. In that moment, all she wanted was to go after her friend, but she couldn't. There was too much at stake in this fight, and she couldn't risk being seen yet.

"Jémys." She whipped around to look at him. "Please," she pleaded. He knew his way around the castle better than them. He was the only one who stood a chance of finding Diyah and making sure she was all right.

Jémys's eyes were wide with shock, flickering between Catanya and the spot where Diyah had just disappeared.

"Please," repeated Catanya, grasping his hands. She didn't want to separate from him, but she couldn't stand the thought of Diyah out there alone. What if Cadyan found her or she got caught in the fray between the Awnadh and the firkon?

"Okay," said Jémys, though he still looked torn. "Okay, I'll go after her, but before I leave—" He hesitated briefly before grabbing Catanya and kissing her firmly on the mouth. "Please be careful," he whispered. His eyes met hers, and she saw the fear in them. "I'll see you soon." He wavered, looking like he wanted to kiss her again, then he tore himself away from her. He stood up, casting off his cloak to reveal the firkon uniform, then he ran off after Diyah.

"Well, this plan is off to a great start," muttered Drayk, closing his eyes and shaking his head in frustration.

"It'll be okay," said Catanya more to herself than to him. She had been working so hard to remain calm and keep control of her emotions, but she was starting to slip. Watching two of the people she loved most in this world run off into the unknown was enough to make her panic.

For a minute she seriously considered abandoning her plan and running after them, but she closed her eyes and forced herself to stay put. There was more at stake here than her own feelings. And after all, Diyah and Jémys had survived in Caerlon for months before without her help. There was no reason to think they couldn't handle themselves now.

She would see them both again. She had to.

Off in the distance, another booming crash echoed. The ground shook even more violently than it had the first time.

The army had reached the city's inner wall.

Catanya took a deep breath and forced herself to focus on the battle at hand. This was the signal she'd been waiting for. "It's time, let's go." She gritted her teeth as she stood up and stepped out from behind the cart. She and Drayk kept their cloaks on and their hoods low as they made their way through the crowd towards the castle.

In the short time that they'd remained hidden, the streets had already filled with Awnadh from the south. The sight of the crimson and black leather set against the cold grey stone of Caerlon filled her with a blast of courage and pride. She had an entire kingdom on her side in this fight.

She kept her head down as countless castle guards and firkon raced past her in the direction of the battle. The swirls of violet and crimson clashed violently against each other.

Catanya's resolve faltered as her concern for the Awnadh seeped through her defences.

The sound of metal on metal clanged and echoed off the buildings, while cries and shouts filled the air. She wanted to know whose cries those were. She wanted to help. Instead, she kept moving without looking back.

Finally, the enormous outline of the castle appeared in front of her eyes. It was nowhere near as domineering as the fortress of Awnell, but it had its own imposing presence as it loomed over the city. A bastion of deathly grey stone, with enormous curtain walls and eight massive towers. It was mounted atop a large hill and enclosed by a plummeting ravine.

The only way across was a narrow, wooden bridge. Catanya squinted at it and realized, almost too late, that the wooden platform was rising. Someone was closing the drawbridge, detaching the castle from the rest of the city.

With a wave of her hand, Catanya halted its movement and forced it back to the ground with a heave. A series of grinding, screeching crunches told her she'd broken the gears and the windlass.

Drayk exhaled beside her. She turned to see him gazing at the castle, his expression bright with glee and anticipation. It filled her with a familiar warmth and self-assurance. She could do this.

"Onwards?" she asked with a stab at light-heartedness.

Drayk's face cracked into a wide grin. "Onwards," he replied, unsheathing his sword and following her across the bridge towards the keep.

Somewhere above, she heard a shout followed by the tell-tale creak of bowstrings being drawn. She looked up just in time. A flock of arrows burst into the sky, careening towards her and Drayk.

She raised her hands instinctively, creating an invisible

barrier that halted the arrows mid-flight. Then she twisted her wrists, forcing the arrows to turn in the sky so their tips faced back the way they'd come. And with a push, she sent them soaring towards their masters.

Shouts and cries rent the air as the guards ducked for cover. Some of the slower ones weren't so lucky. Their bodies toppled over the curtain walls, splashing into the ravine below.

She felt a momentary wrench, as she added them to the list of people she'd killed—a list that grew longer by the minute.

But almost as soon as it had come, the guilt was gone. She turned her attention back to battle.

With another casual flick of her wrist, Catanya ripped the bars off the keep's entrance. She and Drayk marched through to the inner courtyard, then she resealed the bars behind them. They paused, staring back through the arch, and Catanya directed her power towards the bridge. She sensed the wood as her Resonance connected with it, she could almost taste the lacquer and feel the weight of the thousands of feet it had supported over the years. She latched onto those sensations, and twisted. There was a crack and a snap as the planks of wood split and fractured, bursting into kindling shards. The bridge collapsed into the ravine.

A shout drew Catanya's attention back to the castle. Several of the gatehouse guards were charging towards them with spears outstretched.

This time she just closed her eyes and formed a barrier of energy to shield her and Drayk, blocking the guards from approaching. She opened her eyes again to see the men stumbling and flailing in slow, laboured movements as they struggled to move through the dense air around them.

She gave Drayk a half-smile as she proceeded towards the stairs that led to the castle entrance. They climbed the enormous stone steps in silence together and stopped when they reached the top, turning to gaze back at the city below them.

From this height, they could see all the way to the outer wall. It stood largely undamaged, save for several smouldering holes punctured by Zadílar's explosives. Outside the city limits, the vast outline of the ocean was visible to their right, and the dense forest on the left. The city was a labyrinth of winding streets and rolling buildings. It teemed with people running in different directions and screaming, while soldiers skirmished in the streets.

A veritable wall of Awnadh was visible on the south-eastern side of the city, near the forest. Isa was out there somewhere, leading the charge. Through the holes in the outer wall, the Awnadh poured into the lower districts like water through a broken dam. The firkon strode out to meet them in an equally daunting formation. The area in the middle where the two armies clashed was a chaotic jumble of movement and a swirl of colour that spread through the streets like wildfire.

It's now or never, thought Catanya, and she unfastened her cloak, allowing it to fall at her feet. Then she raised her hands above her head and brought them down in one swift movement.

Lightning exploded through the sky, as the rest of the outer city wall came crashing to the ground. She repeated the gesture and brought the inner wall down. It crumbled, sending stones and boulders rolling through the streets.

She took a deep breath, trying to steady the trembling in her body. Then she spoke.

"People of Caerlon!" she cried, her voice magnified across the entire city, reverberating off the walls of the buildings. The sound of cold resolve in it sent a chill down her spine. "Tonight is the night that tyranny fails. Tonight is the night that we take our kingdom back!"

She thought she saw the armies stop, searching for the source of the voice, but she didn't wait to see what happened next. She exchanged glances with Drayk before turning and wrenching open the doors to the castle. They marched through together and slammed the doors behind them, locking the majority of Caerlon's army outside.

"Well, that ought to get his attention," said Drayk, grinning at Catanya. They stood in the entrance hall, listening to the shouts and cries coming from outside. The guards had been released from Catanya's invisible barrier and were chasing after them.

"Now the Awnadh will know it's time," said Catanya, taking a deep breath. She backed away from the door just as they heard the dull thuds of bodies banging against it. "They'll join the fight and before long, the firkon will be subdued. That just leaves..."

"Cadyan." Drayk nodded and looked back over his shoulder into the castle. "Are you ready?"

"Ready as I'll ever be," said Catanya, turning to face the castle interior—the place where she was born. The home of her ancestors. "Let's go."

The entrance hall was eerily still with no guards or servants anywhere in sight. But directly across from them was a large, ornate door. Its wood was so dark that it looked almost black, and it was carved with patterns of golden inlay that shimmered in the torchlight.

Catanya stepped forward and rested her hand on the wood. Her fingertips prickled and her hair stood on end, as she recognized the echoes of residual Resonance.

"This place has known a lot of magic," she said more to herself than to Drayk. She cast him a quick, nervous glance before pushing the door open to reveal the enormous room within.

Catanya gaped at it momentarily. Two rows of massive stone pillars stretched down the centre of the room, drawing the eye towards the gilded throne perched on a dais at the far end.

High above, a set of mullioned windows poured moonlight

into the room. The faint blue-grey rays mixed with the patches of yellow from the torches on the wall. A series of enormous violet banners hung from the ceiling, fluttering as though disturbed by a draught or a mysterious breeze.

The entire room felt unnatural. The slope of the ceiling was too perfect, the pillars were too exact, and the golden throne practically glowed with energy.

"This place was crafted with Resonance," said Catanya, stepping forward and examining the nearest pillar. "I can feel it." She waved her hand in front of her, and the air bristled against her skin.

Out of the corner of her eye she noticed Drayk shudder.

"You feel it too, don't you?" she asked, turning to face him.

"I'm not sure what I feel," he said, glancing around. "But it's not the same as Túir-Avlea. There, everything was alive and vibrant. Here it's—" He broke off, shaking his head.

Catanya knew exactly what he meant. The energy here was strained and fraught, and it made her entire body tense. The magic that built this place was not natural. And generations of kings had left their imprint on top of it, so there was almost a layered patina of power residue that clung to the air.

Catanya's gaze fell on the golden throne. She forced herself to stare at it for a moment, trying to picture herself sitting there, but then she shuddered at the image and averted her eyes.

"We should keep going," she said, as she crossed the room towards the door at the back.

She pushed open the door and emerged in a corridor behind the throne room. She froze in place, momentarily startled to see so many people running frantically in different directions.

In the few minutes that she and Drayk had remained in the throne room, it seemed the rest of the castle had begun to react to the battle.

She and Drayk watched a group of guards run past them

towards the main entrance. A pair of servants ran in the opposite direction, evidently looking for somewhere safe to hide.

No one seemed to notice them at first. Then one servant did a double take, and his jaw dropped. He gaped at Catanya, stumbling as he turned and took off into the depths of the castle.

Someone nearby screamed. Another servant stood in the middle of the corridor, staring at Catanya, evidently frozen in fear.

Their panicked reactions were mildly discomfiting. But right now, Catanya had more important things to worry about.

Cries and shouts echoed from a distant corridor. The guards had opened the door for the ones trapped outside. It wouldn't take them long to get the firkon back into the castle.

"Come on," she said, beckoning for Drayk to follow her as she tore off down the corridor, deeper into the castle.

She and Drayk made their way through the corridors without much difficulty. For the most part, everyone was too preoccupied to notice them. And anyone who did, was too startled to react. The plan had worked so far. There were no firkon in sight, and after a while, the corridors thinned out as everyone sought refuge deeper within the castle.

But there was no sign of Cadyan anywhere.

Catanya was beginning to worry. Maybe Cadyan wasn't even here. Maybe they'd gone through all this effort for nothing.

She was just about to voice her concerns to Drayk when two enormous castle guards emerged from a side corridor directly in front of them.

The guards halted when they caught sight of Catanya. One of them looked like he was resisting the urge to run away, but they both stood their ground. They dropped into a defensive stance, pointing their spears at Catanya and Drayk.

"Evening, lads," said Drayk casually, taking a step back. "Would you kindly point us in the direction of your king?"

A low rumbling drifted down the corridor, reverberating against the walls. The stone floor quaked. They wobbled where they stood and Catanya grabbed hold of the nearest torch bracket to stabilize herself. She glanced out the window beside her. To her surprise, the city walls were being magically rebuilt. Stones soared through the air and stacked one on top of the other like cordwood.

"It's him." She leaned forward to peer out the window, scanning the area for a sign of her brother. "He's up there! On the tower!" She saw his unmistakable silhouette cast against the low-hanging moon. A shudder ran down her spine at the ominous sight. "Let's go!" She turned around to run, nearly colliding with the guards who still blocked their path.

"You're not going anywhere," declared one of the men in a low grumbly voice. He swung his spear out in front of him and attempted to strike them.

But Drayk was faster. He slashed out with his sword and split the wood into two pieces before the guard even had time to blink. Catanya took advantage of the distraction to hurl both guards backwards. They crashed against the wall and slumped down to the ground in a heap.

"Morons," muttered Drayk as he kicked their remaining weapons out of reach.

"Come on!" Catanya turned and sprinted off towards the tower. They didn't have time to worry about guards. From his vantage point on the tower, there was no telling what Cadyan could do.

They hurtled down the corridor, taking the corners so fast that they nearly collided into the walls. Catanya hoped they were moving in the right direction. Rey had sent them castle floor-plans to study in preparation for the invasion, but the chaos made it difficult to remember all the twisting routes.

The ground beneath them shook again. A loud crash came from somewhere deep within the castle.

"They've broken through the gate," called Drayk, pointing out the window at the hordes of soldiers now pouring into the castle over a makeshift bridge. From this distance, it was impossible to tell what uniforms they wore or whose side they were on.

Catanya's panic level rose, and she picked up her pace. She needed to put an end to this before any more people got hurt.

They skidded to a halt at the end of a dead-end corridor. A single stone archway opened onto a spiral staircase that twisted out of sight above them. They had arrived at the base of the north tower.

Catanya glanced around, surprised that no guards were protecting the entrance. It made her uneasy. "You should stay here," she said in a voice like a whisper. She didn't know what they were about to walk into, but this was likely a trap.

Drayk scoffed, shaking his head. "Not a chance, love. I'm coming with you."

"Drayk, I—" She tried to protest but the rest of her sentence was drowned out by a long, chilling scream. A scream of pain and fear that tore at Catanya's insides. It was coming from somewhere directly above them, inside the tower.

24

A SPY, A MURDERER, AND AN ELIXIR

Diyah managed to slip into the castle just as the inner wall blew, distracting the guards and attracting the bulk of Caerlon's fighters out into the city.

She raced up and down the corridors, keeping her head down and her hood up so no guards would recognize her. Swarms of terrified people teemed past her, but there was no sign of Rey or Julyán. She climbed the stairs two at a time and, panting, hurtled to a stop outside the maífirkon's chambers. She pushed open the door, half expecting to find him inside waiting for her, but the room was deserted. The bare fireplace and the empty bed provoked a strange melancholy. It saddened her to see the room looking so blank. She spun around, trying not to let fear overwhelm her.

"Think," she said to herself, "where would he be?" She racked her brain, trying to imagine where Julyán would have gone when he'd heard the city was under attack. The only place she could think of was the armoury. So, she launched back down the hall, towards the stairs that would lead her there.

Her cloak tangled between her legs, and she nearly tripped

as she raced down the steps as fast as she could. She jumped the last two, ignoring the slight ache in her knees. Then she ran through the door at the bottom, sliding on the polished floor and bumping into the wall. She was about to turn the corner towards the armoury when she heard a familiar voice that sent chills down her spine.

"I don't care who they are or what they want. They will all die just the same," said Cadyan, sounding bored. He stepped through a door directly ahead of Diyah. She barely had time to duck back into the stairwell before he was standing right where she'd been only seconds before.

"And when you find the maífirkon, tell him—"

The sky ignited with lightning so bright it was blinding. The rest of Cadyan's sentence was drowned by the sound of tumultuous and unnatural thunder.

"Catanya," whispered Diyah, smiling to herself.

The sound reverberated through the castle halls, vibrating the floor and shaking the doors on their hinges. A heavy silence followed.

"It can't be," said Cadyan, and Diyah heard undertones of horror and outrage.

Then another sound filled the air: Catanya's voice, as clearly as if they were standing right beside each other. Catanya sounded eerily cold and commanding. Even though Diyah knew it was her friend, she couldn't help the prickle of fear raising hairs on her neck.

Deep within the castle, doors slammed, and someone screamed. Diyah waited with bated breath as Cadyan processed what had happened.

Then he let out a hysterical and incoherent cry of rage. "She was supposed to be DEAD!" he shouted. "Why isn't she dead?" He gave another inarticulate cry and a blast of energy exploded through the halls, whipping past Diyah. Then came several muffled thumps.

Diyah chanced a small peek out from her hiding spot. Cadyan stood at the centre of a heap of bodies. Half a dozen guards lay on the floor, lifeless and bleeding. Only one other person remained standing. A tall fírkon with a serious face and a neatly shaved head. Rey wore an expression of mingled shock and relief. He looked surprised to be alive.

"Go find Julyán immediately!" shouted Cadyan, and he turned and stormed off down the corridor, leaving Rey behind.

Diyah waited, watching Rey for a minute. She thought about revealing herself and explaining about Julyán, maybe even asking for help finding him. After all, Rey was supposed to be on their side. But as she watched him from the shadows, something held her back. She didn't know why, but she thought she should wait and see what he did next.

Rey looked around like he was checking to make sure the coast was clear. Then he stepped over the lifeless guards without a passing glance and set out in the opposite direction to Cadyan. If he was going to find Julyán, she needed to follow him. Hopefully she could intervene before someone got hurt.

Diyah waited until he turned the corner before leaving her hiding spot to follow him. She stopped at the end of the corridor and peered around the wall, waiting to see where he went next.

She continued like this, leaving a safe distance and hiding in window nooks and behind statues. But as she crept along the hallway after him, she started to suspect he wasn't looking for Julyán after all. Glancing around, she recognized this area of the castle. The ocean was visible through the windows, illuminated by the glowing moon. They were in the west wing of the castle. Suddenly it occurred to her where Rey was going.

Why is he heading to the dungeons? she thought to herself. But she answered her own question almost immediately. She could have smacked herself for being so slow. Of course, he wasn't looking for Julyán at all, he was going to free Ayr.

Diyah knew she ought to be relieved, but she wasn't. For some reason she still felt uneasy and on edge.

She stood in a dark alcove, behind a large statue of one of the first firkon, peering around the corner. Rey turned down the corridor towards the dungeons, and she hesitated for a second, wondering whether or not she should follow him. Every instinct in her body told her he was up to something, but she didn't know why. She had no reason to suspect that he was doing anything other than following his orders to help Catanya.

Right.

Diyah shook her head, trying to clear it. None of this was important right now. She had to stay focused. She was here to find Julyán, not to follow Rey. And what did it matter if he let Ayr out of the dungeons? Ayr and Rey were on Catanya's side, weren't they?

Diyah sighed in relief. *Yes, of course they are.*

She finally made up her mind not to follow Rey. As she stepped out of her hiding place, she walked headlong into someone.

All of a sudden, she was being slammed against the wall with her hands twisted painfully behind her back. Terrified, she tried to wriggle free but the more she struggled, the tighter the stranger's grip became.

"Who are you?" demanded a familiar deep voice.

Her panic evaporated in an instant—replaced with a much stronger emotion. "Julyán?" She tried to turn her head to see him, but her hood was in the way.

"Diyah?" he said in disbelief, relaxing his grip and taking a step back.

She turned to face him, lowering her hood. He looked just the same as she remembered, though his hair was a little longer and unkempt. Rough stubble lined his jaw and shadows circled his eyes. But otherwise, he looked just the same.

He was staring at her, like he couldn't believe his eyes.

Diyah's heart ached, realizing he must have assumed she'd never come back. She reached forward and put her hand on his cheek.

She wanted to say something, but for the first time in her life she couldn't find the words. Hot tears flooded her vision, streaking down her cheeks.

The corners of his mouth twitched like he wanted to smile but couldn't. Instead, he crossed the distance between them and lifted her up into his arms. He squeezed her tight and buried his face in her neck. Then he kissed her with even more fervour than the last time they'd seen each other.

And until that moment, Diyah had never truly understood how much she'd missed him. Nor how apprehensive she'd been of finding him changed in her absence. She squeezed his arms and breathed him in, happier than she could ever express to be reunited with him now. And gratified that he hadn't reverted to his former, cold and distant self.

A resounding crash farther along the corridor caused the walls to shake. Diyah and Julyán broke apart.

"What are you doing here?" he asked, grabbing the wall to steady them.

"I came to find you," she whispered. She ran her hands along his arms, grateful to feel his touch again. "Catanya's here, she's going to fight Cadyan."

"I gathered that," he said. For a split second, doubt flooded Diyah and she wondered if he would be on their side. Then he suddenly grabbed her and pulled her back into the alcove, out of sight of the dungeons.

"What are you doing?" she asked, but he just shushed her and craned his neck to listen.

"You got the key?" came Rey's voice, drifting down the corridor. Diyah strained to hear over the bangs and shouts echoing through the castle.

"Of course," responded a woman's voice. It was vaguely

familiar. "I wouldn't have killed the old man if I didn't. Here, my queen."

"Excellent." Ayr's voice was dry and raspy from her time spent in the dungeons, but it was unmistakable.

Diyah looked at Julyán curiously. It sounded as though Ayr and Rey were using the distraction of the battle to find something.

"What are they up to?" muttered Julyán.

Diyah's heart swelled with a strong bout of affection. "You don't trust them either?" she whispered, vindicated in her suspicions.

"Not in the least," he replied, frowning as he turned back to listen.

"And are you sure about the final component—what it is?" came Rey's voice again.

"Would you ever doubt me?" drawled Ayr, and Diyah heard the smirk in her voice. "Now let's go, we're wasting time. But, Eva, I need you to find Lia. I promised her all those years ago... Well, now is the time."

Eva? Somewhere in Diyah's memory, that name rang a bell. She looked up at Julyán, and she could tell from his expression that he knew who it was.

"With pleasure," replied the woman called Eva, and something in her voice sent a shiver down Diyah's spine.

Ayr and Rey strode away down the corridor, while Eva's footsteps moved towards Julyán and Diyah's hiding place. Julyán pulled Diyah tighter to him, ensuring they were fully concealed behind the statue, and they watched Eva walk past the alcove. When she passed under the light of the nearby torch, Diyah recognized her with a jolt.

"I know her!" she hissed, when Eva was out of earshot. "She's that maidservant." It was the same maidservant Diyah had treated for sweating sickness—the same maidservant who had helped her during the tournament all those months ago. "I can't believe it, she always seemed so harmless."

"I know," muttered Julyán. "But I've had my eye on her for a while." His eyes narrowed with mistrust. "She killed the chaplain and I expect she's been feeding Ayr information for years." Julyán shook his head, looking displeased. "She was even spying on me—on us." He gave Diyah a significant look. She felt a flash of anger and mortification when she remembered the time Eva had walked in on them during an intimate moment.

"Why would she be spying on us?"

Julyán shrugged. "Looking for weaknesses. But never mind that now. We need to follow Ayr and Rey. I have a suspicion where they're going, and if I'm right, then this battle is about to take a turn for the worse."

He grabbed her hand, and they hurried down the corridor.

They followed Ayr and Rey through the castle towards the northwest wing, all the while trying to stay out of sight as the battle infiltrated the castle. Through the windows, Diyah saw nothing but dark, sprawling ocean. It gave the momentary illusion that nothing was amiss in the city of Caerlon. Then the corridor angled in towards the central castle, and they found the passage crammed with fighters.

"Maífírkon!" shouted a man nearby, but Julyán just ignored him and carried on running. He seemed remarkably uninterested in the fight that raged around them. He tightened his grip on Diyah's hand and swerved in and out of the fighters as best he could. As more fighters recognized him and tried to engage, he ducked and dodged, throwing a few carefully aimed punches to clear their path.

They moved as quickly as they could, trying not to trip over the rubble. Before they made it to the end of the corridor, the wall ahead exploded inwards with a deafening boom. Stones cracked against the opposite wall and the entire corridor shook.

The force of it blasted Julyán and Diyah backwards. As they fell to the ground, Julyán turned to shield Diyah from the flying shards of wood and stone, taking the brunt of the hit. Winded, Diyah coughed on the tangy air, and tried to blink dust out of her eyes. A cloud of thick smoke billowed through the corridor, obscuring everything.

Cries and shouts rang out. A horde of soldiers materialized through the fog, pouring through the gaping hole in the wall.

Julyán made a frustrated sound, brushing debris and blood off his face. He jumped onto his feet and helped Diyah up. Then he spun her out of the way of the skirmish. "Stay here," he said, thrusting her behind a toppled statue of a horse. Then he sprang forward, sword in hand, and was swallowed up by the mass of bodies.

Diyah was helpless, watching the battle rage. Bodies were falling everywhere. Another crash shook the ground beneath her feet. Diyah stumbled backwards and gripped the wall to stop from falling.

A figure toppled through the opening in the wall and landed on his back in front of her.

"Jémys!" she cried.

But he didn't respond. His sword flew out of his hand as he hit the ground. An angry and brutal-looking fírkon was advancing on him, and Jémys had no weapon.

Before Diyah had time to act, someone leapt between them, retrieved Jémys's sword and swung it through the air with such force that the attacking man never knew what hit him. With a dull thud, the fírkon crashed to the ground beside Jémys and moved no more.

Flipping her hair out of her face and holding her hand out for Jémys, the woman turned and said, "Nice to see you two again."

"Fehla!" exclaimed Diyah, gaping at her in awe.

The queen looked down at the slain man on the floor. "I

was raised in Awnell with Ayr. King Ayln trained his children and his wards in all the old arts," she said, shrugging. "I know my way around a sword." She flipped it casually through the air and held it out, handle-first, for Jémys.

"Thank you," he breathed, brushing the debris off his clothes and taking his sword back.

Fehla just nodded before stooping to take the dead man's weapon.

"Diyah!" Jémys turned his attention towards her, looking relieved. "I've been searching everywhere for you. I'm so glad you're all right." He doubled over, panting, and Diyah felt a stab of guilt.

"You shouldn't have come after me," she said, smacking his arm. But she was relieved to see him looking more or less uninjured. "What about Catanya and Drayk—"

But just then Julyán reappeared, sporting a new gash on his cheek and looking harried. "I knew it," he shouted, running over to Diyah. "I found Ayr and Rey, and—" He stopped dead in his tracks when he saw who was with her.

"Oh, hello, brother." Jémys waved his sword in the air. "How are you, then?" he asked, casually wiping the sweat off his forehead.

There was a long pause as everyone just stared at each other, stunned.

"Oh, is he on our side now?" asked Fehla, relaxing. She looked from Julyán back to Jémys and Diyah with a mildly curious expression.

Diyah let out a nervous laugh.

Julyán abruptly regained his composure. "Never mind that," he said, sweeping away the awkwardness. "We have to get it back before they use it."

"Use what?" asked Jémys, frowning.

Julyán brushed the hair out of his face slightly manically. "The elixir," he replied. Diyah was alarmed to see him looking frightened for the first time in her memory. "Ayr and Rey have taken it."

"What?" said Fehla and Jémys at the same time. Diyah stared from them to Julyán, not sure how to react.

"But they can't use it, can they?" asked Jémys. "I thought only the royal family knew how to make it work." He looked at Fehla for confirmation.

"Yes, but also—" She broke off, turning towards Julyán.

"The chaplain," he finished in a defeated voice. "That's why he was tortured and murdered."

Diyah's mind raced as she tried to keep up. "But we overheard Ayr earlier. She needs one last component... If she doesn't have it yet, maybe we can still stop them."

They all stared at each other, silently wondering what that last component might be and just how long it would take Ayr to get her hands on it.

"We have to find Cadyan *right now*," said Fehla abruptly. Her face had gone very pale, and she stood stock still.

"What?" spluttered Diyah. "Why?" Finding Cadyan seemed like the absolute last thing they should do right now.

"Ayr is right. There is one final component... It's him," said Fehla in a dead voice. "It's Cadyan—his life."

Everyone stared at her, stunned into silence.

"What do you mean?" asked Julyán, taking Diyah's hand and exchanging worried looks with her.

Fehla took a long, shuddering breath as though she was trying to muster the courage to say it. "The elixir powers the drinker for as long as he lives," she explained. "But once he dies, his spirit, and the force that was bonded to it, needs to return to the elixir. That's how it works. The elixir was originally powered by the life forces of all the practitioners who were killed during the Quiescence Wars. Their spirits were trapped in it and bound only to flow from spirit to spirit. The power grows stronger and more volatile with each new life force that's added. But it draws its power from death. It contains the life forces of everyone who has ever taken it." Fehla gazed at the wall, wearing a blank expression. "Ayr is going to kill my son."

A long silence followed Fehla's speech until Jémys's panicked voice broke through. "What about Catanya?" he asked, staring at Diyah, eyes wide in terror.

25

THE BATTLE FOR CAERLON

With Drayk hot on her heels, Catanya raced up the slippery spiral stairs two at a time and burst through the door onto the north tower. The scene that greeted her caused her to halt in her tracks.

Half a dozen people hung suspended in the air just outside the tower, grimacing and shouting as they contorted into painful-looking positions. Catanya recognized members of the Awnadh battalion assigned to infiltrate from the eastern front as part of Isa's army.

Cadyan stood at the edge of the tower, gazing out at the city, apparently unaffected by the ghostly figures suspended around him.

"Thank you for joining me," he said without turning around to face Catanya. He stood with his hands behind his back, seeming perfectly calm and at ease. "Would you look at this? It seems my city is overrun with vermin. I found these—" he gestured at the Awnadh through the parapet—"skulking around the forests."

He flicked his wrist, and the six suspended captives flipped through the air so they hung upside down. Several of their swords slipped from their belts and clanged as they tumbled to the ground below.

"Catya!" cried one of the women. Cadyan waved his hand and silenced her so she hung, choking and spluttering but unable to make a sound.

Cadyan turned around slowly and looked Catanya in the eye.

"Well, well, well, you have been busy, haven't you?" He took in her appearance with a sour smile. "I knew you couldn't resist it for long. However, I was under the misapprehension that you'd sadly missed your chance." He paused, frowning as he looked from her to Drayk. "You see," he lowered his voice to a calculated whisper, "I was under the impression that you and your little friend here hadn't survived the siege at Awnell."

"Sorry to disappoint," said Catanya, keeping one eye on the captives.

"I should have known Slaedir was lying," he said, shaking his head. He looked torn between frustration and acceptance. Possibly almost relieved.

Catanya watched him and suddenly a thought occurred to her. "You know what I think?" she asked. "I think you knew it was a lie the whole time. I think you knew I was still alive, and you chose to pretend. You went along with the story because deep down you didn't really want to chase me."

There was a short pause as they both stared at each other.

A wide grin stretched across Cadyan's face. "Really?"

Catanya shrugged. "I find it hard to believe you didn't know," she said. "I've felt your presence from the moment I got these powers." She held her hands out and stared at them. "And I think you've felt me too." She had never known for sure before. But now, standing in front of him again, her power tugged at her, reaching out to his. It was just like Laylian had said. Catanya felt it the same way she had with the man in the cabin, but stronger. Infinitely stronger. Like a thousand cords running between them, pulling and jerking them in the same direction.

"Interesting," said Cadyan. "Well, admittedly, I am somewhat relieved to see you again." Then, seeing the look of surprise and disbelief on her face, he grinned. "It's true. I had always hoped we'd get another chance to talk before the end." He took a step forward.

"Well, here I am," said Catanya, mirroring his movements. Drayk stayed back. "What would you like to talk about?" She tried to keep her tone light as she glanced at the people dangling in the air. Her mind raced, trying to think of a way to get everyone out of this safely.

Cadyan smiled. "Well, for instance. I'm curious. What was it like growing up without a family?" His tone was casual, but he had a cruel glint in his eye. "Living like a peasant in some forgotten little village on the edge of nowhere... What was that like?"

Catanya frowned. His words were obviously meant to injure, but they didn't. She wasn't ashamed of her upbringing. "Lonely," she replied after a pause. She needed to keep him calm, keep him talking until she could free the captives. "It was very lonely. In fact, I always wished I had a brother or a sister to keep me company."

It was the truth. Long before Diyah had ever arrived at the lodge, Catanya had often dreamed about having a sibling, someone to share her life. She had dreamed about that more than she'd ever dreamed about her parents.

Cadyan laughed. "Well, isn't this fortuitous?"

Catanya ignored his glib tone. "What about you?" she asked. "You must have been lonely too. It can't have been easy here with them... with *him*."

Cadyan stared at her. "Oh, it was wonderful, really. Nothing but love and affection. You missed out."

This time his words did sting. It hurt to hear the sarcasm

covering the pain. She shook her head dismally. "Imagine if we had grown up together as brother and sister. I think it would have been nice, don't you?" she asked, moving forward with slow, deliberate steps. "We could have been there for each other. We could have helped each other." She was standing right in front of him now, holding his gaze without flinching. "We still could," she finished.

Catanya felt small and vulnerable as she finally spoke the words she'd been holding in for so long. She held out her hand for him, waiting with bated breath. But Cadyan just stared at her.

Then his expression twisted. "Oh, I'm afraid it's far too late for that," he said, turning and walking back to the edge of the tower to gaze at the ghostly figures suspended in the moonlight. He reached out and pushed the nearest figure, watching as she swung back and forth as if suspended by an invisible string. "You see, I don't appreciate you barging into my kingdom with an army full of my most hated enemies... No, that sends a message, don't you think? A very clear message." He turned around to face her again, leaning against the parapet. He held her gaze and lifted his hand up in front of his face. Then without warning, he snapped his fingers. All six of his captives screamed as the force holding them released, and they fell. They plummeted hundreds of feet down onto the hard, unforgiving ground.

"No!" Catanya lurched forward, wanting to help them, but a blast of energy hit her with the strength of a stampeding horse. It lifted her off her feet and hurled her backwards where she slammed into Drayk. The two of them skidded across the floor and smashed into the staircase railing behind them, which cracked under the force of the impact.

"Now, is *my* message clear enough for you?" asked Cadyan, casually brushing his hands as if he were wiping dirt off them.

Catanya disentangled herself and stood up, enraged and

incensed. "Fine," she said through gritted teeth. "If that's the way you want this to go, then so be it."

In an instant, the Wind was raging around the tower, whipping and pulling at them and threatening to send them all flying off the roof. The sky was full of lightning and the thunder rocked the Earth.

Drayk was forced to seek cover as Catanya and Cadyan sent blast after blast at each other, each blocking them in turn and dodging out of the way. One blast hit the eastern parapet of the tower and the entire wall exploded outwards, exposing the side of the castle. Rubble rained down on the city, and the entire tower trembled. Catanya glanced down. Several small cracks had formed in the floor, creeping through the stones to form one large fracture. The fracture widened, extending towards the staircase. Then the tower framework shuddered and broke, buckling under the pressure of the increased weight of the roof.

With only seconds to react, Catanya grabbed hold of Drayk's hand. Then she stamped her foot down hard on the ground so that the entire floor crumbled beneath their feet.

The three of them fell through the gaping hole, but Catanya managed to keep herself and Drayk elevated long enough to lower them down without injury.

Cadyan, however, had been caught unaware. He crashed through the floor with full force, slamming down several levels amidst the debris from the tower.

And suddenly they were surrounded. The battle had poured through the opening in the castle where the tower used to be. Fighters flooded through the corridors, scrambling towards the remnants of the tower. It was chaos. Everywhere they turned, firkon and Awnadh warriors duelled each other. Swords flew in every direction and the shouts and cries of dueling fighters rang out around them.

Drayk stood a few feet away fighting with two different

men. Catanya used her powers to clear some of the rubble, looking for any sign of her brother.

A sudden tightness clamped around her lungs, and she could no longer draw in air. She clutched at her throat, gasping and choking. And there was Cadyan. He stepped in front of her with his hand outstretched. He was battered and bruised from the fall but he wore a nasty, triumphant expression.

"You may have learned some new tricks, darling sister, but your power is nothing compared to mine. I've used my power to do things you can't even dream are possible." He clenched his fist tighter and his eyes burned brilliant gold, brighter than the torches still clinging to the walls. "What? You thought you could just waltz into my kingdom—my *home* and kill me? ME?"

"N-no. Not k-kill," spluttered Catanya. She tried to summon the strength to resist, but he tightened his hold and she collapsed onto her knees. Her vision was spotted and her body screamed. She reached out with her hand, trying to materialize a gust of Wind, but Cadyan stepped on her arm, crushing it into the rubble beneath her.

"I can feel you reaching out to them," he sneered. "But the Natures can't save you now."

Blinding pain erupted in her head, and darkness threatened to take her.

She heard a shout and recognized Drayk's voice. A flash of metal cut through the air, and all of a sudden, she could breathe again. She heaved in great gasps of air and glanced up. Drayk stood before her with his sword outstretched. Cadyan clutched a wound on his arm. He looked incensed as he raised his hands to retaliate.

"No!" gasped Catanya, and the Wind she'd been trying to summon suddenly swirled around her. She gathered it in and blasted it towards him with so much force that he flew backwards through the tower entrance and out of sight.

"Thanks," said Drayk as he rushed back to help her onto her feet.

"Yeah, you too," said Catanya, rubbing her neck. Her throat was raw, and her lungs felt bruised from Cadyan's assault. "He tried to kill me," she whispered, and realization finally sunk in. She locked eyes with Drayk, and all her inclination towards mercy disappeared in an instant. It was time to put an end to this.

The battle grew more intense. New soldiers joined the fray, stumbling over the bodies and the rubble on the floor. Drayk fended off the firkon as Catanya cast around for any sign of Cadyan, but he hadn't returned to the tower. She launched towards the dilapidated doorframe where he had disappeared. Blocking the attacks of three firkon, she pushed her way through the battle and into the corridor on the other side.

"He's getting away!" she cried as she spotted him running along the hall away from the battle, limping slightly. Without hesitating, she took off after him.

As she ran down the hall, she heard footsteps behind her. She glanced back to see Drayk, covered in blood and debris, running after her. Three firkon were in close pursuit, and they were gaining on him.

"Go!" Drayk called. He spun around and thrust his sword through the first man's chest. "I'll be right behind you!"

But as she watched, the world seemed to slow. Drayk was holding back the attacks of the second man but he hadn't noticed the third coming at him from the opposite direction.

Catanya reacted instantly. She pulled the nearest torch off the wall and channeled its flames towards the third man, engulfing him in Fire. Drayk disarmed the second and knocked him unconscious. The cries of the burning man attracted even more fighters, and Catanya had to think quickly. She stretched the flames out through the corridor, creating a wall of Fire that blocked their path before they could get to Drayk.

She heard muffled shouts of anger and frustration as the men trapped on the other side tried to break through the barrier. The man on fire screamed and collapsed onto the ground, convulsing as the flames overtook him.

Catanya averted her eyes. She didn't have room for compassion, or time for regret.

"Come on," she called to Drayk, and the two of them set off down the hall after Cadyan again.

"Thanks for that," panted Drayk as he caught up with her, wiping the blood from his forehead and wincing as he lowered his arm.

They ran down the corridor, searching for any sign of Cadyan. But he was nowhere to be found.

"Where is he?" asked Catanya. She stopped and looked back the other way, hoping to see something they might have missed.

Footsteps rang down the corridor, and Catanya spun around, bracing to fight. Two people she recognized emerged around the corner.

"Catanya, Drayk!" shouted Ayr. "I'm glad to see you!" She panted as she careened to a halt in front of them and held out her arm in greeting. She looked thin and pale, nothing like the robust queen Catanya had met all those months ago.

"Ayr!" gasped Drayk, gripping her arm. He wore a delighted expression. "Rey!"

"Have you seen Cadyan?" asked Catanya, not wasting a breath. She was happy to see them too, but the greetings would have to wait. They didn't have time for this.

"We just saw him," said Rey, pointing back the way they'd come. "I think he was heading towards the throne room."

Without waiting, Catanya turned and bolted in that direction. She heard the three of them hurrying along in her wake.

"That way!" shouted Rey, gesturing towards a corridor on the right.

Catanya swerved and dodged the onslaught of another group of firkon charging through the broken wall on her left. She reached out her powers to connect with the warmth of their energies. Then she wrenched.

The firkon collapsed to the ground with a series of grunts and groans. Catanya sent a blast of Wind in their direction, sweeping them out of her way. Then she turned and continued running.

After another few minutes, Catanya emerged into an area she recognized. The entrance hall looked smaller than it had at the beginning of the evening. Heaps of rubble blocked the exit. But the enormous ebony and gold doors to the throne room seemed oddly undisturbed by the damage all around them.

With a wave of her hand, she threw the doors open and burst through. The pillars looked remarkably untouched, with only minor dents and cracks. A few lone arrows had lodged into the stone. The high windows had shattered, littering the ground with shards of glass that glittered like droplets of water. And the violet banners dangled from the ceiling in ghoulish tatters.

Several bodies lay in crumpled heaps on the floor. Catanya recognized some firkon uniforms and some Awnadh warriors. There were even a few servants.

Rage and grief tangled inside Catanya.

Cadyan was heading towards a narrow door at the other end of the room. Before he even had time to turn around, Catanya sent a blast of energy in his direction so strong that he went flipping through the air. He crashed into the golden throne behind him with a thunderous crash, smashing his head against the hard stone floor and sending splinters and flecks of gold scattering in every direction.

Catanya faltered, waiting to see if he could still move. Cadyan just groaned and climbed back onto his feet with surprising ease.

"You'll have to do better than that," he said, spitting blood onto the floor. "I've had a lot of experience picking myself up after a beating." He gave a mirthless laugh and turned to face her. When he caught sight of Ayr standing behind Catanya, he laughed even harder, almost like he couldn't stop.

"Of course," he cackled. "Of course! I should have known you were behind all of this." He took a few shaky steps forward, and Catanya noticed he was bleeding quite profusely from the wound on his head. "I must admit, I thought you were smarter than this, sister. Allying yourself with someone like *her*. Are you really that desperate to take the throne from me? Are you really that desperate to rule?"

Catanya was outraged. "You fool!" she shouted. "I never wanted your throne! Never!"

Cadyan's face contorted with rage. "EVERYONE WANTS MY THRONE!" he screamed, and he sounded like a petulant child. "That's all she has *ever* wanted!" He pointed at Ayr. "But she could never take it by force, so now she's using you to do it for her." He laughed again, his voice rising in pitch as he devolved into hysterics.

"I only want what is best for Mórceá, and I want what is rightfully mine," said Ayr in a clear, carrying voice as she strode forward to stand beside Catanya.

Cadyan scoffed and looked up at the ceiling. He took a deep breath as though trying to calm himself. Then he smiled ruefully. "I'm afraid the only thing that is rightfully yours, *Queen Ayr*, is a slow and painful death." When he turned back towards her, his face was masklike. "You never deserved to rule a kingdom," he sneered. "I never understood why my father tolerated your existence for as long as he did." He took another step forward, his eyes full of manic rage. "But I won't make the same mistake. And when I am done with you, I will peel the flesh off of everyone who ever called you their queen." He turned his gaze to rest pointedly on Rey. "Traitor," he spat at him.

For a second, nothing happened. Catanya wondered if he was bluffing. But then all at once, Ayr, Rey, and Drayk crumpled to the ground, screaming in agony.

"You see, darling sister," called Cadyan over the noise. "These people are nothing compared to us. NOTHING! We can kill them without even lifting a finger!"

Catanya didn't know what to do. "Stop it!" she yelled, trying to send another blast of energy at him, but he just deflected it.

"Don't you understand?" he hollered. "These powers make us gods! GODS! We don't have to concern ourselves with *them*. Their lives are meaningless compared to ours."

Horrified, Catanya watched their faces turn a sickly puce as they choked and spluttered on the ground.

"No!" she gasped as she tried to focus her powers on helping them and counteracting whatever Cadyan was doing, but it didn't work. Nothing she tried was working. He was too angry, and that rage fuelled his power. His magic was stronger than hers.

Catanya cast around frantically, looking for any way to stop him, anything at all. And that's when she saw it.

Drayk's sword had fallen out of his hand when he hit the ground. She stared at it for a moment. Time seemed to slow as she considered what she needed to do.

She couldn't let her friends die. Resonance wasn't the only way to fight. She'd trained in Awnell for this very purpose.

She leapt forward and lifted the sword off the ground, spinning it through the air and leaving a deep slash on the side of Cadyan's face. Then without pausing, she kicked out, hitting him in the knees and bringing him crashing to the ground.

The gasping and spluttering stopped instantly, and she loomed over Cadyan, with the sword pressed against his throat.

"You're wrong," she said quietly. "A king is supposed to

protect his people, not terrorize them. He's supposed to lead with hope and courage, not this." She gestured around, shaking her head. "Not this."

Cadyan tried to move, but Catanya raised her free hand and created a barrier, forcing him back onto the ground, immobilized.

"What are you waiting for?" said Ayr, wheezing as she climbed back onto her feet. "Kill him."

Cadyan's eyes widened, and he looked from Catanya to Ayr.

"Do it, Catya! Kill him now!"

26

AN IMPOSSIBLE CHOICE

Catanya was paralyzed with fear and uncertainty. She couldn't hold Cadyan like this forever. Her body was already struggling from the power required to keep him restrained. She needed to act. Now.

This was it.

She'd promised Drayk—promised everyone—that she could do this: kill Cadyan. It was the only way to stop him and restore order and peace to Mórceá. She didn't have a choice. Besides, she'd already killed countless people. Why should his life matter more? Sparing him would be selfish in light of everything else she'd done.

Catanya's mind went suddenly blank as she stood there, staring down at her brother. The same fear reflected in his eyes that was tightening around her soul. It ached to see such vulnerability. It flooded her with pain and sorrow, and in that moment, she knew...

A door opened and slammed.

"Catanya, wait!"

It was Jémys's voice.

She looked around to see him and Diyah running towards her, followed closely by two other people she didn't recognize.

"Catanya, no, don't do it!" Jémys hurtled to a stop a few feet away, looking horrified.

"She's manipulating you!" cried Diyah pointing at Ayr. "She's going to take the elixir. She wants you to kill him because that's the only way for the elixir to refuel. His life force —that's what she needs."

"What?" said Catanya, struggling to make sense of everything. Her arms shook from the exertion of restraining Cadyan. Her focus slipped slightly.

"The elixir binds to each spirit that drinks it. When that person dies, their spirit joins with the elixir, replenishing it and strengthening it for the next drinker," said the woman beside Diyah. She wore an understated green gown and a delicate circlet atop her long, greying hair.

A new blast of tangled emotions tore through Catanya as she realized who it was.

"Catanya," said Fehla, holding out her hands and stepping forward, "please don't do this."

The desperation of her plea startled Catanya. There was so much motherly affection in her tone, but it wasn't meant for Catanya, it was meant for the man lying at Catanya's feet. Fehla was begging Catanya not to kill her son.

Catanya glanced down at Cadyan. He looked similarly stunned, almost like he was surprised his mother cared about him.

"His spirit is bound to the elixir," repeated Catanya, trying to understand the words.

A memory came to her then. A memory of a conversation on a mountaintop far away from here.

Caer was searching for a way to bind Spirit Resonance into a permanently submissive state.

That's what the elixir was, a form of bonded Resonance. But

unlike other bindings, Laylian had told her the elixir would not diminish with time.

It is constantly refuelled, so it does not fade. Instead, it grows stronger and more volatile, siphoning more and more from the Spirits until eventually there will be nothing left.

Catanya glanced up at Fehla and saw the fear and pain in her expression. This was the queen's greatest nightmare, to watch her son die. To have his soul eternally bound to the elixir that had fuelled his cruelty.

"Catanya," said Diyah gently, drawing her attention back towards the others. "Killing him won't solve anything. Ayr will take his power for herself."

"That is ridiculous," declared Ayr with a touch of indignation. "All I want is to put an end to this once and for all. We have to kill him!"

Cadyan started laughing once again, and the sound was jarring against the tense calm of the room. "*I want what's rightfully mine,*" he taunted, repeating her earlier words and cackling as he struggled to stand up. "Of course!"

Catanya redoubled her efforts and slammed him back down. But as she gazed down at him, comprehension dawned on her.

"You think the elixir is rightfully yours," she said, turning to look back at Ayr. "You never wanted to end this, you always intended to take the elixir for yourself."

Ayr looked around at them all impatiently. "Of course not, Catya, don't listen to them. You need to trust me! This was the plan. We set out to stop him, so do it! Put an end to this now! KILL HIM!"

Catanya stared from Ayr to Cadyan, weighing her options. A cruel king or a ruthless queen... Her mind raced faster than it ever had before.

"Where is the elixir?" she asked in a low voice, without moving an inch.

425

"She has it," said the man beside Diyah. He gestured towards Ayr.

Catanya glanced over at him and realized from the similarities in appearance that he must be Jémys's brother, Julyán. He had the same dark skin and broad build, but he had a much more intimidating air as he glared at Ayr with his grip planted firmly on his sword.

Catanya tightened her grasp on her own sword and turned her gaze towards Ayr. "Hand it over," she spoke in a slow, measured voice. Part of her hoped it wasn't true. She liked Ayr —respected her. She couldn't bear to think that the queen had been planning to betray them all this time.

When Ayr didn't move, Drayk stepped forward angrily. "Ayr, give the elixir to Catya, it belongs to her now." Catanya had never seen him looking so agitated before. His eyes were narrowed and his jaw was set. The betrayal was obviously painful for him as well.

"It doesn't!" snapped Ayr, losing her cool. "These powers should have been mine! It was *my* ancestor who led the Quiescence Wars, quashing rebellions and clearing the way for their precious Maílater Caer to take control. The elixir was *my* family's birthright just as much as theirs." Her face contorted into a twisted mask of rage and greed. "But your family stole it from us!" she shouted at Catanya. "Well now I'm taking it back!" Ayr leapt forward.

Then everything happened so fast that Catanya didn't know which way to turn.

Lia and Isa came crashing through the door with two dozen Awnadh and slammed the door shut behind them, barricading it. Rey profited from the moment of distraction to spring forward and disarm Jémys, as Ayr grabbed Drayk's arm, twisting it behind his back and restraining him.

"Finally," she hissed, pulling a dagger from her pocket and waiting for Rey and the other Awnadh to surround them. "Now,

Catya," she said, smiling cruelly as she pressed the dagger into Drayk's throat, sending blood dribbling down his neck. "I'll make this simple for you. Kill him," she nodded towards Cadyan. "Or I kill Drayk, and then everyone else in this room."

Catanya looked around the room, petrified. They were surrounded. Drayk and Jémys were incapacitated, and the Awnadh were advancing on the others.

"Well, *Maífírkon*," spat Rey, moving towards Jémys's brother with his sword outstretched. "I don't think I'll be following your orders anymore. Now, drop your weapons."

When Julyán didn't move, Rey just kept his eyes on the maífírkon and moved his sword to point at Diyah. "Drop your weapon," he repeated with a smug expression.

There was a pause followed by a clang as Julyán let his sword fall to the ground.

"Sentimental fools, both of them!" said Lia as she marched forward. She pulled a long blade from her belt and held it up to Julyán's throat.

"Falia, what are you doing?" asked Fehla, moving to step forward but one of the other Awnadh grabbed her and restrained her.

Catanya watched the scene, frozen in fear and shock, struggling to comprehend how everything could have come to this.

"Get on with it," snapped Ayr. "I'm not a patient woman."

Drayk wrestled against her grasp. He winced as she dug her blade deeper into his throat. "You deceitful snake!" he spat.

"Ayr, don't do this," pleaded Catanya, shaking with anger and exhaustion. "You're better than this." She didn't know what to do. All of her energy was focused on holding Cadyan down. She couldn't risk letting him go.

"It's a simple choice!" shouted Ayr, stamping her foot on the ground. For the first time, she seemed nothing like the cool, charismatic leader she usually was. Now she seemed overcome with greed and bloodlust.

Everyone stood frozen, watching the exchange between the two women with Drayk caught in the middle. But out of the corner of her eye, Catanya noticed movement. A sudden flash of silver flew across the room, and Ayr shrieked in pain, dropping her blade and letting go of Drayk. Everyone turned in open shock to stare at Diyah. She stood next to Julyán with her hand outstretched, watching as Queen Ayr retreated a step, clutching the small, silver dagger embedded in her bloody hand.

Then the room lurched into movement.

Drayk snatched Ayr's blade off the ground and hurled it at one of the men restraining Fehla. Then he jumped forward, grabbing Jémys's sword off the floor and flinging it to him. Jémys knocked Lia away from Julyán and whipped around, striking Rey on the side of the head and distracting him just long enough for Julyán to retrieve his own sword. The maífirkon thrust the blade through the lieutenant's chest.

"Rey!" cried Isa, mad with grief as she watched her husband fall to the floor in a pool of his own blood. She jumped forward in a whirl of rage and pierced Diyah's shoulder. Diyah cried out and fell. Julyán caught her just as Jémys slashed his sword through the air.

Isa fell to the ground, blood seeping from a long gash across her front. It extended from her neck to her waist.

"Diyah!" Jémys whipped around to face her.

"I'm all right," Diyah called as Julyán hoisted her back onto her feet. She grasped at her wound, trying to stifle the bleeding.

Relief flooded Catanya, but it was short lived. In their moment of distraction, Jémys, Julyán, and Diyah hadn't noticed the two other Awnadh advancing on them.

Without thinking, Catanya let go of Cadyan and rushed forward. She slashed out with her sword and cut one of them down. Then she conjured a blast to hurl the other Awnadh away from her friends.

"Diyah, you should go," she said, casting around for somewhere her friend could hide. More Awnadh were already advancing, and they were backed up against the wall. Julyán stepped forward to block Diyah, and Jémys followed suit.

Catanya spun around and found another Awnadh mere inches away. The man struck her hard on the jaw. She stumbled and fell to the ground, winded and tasting the coppery tang of blood. He was bearing down on her now. She reached out with her powers, but before she'd summoned anything, the bloodied tip of a blade burst through his chest, and shock crossed his face. The blade withdrew, and the man slumped down at her feet.

Queen Fehla stood behind him, wiping her bloody sword on her sleeve. Then she held out her hand. Catanya hesitated before reaching out and taking it, allowing herself to be pulled to her feet.

"Thanks," she muttered, not sure what else to say. All her life, she'd dreamed of meeting her mother, but now that they were face to face, Catanya realized they were strangers to each other. An awkward silence swelled between then, but they were saved from having to address it when they found themselves suddenly surrounded by four more Awnadh. The warriors seemed to be trying to cut Catanya off from the others and keep her distracted.

Fehla raised her sword and clashed with the man in front. Catanya lifted the other three off their feet, flipped them in the air, and slammed them back down, where they smashed their heads and didn't get up again. Then Catanya turned around to help Fehla, but the queen's opponent suddenly collapsed to his knees, spluttering and gasping. His veins popped out of his skin, and blood poured out of his eyes and mouth.

"What—" Catanya was horrified, but as she looked around, she spotted Cadyan still standing on the dais amidst the shattered detritus of his throne. He looked deranged as he clenched his fist in the air, his eyes blazing with golden light. The man on the ground spasmed violently before lying still.

The flames in Cadyan's eyes faded back into his natural grey. He stared at Catanya and Fehla, genuine surprise mixed in with the cold anger on his face, and Catanya understood. He hadn't intended to intervene, but when he'd seen Fehla was in trouble...

Fehla rushed forward to join him on the dais, but Catanya stayed behind, watching them and feeling disconnected. She wrenched her gaze away and looked around for Diyah and the others, wanting to make sure they were okay. She spotted them still by the far wall. Jémys and Julyán were fighting with a small group of Awnadh while trying to protect Diyah, who had retreated behind the nearest pillar. She'd yanked a belt off a fallen Awnadh and was struggling to cinch it around her injured arm.

Catanya watched Julyán slice through the wall of soldiers in front of him with ease and precision, all the while keeping one eye on Diyah. In that moment, Catanya knew her friend had been right about this man.

One of the Awnadh feinted left and dodged around the pillar, heading towards Diyah. Julyán spun around and yanked him backwards, hurling him down at Jémys's feet where they both pierced him with their blades before returning to the fray.

Catanya was alarmed, and a little impressed to see how well the two brothers fought together.

"Oh, come on, mate!" came Drayk's voice, bright and jubilant against the cacophony of clashing swords. Catanya spotted him on the other side of the room, in between a set of pillars. He was locked in a battle with two other Awnadh, fighting with a distinctly different approach. Parry, riposte, parry, attack. Left, right, left again. He was hopping in and out of their attacks, grinning widely like he had never enjoyed himself more. "You can fight better than that," he taunted, as he ducked out of the way of another hit. "Or actually, no. Never mind. I was thinking about myself." He snickered as he thrust his sword forward and pierced the man's side. Then he spun around and knocked the other man down with a well-placed blow.

Drayk turned to face Catanya, grinning from ear to ear. Then he brandished his sword at another pair of fighters, daring them to step up next.

But he hadn't noticed Lia approaching from behind.

"Drayk!" cried Catanya. Her stomach clenched as she launched forward. Three Awnadh descended upon her, but she dodged their attack. She raised a heap of nearby rubble and hurled it at them, knocking them out of her way and trapping them on the ground. Then she whipped back around and sprinted towards Drayk. But she was too late. She watched in horror as Lia grabbed Drayk by the neck and plunged her blade into his back, between his shoulders.

Catanya screamed. A blast of primal energy tore out of her so strong it hurled Lia through the air so she crashed against Ayr and the nearby Awnadh. They all smashed into the stone pillar behind them. Catanya skidded forward across the debris and blood, and dropped down on her knees, grabbing Drayk.

"No, no, no, no," she said, frantically trying to stop the bleeding. "No, help!" she called out. "Diyah, help!"

Diyah was at her side in an instant. Jémys and Julyán followed behind, fending off the remaining Awnadh. Diyah's own shoulder bled steadily through her improvised binding as she knelt to examine his wound.

Drayk was shaking and coughing up blood but he barely reacted as Diyah ran her hand along the wound on his back.

Catanya thought that was a good sign but then she noticed Diyah's expression. "I'm sorry," Diyah murmured. She turned to face Catanya and shook her head.

"S'okay, love," said Drayk, managing a half-grin as he patted Diyah on the hand.

But Catanya's head had gone numb. "No, he's fine." She glanced around at everyone, but they averted their eyes. "He's going to be fine," she said more loudly. Then she looked back down at him and saw a sad smile cross his face. That expression of resignation cut through her like ice. "Don't you dare give up," she said in a hard whisper, tears pooling in her eyes. "Not you."

"You can still save him," came Ayr's cool voice from behind.

"What?" Catanya spun around. Ayr had extracted herself from the pileup of injured Awnadh. She stood in the shadows between the two nearest pillars, clutching her bloody hand, but looking otherwise fine.

"The elixir," she said, nodding to something on the floor between them. A small vial had slipped out of her pocket when she'd fallen to the floor.

"If he takes it, he might live," said Ayr, and the emotionless tone of her voice reverberated through Catanya, pounding against her pain.

Catanya snatched the vial off the floor and stared at it. It was almost empty except for a small amount of yellow liquid in the bottom. It looked nothing like what she'd expected for the infamous elixir of Caerlon.

The entire room went eerily still as everyone realized what was happening.

Catanya glanced down at Drayk and then turned her head slowly towards Cadyan. He hadn't moved from the dais. He still stood there, clutching his wounded arm and watching the entire exchange with a tight, inscrutable expression on his face.

"No," whispered Catanya. Tears filled her eyes, and she looked down at Drayk again. It couldn't come down to this. Not after everything they'd been through together.

"It's okay," mumbled Drayk, struggling to smile. "I don't want..." His eyes bulged as he looked at the elixir and shook his head. "You don't owe me anything, remember?" He coughed up more blood and groaned. "And I finally proved it... Proved her —everyone wrong." He chuckled, sounding almost delirious. "And I got him..."

"Who?" asked Catanya. When he didn't answer she squeezed his arms. "Can you hear me?"

"I hear you," he replied in a distant, echoing voice that didn't suit him. "S'okay," he said again, his voice growing fainter by the second. "They showed me, remember? Peaceful... beautiful." He smiled at her feebly. "And I got everything I wanted... almost everything I want..." He was slurring his speech now and his eyes slid in and out of focus. But he raised himself up slightly, struggling to meet her eye as he whispered, "Now it's your turn." He jerked his head in Cadyan's direction and slumped back down on the floor, coughing. "Promise me you'll run towards it... the fire."

Catanya sobbed and nodded. "I promise," she said in a meek voice. She leaned forward and pressed her forehead against his. "Thank you... for everything." Tears poured down her cheeks. She squeezed his hand one last time. Then she stood up and turned around to face Ayr.

"No," she said, taking a deep, shuddering breath to calm herself. "I won't kill my brother. I have to believe he can be saved."

She held the elixir out in front of her and concentrated her thoughts on it. She reached out to the vial. The hardened glass constructed from the Earth centuries ago. The droplets of Water mixed into the remaining fluid, sloshing against the stopper. She sensed the residue of a million trapped souls screaming at her, and she channelled that pain, that rage and anguish, back into the vial. There was a soft crack, and then the glass exploded, shattering into a million pieces as the remaining liquid burned off into mist.

Ayr shrieked and lunged towards Catanya with her dagger outstretched.

Before anyone could react, an unseen force yanked Catanya backwards. She crashed into the dais, winded and confused, and glanced over to see Cadyan standing beside her, looking mildly surprised by his own actions.

Then a brilliant burst of light exploded from his hand, illuminating the room like a flash of lightning. Everyone yelped, momentarily blinded, and Cadyan cried out, stumbling back and clutching his hand like he'd been burned. Catanya instinctively moved towards him, wanting to help, but then she hesitated. He straightened up and turned to face her, raising his hand so she could see. Together, they watched as the iron ring on his finger cracked and broke apart, disintegrating into dust that floated down to the ground.

They stared at each other, lost for words. But they didn't have time to take in what had happened.

A sudden searing pain ignited on Catanya's forearm as a blade slashed through her leather vambrace. She turned around just in time to see Ayr raising her blade for another attack. Catanya reacted in an instant, kicking Ayr in the shins and dodging her assault. But as she tried to step back, she tripped on the shards of wood beneath her feet and fell, landing hard on the stone floor.

Ayr gave an angry shout and launched forward again.

"Ayr, stop it!" shouted Fehla, stepping in front of her children. "This isn't you."

Ayr threw her head back in a manic cackle. "I'm afraid you're wrong about that! This is exactly who I am. I've been waiting for this moment for years—decades! What? Did you think you were the only one with the nerve to kill one of them?"

It surprised Catanya to see Fehla flush.

"That was different," said Fehla through gritted teeth. "I did that to protect my son."

Catanya glanced at Cadyan. He was still rubbing his injured

hand, but he paused to frown at his mother, evidently just as confused as Catanya.

"And a fine job you've done there," cackled Ayr. "All you did was turn him into his father. So why stop me now? If I take him out, I'll just be finishing what you started. Isn't that what you want? Go on, why don't you tell them all?" She gestured around at the room. "Tell them all what you did."

Fehla stood rigid and didn't respond.

"TELL THEM!"

"Fine—I KILLED HIM!" shouted Fehla, matching Ayr's anger. "I killed him, is that what you want to hear? I sent away for the Jade Moss poison, and then I poured it into his evening wine. I killed Casréyan!"

A long silence followed. Everyone in the room exchanged bewildered glances—everyone except Diyah. To Catanya's surprise, Diyah simply nodded, like she'd suspected this for a while.

"Why?" asked Cadyan. He was still staring at his mother.

Fehla exhaled. "Why do you think?" she asked in a small voice. "He was unhinged, and he was getting worse. It was only a matter of time before... before..."

"Before he killed me," finished Cadyan. He stepped back and nodded resignedly.

"I couldn't let that happen," said Fehla in a firm voice. "I did what I had to do then, and I will do what I have to do now." She turned to face Ayr with her sword outstretched. "There was a time when I thought you were better than Casréyan, but now I understand. You were always the same."

Rage twisted Ayr's features. She lifted her dagger and threw it at Fehla.

Without thinking, Catanya launched forward, knocking Fehla out of the way. As she turned to see the oncoming blade, she knew she wouldn't have time to react. She closed her eyes and waited for the impact, but it never came. Instead, a powerful force blasted her to the side.

Catanya spun around to see Cadyan standing where she had been a moment before. He wore a look of total shock, clutching at the dagger now sticking out of his chest.

Everything seemed frozen for a moment, but then Ayr gave a triumphant cry. Cadyan teetered, grasping at the blade.

Catanya blasted Ayr back and caught Cadyan as he fell to the ground.

"No!" cried Fehla, running forward. "No, my son!" She crashed to the floor beside them.

Catanya had gone completely numb. This couldn't be happening. She had finally made her choice, but she had not chosen this. Fehla's anguished face swam before her as the queen scrambled to help her son. But Catanya didn't have any emotion left. She heard fighting above, and she didn't move.

The itching, prickling sensation began in her fingers and she welcomed it. It was all there was left. It stretched along her hands, up her arms and towards her chest where it ignited into a burning wrath.

She closed her eyes, hot tears of rage pouring down her cheeks. She lowered Cadyan onto the ground, then she stood up slowly and turned to face Ayr.

Ayr was defenseless, but Catanya didn't care. The entire world around her blurred with golden light. Her veins awakened with furious power, and she watched the fear enter her enemy's eyes. The temperature in the room plummeted, and the torches along the walls flickered and dimmed. She was the only source of light left in the room. The burning, golden glow that emanated from her bruised and battered soul.

Her head throbbed. As she advanced on Ayr, she imagined that pain reaching out from her and pouring into Ayr's soul. Ayr crumpled to the ground, screaming in agony. But it wasn't enough. Catanya clenched her fists and drew the air from Ayr's lungs, watching her gasp and splutter on the ground like some pitiful insect. Her face turned purple and her skin cracked as her veins erupted, spilling out onto the floor.

Out of the corner of her eye, Catanya saw Lia charge. Rage coursed through Catanya once again at the sight of Ayr's commander. Lia had killed Drayk. Stabbed him in the back like a cowardly traitor. With a wave of her hand, Catanya brought Lia to her knees.

As Ayr took her last rattling breath and slumped down limp, Catanya turned her full attention towards Lia.

"Catanya, no!" she heard someone cry.

She saw a face she recognized as if from a distant memory.

"Jémys?" she asked, her voice echoing through the air. She gazed around the room and saw everyone gaping at her in horror. But their horror meant nothing to her.

She turned back towards Lia, determined to finish it, but then a blinding pain burst through her head and her vision blurred completely. She stumbled backwards, releasing her hold on Lia and clutching at her head.

Doubled over in pain, she cried out. It was like her entire skull was about to explode.

"I knew it," spat Lia, jumping back up to her feet.

Catanya tried to open her eyes to see what was happening, but she was in so much pain she could barely move.

"I knew you would choose *him* over us!" shouted Lia, retrieving her sword from the ground. "Well, one down, one to go!" She charged at Catanya again, but Fehla stepped in front of her.

"Stop!" she commanded.

"Get out of the way," snarled Lia.

"No. Please, sister, they're my children. We're family." Tears poured down Fehla's cheeks.

"*Family*?" spat Lia with disgust. "No. *Ayr* was my family, not you. We haven't been family for a long time. You chose

Casréyan all those years ago. You turned your back on the people who mattered. Now look at you, Fehla. You're *pathetic*. Grovelling to save the lives of his spawn. You should be thanking me. I'm about to set you free. Now move."

When Fehla still didn't budge, Lia lost her composure completely. She smacked Fehla hard on the face so she stumbled out of the way and fell to the ground. Then Lia raised her sword and advanced on Catanya again.

"Catanya!" Jémys dove forward to block Lia's path. In an instant, they were locked in a fight that was nothing more than a whirl of swords.

Panic flooded through Catanya, replacing some of her anger.

Not Jémys too, she thought. She needed to do something. She tried to stand up, but she was too weak. Her vision slid in and out of focus and she could barely see what was happening.

Someone cried out. Catanya opened her eyes in time to see Jémys's sword fly out of his hand. He was clutching a wound on his arm, and blood seeped through his fingers.

He was defenceless.

"NO!" Catanya cried and tried to stand up. A blast of agonizing pain shot through her body from head to toe, knocking her back down so she crashed into the dais, wooden splinters stabbing into her palm. There was nothing she could do. Jémys was going to die.

Lia raised her sword to bring it down on him, but with a deafening clang, her blade was blocked by another—an ornate, gilded sword that gleamed through the darkness. Everyone in the room stood frozen, watching with bated breath.

The fight that followed was unlike any that Catanya had ever seen. The Maífirkon of Caerlon was locked in a duel with the Commander of Awnell. Catanya finally understood why these two were considered the best fighters in their kingdoms. The flashes of metal were blinding as they blocked each other's attacks with lightning speed. They were a whirl of moves and countermoves with no end and no beginning, and the sound of metal on metal clashed and resounded against the stone walls.

For a minute it looked like Julyán might have the upper hand. Then they broke apart and Lia raised her leg up and kicked him in the chest, sending him stumbling backwards into the crumbling pillar behind him. Lia strode forward, looking murderous.

Julyán spun around, unfazed by the setback. He looked poised to block her, but before he could act, Diyah jumped in the way. There was another flash of silver and the dagger she'd thrown earlier was plunged through Lia's ribs.

"No," said Diyah in a calm voice.

The scene seemed suspended in time. Then Diyah jerked the blade deeper and Lia dropped her sword.

"Foolish girl," she spluttered, crashing to her knees as blood pooled at her lips.

"I will do what I must in order to protect my family," whispered Diyah, her voice uncharacteristically cold as she yanked the dagger back out.

Lia cackled as she crumpled to the ground. "Family," she scoffed. "*Children*. You're just as bad as Fehla. Just as *pathetic*. You'll see... That child will only make you weaker."

"That's where you're wrong," hissed Diyah, leaning over Lia. "Unlike you, I'm strong enough to handle anything. My family, my child—they make me stronger because love *is* strength. Hate is weakness. And you are the weakest person I have ever met in my life."

Lia slumped onto the floor twitching and convulsing until, finally, she lay still. Just another fallen warrior of Awnell lying amongst the scattered bodies.

Diyah stood up straight and turned around to find the others staring at her in utter shock.

"Child?" repeated Julyán. Catanya could just make out his searching expression.

Diyah's face flushed, and she looked suddenly nervous. "Y-yes... I was going to tell you after... but..." She trailed off and Catanya was surprised to see her friend so discomposed.

There was a pause like an eternity before Julyán stepped forward and pulled Diyah into what looked like a side-splitting hug. Jémys let out a nervous laugh and clapped Julyán on the shoulder, his eyes alight with affection.

It was strange to see something so beautiful when they were surrounded by so much sorrow.

The pain in Catanya's head had subsided. She turned away from the scene in front of her and made her way over to where Drayk lay sprawled upon the floor. She reached out to take his hand again, but it was too late. He was already gone. His eyes had glazed over and his features were rigid and mask-like, but a faint smile still played at his lips. She squeezed his hand, half hoping he might wake up. But he lay perfectly still. The empty echo of a man once full of life.

Catanya felt a bitter anguish. She wrestled back the tide of pain remounting in her head. Then she turned to look at Cadyan and realized he was still breathing. She slid over to kneel beside him amongst the debris. His eyes flickered towards her.

"Why?" It was the only thing she could say. Her vision was blurring again, and all her emotional resilience was gone. Her soul felt raw and flayed.

Cadyan laughed feebly, wincing at the pain. "I don't know," he said, nonplussed. Then he started fumbling with his jacket, trying to pull something out. "Here," he muttered.

He held out a tattered old book that looked strangely familiar. When Catanya took it, it fell open to a page somewhere near the middle. The spine was well worn as if the book had spent most of its time opened at this page.

Catanya looked down at the sketch she'd done of her brother months ago in Finnua. She let out a soft sniff and closed her eyes, new tears pooling behind her eyelids. "I'm sorry I never got the chance to know you as my brother," she said.

Cadyan coughed, blood leaking out his mouth. "Yes," he muttered, nodding. "I wonder... I wonder how things might have been..." He trailed off, and Catanya watched as the light slowly faded from his eyes.

She knelt there, numb. Gradually, the pain remounted in her body, but she didn't care. Pain was better than nothing.

Then Cadyan's entire body began to glow. It started off faintly at first, but then it grew brighter and brighter. A powerful gust of Wind whistled and blew through the room like a tornado, whipping at them and swirling around Catanya and Cadyan like they were the centre of the storm.

"What's happening?" she heard Diyah shout somewhere in the distance, but she couldn't see through the storm of energy encircling her.

"Catanya!" she heard someone else call.

Then without warning, the energy burst forth in a cloud of debris. It shattered the remaining windows as it broke free into the night air, leaving an eerie stillness in its wake.

Catanya glanced around the room. She saw the faces of her remaining friends eyeing her, with expressions of mingled fear and apprehension.

Catanya exhaled, but when she tried to stand up, her whole body cried out in pain and she crashed to the floor in agony. Every bone in her body seared like it was on fire. Holding out her hands, she saw them glowing gold and flickering uncontrollably. Her muscles twisted and her veins boiled. It was like something was inside her, trying to escape. Like her power had taken complete control of her.

And then the screaming started. Inside her head, she heard

them again just like she had at the monument months ago. Hundreds of thousands of voices screaming in agony, rage, and desperation. The screaming grew louder and louder torturing her and ripping her apart from the inside out. Catanya couldn't contain them anymore. The Spirits.

"R-run!" she shouted at the others. She could barely breathe and she knew she was dying. The Resonance tore at her as it struggled to get free. The heat, the pain—her powers were going to burst out of her and kill everyone.

"You have to run!" she shouted again. The agony was blinding, and she wanted it to be over.

Panicked voices sounded all around her, but she couldn't see. She just had to hope they were doing what she said. It didn't matter if she died as long as everyone else got out. In fact, in that moment, she almost welcomed the end. Any end was better than enduring this pain and grief.

But then a warm hand took hers. A sweet, earthy smell in the air told her it was Jémys.

"What are you doing? You have to go! Save yourself."

"I'm not leaving," he said gently. "I left you once before, and I won't do it again. Not ever."

"You have to, I can't control it!" She tried to push him away, but he tightened his grip and refused to budge.

"We're not leaving, Catanya," came Diyah's voice from somewhere in front of her.

But Catanya needed her friends to go, to leave her here to die. She couldn't bear the thought of taking them with her.

"Just focus," said Jémys. "Focus on what is keeping you here. Focus on living and let the rest of it go."

"I can't!" she shouted. The pain in her head had reached a piercing level. Her lungs constricted, and she couldn't breathe.

"Yes, you can," insisted Jémys. "Don't let these powers destroy you. Let them go! You never wanted them and you don't need them. You never did! Come on, Catanya, you're stronger than this!"

Jémys's voice echoed off the walls. Catanya's body was boiling from the inside out. She couldn't see or hear anything anymore. She was adrift in a sea of flames and screams where there was nothing but pain and sadness.

And then all at once everything went black, and the pain was gone. Everything was gone. She couldn't see or feel at all anymore, and there wasn't a single sound until—

"He's right," said a cool voice in the dark. It was familiar, but Catanya couldn't place it. She tried to see who it was, but the darkness was suffocating. "You cannot contain it, Catanya. You need to stop... Let it go."

"I can't let go. It'll kill everyone."

"No, it won't. You know that. You just don't *want* to let go."

The truth in those words stung, and shame twisted through Catanya. After everything she'd been through, after fighting it for so long, she finally had to admit that she liked it. She liked the power, the strength and the thrill it gave her. She didn't want to give it up.

"Why is this happening?" she cried in anger. It wasn't fair. She had lost so much already. Sacrificed so much.

"You're on the brink, Catanya. The Spirits are overwhelming you. That's why I'm here. Don't you understand yet? We are all connected. It is a heavy burden to perceive that connection and an even heavier one to wield it."

Catanya suddenly realized whose voice was speaking to her. Just like that, everything made sense.

She saw everything that had led her to where she was. Everything Illayan, Caer, and Ana had done centuries ago. The loveless marriage between Casréyan and Fehla. Her mother's decision to give her up, the Oracle Stone with its power for connection, the Natures, the Spirits. The journey from Faltir to Túir-Avlea, and her decision to embrace these powers.

But it was over now. It was time to let go.

Everything ends, Catanya.

Laylian's voice echoed in her memory, and she remembered who she used to be—who she had been long before any of this had happened.

That person had never wanted to be this.

"Do you understand now?" asked the voice in the dark.

"Yes," Catanya replied. "I understand. It was never meant to be wielded. Not like this."

"Exactly. Now you've held on longer than anyone else ever could. But it's time now. Do the one thing none of us ever could. Not me, not Caer, not even Illayan." The cool voice dissipated into the emptiness. "Let go, Catanya."

With every ounce of strength she had, Catanya focused her attention on the present. She allowed the pain to flood back into her. She forced herself to think about Ayr's betrayal. To think about Drayk and Cadyan. Tears flooding down her face, she squeezed Jémys's hand and opened her eyes to look at Diyah.

And then she let go, and the room filled with a blinding, golden light.

EPILOGUE

DIYAH

SMOKE RISES

Streams of thick grey smoke curled towards the sky, unaltered by the mist of early morning and the fog gently rolling off the ocean. The ruins of Caerlon City smouldered and burned atop the horizon. The sun crested the eastern forest, bleeding orange warmth into the embers of the battle wreckage.

Dotted across the city, funeral pyres honoured the casualties of war. The victims of hard-fought change. The city would be burning its dead for days. Awnadh, firkon, civilians... Countless bodies destined to become smoke.

On a small hill, overlooking the ocean on the west side of the castle, two pyres awaited their flames. One person stood vigil beside them, holding a small flaming torch. Its auburn light seemed especially vibrant against the backdrop of the vast, dark ocean.

Diyah hiked up the hill, the damp grass muffling her footsteps. As she crested the top, she slowed to a halt beside her friend.

"How did it go?" asked Catanya, not turning her gaze from the unlit pyres.

"As well as can be expected. Niq and Bir told the others, and the Awnadh are mourning their queen. They don't know what happened. It's up to you to decide what to tell them." Diyah was exhausted. Every inch of her body ached. The wound on her shoulder hadn't closed yet, and she longed to see if her old workroom was still standing and find some bandages. But right now, her friend needed her.

Catanya took a deep breath and turned to face Diyah. "How do you tell a nation that you slaughtered their queen?" Grief wore heavily upon her. The exhausted shadows under her eyes gave her a haunted look that wrenched at Diyah's soul. There hadn't been a chance to rest since the battle ended the previous day—and no amount of rest would heal Catanya's pain. Nothing could undo the losses she'd experienced or ease the sense of betrayal.

Diyah sighed. "Maybe you can tell them the truth... or part of it? You can tell them the elixir killed their queen... People need to know how dangerous it is."

Catanya shook her head, sending her long hair cascading across her shoulders. It had returned to its natural black since the night before. Diyah knew her friend's power was gone. Its loss obviously weighed upon her along with everything else—though she was doing her best to pretend otherwise.

Diyah sighed and turned to examine the wooden pyres. Catanya had insisted on a separate fire funeral for Cadyan and Drayk. The people of Mórceá were reeling from the battle, struggling to recover and make sense of everything. Catanya needed privacy to mourn.

The two figures looked oddly unreal, draped in grey shrouds and lying atop the stacks of wood like statues.

"Do you want me to do it?" asked Diyah, indicating the torch in Catanya's hand.

"No. This is something I have to do."

For a while, they stood in silence together. Then Catanya took a deep breath and dropped her torch. The pyres ignited.

Together, they watched the fire crawl across the wooden logs, creeping up towards the shrouded bodies. The flames flickered and snapped, scattering sparks into the air like fallen stars.

"What happens next?" asked Diyah.

"Now we try to move on, I suppose," said Catanya, her voice choked.

Diyah stepped closer to her friend. "Are you going to stay here?"

Catanya shrugged. "I never wanted to rule. I never wanted any of this."

"Yeah, I know that," said Diyah gently. "But, Catanya, can't you see that's why you have to do it?" She'd been reluctant to say this before now. Diyah knew Catanya better than anyone, and she knew what this would cost. But it needed to be said. "Look at what happened to Cadyan and Ayr. Their thirst for power drove them mad. You're the only one who was able to fight it. Mórceá needs you."

Catanya rubbed her forehead. "I know. It's just... unfair."

Diyah smiled sadly. "Of course it is. But that's what it means to be a leader, right? Making sacrifices and taking responsibility?"

Catanya sighed and turned her gaze away from the fire to look at Diyah. "Will you stay here with me?" she asked in a small, vulnerable voice. "Will you help me?"

"You don't need my help," said Diyah.

Catanya shook her head. "Yes, I do." Then, squinting into the flames, she added, "There's nothing wrong with needing the people you love."

Diyah took Catanya's hand and squeezed it. "Of course, I will help you," she said. "It's you and me together, we're family."

They heard soft footsteps approaching and turned to see Jémys, Julyán, and Fehla climbing the hill towards them.

Jémys and Julyán looked exhausted, but otherwise well. Julyán was as stoic and poised as ever, but his posture seemed lighter, freer than ever before. Despite the exhaustion and grief of the last two days, it warmed Diyah's heart to see him that way.

Jémys gave Diyah a small smile and glanced at his brother before turning his gaze towards Catanya. He was doing his best to look calm and composed, but Diyah recognized the tangled mess of emotions wrestling for control inside him—it was the same jumble of sorrow, affection, and pride that she also felt for her friend right now. It would take some time, but she hoped Jémys and Catanya would find their way back to each other. The deserved to be happy.

In the meantime, Diyah knew Jémys would be there for his brother. Jémys's presence was good for Julyán. He could help him learn to be a father—help him remember how to be part of a family.

Fehla stood slightly separated from the others. Her eyes were puffy and red and her face was drawn in shadow. Catanya and Fehla had spoken a few times since the battle ended but it had been strained and awkward each time. Diyah knew everything Fehla had done had been to spare herself the grief of losing a child. But that pain had found her anyway. And no matter what relationship she managed to build with her daughter, the pain of losing her son would torture her for the rest of her days. Along with the guilt she already carried.

Diyah couldn't condemn Fehla for the decisions she'd made. After all, only a few hours ago, Diyah had taken a life—something she'd always sworn never to do. She'd proven how far she'd go to protect the people she loved, and she didn't regret it.

This war had changed them all. It would take time to heal,

time to find their way forward. But Diyah had faith they could do it, *together*. They had to.

Diyah rested her hand on her stomach and turned to smile at Catanya. "All those years we spent daydreaming at Camlee Lodge... I never realized..."

"Realized what?" asked Catanya without taking her gaze from the fire.

"Family isn't something you inherit, is it?" asked Diyah. "It's not stagnant, or something you can lose. It's something you build and shape over time. It grows and changes along with everything else. And, in the end, it changes us too. That's what life is, right? I mean, everything changes. Sometimes it's painful, but it's important, isn't it?"

Diyah noticed a faint smile tugging at Catanya's lips. "Yes, I suppose it is."

She squeezed Diyah's hand as the others joined them by the fire. They stood there all together, silently watching the smoke stretch up towards the sky.

THE END
of the
QUIESCENCE TRILOGY

ALSO BY KATHRYN KNOWLES

THE QUIESCENCE TRILOGY

The Relics of Illayan

The Warrior Queen

The Age of Resonance

OTHER STORIES OF MÓRCEÁ

The Last Verratrí, a Short Story Prelude

Subscribe to the Mad Endeavour Newsletter to get a free copy of The Last Verratrí.

www.madendeavour.com

ACKNOWLEDGMENTS

Well, here we are. We made it to the end of the story. Thank you, dear reader, for joining me on this adventure. I know how difficult it is to find time for that ever-growing pile of books. So thank you for taking a chance on a new author and making it through not one, but three books! I hope you enjoyed the journey, and I hope you, like me, found some new friends in these characters.

Thank you to the reviewers, social media champions, book peddlers, fans, friends, and supporters. Without you, none of this would be possible. You helped spread the word and you created a support system for me throughout the writing and publishing process. I'm incredibly honoured and grateful for all you do.

To Rebecca, thank you—seriously. THANK YOU. I don't know what I did to deserve a friend like you but I'm overwhelmed with gratitude every day. You were by my side and in my corner every step of the way on this project (and every project I undertake!). The story simply wouldn't be what it is without you, your input, your friendship. I'm so lucky to have you in my life.

To Massimo, thank you for everything. It has been a whirlwind, but you never cease to be supportive and to encourage me in my creative pursuits. This is the beginning of a long life full of creative projects for both of us. Music, poetry, stories, musicals, and so much more! I can't wait to share every part of the journey with you and to live in our own little artsy world together.

To my friends and family. You are the best community I could ask to have. I am overwhelmed by the level of support and encouragement you give me, and I couldn't do any of this without you.

And finally, thank you to Mom—thank you for ALL the things. I love you. You are the bestest.

ABOUT THE AUTHOR

Kathryn Knowles is a composer, cellist, conductor, and writer currently based in Toronto, Ontario. She splits her time between writing, teaching, conducting, composing, and running Mad Endeavour.

Photo Credit: Claire Bouvier Photography

Kathryn received honourable mention in the Writer's Digest 89th Annual Writing Competition for her poem, Beyond the Black Horizon's Crease, and her short story, Lester's Bird Feeder. Her musical works have been played in workshops by the Toronto Symphony Orchestra, the New Orford String Quartet, and the Penderecki String Quartet. She holds a Bachelor of Music and a Master of International Business from Queen's University, as well as a Master in Music Composition from the University of Toronto.

In her spare time, Kathryn enjoys taking on new creative projects (i.e. filling up that "spare" time), spending time with friends and family, tending her ever-growing plant collection (obsession), and looking at pictures of puppies and dreaming of the day she can have one of her own.

Learn more at www.kathryn-knowles.com

 instagram.com/kathryn.knowles_

www.ingramcontent.com/pod-product-compliance
Lightning Source LLC
Chambersburg PA
CBHW020346220726
48290CB00014B/1111